American Midnight

A Damaged Po$$e Novel

B. R. Snow

Copyright © 2012 B.R. Snow

ISBN-10: 984967575

ISBN-13: 978-0-9849675-7-5

Website:www.brsnow.net/
Twitter:@BernSnow
Facebook:facebook.com/bernsnow

Other Books by B.R. Snow

The Damaged Po$$e Series

•American Midnight

•Larrikin Gene

•Sneaker World

•Summerman

•The Duplicates   (*Coming Summer of 2016*)

Other books

•Divorce Hotel

•Either Ore

To Michele

For friendship and support beyond compare.

Chapter 1

I woke at five with an empty heart and a head full of tequila.

Two hours of sleep had no effect on my internal clock that over the years had developed its own on-off switch. I did maintain some control over when to turn it off, but the on-switch flipped at five.

I swayed as I got out of bed, amazed I'd regained consciousness. Knowing all too well that gambling and drinking were a deadly combination, I cursed my stupidity. I had planned on getting drunk, but only after winning a few grand at blackjack. Some plans were meant to be ignored. This wasn't one of them.

I shuffled across the suite. A mirror beckoned but I couldn't bring myself to look. Not yet anyway.

Last night started to return.

Stacks of chips. Green, black, purple. How much had it been? Seventy, maybe eighty thousand? Not major league, but big for me.

The woman in the red dress. Perched on my right shoulder, nuzzling my neck, whispering in my ear. Her words lost in casino noise and my lack of focus on what she was saying. But I remembered the nuzzling.

I remembered my cockiness too. The early evening success following the utter despair of the day.

And the booze. Alcohol was a regular companion, but pounding shots of tequila at the blackjack table were incomprehensible.

And unforgivable.

Don't drink and gamble; the voice had warned.

Absent for the past several weeks, the voice had returned yesterday and refused to leave.

From the corner of my eye, the mirror beckoned. I moved forward cautiously and scanned the dresser top where my clothes and belongings were piled.

No chips. That was probably bad news.

Keys, wallet, cigarettes, cell phone, watch... something was missing. Silently, I repeated the list. Keys, wallet, cigarettes, cell phone, watch...wedding ring. Wedding ring. In a flood of emotions too powerful for a half-drunk, hung over man old enough to know better, I remembered why I came to Vegas in the first place.

Yesterday morning my wife of only a year and a half had announced as I stepped naked from the shower she was leaving. And she left. For Greece. Something about finding a real man, a man bronzed by the sun, to love her and treat her like the lady she was. Or did she say could be? I couldn't remember her exact words because I was busy getting soap out of my ears. I did remember my response.

"Leaving? What a good idea."

At least it had been until I called the bank thirty minutes later to check the status of our joint account. The automated voice on the end of the line was far too unemotional in announcing the account's current balance was $1. That is, it was $1 after my Greek-god-seeking, soon to be ex-wife had withdrawn $187,892 via wire transfer to the Fuck You, Be Glad I Left You a Dollar Bank of Athens.

So the wedding ring was off the list. I had removed one of the six items that told me my life was in order and prepared for another day of battle against the onslaught of the grind. I lit a cigarette and sat naked on the edge of the bed out of the mirror's line of sight.

I silently ran the list again. Keys, wallet, cigarettes, cell phone, watch. It was concise. I liked the rhythm, and it had a nice ring to it.

The ring.

I remembered yesterday's most impressive accomplishment.

I'd been driving to Vegas from LA in a roller coaster mixture of elation and rage with the music loud and the cruise control set at a hundred. For the past hour, I'd been holding the wedding ring, rolling it in my fingers as I pondered its simple beauty and social significance. And it's seamless completeness. I was torn between hurling it out the window or selling it and using the proceeds for one hand of blackjack. A winning hand would be an omen of better times ahead, but a loss would only reinforce my latest financial debacle. The last thing I needed was a reminder.

Thirty miles past Barstow, I passed a dead skunk on the side of the highway. After a quick U-turn, the overpowering stench left me wondering how long a skunk, like my defunct marriage, had to be dead before the smell disappeared. The body, while not decomposing, was in definite stages of decay. I knelt along the side of the road, oblivious to the speeding cars. Whatever questions the drivers may have had about the man dressed in shorts and a Hawaiian shirt kneeling alongside a dead skunk were of no concern to me.

It wasn't very big and, beneath its fur, the skunk looked skinny. I wondered if this was normal or if the skunk hadn't eaten for a while. Its fur flickered as the desert wind gusted. The skunk was on its back, the body rigid with its legs stuck straight up in the air. The feet - or were they called paws - were perfectly symmetrical. Flip him over and he would make a perfect, yet unusual, little table. But where would you put it? Perhaps the zoo? A little zoo table. A place for all the resident skunks that didn't have to worry about getting whacked by speeding cars to rest their feet.

The only sign of bodily damage, apart from it being stiff as a board, was a missing toenail. Clipped off by the wheel of a speeding truck? Broken as he rolled from the impact? Lost in a fight with Mrs. Skunk? I studied the skunk's eyes. What do the eyes say about the last thing in any creature's mind the second before death? I recoiled from my own question. It was at that moment the voice returned.

Don't go there.

I cocked my head and waited.

"Are you back?"

We'll see.

I nodded and refocused on the skunk. Its eyes portrayed shock. Shock from the impact, or maybe it had had time to ponder its impending fate? Few outward signs of damage but an internal system scrambled and rearranged, the ability to function forever lost. I took the wedding ring from my shirt pocket and placed it on the skunk's left paw on the claw most resembling a ring finger.

I stood and stared down at the rigid body. The skunk appeared different. It was now a member of society's most sought after and misunderstood club. It had acquired the means to generate sympathy from passersby who might wonder if the skunk had kids and how the family must be devastated by the loss.

I decided it was time for a drink.

The skunk was dead. But I, although very much alone, was still alive. And I'd stumbled onto the perfect resting place for the ring. Thirty miles outside of Barstow, adorning a dead skunk's foot; its life, like mine, permanently altered in the amount of time it takes to step in front of a speeding car.

Or out of the shower.

The pounding in my head was relentless, and I knew from experience this would be an all-day hangover. I pulled on a bathrobe, sat on the edge of the bed and tried to summon details from last night. I came up blank.

That can't be good news.

I appreciated the voice's whisper. The more I tried to concentrate, the more my head pounded. My stomach churned, and I tried to remember if I'd eaten dinner. A soft constant sound worked its way into my consciousness. Air conditioning? No. Running water.

I hoisted myself off the bed and shuffled to the bathroom door and inched it open. Amidst the steam, I admired the muscular back of a woman washing her hair. I focused on the woman's taut buttocks. I continued the journey down her lean thighs and calves. My eyes drifted back to her bottom.

"World class," I whispered.

Despite the headache and nausea, I began to get aroused and cursed my alcohol consumption. To have shared intimacy with this woman would have been extraordinary. To not remember would be criminal. I pulled the door shut and returned to the edge of the bed. The water stopped, the sound replaced by familiar sounds of post-shower activity.

Who is she and how did she get up here?

"I was hoping you'd be able to tell me."

A hooker, I decided. Given my condition last night, I couldn't imagine any other woman agreeing to a sleepover. The bathroom door opened, and she appeared wearing a towel around her waist and another wrapped around her head. She jumped when she saw me.

"Sweet Jesus," she said, catching her breath. "You're up. I was going to leave you a note. Good morning." She cocked her head at me. "You look like shit."

She smiled as she watched me glance back and forth between her eyes and breasts. Making no attempt to cover herself, she stood still and allowed me some time. I marveled at their slight upward turn. The air conditioning applied the finishing touches.

They're perfect.

I nodded.

"Do you mind if I use one of your robes?"

"As long as you don't mind if I ask you who you are and why you're in my room."

4

She laughed and padded softly across the carpet. She grabbed a bathrobe from the closet. She smiled and released the towel from around her waist.

"I'm Grace."

"Grace. As in the state of?"

"That depends." She focused on untying the knot on the bathrobe's belt. "I'm here because you asked me. Besides, I wanted to make sure you got home safe."

I tried to focus on her words but was distracted by the sight of her sliding into the plush robe. A knock on the door broke what was left of my concentration.

"Oh, good. Breakfast is here." She tightened the robe and went to the door. "Good morning, Ernesto. Just put everything on the table over there."

"Good morning, Grace. How was your evening?"

"Tragically uneventful."

The waiter chuckled as he rolled a large cart across the room. He noticed me sitting on the edge of the bed.

"Good morning, sir." His tone was cheerful and upbeat. I managed a nod in response.

"Thank you, Ernesto."

"My pleasure, Grace. Enjoy your breakfast."

He waved, smiled at me and departed. I continued to sit lifeless on the edge of the bed.

"Why don't you grab a quick shower before we eat?"

I nodded at the woman who'd taken charge. I stood and shuffled toward the bathroom.

"I'll get this ready. How do you like your coffee?"

From the bathroom doorway, I turned. "In solitude?"

She smiled and waited.

"Just cream," I said, closing the door behind me.

When I returned several minutes later, she was fully dressed in a beautiful red evening gown. A memory returned. Green eyes. Red dress. I remembered first seeing her in one of the cocktail lounges late yesterday afternoon.

The shower helped. Now I sought additional assistance. She poured coffee and juice for us and started to eat. I watched the precise strokes she made with her knife and fork. I took a sip of juice and found it lacking.

5

The coffee was more satisfying, so I stayed with that. I warily eyed my breakfast. The woman called Grace noticed and reached into her purse. I accepted a small handful of aspirin and washed them down.

"Thanks."

The woman finished chewing a mouthful of bagel and pointed at me with her fork. "You really shouldn't drink and gamble," she said, sipping her orange juice.

"By themselves, they're fine. But not in combination."

"That was my point." She continued to smile and study my face.

"How long were you with me at the tables last night?"

"Long enough."

My curiosity took over. "I lost... didn't I?" I caught a touch of sympathy in her expression. "How much?"

"About a hundred and fifty."

"We are talking thousands, right?"

She laughed and went to work on her omelet.

"Expensive day," I said.

330 thousand? Nice to meet you, Mr. Rockefeller.

The woman, oblivious to the voice, nodded in agreement. She finished her breakfast in silence as I went back and forth between watching her and staring down at my plate. I picked at my food but did manage to keep down three cups of coffee. The woman pushed her plate away, and I lit a cigarette. She frowned but said nothing. I coughed and sipped my juice.

"Look...Grace. Do I owe you any money?"

Her eyes flared but then relaxed. "Of course not. I'm not a hooker." She then turned playful. "But we should try this again when you're..."

"Sober?"

"I was going to say functional...but yeah, let's go with sober."

"I'm sober now." I forced a weak smile and shook my head. "Maybe not."

She laughed. "That's okay. It can wait. I'll be around."

"You live here in Vegas?"

"I work for the Casino."

Midway through a piece of bacon, I paused. "Doing what? I thought the idea of casino employees dating guests was a no-no."

"We're dating? How sweet." She laughed.

"What would you call it?"

6

"Oh, just keeping an eye out for someone who'd had way too much to drink."

She said it far too casually and, despite his hangover, my instincts kicked in.

"So last night? Did we…?"

"What do you think?"

"I'm betting my plumbing was out of order."

"Finally, you win a bet." She laughed at her joke and cocked her head. "You're staring. What?"

"I'm just wondering what your job is. You're so beautiful."

"You're too kind. Let's call it Guest Relations and leave it at that." She looked at her watch. "I need to run. And I need to change. A woman wearing formal attire at six in the morning can only mean one thing." She stood and kissed me hard. "I'll see you soon."

I watched her leave and stared at the closed door, crawled back into bed and dreamt hard.

Fortunately, the voice slept soundly.

Chapter 2

I pulled two pillows over my head and waited. Eventually, I realized the incessant pounding wasn't coming from my head. It was an insistent fist at the door. I flipped back the covers and shivered from the air conditioning. I pulled on my robe and stomped toward the door intent on inflicting bodily harm.

"Who is it?"

"Mr. White? We need to speak with you."

The voice sounded far too serious. I cracked the door and peered out. Two large Chinese men wearing identical gray slacks and blue blazers stood outside with their arms folded. I noticed the earpieces. Casino security. I opened the door and waved them in. They were smiling, but I remained wary. Anyone that big could afford to smile.

"What can I do for you?"

"My name is Joe, and this is Sam."

Sam, the silent one, nodded.

"Mr. Hedaya requests your company for a brief discussion," Joe said.

I recognized the name immediately. The casino owner was legendary: A penniless Chinese immigrant as a child, Hedaya had ended up in Vegas playing cards as a teenager and parlayed his initial Pai Gow winnings into a fortune. He had built the casino from the ground up and had become a local legend and reluctant national celebrity.

Hedaya was familiar to me for another reason. Given his Chinese heritage and the business he was in, Hedaya was on several lists maintained by various government agencies. As far as I knew, Hedaya had never been officially targeted by the U.S. government, but he was definitely someone they kept tabs on.

Apart from the fact that I owed him a hundred and fifty grand, I couldn't imagine why he wanted to meet me. I planned on paying off the debt. I just didn't have a clue how I was going to be able to do it. I would have preferred to have the conversation at another time, but I doubted the two men standing in front of me would accept no as an answer, their good nature notwithstanding.

"Okay, just let me throw some clothes on."

As we walked toward the elevators, I tried following their conversation but kept going back to Hedaya's request. I did owe the man a chunk of money, but a hundred and fifty thousand didn't seem big enough to warrant Hedaya's personal attention.

"Why the need for a private meeting? Do I look like a flight risk?"

The two men glanced at me, ignored the question and resumed their conversation.

"I'm telling you you're wrong. Lincoln's on the record himself." Joe, the slightly larger of the two men, inserted a key card into a slot adjacent to an elevator door.

Sam waited until he had Joe's undivided attention. "You're gonna stand there and try to tell me that Lincoln wasn't the Great Emancipator?"

"That's not what I'm saying at all. Obviously the results of the Civil War bear that out, but that wasn't his primary objective. It was to preserve the Union at all costs. Jesus Christ, study your history."

"That doesn't diminish the accomplishment," Sam said.

"I didn't say it did. A few minutes ago you were talking about morality in warfare and made the leap to Lincoln's freeing of the slaves. You can't use an example to make your point if it doesn't meet the basis of the argument."

The elevator arrived, and I followed Joe's silent wave into the elevator. The door closed, and we began a rapid descent. Sam, chastised, was angry. Joe noticed his partner's mood.

"What?"

"You don't have to raise your voice. You're always doing that. Especially when you think you're right."

"Here we go again." Joe turned toward me. "What is it? Lincoln's primary motive? Great Emancipator or preserver of the Union?"

I looked cautiously at both men. Despite having opinions on the subject, I wasn't in the mood. I looked up at the ceiling and then back at both men. They stared back, waiting for a response.

"Well, what do you think?" Sam said, still grumpy.

"I think you two should get married."

To my relief, both men laughed. The elevator came to a smooth stop, and the door opened to reveal a large plush room that reminded me of a hotel lobby. The first thing that hit me was the smell. The unmistakable combination of leather and sweat accented with a touch of ammonia and sulfur developed over years of exposure to Zamboni exhaust and chemicals used to make ice. The smell brought back a flood of childhood memories that overwhelmed me. I waited for the familiar sounds of skates cutting ice and pucks hitting boards, but all I heard was a voice speaking in Mandarin barking sharp commands.

I was ushered through two large teak doors with elaborate Chinese dragon handles. The commands were louder now, and I heard the sound of rapid brushing, followed by a series of clicks and soft thumps. I closed his eyes and tried to recall the memory. Eventually, it clicked.

Curling.

Before I had time to consider why a curling rink would be in the basement of a Las Vegas casino, Joe nudged me aside and pulled a second set of doors open.

A regulation ice rink dominated the room. A solitary figure skater was practicing toe loops in one of the far corners of the rink. She was being watched by another woman who appeared to be coaching her. From this distance, I couldn't see them clearly, but their focus was unmistakable.

Two curling rinks ran along one side of the ice rink. On my left was a lounge with plush couches and chairs that overlooked the action. Joe motioned me towards the lounge area. A fully stocked bar behind the sitting area filled one corner. A bartender was on duty, but his only task at the moment seemed to be watching the match in progress. Approaching the couches, I saw a large Oriental rug that sat on top of the protective rubber flooring. It was magnificent, a rug most owners would hang on a wall to prevent feet from ever touching it. I paused at the edge. On cue, Joe handed me a pair of slippers. I removed my tennis shoes and replaced them with the slippers. They hugged my feet and I wondered if anything similar existed for a hangover that refused to go away. I sat down on the couch closest to the ice and looked at Joe and Sam.

"It's like having live sports in your living room," I said.

"Pretty cool, huh?" Joe said, watching the figure skater.

I continued to take in my surroundings. The ceiling was adorned with an elaborate Chinese mural. The teak walls were covered with artwork and photographs. Awestruck, I considered Joe's use of the term cool and decided it didn't do justice to the room; if anything covering at least an acre could still be called a room.

"No, it's more than cool. It's unbelievable."

I focused on the curling. The rules were straightforward, almost identical to lawn bowling and bocce ball. The first time I played, it seemed too simple to hold my interest. The granite rocks weighed forty pounds and had a handle on top that was used to control the release and ultimate path of the rock. A slight twist of the handle produced a rock that curved as it slid down the ice. After my initial attempts, I realized that controlling the direction and length a forty pound rock traveled on ice was a lot harder than it looked. Like most games worth playing, curling had proven easy to understand, but impossible to master.

The one thing about curling that set it apart and always made me chuckle was the sweepers. These team members took direction from the captain and, with precise vigor, swept the ice with various types of brooms. Shuffling their feet to stay a few feet ahead of the sliding rock, they used their brooms to help control the distance the rocks traveled. I watched as the sweepers worked in tandem. A loud command stopped their movements, and everyone watched as the rock continued to glide towards the scoring circle. A small ricochet of other rocks was set in motion. Shouts of glee went up, and I counted two scoring rocks tucked safely behind a ring of three others that sat a few feet in front.

After a short celebration, the team members slid across the ice and stood behind the rocks. At the other end of the rink, a very small Chinese man was preparing to play his last shot. The man shuffled one foot in front of the other as he worked his way down the ice for a closer look at what was facing him. I studied the old man and was drawn to the focused, almost meditative, nature of his eyes. He stalked the scoring circle from every angle, pursing his lips with each potential solution. I thought he was wasting his time. Three of his rocks were forming a perfect shield in front of his opponent's. Without a word, the old man shuffled his way back up the ice.

I continued to study him. He was barely over five feet tall and very thin. And he was old. Probably somewhere in his sixties, but incredibly vibrant. Beneath the loose fitting tracksuit, I sensed power and a sense of grace. The old man squatted and flipped his final rock over on its side. He rubbed the bottom with a small towel to remove any imperfections. With one knee bent and the other leg stretched out behind him, he gently slid the stone back and forth. On the fourth movement, he released the rock with a gentle turn of the handle. The rock began a slow, tantalizing glide and the silence was punctuated by the old man's commands.

"Ni nalai ba."

The sweepers began attacking the ice with their brooms a few feet in front of the sliding rock. I translated the phrase the old man had used. It

11

literally meant 'bring it' and it certainly seemed to have worked on the sweepers.

"Gan kuai. Gan kuai."

The sweepers worked their brooms harder. The old man carefully studied the speed of the rock and shouted, "Xiuxi."

I knew this translated into 'rest', and the sweepers immediately stopped and watched the rock as it approached the others. It hit the outermost rock and was propelled past another sitting nearby. The rock slid at a thirty-degree angle and headed towards their opponent's two scoring rocks. It hit both simultaneously and stopped in the middle of the scoring circle. The two opposing rocks slid away and eventually came to rest outside the scoring circle. A moment of stunned silence followed.

The old man surveyed the scene silently. He looked at his opponents and spoke softly. "Three points. I believe that's match gentlemen."

The opposing captain bowed to the old man and smiled. "Incredible shot, Hedaya. Well done."

The old man bowed back and smiled.

"Thank you, Will." He then addressed the group. "Okay everyone, that's it for today. I will see you tomorrow at our usual time."

The other players departed. The old man turned his attention to Joe and Sam still sitting on the couch. He nodded, and they followed the other men out. The old man stared into my eyes and smiled.

"Hedaya Xiansheng, nin hao o," I said, bowing slightly to the startled man.

"I am very well, thank you. Nin shi Bai Xiansheng ba?" the old man said.

"Yes, I'm Mr. White. But please call me Doc." I shook the old man's hand.

"Bai Xiansheng, I mean Doc." He smiled and bowed. "Nin xuele jinaide zhong wen le?"

"I've been studying Chinese on and off for years. But it's very difficult. My teacher used to apologize to others for my slowness. He was fond of saying, Ta xuede bu kuai."

"He learns slowly." The old man laughed. "Not at all. You speak very well. Tell me, how much time did you spend in China?"

It was my turn to be caught off-guard. Was the old man letting me know he knew I'd been in China or was it just a guess?

"A year and a half," I said, holding the old man's stare.

12

"It's very rude of me for making you stand there. I'm sorry. Zuoxia."

I sat back down on the couch.

"A year and a half," Hedaya said. "Do you write or read Chinese?"

I remembered my futile attempts to understand Chinese characters. In the end, I'd decided that just learning how to speak it was a big enough accomplishment.

"No, it was far too hard."

"Yes, it is difficult. And for business purposes I prefer English. If you don't mind, let's stay with that."

Business purposes? What else would he call debt collection?

I grimaced at the voice's intrusion. But the old man's attention was on the figure skater who had left the ice and was walking towards us. The woman, still on skates, kissed the old man on the cheek and smiled at me. Sweat was dripping off her face despite the constant toweling she gave herself.

"Good morning, Rose. How was your practice?"

"It was fine, Bofu. But I'm afraid, unlike you, I have no chance of ever going to the Olympics."

I knew that Bofu meant 'father's older brother' and noticed the resemblance.

"Doc, I'd like you to meet my niece, Rose. Rose, this is Doc White."

"Nice to meet you, Rose." It was definitely better than nice. The woman was tiny but incredibly beautiful.

"I must warn you, Doc. Rose has a very strong attraction to older men." Hedaya laughed and gently stroked the side of her face.

"Oh, Bofu. Now don't be mean. And don't give away all of my secrets." She kissed his forehead. "I'm going up to shower. Will you be coming up for lunch?"

"Yes. I'll see you later."

"Goodbye, Doc. Nice meeting you." She walked away. I caught myself staring.

"She is an amazing young woman," Hedaya said.

"She's so tiny, but built like a..." I stopped, embarrassed. "What I meant to say was she's perfectly proportioned, but she's so small."

Hedaya chuckled. "Nice save Doc. Don't worry. I'm used to men getting tongue-tied around her." Hedaya's eyes glistened as he stared after her. "My little China Doll. But don't let her beauty fool you. She's

13

brilliant. MBA and a Law Degree from Stanford. Soon she will be running the entire place."

"What does she do now?"

The old man winked at me. "Plays mostly. Which is exactly what she should be doing at this point in her life."

"Are her parents here?"

"No, that was a tragic event," Hedaya said. "They were killed by the communists when she was just a baby. Fortunately, by then I had acquired enough resources to get her out. She's been raised American as you can tell from her sassiness." He sat down on a couch and motioned for me to join him. "Does this place bring back fond memories?"

I was confused by the question. "I've never been here before."

"No, of course not. I meant memories of your earlier years. Your hockey years."

I looked quizzically at the old man. If this was a test, when had it started?

"As a matter of fact, it does. But how do you know about that?"

"Let's just call it background information."

The bartender approached carrying a pot of tea. He placed it on the table and waited. Hedaya prepared to pour.

"Tea?"

I grimaced at the thought. Hedaya noticed and smiled.

"Perhaps something a bit stronger?"

"I don't know. I had a rough night."

"Yes. So I hear. Roger, please bring Doc one of our special cocktails."

The waiter bowed and headed off.

"It will help. It's like a Bloody Mary, but we add some Chinese herbs. It's very good, but it can only do so much to repair the damage of alcohol. Only sleep can do that."

I longed for the comforts of the king size bed in my suite. Sleep was still very high on my list.

"Look, I know I owe you a lot of money. I'll need to free some up." My head continued to pound. "It may take me some time, but you'll get it."

"I'm sorry. Did Joe and Sam give you the impression that I wanted to meet with you to discuss your debt?"

14

"They didn't give me a reason. I just assumed. What else would it be?"

"What else indeed?" Hedaya flashed his smile again. "I know you are good for the money, so let's just wait on that. But I am curious. Your betting pattern was much different from your previous visits."

This revelation didn't surprise me. The sophisticated tracking systems casinos used to monitor betting patterns formed the basis for the comp system, and the fact that I had ended up betting very differently from previous visits wouldn't have gone unnoticed.

"I had a bad day."

"Indeed, you did."

The bartender returned with my drink and departed. I sipped from the large glass and recognized several flavors, ginseng and tomato dominated. I took out a cigarette and lit it after receiving silent approval. I offered the pack to him.

"No, thank you. My smoking these days is limited to the occasional bowl of opium."

I felt my eyebrows go up in surprise.

"Nicotine is not the only habit that's hard to break," he said, laughing. Hedaya leaned forward. "I have a problem, Doc."

I nodded sympathetically and waited.

"No, not with opium." Hedaya's laughter reverberated around the room. "I have a computer problem. Actually, it's a software problem."

The last thing I wanted to hear was anything to do with technology. "Yeah?" It was abrupt, and I regretted it immediately. "I'm sorry. Please go ahead."

"Thank you. To be even more specific, I have a Prophecy problem."

Hedaya watched my eyes and waited for my reaction. I leaned further back into the couch. It was becoming obvious that this man knew a great deal about me.

"Prophecy. Good company. I used to work there."

"Yes, I know. I believe you're even considered somewhat of a leading expert in the field."

"That was a long time ago."

"That's unfortunate. I could really use your help. At least for a short period of time."

I looked at Hedaya, who appeared to be making an honest request. It surprised me that this man would ever admit to needing assistance with

15

anything. I took a deep breath and sipped my drink. I set the glass down and looked at the old man. "Okay. Why don't you tell me a little bit about your current situation?"

"Almost two years ago, I made the decision to implement new financial software for the casino. Ultimately, we chose Prophecy."

"Good choice."

In a previous life, I'd spent several years working with the software, and it was considered one of the best in the industry.

"I thought so too. At least I did until we tried to get it working."

I prepared myself for the conversation. Countless times I'd listened to clients bitch about a multitude of problems technology projects surfaced. I rubbed my eyes. "Okay, where are you at right now?"

"From the latest schedule I've seen, we're still eight months away from getting it in."

"Eight months? When did you start?"

"Over a year and a half ago."

"And you're only installing the standard financial applications?"

"Yes. Doesn't that sound strange?"

I knew better than to respond to that question. Instead, I led back with one of my own. "Do you have any particular requirements that are out of the ordinary?"

"I don't think so."

"How many users will you have?"

"In total, perhaps a hundred."

"Any complex interfaces?" He gave me a blank stare. I'd lost him. "By interfaces, I mean are you connecting the application to other systems that might add some complexity?"

"No, I don't think so. But I can find out."

"That's not necessary right now." I shifted gears. "Are you using external consultants?"

Hedaya rolled his eyes. "I have very many consultants."

"Prophecy consultants?"

"Mostly, yes."

"How many?"

"I'm not sure. It seems to change almost weekly. Somewhere between twenty and thirty."

"Twenty to thirty?" I quickly did the math in my head. "You've got a burn rate of over a quarter million a week?"

16

"How did you know that?"

I smiled. "Background information."

Hedaya smiled back.

"How much have you got sunk into this project?"

Hedaya shifted in his seat and appeared embarrassed having to answer the question.

"Including the cost of the software and new hardware, a little over 30 million. The new estimate to complete is around 40."

I sipped my drink and noticed I was beginning to feel a bit better. Forty million certainly wasn't the biggest number I'd ever seen spent on these projects but, given the size and the apparent straightforward nature of this one, the number seemed outrageous. Hedaya was watching me, waiting for the next question. I took another long sip.

"So how can I help you?"

"I'd like you to spend a week taking a look around," Hedaya said, leaning forward. "I believe I'm getting screwed here and not in the manner I enjoy. Figure out what's happening and make some recommendations. See if you can help me get out of this mess."

I considered the request. I was down over three hundred large and financially crippled. Any other plans I may have had would be on hold until I solved that problem. I looked around the room and decided that perhaps a week in Vegas might do me some good.

"Okay. Let's talk money."

Despite my hatred of all things corporate, I had always enjoyed negotiating about money.

Hedaya perked up. "Go ahead." He relaxed into the couch and crossed his legs, obviously no stranger to the process himself.

"My rate is $500 an hour."

"$500 an hour? That's outrageous. That's more than I pay anybody on the project."

"I imagine it is. But I'm not the one who's spent 30 million bucks of your money."

Hedaya laughed. "No, you're not." Hedaya stared at him. "Are you trying to take advantage of me, Doc?"

"No, I'm not. That's just my rate. I'll cap my hours at fifty for the week. That's twenty-five grand."

Hedaya bit his lip and waited.

"Tell you what," I said. "If you don't like what I come up with at the end of the week, don't pay me. But I keep the suite for the week, plus expenses."

"$300 an hour. You keep the suite, but expenses are for food and incidentals only. Nothing for gambling."

"$400."

"Done." Hedaya nodded, stood and shook Doc's hand. "One week, starting tomorrow."

I nodded and slipped into consulting mode.

"You'll need to call your CIO. Ask him to call me tonight."

"Okay."

"By the way, who's the Project Manager assigned from Prophecy?"

"Jim Barrier," Hedaya said. "Do you know him?"

I lit another cigarette and finished my drink. "Yeah, I know him. But you knew that already didn't you, Hedaya?"

"Yes, I did." Hedaya beamed.

"And what was up with the woman in my room last night? Did you set that up?"

"Oh, Grace. No, I'm afraid that was another one of her attempts to impress me with her abilities."

"So she does work for you?"

"Yes, but I'm not sure for how much longer. She's a total sycophant around me and can't seem to keep her panties on."

"Why do you keep her around?"

"She coaches Rose with her ice skating. And Rose is very fond of her."

"I see."

"And did you get a good look at her? I may be old but women that beautiful don't come along very often. Even here in Vegas."

"She is very beautiful."

"I don't trust her." Hedaya winked at him. "But I'm weak when it comes to beauty."

"I meant to ask you. What's up with the curling?"

"I fell in love with the game several years ago. Now I'm preparing for the Olympic trials."

"The Winter Olympics?" I said.

"It would be a little hard to curl in the summer wouldn't you think?" Hedaya laughed. "It is one of my few remaining dreams."

18

I looked at the old man and wondered what his secret was for keeping dreams alive. "I'm impressed. But why curling?"

The man's eyes twinkled.

"Because I'm too old for the luge."

Chapter 3

As a young soldier, I'd discovered two things about myself: I had an extraordinary innate ability to plan and conduct covert operations, and I had an intense personal affinity for all things Buddhist. In combination, these two created a complex, contradictory lifestyle that, to this day, continues to torment me.

Upon discovering the four sacred vows - a fundamental teaching and tenet of the Buddhist religion - I proudly displayed the perspicacity and invincibility of an eighteen-year-old by adopting the moniker, Bodhisattva. My self-anointment as the enlightened one was initially met with scorn and ridicule by some of my fellow trainees. However, the public nature of their ridicule quickly disappeared as they witnessed the intensity of my conversion and my proficiency with weapons.

During a brief scuffle with a born again Christian lieutenant who, within earshot, had labeled all Buddhists as members of a non-monotheist cult, I pinned him to the ground, applied the tip of a twelve-inch knife to his Adam's apple, and whispered encouragement about his need to either reassess his own path or shut the fuck up. From that point forward my chosen path, while not necessarily understood by other members of my troop, was tolerated. My proficiencies with weapons, however, was both respected and feared.

Upon my release into the world as an authorized covert ops specialist, I embarked on a zealous mission of proselytization counterintuitive to the basic Buddhist tenets. Armed with only a rudimentary understanding of my newly adopted religion along with the latest in high-tech weaponry, I, the young Bodhisattva, went forth into the world's biggest shitholes torn between killing and converting.

Showing enormous potential but demonstrating a reluctance to terminate and violate basic Buddhist tenets, I was ordered to take a mandatory week of R&R by my longtime boss and mentor, Samuels. Telling me to forget contemplating everything except the process I would use to get my holy shit together, he forced me to deal with what would prove to be the first of my ongoing struggles between enlightenment and execution.

I decided on Thailand, a bastion of Buddhist thought and practice, and spent my time in Bangkok visiting temples and debating and negotiating with bargirls spiritual pathways and sins of the flesh. After making a generous offering to a young bargirl for three days personal services, I took her on a temple tour hoping she could provide additional insights into the nuances of the Buddhist way of life. Eager for the chance to spend a few hours in a vertical position and intrigued by her new farang's focus on perspective rather than penetration, she locked arms and led me to her favorite temple.

Perhaps Buddha himself was looking down favorably on me that muggy, carbon-dioxide-filled afternoon where I experienced an event that would forever alter the course of my life. A small, bald, orange-clad monk was orating to several dozen curious tourists and a handful of worshippers. We approached the monk and sat reverently at his feet.

"What's he saying?" I whispered.

"He's talking about how many Buddhists mis...what's the word... misinterpret the teachings concerning the concept of non-violence."

I nodded and ignored the girl's proximity and perfume. I stared up at the monk who continued to speak in a soft, yet firm, tone. I looked at her and waited for the translation.

"He's saying that sometimes it is not only okay to kill, but that is what Buddha expects."

"Really?" I said, nonplussed. "Who can you kill?"

"At the moment, he's talking about communists."

"Communists, of course."

"This monk is very controversial. He was just released from jail for saying such things."

"So he's courageous."

"Perhaps," she said, yawning. "Many think he just likes to, how do you Americans say it... stir the shit?"

"I think he's great." I nodded my head vigorously and stood. "I've got what I need. Let's go get a beer."

I spent that afternoon watching her gyrate solo in front of a jukebox and reflected upon the first of the Four Sacred Vows: I vow to liberate all beings, without number. Using a broad brush to define the term liberate, over several cold, sweaty Singha, I modified my thinking thereby opening up a fork in the pathway I could take, and I returned to work refreshed and focused.

As the scope and secrecy of my missions deepened, the number of enemy combatants seemed to multiply faster than I could kill them. As the count of my liberations approached one hundred, doubts again surfaced, wore me down, and, for the second time, I began to question my chosen path, certain that this wasn't quite what Buddha had in mind.

Highly decorated but extremely confused, one night I sought solace at a Buddhist temple outside of Washington and was approached by a monk. I placed my palms together and bowed my head.

"Namaste."

"Right back at ya."

I dropped my hands and raised my head. "Samuels?"

"Hard to tell with the robe and finger cymbals, huh?"

"Why can't you ever show up in public as yourself?"

"Because I'd be dead in an hour." Samuels looked around the temple and nodded. "Nice place."

"How did you know I was here?"

Samuels stared at me and waited.

"Never mind. I forgot who I was talking to. What do you want?"

"Slight change of plans. Actually, it's a major change of career path."

"For whom?"

"Both of us."

"Do I get to stop killing people?"

"Well, I doubt that's ever going to happen," Samuels said. "But you should be able to cut back."

"That's a start. What's up?"

Samuels glanced around the temple to make sure we were alone and rang his finger cymbals. "I'm changing organizations."

"You're leaving the Agency?"

"Yes…and no. They've asked me to set up a new group with a technology focus."

"Interesting. So I get to sit behind a computer monitor all day? That doesn't interest me."

"Nothing like that. You're going to head up our corporate side."

I stood and worked the cramps out of my legs. "I'm confused."

"Yeah, I know. It's all this Buddhist crap." Samuels smiled. It wasn't much of a smile, but it was all he had. "Given globalization and the way technology is moving, we've decided that corporate infiltration is an indispensable component of our efforts."

"You're asking me to infiltrate U.S. companies? Isn't that something the FBI does?"

22

"The FBI? The Feebs couldn't infiltrate their own Christmas party dressed as Santa. Besides, we're talking global companies. And if they just happen to be headquartered here in the U.S., that's their problem." Samuels glanced around and tapped his fingers together. The soft ping reverberated around the temple. "I don't get the infatuation you have with this religion. It's too confusing. Give me the Catholics. Right and wrong. Guilt, then forgiveness. Say ten Hail Mary's and pass the wine."

"I don't know, Samuels. Do I have a choice?"

"Of course. You've got two. Come with me or end up in the middle of the fucking desert somewhere. In case you haven't been watching the news, Saddam just invaded Kuwait. The stupid bastard. If he thinks we're a pain in the ass now, let's see how he feels after we drop about a half million troops in his backyard."

"The Middle East?"

"Ever been on a camel before?"

"No."

"Nasty creatures. I got bit by one once." Samuels raised his robe and exposed his calves. "See that scar? Fucker bit me right there."

"You probably deserved it."

Samuels rang his finger cymbals. "Probably. So what's it gonna be, Doc? Women covered head to toe and not a drop of alcohol for a thousand miles in any direction or the corporate lifestyle?"

"Well, when you put it like that."

Samuels tapped his finger cymbals together, bowed his head and wandered off into the night.

Chapter 4

Summerman closed his eyes and listened as his right hand took off in a new direction. Playing piano while cruising at 40,000 feet would probably seem odd to most people, but Summerman found it to be the perfect way to pass the time while flying cross country. He paused and looked under the baby grand piano that was bolted securely to the cabin floor. Murray glanced up and waited for the head rub he knew was coming and thumped his massive tail.

"You like that one, huh?"

Murray stretched, then climbed out from under the piano and draped his paws over Summerman's shoulders. He nuzzled Summerman's neck and licked the side of his face, leaving behind a well-defined trail of slobber.

"Jesus, Murray. If you wanted a Guinness, why didn't you just say so?"

Murray woofed once and picked up the pace of his tail wag. Summerman laughed, worked his way out from under the dog and headed to the small refrigerator. He grabbed two Guinness, carefully poured one into a glass, the other into a metal bowl. He placed the bowl on the carpet and sipped as he watched Murray make short work of the foaming beverage. Murray finished his Guinness and looked up expectantly at Summerman.

"One more, but that's all for now," Summerman said. "It's going to be hot in Vegas and I don't want you getting dehydrated."

Murray woofed and waited. Summerman poured a second Guinness into the bowl and smiled as the dog lapped furiously at his fresh drink.

Summerman heard the landing gear drop and checked his watch. He rinsed the empty bowl and closed the piano lid.

"We're landing soon," Summerman said. "Let's go."

Murray trotted towards the main cabin with Summerman trailing behind.

"Five minutes out, Summerman."

Summerman pressed the intercom. "Got it. Thanks, Captain Wilbur. Smooth flight."

"Yeah, beautiful day for flying," Captain Wilbur said, through the intercom. "But aren't they all."

Summerman pressed a button next to his chair and a large, plush container emerged from the floor of the cabin. Murray stood next to the door of the container and waited. Summerman opened the door then closed it behind the dog that'd entered and immediately stretched out. After years of trying to figure out how to put a seat belt, or some form of effective safety harness, on a recalcitrant 200-pound dog during takeoff and landing, Summerman had finally hit on the idea of the container. The device had increased the cost of the plane by two hundred thousand, but it was worth every penny. While Murray loved to fly, he hated being restrained. And when Murray hated something, he could be a real pain in the ass.

Summerman buckled his seat belt and waited for the plane to touch down. Captain Wilbur effortlessly brought the Gulfstream back to earth, taxied, then stopped. He entered the main cabin. Murray woofed, and both he and Summerman laughed. Summerman opened the container door and Murray climbed out and stood on his back legs and draped both paws over Captain Wilbur's shoulders.

Captain Wilbur laughed and scratched Murray's ears. "You're welcome, Murray. Thanks for flying with us today." He extricated himself from the dog and sat down in a leather chair facing Summerman. "We're done for the day, right?"

"We certainly are." Summerman reached into a refrigerator next to his seat and tossed Captain Wilbur a can of beer. Murray immediately went on point. "No, Murray. If you're good, maybe you can have another one later on."

Captain Wilbur removed his pilot's cap and took a long sip. "What's our schedule?"

"I think we'll be here a day or two. Then I need to head down to L.A., but if you want to spend some extra time with your mom, I can drive down."

"Nah. Who wants to drive when you've got this baby?" Captain Wilbur glanced admiringly around the plane.

"I'm thinking about upgrading," Summerman said. "That reminds me. Would you be willing to work year around if I needed you?"

Captain Wilbur stared at Summerman with a confused expression. "Summerman, you know I don't have a clue about how you and Murray happened to get into the state you did. But I do know that the two of you are only here for about three months a year. What exactly would I be doing the other nine months? Flying around the world by myself?"

Summerman gulped down the rest of his Guinness. "I have an idea, but I'm going to need some help to make it work."

"Okay," Captain Wilbur said, then waited. "I'm going to need a little clarification here, Summerman."

Summerman laughed. "That's my line. You stealing my material now?"

"Well, since I already feel like I'm stealing your money, it seemed like the logical progression."

Summerman stroked Murray's head. "I figured, as long as we have one foot in this world, I might as well see if we can make a contribution."

"You lost me."

"It's complicated. I'll explain it to you when it's time. Who knows, it might not go anywhere, but I need to give it a shot."

Captain Wilbur took a sip of beer. "Just be careful, okay? If word gets out about the two of you being part-timers, you'll either end up in a traveling freak show or the focus of a government study."

"Yeah, I know. But I think I've identified a couple of people I might be able to work with."

"What are they like?"

"They've got the right background to pull this off, but they're pretty damaged."

Captain Wilbur grinned and shook his head. "Summerman is going public. And putting a posse together. This ought to be fun."

"Only with a very small handful of people. And they'll be sworn to secrecy, just like you."

"Damaged people sworn to secrecy?"

"Exactly."

"Like some kind of superhero gang?"

"Maybe, but no capes. I hate capes."

Captain Wilbur laughed and drained the rest of his beer. "This is classic. The Damaged Posse."

"Hey, that's not bad."

Chapter 5

I heard the knock at four. I'd spent the rest of the day in my suite napping and snacking and watching sports. Assuming it was Hedaya's CIO showing up early, I opened the door and was surprised to see Grace. She was wearing a casual summer dress and sandals. She walked in, turned off the television and looked me over.

"Feeling better?"

"Much." I watched her kick her sandals off. "Did you forget something this morning?"

"No. Am I interrupting anything important?"

"Actually-"

"Good. I need a shower."

I watched the dress drop to the floor, and she strolled towards the bathroom. At the door, she turned.

"Well, are you coming or not?"

"What?"

A little slow on the uptake today are we?

I ignored the voice. After dealing with it all day, I'd accepted the fact that it was back and wouldn't be leaving for a while.

"I said, are you coming?"

"Right behind you," I said, heading towards the bathroom.

"You should be so lucky."

I had no idea if she had an ulterior motive for showing up or if she was just a big fan of the horizontal mambo. After an hour, I still wasn't clear on the ulterior motive, but I had confirmed one thing.

The woman sure loved to mambo.

Chapter 6

Another knock just before six. I walked to the door and pulled it open. A short man carrying a large briefcase and an extra fifty pounds stood waiting. Definitely a downgrade from my earlier visitor.

"Mr. White? I'm George Jenkins."

"Hi, George. Nice to meet you. Call me Doc."

We shook hands perfunctorily, and I escorted him to the suite. Jenkins placed the briefcase on a table and stepped into the living room. He looked around.

"Very nice. I've never been in one of the suites before. Hedaya has a good sense of style." Jenkins stared at me. "Have you known him long?"

I returned the stare. It was starting already. A casually delivered question designed to elicit a revealing response. I sized him up. The man was tired. But who wasn't these days? Jenkins slowly rocked back and forth on his feet, waiting for an answer. He was going for aloof, but I recognized anger. This didn't surprise me. No one, especially people in positions of power, liked having outsiders poking around their business. I waited until I saw what I was looking for. The nervousness appeared via a slight tug of an ear, followed by an almost inaudible exhale.

I smiled at Jenkins. "Not long." It was an honest, yet unrevealing response.

"I see," Jenkins said. He folded his arms behind his back and walked in a small circle taking in his surroundings. "It's magnificent. Do you mind if I ask you what these go for a night?"

"I think these smaller suites go for about a fifteen hundred a night." I smiled at him. "But I'm not sure since I always get comped."

"I see."

Formalities over, I moved on. "Thanks for taking time out of your Sunday. I assume the briefcase is for me?"

"Yes, it's all there. Everything you asked for."

And nothing else. I was certain of that. "Great, thank you. And the meeting?"

"Eight o'clock tomorrow. They'll all be there."

"Did you tell them why?"

"Absolutely not. I simply announced an all hands meeting for eight o'clock. Mind if I ask you why you wanted the purpose kept secret?"

"Well, I've done these before. What shall we call it… a review? I've found that it's better to prevent, as much as possible, the creation of shared memory."

"Are you saying that I would ask my people to feed you a line of shit?"

I was surprised by the sudden and direct question. His anger appeared genuine, and I ratcheted up my respect for the man. "Not at all. It's just that in times of perceived threat people tend to rally against common enemies."

"So you want to catch them off guard?"

"No, I just want them all to be at the same place when I start."

Jenkins dropped himself into the large leather couch that dominated the living room. He looked up at me. "Mind if I smoke?"

"I wish you would."

I sat down in the chair opposite Jenkins, and we spent the next few minutes smoking in silence.

"This project is going to be the death of me."

"These projects are always hard," I said. "And they often take on a life of their own." I paused to let the comment sink in, but didn't expect Jenkins to bite.

It was Jenkins turn to smile. He finished his cigarette and vigorously crushed it out. Then he stood up. "Is that everything for now?"

"Yes. I'm sure I'll have questions, but I need to review these things first."

"I'll be in the office by seven if you want to stop by."

"Okay. Oh, by the way, would a daily update be sufficient for you?"

"Daily? That would be a nice change. I'll see you tomorrow."

Jenkins walked to the door and let himself out. I watched him leave and wished I felt at least a bit bad about lying to the man. While I didn't want to give the group a chance to develop a collective memory, I was primarily interested in the reaction of one person. I began organizing the contents on the coffee table and, judging by the size of the stacks, I was in for a long night. I ordered dinner and a bottle of wine from room service.

Chapter 7

At a quarter to eight, I took the elevator to the second floor and saw Joe standing with arms folded as the doors opened.

"Morning, Doc. Sleep well?"

"Like a baby. Tell me, Joe. Are you following me or do you just think I'm cute?"

"You're okay. Just don't get too cute."

"Where's your partner?"

"Getting coffee. He lost a bet."

"What is it today? Whether a Lincoln or Ford is the better presidential car?"

Joe laughed. "You're pretty funny aren't you? No, we're off presidents. Today, it's philosophers. You know, the meaning of life stuff."

"Well, when you figure it out, let me know."

I started down the hall, then turned back. "Hey, where's Jenkins office?"

"Past the surveillance room. Third door on the left."

I strode off but slowed as I walked past the surveillance room, the place where casino security watched everything that went on inside their walls with the exception of public bathrooms and the guest rooms. And these days, I wasn't too sure about those.

Fighting back the urge to wave to the cameras, I continued down the hall and knocked on the open door. Jenkins, wearing a suit and tie, was sitting behind his desk. The office was immaculate. Either Jenkins had a neatness fetish or a very organized assistant.

"Good morning, Doc. Are you ready?" Jenkins said.

"Absolutely. Are they all here?"

"I just got the call. They're waiting in the conference room."

"Let's do it."

Jenkins led me down the hall into a large conference room. The room was filled with an enormous table surrounded by people sitting in plush chairs. Other people sat in identical chairs that ringed the room. I shifted my attention to the man sitting at the far end of the table. His head was down, and he was flipping through a stack of papers. I settled into a chair, and Jenkins sat down next to me and opened a thick manila folder.

I studied the man at the far end of the room. I noticed the gray hair that was beginning to dominate. I also noticed the weight gain. Too many airplanes and too many corporate dinners. Also evident were the bags around his eyes. I knew it wouldn't be long before the man had some work done.

The man sensed the change of tone as the chatter died down. He removed his reading glasses and looked up. Our eyes locked immediately.

Watch the eyes. Always watch the eyes.

I saw surprise, then confusion. The man smiled, nodded briefly, and leaned back in his chair. He stroked his chin and waited.

Jenkins called the meeting to order. I surveyed the other faces in the room. I ignored their quizzical glances and stares.

"Good morning everyone. I hope you all had good weekends. I'd like to introduce you to Mr. Doc White."

Jenkins reached for his manila folder and proceeded to knock it onto the floor between their two chairs. I leaned under the table to help Jenkins collect the scattered papers. From under the table, I heard the conference room door open. Seconds later I smelled the perfume. Memories flooded my brain, but before I could organize them, I heard her voice.

"Sorry, I'm late. We got six inches of rain in New York. Can you believe that? A twelve-hour delay."

I heard the murmurs of sympathy around the table. From my vantage point, I looked in the general direction of the voice and caught a fleeting glimpse of her calves as she walked past. They were still magnificent. My mind was racing. And so was the voice.

Her? That's not possible. Now what?

Now what indeed.

Jenkins finished collecting the papers and popped up from under the table.

"Good morning, Maya. Sorry about your flight."

"Thanks, George. I should have just stayed here."

Still crouched under the table, I took a deep breath and waited for the voice to provide counsel. None was forthcoming, and I cursed its unreliability in times of need.

Hey. Don't blame me. I'm as surprised as you are.

31

I took a deep breath and slowly settled back into my chair. Our eyes locked and her initial shock was powerful but brief. I tried unsuccessfully to look away, but her beauty held me captive. Her face flushed, and she brushed a strand of hair away from her face. She shook her head and sat down. I glanced around the room. It appeared that the other participants, preoccupied with their own concerns, had missed the moment. Except for Barrier. I knew from his expression that he hadn't missed anything.

Just get through the meeting.

Maya opened her bag and extracted a writing tablet and pen. Her hand shook slightly. Jenkins continued.

"As I was saying, this is Doc White, and he'll be spending the week with us. I'll turn the meeting over to him."

Jenkins leaned back in his chair and smiled at me. I stood and prepared to address the group.

Thanks for providing some context, George.

"Thanks, George. It's nice to see all of you. Although I'm sure you're not exactly feeling warm and fuzzy about me."

A nervous chuckle filled the room.

Good. Keep it up.

"Mr. Hedaya has asked me to spend the week taking a look at your project."

From my immediate left, a voice spoke.

"Might I ask what the purpose of this is? After all, we are very busy people."

I sized up the woman who had asked the question. She was in her late twenties and very pretty with an elegant style. From the tone of her question, I surmised she was relatively inexperienced. Taking offense at my silence, she pushed harder.

"Are you here to help or just look?"

The challenge came earlier than I had expected and I'd have to deal with it directly. And forcefully. I felt bad that it had to be her. I continued to smile at the woman.

"Hopefully to help. And I'm more than happy to explain the purpose of my visit. What is your name by the way?"

"Cynthia Simmons."

I grabbed the list of project team members and scanned it quickly. "Ah, yes. Ms. Simmons. Definitely someone I wish to speak with."

I let the comment sink in before continuing. The woman continued to stare back. She had taken her training very seriously. I sharpened my tone.

"Well, Ms. Simmons, Mr. Hedaya has some concerns with the quality, cost, and timeliness of this project. In fact, he's beginning to wonder if you folks will ever finish, if it will ever work, and if he will have any money left should you ever finish. So he's asked me to review the project and make recommendations as to whether certain individuals, such as you, should be allowed to remain on it."

"How dare you talk to me like that."

I stared and held her eyes.

Maybe there's a puppy around you could kick.

Eventually, the woman blinked. I focused on the group, but she began to speak again. She was abruptly, yet safely, cut off.

"I think we all understand why you're here Doc. Please, continue," Barrier said, glancing at the young woman who was silently protesting back at him. Barrier smiled, then shook his head. The woman sat back in her chair dejected.

He's sleeping with her.

"Okay. Here's the deal. I've got a week to do this review, and I will do my absolute best not to disturb your work."

I delivered this comment in the direction of the woman, but she had decided not to play. I looked at Maya, but she was staring down at her notebook, deep in thought. I felt another surge of emotion.

"Today and tomorrow will be interview days. I have a schedule here for all of you. I would prefer to do individual ones, but the team is too big, so some will be in small groups. Wednesday, I will do any necessary follow-up interviews. I'm keeping Thursday open for now, and I'm setting Friday aside for my write up. I'll be working next door in the small conference room, and George's assistant will handle my schedule. Talk to her if you want to schedule some time with me. Any questions?"

I looked around the room and was greeted with silence.

"Okay, that's it. Jim, you're up first. I'll see you at 8:30."

I walked out of the room and headed for the elevator. I exited directly into the noisy casino and walked outside. I felt the heat and tasted the dust of Vegas. I leaned against a wall, fumbled for a cigarette and took a long drag.

"You look like you've had a tough morning," said a bellman.

"Yeah."

33

"Well, don't worry. Your luck will change soon."

I looked at him. "From bad to worse?"

The bellman chuckled. "Let's hope not. You know you can smoke inside?"

"Force of habit I guess."

"It's tough for smokers these days."

I nodded, not paying attention. I closed my eyes and recalled the memory of the last time I'd seen her. It had been almost five years since we'd said goodbye. The intensity we'd generated together had taken me by surprise and, when it was over, had left me exposed and vulnerable. Eventually, the memories had been safely tucked away but now, with one glance and one soft toss of her hair, she was back.

And she was back with a vengeance.

Chapter 8

I surveyed the small conference room and was satisfied. Compared to some of the places I'd worked in the past, this was plush.

Are we all set?

I shook my head; both at the voice and for being back in an environment I thought I'd left behind forever. I reviewed the items on the desk. Writing tablets, Post It notes, stapler, paper clips, a casino coffee mug and an electric pencil sharpener. I grabbed one of the writing tablets and moved to the small table. I put the tablet down and took out my pen. I paused and looked at the pencil sharpener.

I was thinking the same thing. Where are the pencils?

I got up and moved to the corner of the desk. I studied the pencil sharpener from a distance. It wasn't an unusual piece of equipment, but for some reason, it seemed out of place. I stood with my back against the wall and studied the angles. I realized that almost the entire room was in full view through the opening of the sharpener. I leaned in, careful to stay behind the opening and smiled as my suspicions were confirmed.

These guys don't screw around.

I sat back down at the table, picked up my pen and wrote on the top of the first page.

Jim Barrier. 8:30. Monday.

I tossed the pen on the table and stretched. The quick, sharp knock startled me. Barrier, not waiting for an invitation, entered and sat down opposite me. We stared at each other, neither wanting to speak first. A small smile was attached to Barrier's face. I studied the man who had been an enemy for years. As with any enemy, wariness was required. I felt the adrenaline rush begin. I'd spent hours preparing and was anxious to get started, but waited. Eventually, as I knew he would, Barrier spoke.

"What did you do? Lose a bet?"

"Actually, I lost several."

Barrier laughed and shook his head.

"I heard you quit years ago. Gave all this nonsense up."

"It's a curtain call."

"Whatever. You look good. What's it been?"

"A long time."

"Yeah, the project in Chicago. Now there was one fucked up organization. Hey, remember the CIO there? What was his name?"

I recalled the memory. By the end of the project, Barrier had single-handedly destroyed the man's reputation.

"Walter Berger."

"Berger. That's right. You ever hear from him?"

"He died a couple of years ago."

Barrier was mildly surprised. "Really?" He thought for a moment. "Good. I hated that cocksucker." Barrier sat back in his chair and folded his hands. "Okay, Doc. That's enough memory lane for me. How can I help you?"

Refusing to take the Berger bait, I leaned forward. "First of all, what the hell are you doing running projects again? The last I heard you were running the entire western region."

"I was getting bored sitting around corporate and having to deal with Billy Boy's mood swings."

Despite my best attempt to remain neutral, I laughed. Lawrence, Prophecy's CEO, temper was legendary.

"I swear," Barrier continued, "if the man doesn't make at least five million and get new pussy by noon, his day is ruined." He laughed too loudly at his joke. "So one day I went in and told him I wanted to get back in the game. Get the skill set sharpened up."

I ignored the lie.

"You've been here since day one?"

"Yeah, I came in and pitched the old man. What a piece of work he is, huh? I sold it, put the team together, and here we are."

"A year and a half later."

Barrier smiled and rolled his tongue over his lips.

"So it's going to be that kind of review is it? Okay, take your best shot."

I smiled and led with one I knew would put him immediately on the defensive.

"Tell me about what the hell you're doing with the purchasing application."

"I'm just trying to make the software do what the client wants."

"Multiple vendors on the same purchase order? C'mon, Jim. We both know that you just can't teach that kind of stupid."

"Hey, they need to track a lot of their costs in one place for certain activities. We're giving them the ability to set up big purchase orders as collection buckets and then release funds for different vendors. What's the big deal?"

"How long have you've been trying to make that work?"

Barrier lost some of his cockiness.

"About a year."

"How many people have you got working on that one?" I knew the answer, but I wanted to hear it.

"Six, maybe seven."

"How much source code are you stepping on?"

Barrier grinned.

"A shitload."

"Have they figured out yet that they'll never be able to upgrade? I don't imagine you've gotten around to telling them that yet."

"Jenkins knows. But he's on his last legs and just hoping to slide into retirement. So he's not saying a thing. Hey, what the hell? I'm just doing what they asked me to do. Rule number one, keep the client happy. Besides, aren't these the kind of decisions that keep people like you in business?"

"I'm not in the business."

"Well then, why the hell am I sitting here wasting my time talking to you?"

"Good point." I forced a smile. "Let's talk about the data warehouse."

"What about it?"

"The schema will never work."

"How the fuck would you know? You're no system architect."

I maintained the smile. I wasn't a data architect, but I knew I was right. My smile seemed to be pissing Barrier off even more. I widened it.

"Besides, it's already working," Barrier said.

"Really? I must have missed that in the status reports."

Barrier shifted in his seat.

"Yeah, we ran a bunch of test data last night."

"You'll have to excuse my lack of technical expertise. Tell me, in laymen's terms, how many are in a bunch?"

"Go to hell, Doc."

"How many?"

"A couple of hundred records."

"They want the warehouse for reporting on weekly stats right?"

"Yeah. They've got a bunch of reports they run weekly. Pretty standard stuff."

"How long did it take to load and process the two hundred?"

Barrier's eyes narrowed. I'd seen this expression many times before.

"A couple of hours," Barrier said.

"A couple of hours? You could do them faster on an abacus, Jim."

"So the database needs a little tuning. They always do. Hey, they wanted a data warehouse, I'm giving them a data warehouse."

"The weekly volume around here is what? About twenty thousand transactions?"

"Something like that."

"At the rate you're going, it's going to take over a week to process seven days of data."

It was a total exaggeration, but I wanted to see if I could make the veins in his neck pulsate. What's the point in coming out of retirement if you can't at least enjoy your work?

I grabbed the master diagram for the overall design of the system and spread it out on the table. With the large number of lines that crisscrossed the page, it resembled a road map.

"You're building fifteen interfaces."

"Sounds about right."

"For what? From what I've read, most of them don't do anything other than copy data from one place to another. Why don't you have them look for the data where the system puts it in the first place?"

"We're trying to make the system more user-friendly, Doc. That's all we're trying to do."

My head was beginning to throb. I put down my pen and rubbed my eyes.

"A little out of practice, huh?" Barrier said, chuckling.

"Yeah, I guess. That's enough for now. We'll talk later after I talk with some of the others."

"Okay, they're your cards. Play them the way you want." Barrier stood up and stared at him. "The old man's using you. You know that don't you? He's just trying to dig up some dirt in case he decides to sue us."

"I don't give a shit what his motives are. Or whether he sues your ass or not. My objective is to get through this week and go home."

38

"This is just one more fucked up technology project, Doc. It's the same shit every time. Some end up worse than others. Want me to send in your next interview?"

"Sure."

"Who is it?"

I scanned my interview schedule. "Cynthia. The young blonde who doesn't like outsiders." I remembered my previous interaction with the woman and realized my headache was about to get worse.

"Go easy on her? She's just a kid."

"I bet you don't tell her that late at night."

Barrier stared at me and then broke into a big grin.

"No, I don't. But when it comes to late night activity, she's no kid."

Chapter 9

Hedaya tested the steaks with his finger and decided they needed two more minutes. He removed a huge piece of salmon from the grill and gently slid it onto a warming plate. He sipped his wine, glanced up at the midday sun and then at the pool where four of his favorite cocktail waitresses were splashing, sipping cocktails, and enjoying their day off. He watched Rose emerge through a door carrying two large bowls of salad. She winked at Hedaya, placed the bowls on the table set for seven and joined the other women in the pool.

Hedaya smiled and raised his glass to the good life.

A door on the other side of the rooftop garden opened, and Hedaya waved to the man and his massive traveling companion. Spying Hedaya, the dog raced towards the old man, paused to stand on his back legs and gently draped his front paws over his shoulder.

"Murray, it is so good to see you," Hedaya said. "What a good boy. Summerman. Welcome. It's been too long.

The men shook hands, then watched Murray race towards the pool and the five scantily clad women. They laughed as Murray dove in, surfaced and swam in small circles barking loudly.

"Don't mind him," Summerman said. "He had a couple of Guinness on the flight in."

"I just can't get over how much he looks like a tiger. Especially when he's wet."

"He'll settle down in a few days. He's pretty excited the first few days after we cross over."

"Three days ago, right?"

"Yes. It's been non-stop since we got back on this side. I had a lot of stuff to write up." Summerman handed Hedaya a thick folder. "I think you'll be pleased."

"I'm sure I will." Hedaya turned towards a man standing near the grill. "Henry, please pull the steaks and prepare the table for lunch." He sat in a chair and began flipping through the enclosed document. "Wonderful. This is wonderful, Summerman."

"There are some interesting things going on in Guangdong and Sichuan provinces. It'll take years, but I think they'll be very useful."

"Patience is one thing I have in abundance, Summerman. Let's eat. Ladies, if you're hungry, lunch is served."

Murray climbed out of the pool and shook vigorously, sending all five women scurrying. Murray trotted towards the table and stretched out in the sun to dry off.

Rose led the other women to the table. She kissed Summerman on the cheek and sat down on the other side of Hedaya.

"You're looking beautiful, Rose," Summerman said. "Has that special person stolen your heart yet?"

"I'm still waiting for you to come to your senses, Summerman." She winked at him and filled her plate.

Hedaya introduced Summerman to the four waitresses and, with the exception of Hedaya, they began eating in earnest. Hedaya was busy cutting two large steaks into manageable pieces. Murray stood transfixed, drooling.

"Hedaya, eat your lunch," Summerman said. "I can do that."

"Nonsense. It's my pleasure."

"I'd say you're going to spoil him, but it's way too late for that."

Hedaya chuckled and grabbed a baked potato. He cut it in quarters and added it to the plate filled with steak. He reached for a bowl of sautéed spinach but paused when he heard the low growl.

"Oh, that's right," Hedaya said, laughing. "You hate spinach don't you, Murray?"

He placed the plate on the floor next to the table, watched the dog begin eating, and then filled his own plate.

"Before I forget, Summerman. How long are you planning on staying?"

"I need to get to LA at some point, but there's no rush. Why do you ask?"

"I'm having a small dinner party tomorrow night, and I'd love for you to come."

Summerman raised an eyebrow at the old man. "And?"

"And nothing," Hedaya said, chewing a mouthful of salad. "Of course, my guests would be most disappointed if the great Summerman Lawless was present, but failed to play."

Summerman smiled.

"What did you have in mind?"

"Two, forty minute sets, an hour break between them for dinner."

41

Summerman laughed.

"You're a real piece of work, Hedaya. Any special requests?"

"No, I'll leave that to you." Hedaya bit into a piece of steak. "Of course, a mixture of jazz standards and a few interpretations of some of your old hits would make for a great first set. And the second set would be perfect for one of your wonderful extended improvisations." Hedaya sipped his wine and winked. "But, of course, I'll leave that up to you."

"Of course." Summerman looked down at the wet nose buried against his hand. "You finished already? You little pig."

Hedaya waved to a waiter standing nearby.

"James, if you'd be so kind. A Guinness in a bowl for my furry friend."

Chapter 10

I spent the rest of the day interviewing consultants and casino staff working on the project. By late afternoon, I already had ninety percent of the information I needed, but the process had to be rigorously followed. Input from everyone was necessary to validate findings and minimize later outcries of bias and unfairness, which I knew would come.

I'd found the Prophecy consultants as expected; indignant about having to answer questions regarding their performance from an outsider; their perceived expertise challenged. I had also found them inexperienced, and many had shared that this was their first project. The casino staff was more cordial, but it was apparent they'd been kept out of the loop and only given piecemeal information.

Hungry, I looked at my watch. I had one more interview left for the day, and it was the one I was both dreading and eager to start. On cue, she knocked softly on the door.

"Are you ready for me?"

I looked into her eyes. They were wary, but inviting.

"Now there's a loaded question. Hey, I missed lunch. Do you mind if we do this downstairs?"

"As long as it's out of earshot of those damned slot machines."

We walked to the elevators and took the short trip down to the casino floor in silence. We found a small lounge in a far corner of the casino and sat facing each other across a small table. A waitress was ready and waiting.

"What can I get you?"

I quickly scanned the menu and ordered. I looked at Maya, who shook her head no.

"What would you like to drink? Wine?"

She stared at me.

"For old time's sake."

"Well, okay. A glass of cabernet."

"Make that two, please."

We sized each other up, silently noting the changes and similarities, both wondering how we'd come to be sitting together in a casino cocktail lounge in Vegas. Finally, she spoke.

"You look good."

"You're still so beautiful."

"Don't start. Please." She blushed and flipped her hair back from her face.

"So. How are you?" A gentle probe.

"I'm…okay."

I saw the sadness in her eyes. Was it for her? For me? Or perhaps both of them? The waitress returned with our drinks.

"Your food will be right out," she said, then scurried away.

I watched her leave.

"She's a good waitress."

Maya smiled. "You still have the need to comment on everything, huh?"

"Only on what I understand." I picked up my glass. "I've been pretty quiet lately."

She picked up her glass and raised it to her lips.

"What?" I said. "No toast?"

"I thought we stopped toasting."

"That was a long time ago." I raised my glass. "To good friends."

We touched glasses and sipped. She set her glass down and smiled at me.

"Go ahead."

"What?"

"Have a cigarette."

I laughed and retrieved the pack from my jacket. She watched the once familiar scene play out.

"You're never going to stop are you?"

"Stop what?"

"Funny." She took another sip of wine. "So tell me, Herr Doctor, what on earth are you doing here?"

"I was about to ask you the same thing. You quit working a long time ago."

Maya chose silence, so I recounted the events of the past few days. I chose not to enlighten her on my energetic shower session with Grace. The waitress arrived with my food, and I chewed in silence for several minutes. Between bites, I snuck glances and marveled at her beauty. I'd seen the name Maya Helton on the project list, but I'd never known her married name. For me, not knowing it made her decision less real. Now, as I looked at the diamond ring and wedding band, reality glittered at me. I finished eating and sipped my wine.

"Okay, what's up with this project?"

"It's the most screwed up thing I've ever seen. We both know that Barrier's a total asshole, but he's always been good at putting these things in. I guess he's been in corporate too long."

"Any special requirements from what you've seen?"

"No, it's a slam dunk," she said. "Or should be. There's nothing unusually complex here. And the purchasing side. Have you seen what they're doing to that application?"

"Yeah. It's a mess."

"It's never going to work."

I listened closely to her comments. Most telling was the fact she rarely talked in absolutes.

"What do you think would fix it?"

"A bomb."

Satisfied my observations had been confirmed, I sat back and lit another cigarette. I found her indignation arousing.

"What?" She looked at him quizzically. "I'm serious. It's a total piece of shit."

"I just love it when you get cranky."

"You love everything I do." She gulped down the last of her wine. "Why is one of life's great mysteries."

"How did you end up in Vegas? You hate this place."

"A couple of months ago I decided to go back to work, and I put out a few feelers. I figured, given my history with Billy Boy, it would be the fastest way to get working. So I talked with him, and he told me about this project. He said it needed help for a couple of months."

She looked over at me. "Yeah," she said. "Billy Boy lied to me. What a shock, huh?"

"You should know better." I laughed

"Anyway, I figured with Barrier running things it would at least be organized, so, I said what the hell. But when I get here I find out it's a complete mess and I'm looking at a year. Unless, of course, you kill it."

I ignored the comment. "There's a camera in the small conference room."

"What?"

"Yeah, it's in the pencil sharpener. That's why I wanted to do this down here."

"Spooky. But they're everywhere else, so why should that room be any different?"

"Don't tell anybody, especially Barrier. I want him on his worst behavior this week. What do you know about Jenkins?"

"He's okay, and the rest of the systems all seem to work fine. It doesn't make any sense. This place is an incredibly high-tech operation, but they can't install some financial software?"

"It looks like Jenkins has given the keys to Barrier."

"Yeah, a set of keys but no engine or tires. I guess thirty million doesn't go as far as it used to."

I was pleasantly surprised by how quickly we'd slipped back into our comfort zone with one another.

Why did you ever let her get away?

I shrugged and checked my watch. I was late for my meeting with Jenkins. I signed the check, grabbed my jacket and bag, and stood.

"Dinner?"

She searched my eyes. "Best behavior?"

"You know I can't promise that. I never could."

"Where?"

"Room service in my suite."

She cocked her head.

"We won't have to worry about other people being around."

"Liar."

"Okay. So I want you all to myself for one night. After five years that's not much to ask, is it?"

"It's a lot to ask, and you know it."

"Seven o'clock?"

"Yes."

Chapter 11

I left Jenkins' office at 5:30 and headed down to the casino. Although the meeting was brief and uneventful, Jenkins seemed to appreciate the update. I had hoped to develop a better understanding of the man, but Jenkins appeared preoccupied with other matters. Over the years, I'd developed great respect and sympathy for Chief Information Officers. Their jobs were brutal, and the average lifespan of a CIO was around three years. The technology landscape changed daily and the expectations of executives and system users were constantly going up. I wondered how Chief Financial Officers, always quick to beat the shit out of their CIOs, would handle the pressure if they were forced to change their accounting structure every couple of months. As I rode down in the elevator, I wondered where my mental tangents came from. What was it that caused my neurons to spark and set off brush fires in the far corners of my brain?

Probably the same thing that's given you, me.

"Thanks. That makes me feel so much better."

I walked towards the blackjack tables, found a ten dollar table with only one other player and sat down.

"Good afternoon, sir," the dealer said.

"Hi. How are you?" I extracted a hundred from my wallet. I watched her crisp, efficient movements as she changed the bill into a small handful of chips.

"Change one hundred."

A woman wearing a casino blazer walked over and nodded at me. She made a quick note on a pad, maintaining her carefully studied air of indifference.

"Hey, man. Whassup?"

I looked at the young man sitting to my immediate left. His baseball hat was turned backward. "I'm good. How do you like being a catcher?"

"What?"

"Nothing."

"Please don't touch your money, sir. No touching your bet after I've started dealing the cards."

"Gee, I'm sorry. You've only told me that about six times."

I looked at the face-up ten and checked my down card. Another ten. I pushed my cards forward and lit a cigarette. I watched the man on my left,

47

deep in thought. I peered over and saw the ten the man was holding along with the three face-up on the table. I glanced at the dealer's five.

Stay. Just sit.

I silently cursed the voice. The man tugged the baseball cap down further.

"Give me a card."

Moron.

I rolled my eyes.

"Sir, you need to make a hand motion for another card," the dealer said, the edge in her voice impossible to miss.

"Oh, yeah right. Give me another card." He flicked a finger in the general direction of the dealer.

The dealer pursed her lips. "Okay." She flipped a ten from the shoe.

"Damn. What's up with these cards?"

The dealer flipped her hole card over. Ten. Fifteen. I bit my lip and said nothing. The dealer reached into the shoe and flipped a six. She looked at me, a touch of pity in her eyes as she took my money.

"Sorry," she said.

I shrugged.

That's what you get for playing the ten dollar tables.

"Why can't she just give me another card when I ask for it? Why do I have to make some stupid hand gesture?"

"It's for the cameras," I said.

"Cameras?" The man looked around. "What cameras?"

I ignored the question since I was focused on the man's left hand, shocked by what I saw.

"That's quite a ring you're wearing."

The man proudly held up his left hand. "It's great, isn't it? My wedding ring. Me and Sylvia just got married today."

"Sylvia, huh?"

Perfect.

"Congratulations."

"We drove up from Riverside today just to get hitched." He leaned over and whispered. "I found it on the side of the road on the way up. Amazing. It was like a sign from above. Perfect fit, too."

"Did you also take the table?"

"What?"

"Nothing. Riverside, huh?"

"Yeah. How about you?"

"L.A."

"L.A." The man almost spit it out. "What a cesspool."

I smiled at his reaction. Los Angeles wasn't a place that generated ambivalence.

"Well, it's certainly no Riverside."

I heard the dealer laugh and checked my new hand. Another twenty. I slid the cards forward and looked back at Baseball Cap, who was studying his cards. He held fourteen against the dealer's six.

"Say would you mind if I helped you out a little?"

"I could sure use some," the man said.

I spent the next half hour slowly explaining basic blackjack strategy. How to play against the dealer's hand. When to double your bet. How to minimize your losses. As a big believer in Karma, I couldn't help but wonder how much baggage this man now carried on the third finger of his left hand. But, for the moment, his luck was improving. Over the next several hands, Baseball Cap won back his losses plus another two hundred. I broke even but didn't mind. I was more interested in the success of my new blood brother from another world.

A very pregnant woman waddled up to the table. She was young and pretty, but I noticed her fatigue and could only imagine what childhood wedding dreams had been put to death today. Still, I saw the love in her eyes.

"Hi, hon. Are you winning?"

"Just look at this," the man said, proudly revealing his winnings.

"Wow. You won all that?"

"Sure did. And you thought I didn't know how to play. Hey, Sylvia, I'd like you to meet…"

"Doc."

I smiled and shook the bride's hand.

"Nice to meet you." She turned back to her new husband. "Hon, I'm hungry."

The man softly rubbed the woman's stomach. "Okay, buffet, here we come. Doc, we gotta run."

He pushed his chips in the direction of the dealer who quickly counted and stacked them in front of her. She removed three black chips from her tray and placed them next to the stack.

"Three hundred out. There you go, sir. Enjoy the rest of your evening."

The man clutched the chips in his right hand.

"I hate to leave Doc. You're my good luck charm."

"Only time will tell about that."

"What?"

"Nothing. Well, congratulations to both of you. Have a nice honeymoon."

"You bet."

They walked off in search of food. The dealer watched them go.

"Something tells me it's going to be a short one," she said.

"Let's hope not."

"You did a good thing there. You're a nice man."

My eyes suddenly welled up.

Wow. Where did that come from?

"I couldn't afford not to help him out. I owed him that much."

The dealer gave me a confused smile.

"Well, it was sweet."

I left the table, my mood better than it had been in several days. Near the elevators, I saw Baseball Cap and Sylvia standing in the long line waiting to get into the all-you-can-eat buffet the casino was famous for. I passed unseen but overheard the man asking his new wife if she had seen any television cameras.

"No. Are they filming something here?"

"Don't know, but let's keep our eyes open."

"I'd love to be on TV. That would be so cool."

Chapter 12

My good mood was short-lived.

I'd started pacing the suite at 6:45 and hadn't stopped. Seven o'clock had come and gone, and I began wondering if she'd changed her mind. Instinctively, I knew she was as intrigued as I was about catching up. I also knew she would be wary and nervous. At least we'd begin the evening with something in common.

The knock was soft. I opened the door. She had changed clothes and was wearing a soft cotton dress that hung from her shoulders by two small straps. The dress flowed off her legs whenever she moved. I checked the length of the dress. It wasn't short, but short enough. She kissed me on the cheek and looked around.

"Nice. How do you rate? I've only got a room."

"It's amazing what they'll give you if you play enough."

"Hmmm," she said, dismissing the comment. I knew she wasn't much of a gambler.

She walked over to the table for two that had been arranged earlier. It was elaborately set, and candles lit the darkened corner of the room. She played with the centerpiece and cocked her head at me.

"You know this is just dinner, right?"

"Yes. But if this makes you nervous we could order a pizza."

She smiled and sat down on the couch, appearing more relaxed.

"Glass of wine?"

She looked down at the opened bottle on the coffee table in front of her.

"Two glasses tonight. That's it. I know how you get."

"Me?"

"Okay, how we get."

"I already ordered for us. I think you'll like it."

She nodded and sipped her wine, deep in thought.

"Do you remember that little bar in Belize?"

"The one on the beach?"

"Yes. What was the name of the drink they served?"

"The Snapping Turtle."

She smiled at the memory.

"That was the best week I ever had. And the shortest."

51

"Me too."

I felt my eyes moisten again. I turned and reached for my cigarettes. I fumbled for the lighter.

"The place hasn't changed much."

She raised an eyebrow and waited.

"I go back every year."

"For your birthday?"

"What else?"

"Jesus, Doc," she said, shaking her head.

"What can I say? I like the place."

She remained silent for several moments.

"How does your new wife like it down there?"

"I always go alone."

"I see."

I could only sit and wait for the question.

"So how is…Sylvia, right? How is she doing?"

"She's in Greece."

"Nice. We recently spent a month sailing the islands. It was beautiful."

"No. I mean, she's gone. We're done."

A flash of surprise crossed her face.

"I'm sorry. I truly am. What happened?"

"Lack of effort, I think," I said. "Well, that's half the story. How's Jeremy?"

"He's…active."

The knock on the door startled us. The waiter, sensing the mood in the room, quietly and efficiently set dinner up. I over tipped him, and he was gone. We moved to the table and began to work our way through pork tenderloin with asparagus and Portobellos and an incredible potato dish laced with various cheeses. She chewed slowly, then put down her fork and sipped wine.

"This is my favorite meal."

"I know."

From across the table, she frowned.

"So I remembered. It's no big deal."

"Hmmm."

She resumed eating.

"You were saying?"

She smiled at me through the candlelight.

"Subtle as a truck, Doc."

"I'm a curious guy. What can I say?"

She put down her fork and wiped her mouth with her napkin. She picked up her wine, sipped, then shrugged.

"Jeremy is sleeping around. Is that what you wanted to hear?"

I sat back in my chair and saw a single tear roll down her cheek. She made no effort to wipe it away.

"That's impossible."

"Really?"

I caught the brunt of the flash of anger and immediately regretted the comment.

"Well, at least it would be for me."

She studied me long and hard from behind her wineglass.

"You believe that, don't you?"

"Yes."

"Well, maybe you should explain some things to him."

I laughed and shook my head. I had never met the man and planned on keeping it that way.

"Never help your competition. Especially after they've won. Who's the woman?"

"Women. Once you cross that line, why stop at one? It's funny. Given everything that happened with us, I always thought that if one of us cheated, it would be me." She softened a bit. "And no, that's not an invitation."

"I'm so glad you told me. I was just getting ready to turn down the sheets. Are you guys separated?"

"No, it's more like mutual co-existence at the moment. That's why I'm here. I figured if I was going to be that alone, I might as well work for a while."

"It's amazing."

"What?"

"Ever since I met you, you've gotten everything you wanted, but it seems to just fall short of what you truly deserve."

"Some of us have lower standards of happiness, Doc. Or maybe it's a lower threshold for pain."

"When all else fails, lower your expectations?"

"Maybe you should try it sometime. From what I've seen, you don't seem to be sending the bliss factor off the charts."

"Touché."

We sat in silence as we finished our dinner. I hadn't bothered to order dessert. We never ate it. I studied her as she studied her half glass of wine. Apart from her eyes, traced with a few age lines and a different hairstyle, her outward appearance was identical to the woman I'd last seen five years ago. Not looking up from her glass, she finally spoke.

"What was the question you asked me when we were saying goodbye?"

"Is this the end of the beginning or the beginning of the end?"

"That's it. I liked that question."

"I thought you hated it. You always hated it when I pushed you to think too hard. Or talked too much."

"I didn't hate it. It was just unfair."

"You started to slip away. I had to push. Maybe I pushed too hard."

"Maybe you should have been a little more open."

She stared at me and waited.

"You never were one to beat around the bush." I glanced around the room, then exhaled loudly. "The voice is back."

"Oh, no. Since when?"

"Couple of days ago."

"How bad is it?"

"Still under control, but getting worse. Strangely, it's been pretty quiet tonight."

"I'm sorry. It must be horrible."

"No, it's okay. I've learned to live with it."

"The medication never worked?"

"Oh, it worked great. We went around stoned all day just talking to each other."

"I heard you were seeing a therapist. How's that working?"

"I get better advice from the voice."

She laughed.

"Do they still think it's stress related?"

I nodded my head slowly.

"Yeah, and if they're right, it's going to be a long week."

"Let me know if there's anything I can do." She caught herself and smiled at me. "Within reason of course. Look, I should go."

"Yeah, long day tomorrow."

She stood and I followed her to the door. She leaned in and kissed me softly on the lips. I gently brushed her cheek with the back of my hand.

She closed her eyes and enjoyed the moment. "Thanks," she said. "I had a nice time."

"Me, too. Let's do it again."

"We will. Soon."

"How about tomorrow?"

She laughed and pulled her shoulder straps further up.

"Goodnight, Doc."

I watched her walk down the hall before closing the door. I refilled my glass, sat down on the couch and lit a cigarette. I enjoyed the darkness and silence that existed far above the action down below.

Even the voice seemed content.

I was still sitting there when I noticed the first rays of sunlight working their way through the curtains. For me, it was just one more sleepless night.

But I had a feeling that, last night, I wasn't the only one.

Chapter 13

"Your car, sir."

Barrier reached into his pocket and pulled out a crumpled dollar bill. He handed it to the attendant who looked at it, then back at Barrier with a blank stare.

"What? A dollar's not enough to open a fucking car door?"

"Have a nice evening, sir."

Barrier slammed the door and checked the rear view mirror catching the final seconds of the finger he was getting from the attendant.

"Insolent little prick."

He gunned the car past the immense fishpond that surrounded the casino entrance. He turned left at the end of the driveway away from the Strip and began to crisscross his way through several side streets in the general direction of North Las Vegas. The neon, while ever present, began to lose some of its power over the surroundings, and he began to see the deterioration. Away from the neon, Vegas was like any other city.

Rather than navigating the Strip filled with tourists, he'd chosen reality and found himself amid the regular folks. And the hookers and dealers. He hated dealing with regular folks, especially when he was in Vegas. He came here to get away from reality, not to be reminded of the scum that infringed on his daily life. He drove slowly and watched street people lingering in the shadows. Cursing his decision to avoid the Strip, he stopped for a red light and saw a woman standing on the corner. He checked the rearview mirror and opened the window.

"Hey, Sugarlips. How much for a blowjob?"

"Sixty bucks. Unless you're a cop."

"Nah, I'm not a cop."

"Too bad. I do cops for free."

"You make me want to protect and serve."

"And you make me want sixty bucks. What do you say?"

"I'll give you twenty."

"I don't even blow a kiss for twenty bucks. Drive on, honey."

"And no condom."

"From the looks of you, sweetie, you'd be lucky if I didn't make you wear two."

"Your loss."

56

The light changed, and he gunned the car down the street. He laughed and turned the music up. About a quarter mile ahead, he saw the sign for Pete's. He parked in back and entered the bar through a side door. It was dark, and Barrier stood in the doorway waiting for his eyes to adjust. A cloud of smoke hung a few feet above the patrons, and he cringed at the smell of stale beer and urine. A pool game was in progress, and a line of slot machines ringed the outside wall. The clatter of coins punctuated the country music coming from the jukebox. A woman in a short skirt with big hair was rubbing herself against a drunk playing video poker at the bar. Scanning the room, Barrier eventually recognized the man sitting in a booth near the back. He nodded in his general direction, walked over and sat down opposite him.

"Nice. This city has some of the most upscale places on the planet, and you drag me here."

The man crushed out his cigarette and tugged his baseball cap further down. He studied Barrier's face before speaking.

"There aren't any surveillance cameras in this place."

"No shit. It's not exactly a Kodak moment. Where's Jenkins?"

"Playing the slots. Where else?"

Barrier followed the man's gesture and saw Jenkins working a machine near their booth. The man produced a sharp whistle and Jenkins turned toward them. No one else had the energy or interest to notice. Jenkins cashed out, collected the coins in a plastic cup and walked over to the booth.

"Won forty bucks. Not bad, huh?"

"There's obviously no waitress here. I'm getting a drink," Barrier said.

Without asking if his companions wanted anything, he left for the bar. Jenkins sat down and looked across the table. The man ignored him and leaned back and waited while Barrier ordered and paid for a beer. Barrier slid into the booth next to Jenkins and took a long pull of beer.

"Okay, let's start. What happened today?"

"He did interviews and pissed off my entire staff," Barrier said.

"My staff liked him. They said he's the only person who's ever made any sense on this project," Jenkins said, running his fingers through the coins in his cup.

"Will you stop playing with those things? Jesus Christ, you're worse than a little kid." Barrier grabbed the cup and moved it to his side of the table. "Well, what the fuck does your staff know about anything? They're still trying to figure out how to log on."

"No thanks to you," Jenkins said.

Ignoring the exchange, the man in the baseball cap continued. "So what did he find?"

"He found exactly what I told you he would find. That the project is completely out of control."

Barrier took a long drink from his beer and set it down hard on the table.

"He's smart," Jenkins said.

"Big deal. We're all smart," Barrier said.

"Yes, but we're the ones with the problem," Jenkins said.

"We don't have a problem," Barrier said, rapidly working his way through the beer. "We get through the week, listen to his recommendations and then we get back to work. If we need to make some changes to keep the old man happy we do it,"

"I don't know. I'm worried," Jenkins said. "I think I'll get a drink. Roger, you want one?"

"No, I'm good."

Jenkins headed to the bar. Barrier watched him go and shook his head.

"Fucking gamblers. They'd sell their own mother."

"Is he going to make it?"

"Jenkins? Who knows? I guess it depends on how long he can stay ahead of the loan sharks."

"He doesn't look good. We need him, but if he is going to go over the edge, maybe-"

"Look," Barrier said, interrupting. "Whatever you and the Bureau decide to do with Jenkins, I don't want to know about it. I'm already up to my chin on this thing, and I don't need any more waves."

"It's a little late to worry about that, Jimbo. Trust me; you're in."

The man smiled at Barrier and lit a cigarette. Jenkins returned with his drink.

"What did I miss?"

"Nothing. Just another chapter in the sad life and times of Roger Gentry," Barrier said. "When are you scheduled to meet with him?"

"Tomorrow afternoon."

"Well, if he gets his hands on your resume, Roger, let's hope it holds up."

"I forgot about that. Damn."

"Don't worry about it. He probably hasn't even looked at them," Jenkins said.

Both men turned toward Jenkins, who stared back, oblivious.

"What?"

Gentry was angry.

"What are you talking about? He's already got it?"

"Way to go, George," Barrier said.

Jenkins turned defensive.

"He asked for them. I couldn't refuse to give them to him. Hedaya made it clear that I had to give him everything he asked for. If I refused, that would have been even worse."

Gentry and Barrier let it go. Gentry turned his attention to Barrier. "It's too late to develop some cover."

"Yeah, there's not enough time. Let's just hope it doesn't come up," Barrier said.

Barrier frowned. Gentry noticed.

"What?"

"I was just trying to remember what we put on it."

"How many people does he know in the industry?"

"He used to know everybody. But he quit working in technology years ago. Look, don't worry about it."

Gentry slapped the table, and his voice dropped about an octave. "Don't tell me what to do. It's my job to worry."

"Does the Bureau teach you to do that with your voice?" Barrier mimicked the voice. "Oooh. Don't mess with me. Especially when I sound like James Earl Jones."

Jenkins laughed but stopped when he saw Gentry's expression.

"Barrier, I'm most dangerous when you don't hear me coming."

"Then remind me not to buy you slippers for Christmas. Just cut the intimidation crap, Gentry. I don't scare easy. You might work for the FBI, but I've been in the private sector for twenty years."

Barrier got up from the table and walked to the bar. Jenkins and Gentry watched him go and then looked back at each other.

"He's a despicable human being," Jenkins said.

"I'd like to shoot him."

Chapter 14

At four o'clock sharp, Gentry knocked on the conference room door. Doc looked up from behind his desk and stood.

"Roger, right?" Doc extended his hand.

Gentry accepted the handshake.

"Right. Nice to meet you, Doc. Everything going okay so far?"

Be careful with this one.

"Yeah, I think so, but I've still got some questions."

"Well, that's to be expected. It's a big project."

"Yes. Sit down."

Both men sat at the small table. Doc flipped his notebook to a fresh page and jotted down the name and time. He put his pen down and smiled.

"So, you're coordinating the training and documentation side."

"Yeah. It's a lot of work. But after you've done it for as long as I have, it gets easier."

"I noticed on your resume that you were an independent consultant for about ten years. What made you accept a permanent position here?"

"I burned out on airplanes. Plus, my girlfriend lives here in Vegas. She works here at the Casino."

"Really? What does she do?"

"Guest relations. Or something like that."

"Sounds interesting."

"It sounds pretty boring to me, but Grace seems to like it."

Uh-oh.

"Grace?" Doc glanced up.

"Yeah. What?"

"I like that name."

"Yeah, she's pretty special," Gentry said. "And very good at what she does."

You got that right.

Doc shook his head at the voice and refocused on Gentry. The majority of people he knew who worked in the training field had warm, outgoing personalities. Gentry's seemed anything but.

"So, you're just here for the week."

"Yes."

"You got any real recommendations or are you just going through the motions?"

"What motions would those be?" Doc sat back and waited.

Gentry frowned, then forced a smile. "Oh, you know. Take a look, write the report, collect your fee."

Doc remained silent. Gentry, sensing he had dug himself a hole, attempted to climb out.

"Look, it's nothing personal but we've all been through these reviews before. Usually, nothing comes out of them."

"Usually."

"But not this time?"

"We'll see. That's out of my control. But don't worry, whatever happens, people will still need to be trained."

"Oh, yeah. Right. They certainly will."

"Let me ask you something. How are you filling your day?"

"What do you mean?"

Good one. He's edgy.

"Well, all the actual training is being handled by Prophecy. And it looks like you have two staff dealing with the documentation. Plus, given the current schedule, actual training sessions won't even begin for another three or four months."

"What are you saying?"

Doc smiled at the reaction he was receiving.

"I'm not saying anything. I'm asking how you stay busy. Aren't you bored?"

"No, I'm not bored. I do other stuff around here. I help other people when they need it."

"That's good. It's always nice to see teamwork. Who?"

"Who do I help? Well, lots of people."

"Such as?"

"Well, Jim Barrier for one."

"What do you do for Barrier?"

"Stuff. Just general stuff."

Doc picked up his pen and jotted down a note. He then flipped to a fresh page. He noticed Gentry watching. He put the pen down.

"One idea per page," he said. "That way I don't get confused."

"Was it a good one?"

"The idea? It's a great idea."

Doc sat back in his chair and waited for the man's next question. Gentry sat quietly staring at the notepad.

"Okay, I think we're done."

"Already. That was quick."

"I don't see much there. Unless you have something else you want to discuss," Doc said.

"No, I can't think of anything. I guess I'll see you around."

Gentry headed for the door.

"Oh, Roger. Just one more question."

Gentry stopped and turned back.

"Sure. What is it?"

"About your resume."

"What about it?"

"I worked on that project in Chicago for about a year. It's strange. For the life of me, I don't remember you."

"Well, I had a beard then. Plus, I've lost a bunch of weight."

"I see. How'd you do it?"

"Diet and exercise. It's a constant battle to keep it off."

"Yeah, I know. Me too."

"You look pretty fit. How do you do it?"

"Cigarettes and stress."

"Whatever works, huh? Well, I'll be seeing you."

Gentry turned back to the door and left. Doc watched him go, then picked up the phone.

Chapter 15

Doc had been under the false impression that his suite on the top floor was about the best the casino had to offer. As the elevator door opened, he was engulfed by a magnificence that made his plush accommodations pale by comparison. Like the massive room at the bottom of the Casino that contained the ice rink, the rooftop garden was enormous and magnificent.

Doc scanned the plants, lighting, and furnishings that stretched in front of him. A massive pool with a waterfall running the entire length of one side was lit from below. Dozens of splashing, laughing bodies barely made a dent in the square footage. The entire rooftop was an eclectic mix of contemporary Western and traditional Chinese, yet everything blended perfectly.

Doc, absorbed in his surroundings, didn't notice the young Chinese woman standing next to him, holding out a pair of slippers.

"Oh, I'm sorry," Doc said, accepting the slippers. "Slippers, outside?"

"Hedaya considers this part of his home. And tradition dies hard."

"I understand. Thank you."

He took his shoes off and handed them to the woman before putting on the slippers.

It's like being back in Shanghai.

The woman extended her arm, inviting Doc to follow her. As they walked past a massive fireplace, the woman smiled and gestured to a sitting area near the grand piano. Doc sat down in a huge chair that welcomed him.

"Hedaya has asked me to take good care of you while he finishes a phone call. But he won't be long. Can I get you anything?"

"Yes, I'll take one of these," Doc said, gesturing to indicate the massive garden. "Just have it shipped to Los Angeles."

The woman smiled and looked around.

"It is beautiful, isn't it?"

As she walked away, Doc could hear the soft shuffling of her feet. He relaxed into a chair and let the garden's tranquility wash over him. A few minutes later, he saw Hedaya walking towards him. He was wearing tailored black silk pajamas. Doc stood and shook the man's extended hand.

"Good evening, Hedaya. Nin hoa ma?"

"Wo hen hao. Couldn't be better. Thanks for coming, Doc. It's good to see you."

"No, thank you. I wouldn't have wanted to miss seeing this place. What can I say? It's magnificent."

"Thank you. It's still a work in progress, but it's coming along."

"Yes, I can see that it must be quite a burden." Doc laughed. "It fills the entire roof?"

"Of course. It's an indulgence, but one must feel comfortable in one's home, don't you think?"

"I'm sorry, but I have to ask. How many square feet?"

"About sixty thousand, I think."

"Sixty thousand square feet?"

Doc thought about his house in L.A. and how often his four thousand seemed excessive.

"Not counting the heliport." Hedaya smiled and winked. "To count that would be cheating. Come, there's someone I'd like you to meet."

Hedaya led him across the garden. They walked through tall rows of hibiscus and palm trees until they reached a glass building. Hedaya opened the door and motioned Doc through. Doc stepped into yet another world, this one a massive atrium. The room was hot and shrouded in mist. He followed the old man onto a wooden bridge spanning the small stream that ran through the glass structure. Doc stopped on the bridge and looked around. Hedaya waited, watching Doc as he tried to comprehend his surroundings.

"Rainforest?" Doc looked at Hedaya, perplexed.

"Yes. I'm afraid it's the only climate that Bugsy can handle."

"Please don't tell me you have Bugsy Siegel's corpse in here."

Hedaya laughed.

"Goodness, no. Only his namesake. Come."

Hedaya escorted him from the bridge onto a stone walkway. From his vantage point, Doc noticed a polished black granite wall that crisscrossed the entire perimeter of the room.

"Here. Come closer." Hedaya gently took Doc's arm and led him to the edge of the wall. "Look," Hedaya said, guiding Doc forward.

"I don't see anything."

"Just down there," Hedaya said, pointing down into the thick underbrush that lay inside the wall.

65

"No," Doc said. "All I see is a bunch of plants. I'm sorry but I…aaaahhh." Doc jumped back several feet. "Jesus Christ. What the hell is that?"

"That's Bugsy." Hedaya laughed. "I'm sorry, but I just love doing that."

Doc slowly moved back to the edge of the wall and looked down at the giant lizard staring back up at him.

"What is that? A Komodo dragon?"

"Very good. Yes. And it appears that he is hungry."

Hedaya pressed a button on the wall. A voice came back within a few seconds.

"Yes, Hedaya."

"Charlie, did you feed Bugsy yet?"

"I was just on my way, sir."

"Very good. Thank you." Hedaya turned back to Doc and smiled.

"What does he eat?"

"Usually, everything that gets inside that wall. He's quite magnificent, isn't he?"

"Well, he's big. I'll give him that."

"Almost thirteen feet the last time we measured him. Usually, they don't grow past ten feet, but he's quite pampered here. He's more of a pet than anything. The last time we were able to measure him was three years ago. Bugsy may like living here, but he doesn't like having his measurements taken,"

Hedaya stared down at the dragon that appeared to be wagging its tail.

"So he's named after Bugsy Siegel?"

"Yes, my little tribute to the history of Las Vegas."

Hedaya motioned for Doc to follow him. They went back down the walkway, across two more bridges, and eventually reached the far side of the atrium. As they walked, Hedaya chatted casually about the history of Vegas that included anecdotes about Siegel, Howard Hughes, and the nuclear testing the federal government conducted in the area during the 1950's.

"So, you see, Doc, the real history of Vegas is somewhat different from the legend that attributes its origins to Bugsy.

"You mean the mob."

"That's such an unfortunate term. Mob." Hedaya shook his head. "I know many people who work for those organizations, and the majority of them are wonderful people. They have a well-defined code of ethics I find appealing these days, given the total lack of business principles I see from many of this country's more *legitimate* business people."

"Unless you cross them."

"Doc, even though I've been in this country a long time, you must remember that I am Chinese. I am very familiar with violence as both a tool and a consequence of business. Anyway, our city leaders have always preferred the image of gangsters creating Vegas. It has a more romantic appeal, I imagine. We are here."

Hedaya led Doc through another door into a smaller glass room that contained a bar and a single blackjack table. A solitary man was playing and laughing loudly at something the dealer had said. Doc looked down at the massive beast sitting next to the player's stool. The beast stared at Doc.

"Uh, Hedaya?" Doc said.

"Yes?"

"Given your penchant for exotic animals, I need to ask you a question."

"Go right ahead."

"Is that a tiger?"

"No, that's Murray."

The man playing blackjack looked up from his cards to greet Hedaya.

"Summerman Lawless," Hedaya said, "I'd like you to meet-"

"Doc White."

"Have we met?"

"Not officially," Summerman said.

Doc accepted the handshake and looked down at the dog that continued to stare up at him.

"Does he bite?"

"Only if you get in his way when he's eating," Summerman said. "Or when I tell him to."

"I'll try to remember that."

Murray stood and inched his way closer to Doc. Doc slowly lowered his hand and scratched the side of the dog's head. Murray accepted the gesture of friendship but continued to stare up at him.

"Why is he looking at me like that? He looks like he's seen a ghost."

"Interesting choice of phrase," Hedaya said. He winked at Summerman who smiled at the old man. "Well, I'm sure the two of you will get a chance to chat later. Are you ready to sing for your supper, Summerman?"

"I certainly am. Billy has been kicking my ass the last hour and I'm down ten grand."

"That makes me happy," Hedaya said.

Hedaya turned to go, then stopped.

"Billy, go ahead and take a break for an hour or so. After dinner, I have a nice young couple from Denver that is dying to give me back the million they won last month. I'll send them your way."

"Yes, sir. Would you mind if I spent my break listening to Summerman's first set?"

"Of course not. Let's head out. I'll lock up behind you."

Chapter 16

Doc wasn't sure what was moving faster; Hedaya's legs or his mouth.

"The city grew and during that time it was quite wild. And in the late 1940's, Mr. Hoover decided to make an example of how it was being run. After a round of comical congressional hearings, the state was forced to institute the Gaming Control Board, the group that decides who can own a casino. That was the beginning of the end for organized crime."

They reached the head table, and Hedaya gestured for Doc to sit down. They settled in, and Hedaya took a sip of champagne.

"I'm not boring you with my history lesson, am I?"

"No, not at all," Doc said.

Doc nodded at Summerman, who was approaching the grand piano followed by the massive dog.

"Who is that guy?"

"I'm sure you'll find out soon enough." Hedaya smiled but turned quiet. "As I was saying, most people choose to either ignore history or rewrite it."

"And repeat it."

"Of course. One of our fatal flaws as a species. Anyway, Vegas was faced with a serious problem."

"No new money."

"You're very good, Doc. Exactly.And in the early 1950's help came from a most unusual source. Mr. E. Perry Thomas, a Mormon banker."

Doc shook his head.

"Never heard of him."

"You're not alone. But for the people who matter in Las Vegas, he was a very special man. He helped establish local banking and identify more legitimate funding sources. A true visionary."

"So he provided access to money."

"Yes. A lot of money." Hedaya smiled at something in the distance. "Ah, there she is."

Rose, dressed in a forest green silk dress, strolled towards the table. Her long hair was woven and tied on top of her head, and Doc found himself, once again, stunned by her beauty.

Talk about good things coming in small packages.

Doc nodded and continued to stare.

She kissed Hedaya softly on the cheek.

"Good evening, Bofu."

"What a lovely dress, my dear. Doc, what do you think?"

"Rose, xiaojie hen hao kan," Doc said.

"Yes, she is very beautiful tonight," Hedaya said, beaming proudly.

"Hi, Doc. It's so nice to see you."

Hedaya pulled her chair out, and she delicately sat down and looked around the table.

"Oh, champagne," she said, casually.

Doc took his cue and poured her a glass. She sipped, put the glass down, and folded her hands in front of her on the table.

"Oh good, Summerman hasn't started. I was afraid I was going to be late."

"We were waiting for you. I was just giving Doc a short history of our beautiful city."

"More stories about the crazy billionaire who refused to cut his toenails? Really, Bofu, you must get some new stories. Do you like Chinese food, Doc?"

"Yes, very much."

"Then you will love this," Rose said. "Lotus Flower is our best restaurant."

"I must agree," Hedaya said. "We truck our vegetables in from Los Angeles. One of my good friends has a wonderful produce market in Chinatown."

Doc nodded, finding the vegetable conversation less than interesting.

"Have you had a chance to talk with George about my preliminary findings?"

Hedaya frowned.

"I would prefer not to talk business this evening."

"My apologies, Hedaya."

"Don't give it another thought. But in answer to your question, I have only spoken briefly with Mr. Jenkins. It can wait until tomorrow for your presentation. Will you have numbers for me to look at?"

"Yes, I will."

"Excellent news. I'm sure Mr. Lawrence will find the meeting most interesting."

Hedaya sat back in his chair, a small smile fixed on his face.

"Bill Lawrence is coming?"

"Yes. I have some matters to discuss with him, and I thought he might find your presentation interesting," Hedaya said. "How long has it been since you worked for Mr. Lawrence?"

"I think you already know the answer to that question, Hedaya,"

Hedaya laughed.

"Well, one thing emphasized during my brief stay in law school was never to ask a question unless you already know the answer."

"Your sources of information are most impressive, Hedaya."

"Obtaining information is easy in today's world. Keeping things private is the problem."

"Have you met Lawrence before?" Doc said.

"No," Hedaya said. "But I am looking forward to it. I always enjoy meeting people like Mr. Lawrence."

"You mean meeting other billionaires, like yourself?"

Hedaya feigned surprise.

"Have you been peeking at my balance sheets, Doc?" His eyes twinkled, and he patted Doc's arm. "I just wish the circumstances of our initial meeting were more positive."

"I wouldn't worry about Bill. He's used to angry clients."

"Oh, I'm not worried. Because you're going to take good care of my interests."

Hedaya stood.

"Okay, no more talk of work. It's show time."

Hedaya walked to a table near the stage and whispered in Summerman's ear. He then reached down and petted Murray before stepping onto the stage. The crowd fell silent.

"Good evening and welcome to my home. This is the first of what I hope will be many wonderful get-togethers this summer. And I can't think of a better way to start than by introducing someone I'm sure you remember. He'll be performing before and after dinner and, if you've never heard him before, I'm envious because I remember how I felt the very first time I listened to him play. Ladies and gentlemen, please join me in welcoming Summerman Lawless... and Murray to the stage."

The crowd erupted, and Summerman sat down at the piano. Murray crawled under the piano and stretched out, draping himself over Summerman's feet.

"Who is this guy?" Doc said.

"Summerman?" Rose said. "Don't you remember the band Life's Eclectic Nightmare?"

"No, who were they?"

"A very popular rock band that got killed in a boating accident. Well, except for Summerman, of course."

"Never heard of them."

"Really? Do you live under a rock?" Rose said, laughing.

"I'm just not a fan of rock. I'm more of a jazz fan."

"Then you, my friend, are in for a very special treat."

And she was right.

Chapter 17

Summerman felt sweat dripping into his eyes, and he blinked it back as his hands hammered the keys. He'd taken the small riff he'd experimented with on the flight and turned it into an extended improvisation that now approached forty-five minutes. Fighting back the fatigue he always dealt with during his first week back on this side, he pushed himself forward. He moved both hands left on the keyboard and created a furious sound that resembled a distant rumble of thunder. He raced up and down the keyboard three times, softly repeated the small riff that had started the piece, then spread all ten fingers to play a chord that stretched three octaves. He nudged Murray under the piano with his foot. The dog took his cue and placed a paw on the sustain pedal. The chord hung in the air, then faded.

The crowd, led by Hedaya, roared and leaped to its feet.

"Holy shit," Doc said. "What was this guy doing wasting his time playing rock and roll?"

"Making millions, I presume," Rose said, clapping wildly.

Summerman took a small bow, and Murray approached the edge of the stage wagging his tail. The crowd roared again.

Summerman laughed and stroked the dog's head.

"Don't mind him. He's a total ham."

Summerman toweled off and sat down at his table in front of the stage. A waiter approached with a glass and a bowl of Guinness. Summerman and Murray made short work of them.

Doc approached the table and sat down. "That was incredible."

"Thanks. It still feels great to play in front of an audience."

"If I could play like that, I'd never stop."

"I've been known to do that," Summerman said. "Keep playing, that is."

Doc extended his pack of cigarettes towards Summerman. He waved off the offer, and Doc lit one and sat back in his chair. "What did you mean earlier when you said we've never met officially?"

"I don't think I have the energy to do this tonight. I'm pretty tired."

"Do what?"

"Have the conversation we need to have."

I'm not sure I like the sound of that.

73

Doc stared at him and rubbed his forehead. "I'm not used to people telling me no."

"Yeah, I know."

"Excuse me."

"Sorry. Like I said, I'm just tired. How about tomorrow?"

"To do what?"

Summerman stood up and arched his back. "To have the conversation we need to have."

"I don't see any reason why we would need to have a conversation."

"You will." Summerman glanced under the table. "You ready to go, Murray?"

The dog climbed out from under the table and stretched.

"Good night, Doc. Hope to see you tomorrow."

"Hey, wait a minute."

Summerman paused.

"Just answer this. Why do you need to talk to me?"

"Because I'm here to help you. And, after that, I think we can help each other."

"You're here to help me?"

"Yes, I am."

"With what?"

"Well, for starters, with the voice."

Doc stunned into silence, watched him and the dog wander off into the night.

Chapter 18

I worked through the night rechecking facts and cross-referencing the mwith my interview notes. Finally satisfied, I finalized the recommendations I'd been formulating all week. The clock next to my bed read 2:50.

Needing a break, I ordered coffee and took a quick shower. By the time room service arrived I was back at the desk in my robe. Hot coffee in hand, I did a final review as I sipped.

They're going to be really pissed.

I shrugged and began work on the new schedule and budget. Two hours later, I looked at the final number and compared it to the current projected budget. I sat back, smiled and lit a cigarette.

But Hedaya is going to love you.

At six, I glanced at the phone but decided it was too early. I killed the next half-hour channel surfing then picked up the phone next to the bed and dialed. An angry voice answered.

"Jeremy, I told you we'd talk about it when I got home."

"It's me."

"Oh, I'm sorry." A long awkward moment of silence followed before she regrouped. "Good morning. Did you sleep last night?"

"No. I tried to call, but your phone was busy."

"Yeah, I was on a long time."

The silence continued. I finally gave the conversation a nudge forward.

"Hey, since we're both leaving today I was wondering if you'd like to have a goodbye breakfast. But if you can't, that's fine."

"Relax, Doc. I'm just checking my schedule. I'm clear until nine. Your place I assume?"

"Sure. Come on up when you're ready. The usual?"

"Give me fifteen minutes."

I placed the order with room service and got dressed. I opened the curtains and looked out at the vast expanse of desert interrupted only by the adult Disneyland that was Las Vegas. Tonight I'd be back in my house, sleepless in an empty bed. Somehow that seemed more inviting than the bleeding brought on by my recent trip down memory lane. I knew this set of fresh wounds would heal. I just needed time and distance. Maybe even the voice would disappear.

We'll see.

I heard the knock and opened the door and was greeted by both Maya and the waiter. "Good timing." I stepped back to let the room service cart pass and greeted Maya with a quick kiss on the cheek. I caught a whiff of her perfume. It worked its usual magic on me.

"You look great."

"Thanks."

She placed her bag on a chair and poured two cups of coffee. She was biting her lip as she handed me a cup. She sat down on the couch and sipped.

"Tough night?"

"Very."

"Anything I can do?"

"No." She looked at me with tears forming in the corner of her eyes. "But thanks."

"What time are you flying out?"

"Noon. I should get home by nine at the latest. You?"

"Depends, I guess, on whether I make it out alive. I'd like to be on the road by five. I'll be going against traffic, so I should be home by…nine." I smiled at the irony. "Let's make it a race."

"How does the presentation look? Everyone's dying to know what you're going to say."

I retrieved the laptop and slid it in front of her. She spent several minutes reviewing the presentation.

She pushed the laptop away and sat back.

"Impressive. Make Hedaya happy and piss Barrier off the same time. Good job. Did you leave a role for me?"

"Do you want one?"

She sat quietly and thought about it.

"I think I do. I'll know better after this weekend."

"I'll let Hedaya know. Just call him when you've decided."

I stood up, uncertain what to do with my hands.

"It's been great seeing you. Short, but great."

"Yes, it has," she said.

"Maybe we're better in short bursts, huh?"

She laughed.

"Probably. But let's not wait another five years. Okay?"

"Okay." I felt a surge of emotion rip at my chest.

"Take care of yourself, Doc."

"You too. And whatever you do, don't settle for less than you deserve."

"Good advice. Maybe you should take some of it yourself."

She leaned in, touched my face and kissed me softly on the lips.

"Be good."

She grabbed her bag, tossed it over her shoulder and left without looking back. I watched the door shut, closed the curtains and climbed back into bed.

Chapter 19

Barrier and Gentry watched Jenkins pace the small conference room that, given the size of the room, was more like a nervous shuffle.

"Jesus, George," Barrier said. "You look like a rat in a tunnel. Sit down."

Jenkins stopped and looked at Barrier.

"I'm fucked. If the presentation is anything like the notes he gave me, I'm going to be fired on the spot. How did I let you two talk me into this?"

"You didn't have a choice, George," Gentry said, clipping his fingernails. "So just sit down and deal with it."

Jenkins sat at the table and fidgeted with a paper clip. Barrier reached over and grabbed Jenkins forearm.

"Ow. Stop that," Jenkins said, pulling his arm away.

"Relax, George. Give us a few minutes to work this out," Barrier said, not releasing his grip. "Okay, so what do we know?"

Jenkins, on the verge of a full meltdown, let loose again.

"Only that he is going to turn this thing completely upside down. And I'm going to be out on the street. Do you have any idea how hard it is for a fifty-year-old CIO to find another job? I'll end up doing PC maintenance in Fresno."

Barrier looked at Gentry who continued his clipping.

"You know, I spent a week in Fresno once," Barrier said.

"Yeah," Gentry said. "Why?"

"I won first prize in a contest."

"What was second prize?" Gentry said, stifling a yawn. "Two weeks?"

Jenkins jumped up from the table.

"Goddamn it."

"George, sit down and be quiet." Gentry looked at Barrier. "Will Lawrence be any help?"

"He certainly won't hurt. He's a magician. The problem is he and Doc go way back. They're not tight like they used to be, but he will definitely listen to what he has to say. The worst thing that can happen is for Doc to come up with a way to shorten the schedule. That puts more pressure on you."

Gentry nodded and began to collect the nail clippings scattered around the table.

"We can deal with that. Once he's out of here, we'll find a way to stall for more time."

"I don't know. The old man is getting pretty tired of writing checks." Barrier massaged his forehead.

"What?"

"Billy Boy is going to have me by the nuts. He's too busy to get involved in these projects, but as soon as you get on his radar screen, look out. I'm a dead man."

Gentry tossed a handful of nail clippings into the wastebasket.

"Sorry, Jimbo, but I don't give a shit. You made your bed."

"You're a real piece of work, Gentry. I feel so much safer knowing the FBI is filled with people like you looking out for our best interests."

"I'm not here to make friends, Jimbo. We know the old man is moving money to the Caribbean. I'm here to find out how and how much. And so far the two of you have been remarkably consistent in your total lack of help. So excuse me for not giving a shit about what happens to either of you."

The phone rang, and Jenkins answered.

"Jenkins. Hi, Doc. Now? Okay. I'll see you in my office." Jenkins hung up and looked at the two men. "He wants to go over the presentation with me."

Barrier shook his head and looked at his watch. "An hour before the meeting. How considerate of him." Barrier stood up. "Okay, George let's go warm up the band."

"No," Jenkins said. "He specifically said you weren't invited."

Chapter 20

Doc walked down the hall towards Hedaya's office. He was wearing a new suit. His shirt collar, although perfectly tailored, still seemed determined to choke him. He waved to Hedaya sitting at his desk and continued past the main office into the adjoining conference room. Hedaya's assistant was preparing the room for the meeting. Doc handed her the stack of papers he was carrying.

"Hi, Shirley. Could you keep these away from prying eyes for the next few minutes?"

"Sure, Doc," she said. "Don't you look nice today?"

"Well, if you're going to swim with the sharks, you should at least wear the right equipment, huh?"

"I'll alert the Coast Guard," she said, laughing.

**

The corporate jet taxied to a stop on the runway. A large black limousine pulled up, and the driver got out and stood ready to open the back door. At the top of the stairs, a freshly showered Bill Lawrence entered the heat from the air-conditioned comfort of the plane. Squinting from the glare, he pulled on sunglasses and walked briskly down the stairs. Two young women, wearing identical blue business suits and carrying briefcases, followed him into the back seat.

Lawrence looked at the two Chinese women sitting across him. He didn't know if bringing them would soften the old man, but he decided it couldn't hurt. He stared at the faces smiling at him. They could be twins, he decided.

"I love Vegas. Are we staying the night?"

"I doubt it. I have a speech in Miami tomorrow."

"Oh, please Bill. The three of us could have so much fun here tonight.

Lawrence, remembering the previous hour on the plane, had to agree with her.

"Let's see how the afternoon goes."

"Who's Doc White?" asked one of the women reading her email.

"He's somebody who used to work for me. He went independent several years ago."

"Oh, another consultant too good to work for a real company, huh?"

"What? Yeah, it was something like that."

"What's he doing on one of our projects?"

"Trying to kill it," Lawrence said.

"Well then, you'll just have to stop him, won't you?"

"No, I'm afraid I'm too late. This trip is straight damage control. But that stays with us. Understand?"

He stared hard at both of them for emphasis. Both women nodded and went back to their reading.

**

Doc headed outside for a cigarette. He leaned against a wall near the main entrance. He saw the limousine pull up and watched two women get out, followed by Lawrence.

Their eyes met almost immediately.

Lawrence spoke briefly to the two women who nodded and walked briskly into the casino. Lawrence approached Doc with his arms extended. They shared a brief, but genuine, embrace.

"Jesus, Doc. You look good."

"You too, Bill. It looks like being a billionaire agrees with you."

"Yeah, it has its moments. I see you still haven't quit those things."

"As soon as they hit fifty bucks a pack, I'm quitting."

"Won't be long." Lawrence laughed.

"Want one?"

Lawrence glanced around.

"What the hell. Sure."

Doc took out two cigarettes, lit both and leaned back into the wall.

"Thanks," Lawrence said, taking a long drag. "Damn things. They're just like women. Eventually, they'll kill you, but just try to give them up."

"By the way, nice touch with the women. But Hedaya won't buy it."

"No, I didn't think so. But what the hell, they're still fun to travel with."

"I bet they are. Same old Bill, huh?"

Lawrence smiled.

"So what's the old man like?"

"Pretty amazing. The kind of guy that makes you not worry about getting old."

"Is he actually trying to qualify for the Olympics?"

"Yeah. He's dead serious about it. I wouldn't bet against him."

Lawrence took another long drag on his cigarette.

"You've got me on this one, don't you, Doc?"

"Yeah, you guys are hosed. But you've got to believe that I didn't go looking for it. I've made a very good living off your stuff, and we go way back. Barrier fucked you on this one."

"I knew I shouldn't have let that prick out of the office. I should have kept him doing what he's good at."

"Scaring the shit out of the troops?"

"Exactly. So how much am I going to have to give back to the old man?"

"That's really your call, Bill. You've gotten over thirty million out of him, and all he has to show for it is a copy of the software. Have you seen any of the documentation on this thing?"

"Yeah, I read it last night. Not one of our finer moments. You know, this wouldn't happen if you were still around. By now, you'd be running the whole consulting operation."

"I know. Such is life, huh? Anyway, you're looking at a giveback of somewhere between five and ten million. Plus, you'll have to promise to bring in a whole new team to finish it. Do those two things and Hedaya will probably agree not to sue your ass."

"I hate dealing with this shit."

"Well, at least you're here. That's more than a lot of people would do."

"Whatever. Okay, let's go do this."

He buried his cigarette in a sand-filled ashtray.

"You better be good because I'll be paying attention."

"Don't worry; I promise to go slow."

**

Hedaya stood at one end of the conference table and looked at the four men waiting for him to speak. Doc, at the other end, was sitting with his hands folded in front of him. Barrier and Jenkins sat on one side of the

82

table with Lawrence directly opposite Barrier. Lawrence kept firing sharp glances at Barrier, who carefully avoided eye contact.

"First of all, I would like to welcome you, Mr. Lawrence. I am a great admirer of you and your company. I hope that whatever takes place this afternoon does nothing to diminish the respect I hold for you."

Nice start.

"We are here to discuss the future of this project. I stress that because I pride myself on being someone who looks forward rather than dwelling on the past. Any remedies we come up with for previous mistakes will be dealt with at a later date."

Hedaya glanced at Barrier and then at Jenkins. Both men sunk a little deeper into their chairs.

"I want to assure you that I have no advance information about what Doc is going to present today. I thought this process would be fairer if I stayed out of this week's activities. It is my understanding that the only person who has seen the presentation is George, who was briefed a short time ago. I do need to say that I have very strong opinions on this matter that I chose to keep private until the appropriate time presented itself. That time has arrived. Doc, please proceed."

Doc passed out copies of the presentation and waited until the room resettled.

"I'm going to sit if that's okay. Let's keep it as informal as possible. If you have questions, ask them as they come up rather than wait until the end. I think that will help the flow as long as the questions stay on point."

He looked around and received silent agreement.

"Okay," Doc said, taking a deep breath. "This will be uncomfortable for some of you. George, you've already seen it, and I think you'd agree."

Jenkins nodded without looking up.

"Jim, you aren't going to like this at all. Since you're in charge, I'm afraid it all comes back to you."

"I'm a big boy, Doc. Go ahead."

Doc nodded at Barrier and took a sip of water.

"This project was doomed from day one. The initial design was too complex for the relatively straightforward requirements. I have no idea why some of the design decisions were made, nor do I care, but they were some of the worst decisions I have ever seen."

Barrier started to interject, but Lawrence waved him off. Doc looked at Barrier and tried to find a trace of sympathy for the man. Coming up empty, he pushed on.

"During my interviews, I repeatedly heard from Prophecy consultants that the design was driven by the casino staff. But based on my conversations with the staff, as well as my review of the documentation, I found little evidence to back that up. It's obvious that most of the design decisions were made independently by Jim and George. With that initial design as a blueprint, you then began dismantling the basic functionality of several applications. As a result of massive customization, they are now virtually unrecognizable. Assuming you were able to get it working, it's unlikely the casino would ever be able to upgrade to newer versions of the software without spending several million dollars."

"Several million?" Hedaya said. "Can you be a little more specific?"

"Probably somewhere between five to seven million. And that would be an expense you would face every three to five years. That's a nice annuity for Prophecy, but certainly not good for you, Hedaya. Okay, let's go through the findings section. They start on page three."

Doc spent the next several minutes reviewing his detailed findings. As he continued, he noticed Barrier's anger build. The other three men sat quietly following along with the presentation. At the end of the section, Doc paused, took another sip of water and waited for questions.

"It seems that we are like a dog constantly chasing its tail," Hedaya said.

"You are," Lawrence said. "For that, I apologize to you right now."

He glared across the table at Barrier, who had turned a light shade of red.

Welcome to the shark tank, Jimbo.

Doc looked around the table, then continued.

"All right, let's move on to the recommendations."

"There are no numbers here," Barrier said. "How can you expect us to deal with recommendations without a new set of numbers?"

"He has the numbers, Jim. I'm sure you'll see them when he feels the time is right," Lawrence said.

"Yes, I have numbers," Doc said. "I didn't want you getting ahead of yourself, Jim."

"Fuck you," Barrier whispered.

Unfortunately, it was just loud enough.

84

"Please, Mr. Barrier," Hedaya said. "Go ahead, Doc."

"First of all, it's my recommendation that the entire design be scrapped."

"Sure, let's just start over," Barrier said, shaking his head. "What planet are you from?"

"Next, I would go back to the standard functionality and add the projects module to handle the bulk of your cost collection. Stop trying to do that out of the purchasing module."

"Add another module? What is that going to cost me?" Hedaya said.

"Well, I can't speak for Bill, but I would imagine you're going to get that for free."

"Absolutely," Lawrence said, nodding.

"I would eliminate virtually all the interfaces you currently have and replace them with one primary interface that would meet all your needs. Also, the data warehouse disappears. Since all your reporting requirements can be met out of the production system, you don't need it. You can easily run your weekly reports over the weekend, and everyone will have the information they need on Monday mornings."

Doc paused and waited for questions. He saw Lawrence shaking his head with a disgusted look on his face. Doc shrugged his shoulders and continued.

"That's the guts of it. There are several smaller recommendations listed on the last page. But let's move on to the schedule and budget."

Doc turned on a laptop, and a large chart appeared on the projection screen behind him. The various project phases were outlined, and the current project schedule was displayed in red bar graphs that ran horizontally across the chart. Standing to one side of the chart, Doc continued.

"This is your current schedule. It shows you have a minimum of eight months remaining. Given your current progress, I think it's at least a year and, when you do finish, you will have succeeded in implementing a sub-optimized solution."

"A sub-optimized solution?" Hedaya said.

"Please excuse my crassness, Hedaya," Doc said. "But by the time it's finally done, you will have spent over forty million dollars on a piece of shit

"No, that is quite all right," Hedaya said. "The image is very clear. Okay, what do I do?"

Doc looked at Lawrence, who nodded his head.

"The first thing you do is get rid of the current group of consultants and bring in a smaller, more experienced team."

"Hey," Barrier said. "Now just wait a minute."

Hedaya shook his head and whispered, "Neige ren hen tebie."

Doc smiled at Hedaya's comment about Barrier being a peculiar man. He was shocked when he heard Lawrence's response.

"Ta xuede bu kuai."

Lawrence's Chinese was impeccable.

"Indeed," Hedaya said, laughing. "He does learn slowly, doesn't he?"

Hedaya sat back down and nodded at Doc. Doc worked the smile off his face and continued.

"Unfortunately for you, Jim, that includes a new project manager. George, as we discussed, you need to reduce the number of your staff working on the project. Send two-thirds of them back to their real jobs. You have too many people working on this thing. The coordination effort required is enormous and wastes too much time. Plus the effort you spend coddling everyone is not a good way to run these projects. While they are collective efforts, they are not necessarily democracies."

Doc flipped to the next slide and a new project schedule in green was overlaid onto the current schedule.

"From a schedule standpoint, here's what you get."

He waited while the reality sunk in around the table.

"What am I looking at?" Hedaya said.

"You're looking at a ninety-day schedule, Hedaya," Jenkins said.

"Three months? You're telling me that I can have this system in three months?"

"With the right project team and a little focus, yes," Doc said.

Hedaya turned to Lawrence.

"Do you agree with that assessment?"

Lawrence looked at the schedule projected on the wall and turned back to Hedaya.

"I would have to say that if you implement according to the recommendations Doc has made, it is possible. It is an aggressive schedule, but it is possible."

"I'm starting to like this meeting," Hedaya said, sitting back in his chair. "Continue."

Doc flipped to a new slide that showed the current project's budget. "That leaves us with the numbers. Here is your current expenditure chart along with each team member."

Hedaya impatiently waved the screen away.

"I've seen those numbers. Show me the new ones."

Doc flipped to a new slide. Again, he waited. Lawrence was the first to respond. It was a low, soft whistle.

"Am I seeing correctly?" Hedaya said.

"Yes, sir," Jenkins said.

"What game are you playing, Doc? Name That Tune?" Barrier said.

"If you immediately transition to a team of six consultants, assuming they are the right ones, you can implement this system in three months for approximately two million dollars."

Doc sat down. The room was quiet.

"You just saved me over ten million dollars."

"Yes, he did," Lawrence said.

Hedaya removed his glasses and rubbed his eyes.

"George, please excuse yourself and take Mr. Barrier with you. I need to speak with Mr. Lawrence and Doc privately."

The two men looked at each other, then Barrier glared at Doc. They quietly left.

"A most interesting morning," Hedaya said. "Mr. Lawrence, I'm afraid the services of your consulting group are about to be terminated. Please do not take that decision as a personal attack on you. I think your mistake in this matter is principally a lack of oversight. One I can understand given your schedule, but I would expect better from your management staff."

"So do I. Rest assured that I am committed to making adequate restitution for the problems we have created."

Hedaya dismissed the comment with a wave of his hand.

"Of course. I'm sure you are. Neither one of us wants bad feelings. But let's allow our respective legal staffs to earn their money and handle those negotiations, shall we?"

"That would be fine. Just for the record, I was thinking somewhere in the neighborhood of five million."

"Interesting," Hedaya said, "but I was thinking of a somewhat larger neighborhood."

Hedaya smiled and motioned for the two men to follow him.

"Come, let's go upstairs and have something to drink."

Hedaya led them into his residence on the top floor. He escorted them into a portion of the penthouse Doc had not seen on his previous visit. Doc found himself in a small rustic room that resembled an Irish pub. The more he looked around he realized that, in fact, he *was* standing in the middle of an Irish pub. Hedaya noticed Doc's bewilderment.

"I have some Irish clients who visit several times a year," he said. "The more they feel at home, the more they gamble." He pointed to a corner of the room. "A few weeks ago one of them lost three million dollars right at that table. Serves the bastard right since a few months earlier, he won two million in that same spot."

"You built them their own pub?" Doc said.

"Yes. Despite the large number of people that visit the Vegas casinos, it is the big players that are most coveted. Individuals like Mr. Lawrence here. You usually stay at the Bellagio, correct?"

"Yes."

"Well, tonight you must stay with us. As my guest, of course. How about a pint of Guinness?"

Hedaya walked behind the bar and proceeded to draw three drafts from the keg. Doc and Lawrence sat down on bar stools and watched.

"Hedaya, there is one more piece of business we need to discuss," Lawrence said. "Mmmm, that's good."

"I assume you are referring to the clause in the contract that mandates, at a minimum, one Prophecy staff member must be assigned to the project, regardless of who I use for consulting assistance. Yes, one of my lawyers pointed that out to me this morning."

"We've found that having at least one technical advisor on all projects that understands our technology prevents many problems. It is, I'm afraid, non-negotiable."

"I see. Well, I'm sure that is a role Mr. Barrier can adequately handle."

"What?" Lawrence glanced at Doc, who was also baffled. "I'm sorry, but after all you've been through, why on earth would you consider keeping him around?"

"Let's just say he has some unfinished business to attend to and leave it at that shall we?"

Hedaya smiled and took a long swallow from his glass. He put down the glass and wiped his mouth with the back of his hand.

"Besides, Doc will certainly know how to handle him."

This oughta be good.

Doc stared at Hedaya, who was smiling at him from behind the bar. "Excuse me?"

"I said that you will know how to handle Mr. Barrier. I am in need of a new project manager, and you are the perfect choice."

"Now wait a minute. I need to get home."

"Why? From what I understand, there is nothing waiting for you there."

Doc again wondered about the old man's information network.

"No, I'm done doing these projects. Sorry, Hedaya. I'm flattered, but no way."

"What do you think, Mr. Lawrence?"

Lawrence, down somewhere between five and ten million for the day, shrugged his shoulders. "I think I'll have another Guinness."

"No," Doc said. "I'll find somebody to run it. Somebody really good."

"I'll even increase your rate. I came into some extra money earlier today. Just think about it, Doc. A painless way to pay off what you owe me."

That is something worth considering.

"I don't care. No."

"You get to pick your own team." Hedaya raised an eyebrow and held Doc's stare.

With that comment, Doc stopped. Three months with her by his side. Conflicting thoughts and emotions surged through his mind. He remembered her smell and the softness of her kiss. He remembered months when the voice had been relentless. He waited for it to come. Finally, it spoke.

What if?

"Okay. I'm in."

Chapter 21

Doc tossed the last of his three suitcases into the Explorer and pulled out of the driveway, plotting a route that, with luck, would get him back to Vegas in a little over four hours. He pulled a piece of paper from his shirt pocket and taped it to the console. He scanned the list of phone calls he needed to make and put on his headset. He called the first number on the list.

"Hello." The voice was angry and abrupt.

"Hi, is Maya there?"

"Hang on."

"Hello?"

"Hi. It's me. What are you up too?"

"Packing."

"So you're going to come back?"

"Yes. I get in late tonight."

"Are you okay?"

"Let's just say Goldilocks found out who's been sleeping in her bed and leave it at that."

Doc remained silent.

"Not a good time, Doc. I'll call you when I get in."

"No problem. I was just checking in like I promised."

"Okay. Thanks. Bye."

Before Doc had time to ponder their conversation the phone rang. He looked at the display screen and didn't recognize the number.

"Hello, this is Doc."

"Hi. How are you doing?"

Doc steered the Explorer into the slow lane and prepared for battle.

"Hi, Sylvia."

"So, how are you?"

"I'm poor," he said.

"Well, if it's any consolation, I don't want anything else."

"Good. That will make it easier. I'll have the papers drawn up."

"No, don't bother. I've already done it. I had Larry take care of it."

Doc remembered the lawyer they'd used in the past.

"Did you have him change the will as well?"

90

"Yes, he's taken care of everything. But you'll see it. I'm mailing it today."

"Don't send it to the house. Mail it back to Larry. I'll get it from him. I'm going to be working in Vegas."

"I see. I suppose you're blaming me for that."

"No, I'm not. How's Greece?"

Her mood brightened.

"It's so beautiful. I'm on a boat right now. We're island hopping. It's too bad I never learned how to swim."

"That's one opinion."

"Don't be mean," she said. "What happened, Doc?"

Doc sat silently in the stalled traffic. Rain started to pound the car.

"We weren't in love. I'm not sure if we ever were."

"That's probably true." She fell silent, then coughed. "Well, I should let you go."

"Okay. Take care of yourself."

"No hard feelings, Doc?"

"Actually, Sylvia, I'm not feeling much of anything."

"Me neither. That must be a good sign, huh?"

"As far as we go, probably. But I'm not so sure what it says about us as people."

"Don't be too hard on yourself. We're just still searching. Goodbye, Doc."

"Goodbye, Sylvia."

Doc hung up wondering where to lay the blame. The secrets he kept from her were a testimony to his own culpability, but her inability to take any real interest in his life must have contributed to his unwillingness to let her in.

Fifty-fifty.

The rain slowed to a drizzle, and Doc's spirits improved. Rather than let the traffic ruin his mood, he slid his seat back for comfort and turned on some music. He tested several CD's and finally settled on mellow jazz.

I like this.

"I know you do." Doc checked his list and turned the music down. He dialed and waited. A sleepy voice answered on the third ring.

"I'm not here."

"Hey, Merlin. It's Doc."

"Doc? Jesus, Doc. What are you up to?"

"Right now I'm looking for the freeway lane designated for Californians who know how to drive in the rain. Where are you?"

"I'm in Rio."

"Bad news for the Brazilians."

"Yeah, you know me. I had some odds and ends to take care of so I've been down here for a few days. I'm done, but I thought I'd pay a visit to the doctor while I was here. Speaking of which, hang on a second."

Doc heard a faint tapping sound followed by two long sniffs.

"That's better. So, how's retirement?"

"For the time being it's over. That's why I'm calling."

"What have you got going?" Merlin said.

"It's a project in Vegas."

"Vegas? Jesus, I hate Vegas."

"I know. Will the Company let you take some vacation?"

Merlin laughed.

"After what I just did down here, I'm sure that won't be a problem."

"You been bad?"

"Good, bad? Who the hell knows the difference these days? But I think the Company and I are about to part ways. Which is exactly what I've been hoping for."

"Be careful what you wish for, Merlin."

"They won't fuck with me. So what's this project?"

"It's completely legit. A Prophecy implementation."

"What? What the hell did you do, lose a bet?"

"Actually, yes. You can do this one standing on your head. It's a restart, but pure vanilla from here on. Barrier's been running it."

"Barrier? He's running projects again? What'd he do, sleep with one of Bill's girlfriends?"

"I'm still not clear on that. Have you got three months open?"

"Yeah, I could probably make it work if the price is right."

Doc smiled.

"All right, let me have it."

"Well, since it's you, I'll do it for ten a day."

"You'll do it for five and like it. Ten thousand a day, nice try."

"Hey, if you don't ask, you don't get. Five's cool, but I want a seven-day billing week."

"Deal. I need you in Vegas as soon as possible."

"What's today? Sunday, right? Uh, let's see. I can get there by tomorrow night."

"That's great, Merlin. Looking forward to it. And do me a favor. See if you can dig anything up about what Barrier might have gotten into. Also, there's a Roger Gentry, who I think might be with the Feds. See what you can find." Doc paused, then continued. "And Gentry's got a girlfriend named Grace. Check her out too."

"I thought you were done with this stuff."

"Me too. Hey, I hear the beaches down there are great. How's the water?"

"I'm not going anywhere near the water down here. Did you know they have a tiny fish with barbed fins called the Candiru? It's attracted to warmth and, if you urinate while swimming, it will follow the urine stream back to its source and enter your body. Then it flares it fins, and it stays stuck inside your wee-wee until it's surgically removed."

"So don't pee in the water."

"Thank you very much. I'll stay in the pool. With all the snot-nosed, ankle-biters around that's bad enough."

Doc laughed.

"This should be fun. Maya's working on it, too."

"Maya? Geez, I haven't seen her in a long time. How is she?"

"She's miserable."

"Well, you always did have that effect on her."

Chapter 22

"Are you familiar with the term shin-ken, Doc?" Hedaya said.

"What's that?" Doc said, caught off guard. "Oh, shin-ken. Yes, that's the Japanese term for real sword. It means to do something with the utmost earnestness."

"Exactly," Hedaya said. "Perhaps you would perform better if you paid more attention to this piece of ice."

Doc felt his face flush. He had been staring at Rose, who was wearing a pink spandex body suit practicing spins on the rink adjacent to the two men.

"Sorry," he said. "She's very distracting."

Hedaya smiled in the direction of his niece.

"She does have that effect on most men. You know, Doc, she is very fond of you. You have treated her with the utmost respect and I thank you for that. My hope is for her to find someone who truly cares for her. She deserves to have her heart stolen."

Hedaya winked at Doc.

"You understand what it's like to have your heart stolen, don't you?"

He looked at the old man and caught the coy smile. Doc decided to ignore the question and knelt down.

"Okay, let's see what I can do with this one."

He rocked back and forth and released the rock down the ice. Immediately, he knew this one would have the same result as the last three. Doc watched it race down the ice and hit the back wall with a loud thud.

"Hockey players," Hedaya said, laughing.

He turned his attention to his next shot and Doc admired the man's total concentration. Hedaya released the rock and Doc watched it gently slide down the ice and come to rest alongside three more of his own. Hedaya, pleased with the result, turned back to Doc.

"Tell me how you and Mr. Barrier came to share such enmity."

"Is it that obvious?"

"Oh, my yes. But it's understandable. The man is very easy to dislike."

"Then why did you decide to keep him on the project?"

"I have my reasons."

94

Doc waited for an explanation that wasn't offered.

"Well, we used to work together, and we have different perspectives on most things. Especially about how to deal with people."

"You like people; he doesn't," Hedaya said. "But I already know all about your work history. I'm talking about your days in hockey."

"You know a lot, Hedaya. Sometimes I worry you may know too much," Doc said, raising an eyebrow. "We started playing hockey against each other as kids and disliked each other immediately. We had our first fight when we were about thirteen, and it continued through high school. We ended up playing for rival colleges. So, it continued for another four years."

Doc prepared for his next shot. This one bounced off the back wall even harder.

"See the effect he has on me?" Doc laughed. "Barrier likes to use his stick. You know, jab you in the ribs. Slash your ankles."

"That doesn't surprise me."

"Late in our junior year we were taking a face-off, and he got literal."

"I'm sorry, I don't understand."

"He tried to take my face off. The referee dropped the puck and Barrier jammed his stick right into my face." Doc showed Hedaya the scar that was on top of his nose directly between his eyes. "An inch on either side I lose an eye."

"Nasty man," Hedaya said. "What did you do?"

"Well, I bled for a long time and then I waited. We opened our senior season against them, and I caught Barrier coming across the blue line with his head down. I lined him up and hit him low. I broke his leg in four places."

"The limp," Hedaya said.

"Yes, he still believes I cost him his shot at the pros."

"Was he good enough?"

"No, but you'll never convince him of that."

"Was the check legal?"

"It was… marginal. Have you ever met anyone who brings out the absolute worst in you?"

"Of course. Fortunately, most of them are several thousand miles away. Come, let's sit down."

They walked to the other end of the rink and sat in the lounge area. Hedaya motioned briefly, and the bartender appeared. Hedaya looked at

Doc, who checked his watch. It was nine o'clock. Maya wasn't getting in for another hour.

"Two Tsing Tao, please," Hedaya said.

Doc lit a cigarette and watched Rose approach. She had removed her skates and put on a sweater, but her pink legs were still on display. She leaned over to kiss her uncle, then kissed Doc on the cheek.

"I understand you'll be spending more time with us, Doc," she said, beaming.

"Yes."

"Well then, we'll have to get together soon."

Hedaya laughed.

"You are the persistent one, my dear. Would you like something to drink?"

"No, thank you. It's Sunday night, and I have some things to take care of."

"Yes, of course."

"Stop by when you come up. I need you to review some numbers. Good evening, gentlemen."

She turned and walked away. Both men watched her leave. Doc again shook his head in amazement.

"Like I said, she's very fond of you," Hedaya said.

"Yes, I know.""Perhaps you should consider it."

That's what I said.

"I have." Doc looked at the old man. "But I wouldn't be doing it for the reason you mentioned a moment ago."

"You mean for the purpose of stealing her heart?"

"Yes. I mean, I would just be doing it for another reason. And I don't think you would approve."

"Her size notwithstanding, she is a big girl, Doc."

"She's your niece, Hedaya. And if I did anything with her for the wrong reason, I would see that as a betrayal of both of you."

"How very old school of you, Doc."

Hedaya smiled and stared off into the distance.

"You don't like being betrayed."

"No, I don't," Hedaya said, glancing back at Doc.

"Plus, I think I'll more than have my hands full the next few months."

"If it plays out the way you're hoping, I'm sure you will. What time does she arrive?"

96

Doc laughed.

"I was talking about the project."

"Of course, you were." Hedaya smiled. "Well, it's such a pity. Rose will be most disappointed."

The bartender returned and poured their beer. They both took long sips. Hedaya sat back pleased.

"Life is good," he said. "Now you must tell me about your time in China."

Doc lit another cigarette and thought about how much information he should share. He leaned into the couch and thought back to the year and a half he spent in that world. He remembered the mind-numbing tasks he had undertaken. He remembered the close encounter with Chinese authorities that had almost cost him his life. But most vividly he remembered the day the voice entered his life. The events of that day, buried just under the surface, rose and overwhelmed him. He fought back against the lump that was forming in his throat.

Forget about it. It wasn't your fault.

"Are you okay?"

"I'm fine," Doc said. "Just a bad memory, that's all." Doc smiled at Hedaya. "I was over there working on a project for a bank. Usual stuff. They were putting in a new financial system, and I got hired to run it. It was based in Beijing, but I also spent time in Shanghai and Hong Kong, as well. It was a good experience for the most part. It's an amazing country."

"Very different from this one."

Doc nodded in agreement.

"It's changing and opening up, but when you're there as a foreigner, you get the feeling that at any moment the government might lock down the whole place. It's tough to get comfortable in that kind of environment."

"That's the point. They don't want you to get too comfortable."

"Yes, that's right," Doc said, sipping his beer. "Still, living in a place like China helps put this country in perspective."

"How so?"

"Well, it's interesting to see the overwhelming influence the U.S. has. You can go into any remote village and buy a Coke or get asked about Michael Jordan. But the love-hate relationship they have with the West is obvious. The government is forced to deal with us because they need access to technology. Fortunately for them, there's no shortage of Western countries willing to sell it to them. And in those areas where they can't buy it, they try to steal it." Doc stopped, concerned that his last comment may have offended his host.

"Please continue," Hedaya said, leaning forward on the couch.

"Watching the Chinese government inch toward a more capitalistic economy is a lot like watching swimmers stick their toe in the water to gauge the temperature. Even if the water is perfect, there is no way they will just dive in. It's a cautious society. The government's biggest fear, I believe, is to have the people get out in front of them."

"Yes, and you know what you get when over a billion people start thinking for themselves."

"Well, I suppose the Chinese authorities would call it chaos."

"I would call it democracy."

"A democratic China? It's possible, I suppose. But it would be very difficult."

Hedaya leaned back into the couch and looked at Doc.

"What would it take?"

"What? For a democratic revolution to take place in China? That's a little out of my league, Hedaya."

Doc, uncomfortable with the direction the conversation was headed, forced a laugh.

"I have a suspicion that it's a league you're very comfortable playing in, Doc. Please, if you would, indulge me."

Be careful.

Doc rubbed his forehead and thought for several seconds. "I imagine it would take a number of things occurring simultaneously on several fronts. First and foremost, it would have to be internally driven. If any attempt at some overthrow were perceived as being driven by an external force, like the U.S., there would be a huge outcry. Xenophobia would rule the day and crush the effort."

"Yes, nationalism is always a good card to play in such matters."

"But if it did come from inside, you would need a way to neutralize the military. They are so woven into the economic base that it might prove impossible. I'm not sure of the number of Chinese companies that are owned and operated by the PLA, but it has to be in the thousands."

"Yes, the People's Liberation Army would be a major concern, but assume that could be handled."

"That's a big assumption, but as far as other groups go, you would need the media at some point to reinforce whatever the message was. Having the youth on your side wouldn't hurt. The bourgeois would be helpful, and they would likely fall in line if the changes didn't hurt their pocketbook. Plus, the Overseas Chinese living here and other places would be very useful. The rural villages probably could wait. In fact, there are many places in China that wouldn't notice if a revolution had taken place."

"So it would have to be primarily an urban effort?"

"One would think. You'd have to control the cities. But you'd need more than that."

"Such as?" Hedaya said, motioning for two more beers.

"You'd need a big event that would outrage and rally the people. Some crisis that could be laid at the feet of the authorities."

"Yes."

"But even if the authorities did something stupid, an opposition group would have to be extremely organized and very well funded. If you had all those things working for you, you'd still have to be incredibly lucky to pull it off. As a betting man Hedaya, you'd have to give me some very long odds."

"How did you come to such an understanding of China?"

"Asia has always been an interest of mine. It's like a hobby."

The lie rolled effortlessly off Doc's tongue.

"It's interesting. You seem to spend as much time trying to understand my country as I do yours."

Doc looked around the magnificent room.

"I think you've figured out what makes this country tick, Hedaya."

"Making money is easy. I'm more concerned with how it's used and its long-term effect."

"Well, that's been the basis for over two hundred years now."

"Yes, but two hundred years for a civilization is nothing. I worry about the many signs of decay I see."

"All great civilizations eventually decline, Hedaya."

"Yes, but only the chosen ones are reborn," Hedaya said, staring at Doc. "Don't you worry about the future of this country?"

"Yes, I do."

"And what is your biggest concern?"

Doc fired up another cigarette and thought for a moment.

"Internally or externally?"

"Internally," Hedaya said.

"The death of the middle class," Doc said.

Hedaya sipped his beer.

"The Haves and the Have Nots. Yes, I can see that. Take away the middle and the choices for people become much clearer. How about externally? The terrorists?"

Doc laughed.

"They're everywhere. Haven't you heard?"

Hedaya returned the laugh.

"Yes, I have."

"Terror is a problem, and it's going to get bigger. But I'm afraid that it's often used as a distraction to what is really going on."

"Interesting."

"You can kill as many terrorists as you can find, but with three billion people on the planet trying to live on less than a dollar a day, they're being made faster than you can kill them. And you can't kill them all."

"No, you can't," Hedaya said. "You know what I worry about most, Doc?"

"Apart from Rose and your curling, I wouldn't have a clue, Hedaya."

Doc smiled at the old man.

"I worry about the culture of celebrity in this country. Personality over performance. Fashion before form. For the popular culture, it makes interesting fare, but I think in the long-term the negative consequences are enormous."

"Short term perspective almost always leads to decline," Doc said, nodding his head.

"We have enormous problems that are currently masked by our apparent success. I fear that our leaders have lost control of the system. The money has worked its way into every facet of every nook and cranny. This bothers many people, but most feel powerless to stop it."

"They are powerless," Doc said. "I'm glad people feel better when they vote, but they're only choosing between two candidates who are bought and owned by the same special interests."

"Yes, but in China, you don't even have two choices. But it is a new day in China, and there's hope and anticipation for what might happen," Hedaya said. "And it pains me to say this since I love this country more than anything, while it may be morning in China, I believe it could be almost midnight in America."

Hedaya sunk back into the couch then bounced to his feet.

"Enough morbidity," he said. "Come. Walk with me."

Hedaya waited as Doc finished his beer. He led Doc out a side door into a section of the casino he had never seen before. Doc looked up and down the well-lit hallway and waited for Hedaya's direction.

"You'll enjoy this," Hedaya said.

Chapter 23

They walked down the hallway and made several turns as the catacomb wound its way through what Doc believed to be the basement of the casino.

"It's spooky down here," Doc said.

"Don't worry, you're completely safe," Hedaya said. "You're never alone."

Hedaya pointed up to row of lights that ran down both sides of the narrow ceiling. Doc noticed the tiny cameras interspersed between the individual lights every few feet. They approached a locked door, and Hedaya swiped an electronic keycard. The light turned green, and the lock clicked open. Hedaya led him through the door, and it immediately closed behind them. Doc saw another identical door ahead and two large mirrors on either side of him.

"They're one-ways aren't they?" Doc said, nodding at the mirrors.

"Of course."

"Good evening, Hedaya," said a voice through the intercom.

"Hello, George."

The second door clicked open, and Doc stepped into one of the most brightly lit rooms he'd ever seen. He squinted and waited for his eyes to adjust.

"The lighting is quite different down here, wouldn't you say, Doc?"

"What do you do in here? Conduct interrogations?"

Hedaya laughed.

"Only when necessary. This is one room where a lot of light is necessary."

Doc looked around and saw about a dozen people working at a feverish pitch, oblivious to their presence. He glanced up and saw the balcony that wrapped around the entire room. Security guards were strategically positioned near the corners.

"This is our hard count room," Hedaya said, above the clatter rattling through the machines counting the thousands of coins being fed into them. "It's usually not this crowded, but I like to bring in extra staff on Sunday night to handle the weekend processing."

A man wearing a smock over his shirt and tie approached and nodded to Doc. "We're only about halfway done, but it looks like we had a very good weekend, Hedaya."

"Yes, I can see that, George. Well done." Hedaya looked around the room very pleased with the proceedings. He turned to Doc. "What do you think?"

"I think a lot of people are going home unhappy this weekend," Doc said, admiring the stacks of wrapped coins that filled dozens of identical carts.

A man wheeled an empty cart into place and began filling it with trays of wrapped quarters.

"Come. Let me show you my favorite room in the whole place." Hedaya waved goodbye to the staff and led Doc through another locked door on the opposite side of the room. Doc found himself once again in the hallway. He looked around trying to understand the layout.

"Don't bother," Hedaya said, noticing his confusion. "Even the rats get lost down here."

Hedaya swiped the keycard and soon they were standing in a much quieter room. Several people were hard at work. Doc whistled unconsciously.

"How much is in here?"

Hedaya looked at him and winked. "That's one secret I don't share. Let's just say several million and leave it at that. This, of course, is the soft count room."

Doc watched as stacks of bills of various denominations whirred rapidly through machines that were sorting and counting the cash. He noticed a table piled three feet high with stacks of hundred dollar bills.

"There's just something about this room that relaxes me," Hedaya said.

"Yeah, I can imagine," Doc said, looking around the room. "Do you ever have employees who get tempted?"

"Rarely. That would be a most unfortunate choice on their part."

Hedaya walked to a table and picked up a stack of hundred dollar bills. He flipped through it and listened to the soft ripple.

"For somebody who claims that money isn't all it's cracked up to be, you certainly seem to like being around it," Doc said.

"No, what I said was that making money was easy. I never said I didn't enjoy doing it." Hedaya smiled and put the stack down. "Let's continue."

They left the room and walked a short distance down the hallway to an elevator. Hedaya swiped the electronic key into the slot, and the door opened immediately. Hedaya pushed the up button. Moments later they were walking down a hallway that Doc recognized as the second floor. Hedaya turned left, and they arrived outside the casino's surveillance room. Hedaya swiped the card, and they stepped inside.

"This is the nerve center," Hedaya said. "Very few outsiders ever get the opportunity to see this first-hand."

"Hedaya," Sam said. "I'm glad you're here. We need you to settle a bet. Hey, Doc. How's it going?"

"Hi, Sam. Joe."

Doc looked around at the banks of video monitors that filled the room. Several people were reviewing the scenes playing in front of them. Two men sitting were focused on the activities of a roulette table.

"See, right there." The man stood and pointed his finger at the screen.

"Son of a bitch," said the other, shaking his head. "Hedaya, you need take a look at this."

Hedaya walked over and stood behind the two men. He studied the monitor. Doc fell in behind the small group. He watched as the bets were placed on the table and the wheel was spun. Gradually, it came to rest. A large shout went up around the table, particularly from two scantily dressed women at the far end of the table who were noisily jumping up and down.

Hedaya's eyes narrowed, and he turned toward Doc. "Did you see it?"

"See what? I was checking out the two women."

"Precisely," Hedaya said. He turned back to the men watching the monitor. "Give them another roll. How much are they up?"

"It looks like around fifteen grand."

The wheel whirled and began to slow down. Hedaya turned to Doc. "Watch closely."

Doc watched as the wheel came to a stop and the women repeated their display. He saw a hand quickly dart into view and disappear.

Hedaya shook his head and looked at Doc. "Did you see it?"

"He made his bet after the wheel stopped."

"Yes. It's called past-posting. He's working with the two women." Hedaya turned back to the men reviewing the monitor. "Who's on the table?"

"I don't know his name. I think he's new." He zoomed the camera in on the staff member's name badge, then pulled back. Zoom. "First name is Jeffrey."

"Gerber," Sam said. "Jeffrey Gerber. He started Monday."

"Well, get him back on five-dollar blackjack and tell him to start paying attention to what he's doing down there. If he's that easily distracted by beautiful women, he's chosen the wrong career." An angry Hedaya turned to Sam and Joe. "Okay, let the dogs out."

Joe spoke briefly into the headset he was wearing. Doc turned back to the monitor. Seconds later two security guards approached the table and soon escorted the three people away.

"What happens to them now?" Doc said.

"They give the money back and get turned over to the police. When they see themselves on video I don't expect they'll put up much defense," Hedaya said, still angry. He looked at Joe. "So what was the bet you wanted me to settle?"

"The top grossing Vegas act of all time. I say it's Wayne Newton, but moron here thinks it has to be Siegfried and Roy."

"Neither," Hedaya said. "Before it's over, it'll be no contest. It's O." He looked at Doc. "Have you seen the show?"

Doc remembered the Cirque de Soleil water extravaganza permanently housed in the Bellagio. "Yes, it's amazing."

"I don't know Hedaya," said Sam. "It's a pretty new show. The others have been around a long time."

"Yes," Hedaya said, still cranky. "But eighteen hundred seats at a hundred a pop with ten shows a week. And it is going to run forever. You do the math."

"Big number," Doc said.

"Yes," Hedaya said, "and it should have been mine."

Doc looked at the old man witnessing, for the first time, his darker side. He looked back at the monitors, and an idea came to him. He thought it might not be the best time to ask for a favor, but went ahead.

"I was wondering if you could make a copy of the tapes from last week for me."

The three men looked at each other.

105

"What are you talking about?" Sam said.

"The conference room. I've got new staff starting this week and rather than rely on my notes, it would be easier to have the tapes of my interviews."

"What makes you think there are tapes? We don't have cameras in that room," Hedaya said.

Joe and Sam fell silent and looked down at the floor. Finally, Joe spoke.

"Actually, Hedaya we do. Remember when we upgraded the surveillance system a few years ago? We had a bunch of old stuff lying around and rather than toss it we hooked a few rooms up."

Hedaya frowned. "Which cameras were they?"

"I think that one was the old pencil sharpener," Sam said. He looked at Doc, who nodded in agreement. "The question is how did you know about it?"

Doc felt his face flush. Sam kept staring at him, waiting for an answer.

"Just a lucky guess."

Hedaya's attention remained on the two security men. "You guys are amazing," he said, shaking his head. "Are there any more floating around I should know about?"

"No, nothing you need to worry about," said Joe, turning back to Doc. "I don't know Doc. That's a lot of tape to copy." He looked at Hedaya, who thought for a moment, then nodded.

"Do it."

Chapter 24

Doc entered the rooftop garden and glanced around. It sparkled clean. A handful of staff, setting tables for dinner, ignored him. Doc pulled on sunglasses and headed for the pool. It was empty except for the man and his dog. Doc dragged a lounge chair to the edge of the pool and stretched out.

"Murray, give it up. You can't get all six in your mouth at the same time." Summerman shook his head as he watched the dog do his best to prove him wrong. "Hey, Doc."

"Summerman." Doc nodded and watched the dog. "He's an amazing swimmer."

"Just wait," Summerman said, collecting the tennis balls from Murray's mouth.

He climbed out and stood near the edge of the pool. The dog followed and stood next to Summerman, his eyes fixed on the balls. He shook and drenched Doc.

"Sorry about that," Summerman said. "You want a towel?"

Doc laughed. "No, I'm fine."

Summerman held up one of the tennis balls and looked at the dog. "You ready?"

The dog went on point. Summerman fired the ball into the distance, and it landed in the middle of the massive pool. Murray took a running leap and was soon furiously churning through the water.

"Jesus. He's fast." Doc sat up and watched the dog grab the ball and immediately reverse direction. "What kind of dog is he?"

"He's a mix of Newfoundland and Golden Retriever. I call him a Goldenland."

"I've never seen anything like him."

"Murray's one of a kind."

Doc couldn't miss the love and affection in the man's voice.

"Where did you get him?"

"Out of a dumpster in Amsterdam," Summerman said, firing another tennis ball into the distance. He glanced at Doc. "Long story."

"All of the good ones are."

Doc returned to the prone position in the lounge chair.

"Okay, Summerman, I'm here. What's this conversation we need to have?"

Summerman tossed the remaining tennis balls into the pool and dragged a lounge chair next to Doc and dried himself with a towel.

"Before we get started, I want you to know that this wasn't my idea."

"Backtracking already? You're not exactly starting from a position of strength."

"I'm not trying to stake out a position here, Doc."

Summerman waved to a waiter and held up three fingers. He looked at Doc. "Guinness okay?"

"Sure. Okay, Summerman. I'm a patient man, but let's get on with this."

"No, you're not. Patient, that is. I mean you have your moments, but patience isn't one of your strong suits is it?"

"Now you're starting to piss me off."

"Kind of proves my point, doesn't it?"

Summerman chuckled and looked at the dripping dog standing two feet away holding three tennis balls in his mouth. "I need a break, Murray. I ordered you a Guinness and after that why don't you take a nap in the shade?"

Murray woofed his displeasure but stretched out under Summerman's lounge chair.

"It's like he understood exactly what you just said," Doc said.

"He did."

Doc raised an eyebrow behind his sunglasses. "Okay, Dog Whisperer, let's get on with it."

Summerman held up a finger as the waiter approached with their drinks. He departed, and they sipped and listened to Murray lap furiously at his Guinness. Summerman held his glass in his lap and looked at Doc.

"What I'm about to tell you is known by only a handful of people, and I must ask you, before I start, to keep it in the strictest confidence. Even if you don't believe a word I say, you must keep it to yourself."

"I can do that," Doc said.

"I would certainly hope so. Given your background, I would imagine keeping secrets is second nature."

"What do you know about my background?"

"I know pretty much everything, Doc."

Doc removed his sunglasses and sat up in his chair. He stared intensely at Summerman.

"Again, I remind you, Doc. This wasn't my idea."

"I'm waiting. But be very careful, Summerman."

"Everything I do is careful, Doc. And in a few minutes, you'll understand why." Summerman sipped his beer and poured the remainder into Murray's bowl.

"Okay, here we go. My situation, Murray's too, is…unique. You probably know that I used to be in a band that had a tragic boating accident some years back."

"I heard. Everyone in the band, except you, was killed."

"Yes, that's the story."

Murray climbed out from under the lounge chair and draped his paws over Summerman's shoulders. He licked the side of his face and panted happily.

"You're very welcome," Summerman said. "Why don't you go stretch out in the shade?" He watched the dog trot off and looked back at Doc. "Actually, I did die. Murray did too. But we came back."

Doc laughed and put his sunglasses back on.

"You came back?"

"As a Buddhist, certainly the concept of rebirth isn't foreign to you."

"No, it's not, but a rock star and dog coming back as…hey, how did you know I'm a Buddhist?"

"How indeed?"

"Summerman, if you want to play the part of a mystic, I'm sure Hedaya can find you a slot as one of his lounge acts."

"I'm not a mystic. Actually, I'm a part-timer."

"What the fuck is a part-timer?"

"You're getting angry. There's no reason to get mad, Doc. We're just talking."

"Well, I don't like where this conversation is headed."

"I didn't think you would. But bear with me. I think it will help."

"With what?"

"Well, like I said the other night, with the voice for starters."

"What voice?" Doc stared off into the distance.

"I know, Doc. I know the whole story."

Doc leaned closer to Summerman and whispered. "Who do you work for? Are you one of us, or with some foreign intelligence group?"

"I work for myself. For the moment anyway. But, when the time's right, that is one of the things I want to talk with you about."

"Jesus Christ, I only came to Vegas to play a little blackjack."

"What can I tell you? Things have changed. My original plan was to visit you in LA. Imagine my surprise when I found you already here."

"Yeah, that must have been a real shocker for you. Okay, Summerman. Order us two more Guinness and then you have until I finish mine to explain yourself. If I'm not happy with the explanation, you're going off the roof. Or can you fly too?"

Summerman laughed.

"No, I can't fly. At least on this side. You could kill me, Doc. But next June, I'd be back."

"June, huh? Just in time for Flag Day."

"No, we cross over about a week after that. But I am back in plenty of time for the 4th of July."

"Now you're just fucking with me, right?"

Summerman smiled up at the waiter who arrived with their fresh drinks.

"Would you like me to bring one more for Murray, sir?"

"No, Arnie. He's fine for now. But check back in about a half-hour. Thanks."

"Should you be giving your dog that much alcohol?"

"He likes it. And Guinness is one of nature's perfect foods. Besides, he resets every June so it doesn't matter what he does each year during his time on this side." Summerman beamed at Doc. "That's one of the benefits of being a part-timer."

"This is too fucking weird." Doc drained half of his Guinness and peered over his shoulder.

"Looking for something?"

"I keep waiting for a camera crew to pop up."

"You mean as in Candid Camera?"

"Or some weird reality show."

"No, Doc," Summerman said, "no cameras. Just you and me. And the voice."

Doc blanched, but let the remark pass.

"So, how did you manage to come back?"

"Murray pulled me out of the boat and dragged me to shore. My grandmother's companion, a Native American shaman, worked his magic.

110

But he got something wrong. Instead of coming back as someone like him… he's over 200 hundred years old by the way, I only return during the summer solstice. Weird, huh?"

"Weird? No. Weird is some nut job walking down the Strip telling everybody he's Jesus. This is… insanity."

"I'm sorry you feel that way." Summerman sipped his beer as he stared off into the distance. "Your brother will be most disappointed."

Doc, stunned, dropped his drink. The plastic glass bounced off the tile and into the pool.

"Time for me to go off the roof, Doc?"

"What do you know about my brother?"

"Like I said, pretty much everything. He and I have grown very close."

"What the hell are you talking about? My brother has been dead for…"

"Yes." Summerman handed his Guinness to Doc. "Questions?"

"Tell me," Doc whispered.

"What?"

"Tell me the story, smart ass."

"Okay, you were in China. You were supposedly there working on some computer project, but that was merely cover. The CIA had you there to infiltrate China's technology infrastructure and see if you could identify a mole who was selling military secrets to them." Summerman glanced at Doc. "How am I doing so far?"

Doc, wide-eyed, sipped his Guinness in silence.

"You'd been there about six months when you talked your twin brother into visiting you. And I must say the resemblance is remarkable. Unfortunately, your cover was blown, and the Chinese government started looking for you. They thought they'd found you in a restaurant and gunned you down while you were working your way through a bowl of hot and sour soup. At least they thought it was you. But it was your brother wearing one of your shirts. You made your way out of China and back to the States. Around that time, the voice started."

Summerman watched Doc sob softly in the lounge chair. Murray heard the crying and trotted across the garden. He placed his head in Doc's lap and waited. Doc began to stroke the dog's head as he struggled to regain his composure.

"Can… can you see him now?"

111

"No. When I'm on this side, I'm completely human. I can't see or hear the spirits, but I can sense them. He's here now."

"How do you know that?"

"Because he's always around you. He won't leave. At least until you're able to deal with the guilt you're still carrying around. And get some control over the voice. His message to you is that is wasn't your fault."

"Of course, it was my fault. If he hadn't come to visit me, he'd still be alive."

"No, he wouldn't, Doc."

"What are you talking about?"

"The reason he decided to visit you was to tell you he'd just been diagnosed with a malignant brain tumor. He wanted you to hear it from him. Unfortunately, he never got the chance to tell you. But he wants you to know he's doing fine. And he is. We have a great time on the other side."

"This is too much to process." Doc stood and began pacing.

"I'm sure it is."

"I need to go now."

"I understand."

Doc started to depart, then stopped and turned back.

"You said there was something else you wanted to discuss."

"It can wait, Doc."

Chapter 25

Doc, still processing his conversation with Summerman, was in a mood. He looked around the conference table assessing the mixed reviews he was receiving from the group. Jerome Johnson, the manager of the casino's purchasing department, was the first to speak.

"Three months. You're joking right?" Johnson tossed his pen down, sat back in his chair and waited.

From the corner of the room, Barrier smiled.

"I don't joke about this stuff, Jerome," Doc said.

"How you go from eight months to three over a weekend is beyond me."

"You gut the project, that's how you do it," Barrier said, just loud enough to be heard.

Doc ignored the comment and stayed with the indignant purchasing manager. "I'm about to show you how we're going to do it, Jerome. After I'm finished, if you're still not happy, feel free to discuss it with Hedaya."

My, aren't we in a good mood today.

"Aren't you supposed to go away now?"

"Excuse me?" Johnson said.

"Nothing. Never mind." Doc said.

Johnson looked over to Jenkins, anticipating some support, but the CIO chose to sit quietly picking at a small scab on his wrist.

"What about the new staffing plan?" Johnson said.

"For now, it's gone. And you won't need any additional staff when this is over."

"Three months and no additional help," Johnson said, under his breath. "That's ridiculous."

Doc let the rush of anger pass. He glanced at Maya, who was smiling to herself at the other end of the table. A roomful of curious eyes watched to see how he would deal with the direct challenge.

He looked back at Johnson. "Suppose I told you Hedaya has thrown a million bucks in the pot to be divided up among the team for getting this thing done in three months. Would that change your opinion?"

Johnson raised his eyebrows. "Why yes, it would. Has he?"

"No," Doc said.

A ripple of laughter filled the room. Red-faced, Johnson sat back in his chair. Doc glared at him, then refocused on the group.

"Okay, this week is for confirming the requirements. Focus on the standard transaction processing. We'll deal with reporting requirements next week. I'm going to handle the purchasing side. Maya has the rest of the financials. You folks on the technical team should spend your day preparing to brief Merlin tomorrow. He'll be here first thing in the morning. For those of you that haven't worked with him before, get ready for a wild ride. If you think I'm a pain in the ass, wait until you meet him. But if you pay attention you'll learn more in three months than you've learned in your entire career. Also, if you even have the slightest sniffle, keep your distance. He can be a little phobic."

"A little?" Barrier said. "The man is hypochondria's poster boy."

Even Doc had to smile at Barrier's comment.

"Hedaya will sign off on the requirements Friday, so early next week we move right into application setup. You've got three days for that, so those of you who are assigned to write test scripts stay on top of what's going on. Next Thursday we're going to start taking the system for a test drive."

A loud groan went up around the room from the casino staff members. Doc gave them a few moments to get it out of their system then continued.

"Look, I know you folks are tired, but that's the deal. Besides, how can I justify giving you a week off next month if we don't show some real progress?" Doc smiled and waited.

"A week off?" Johnson said. "Oh, I get it. Another joke."

"No, it's not. Hedaya has approved a paid week off for the staff in week five if I recommend it." Doc looked around the room. "But that's just for the staff. The consultants will be working that week."

Doc again waited as the room buzzed, then turned quiet.

"That's enough for now. Is there anybody in this room who doesn't know what they need to do next?" From the corner of the room, Barrier raised his hand. Doc caught the gesture and nodded before ending the meeting. Doc watched Maya depart, already deep in conversation with several members of her team and turned back to Barrier.

"How did it go with Lawrence on Friday night?"

"Apart from being about a foot shorter? How the fuck do you think it went?"

Doc turned his attention to collecting the papers strewn across the table. Barrier stood waiting.

"So, what's my role going to be?"

Doc closed a folder and looked up.

"Well, you're on the org chart as the technical advisor, so you need to attend all the meetings and help answer software questions when they come up. If we have any problems with the software, I'll need you to run interference with your customer support people. That's about it. As far as I'm concerned, you can spend the rest of your time working on your tan."

Barrier leaned closer.

"I hope you haven't overextended yourself, Doc. There's a lot going on here."

"I know," Doc said. "A pity it swallowed you up."

Doc picked up his folders and left the room without looking back. He walked down the hallway and knocked on the surveillance room door. Sam pulled the door open and let him in.

"What's up, Doc?" Sam said, doing a bad rabbit impression. The others in the room chuckled.

"Morning, Sam. Good one. I've never heard that one before. Do you have those tapes for me?"

Sam reached under a table and pulled out a small box.

"Here you go. I hope DVDs are okay. There's one for each day, and they're all labeled."

He handed the box to Doc, who added it to the pile he was carrying.

"Thanks, Sam."

"They should make for some riveting television. You're not an insomniac by any chance are you?"

"As a matter of fact, I am."

"Well, these should help," Sam said, returning to his coffee.

Doc fought the brief surge of adrenaline. "Did you watch them?"

"Yeah, right," Sam said. "Like I've got nothing better to do than watch you ask some tech weenies about their problems."

The room laughed and Doc, both hands occupied, exited with a nod of his head.

Chapter 26

For the third time, Doc turned the machine around and reviewed the labels on the back. Cursing his ineptitude he unplugged and reinserted the various cables into the DVD player. He pushed the play button and turned his attention back to the television. He saw his reflection in the blank screen.

The computer genius in his element.

"Shut up. You're no help," Doc said. He lit a cigarette and stood looking back and forth between the DVD player and television.

Yeah, that'll help. Why don't you try putting the TV on channel three?

Doc followed the suggestion and immediately the image of one of the casino staff members appeared on the screen. He turned the volume up and watched for a few seconds, then stopped and ejected the DVD. From the box, he removed last Friday's tape and hit the play button. The image of the empty conference room appeared, and he held the fast forward button down, watching until he saw a nervous Jenkins walk in and begin to pace in small circles. Barrier and Gentry entered soon after. Doc removed his finger from the remote and sat down to watch.

After viewing the tape three times, he turned the television off. He leaned back in his chair with his feet propped up on the coffee table. He lit another cigarette, took a sip of beer, and closed his eyes. A smile slowly appeared.

What's so funny?

"Life."

Doc remained in that position until he heard the knock on the door. Startled, he removed the DVD and looked around the room holding it in his hand.

Relax. Do you think they're coming to get you already?

Doc laughed at his paranoia and tossed the DVD onto the desk. He walked across the room enjoying the way the plush carpet enveloped his bare feet. He peered through the fish eye in the door and saw the tiny man in a Hawaiian shirt waiting. Doc pulled the door open and spread both arms wide.

"Come here, you," he said.

The man smiled but didn't move.

"How are you, Doc?"

Doc laughed and grabbed the man by the sleeve.

"I'm healthy as a horse, Merlin. Now get in here."

Doc hugged the man who returned the embrace with a couple of short pats on the back then stepped back. Despite the distance he kept, Doc knew the man was glad to see him. He ushered him into the living room and they sat across from each other. Merlin looked around the suite.

"You must have some serious pull around here, Doc."

"Is your room okay?"

"Yeah, it's identical. Does everybody on the project get one of these?"

"No, just the three of us."

Merlin nodded. "How is she?"

"Still bleeding."

Doc briefly sketched out the details of her current marital situation. Merlin waited for more, but Doc had finished.

"Want something to drink?" Doc said, walking to the refrigerator.

"Any vodka in there?"

"Of course. I ordered a couple of extra bottles. By the way, how was your flight?"

"It sucked. I left my headphones in Rio, so I ended up sitting for twelve hours with no movies or music."

"I think the airlines have added headphones to their list of amenities, Merlin."

"Yeah, like I'm going to put a pair of those germ factories over my ears. Did you know wearing airline headphones for an hour increases the amount of bacteria in your ears over seven hundred percent?"

Doc laughed and grabbed two glasses and a small plate of lime wedges along with a chilled bottle of Grey Goose. He returned to the living room, sat down and poured. Doc watched Merlin grab a handful of tissues and wipe the glass surface of the coffee table. He pulled a small glass container from his shirt and dumped a pile of cocaine onto the glass. Doc frowned, and Merlin paused.

"You don't mind do you?"

"About having it in my room? No. I just worry about how much you're doing these days."

"I'm fine. Cocaine killed a couple of hundred people in this country last year. Cigarettes killed about 450,000. Frankly, Doc, I'll take my chances. Besides, it's still the weekend."

"It's Monday night."

"Yeah, but I had the day off."

"You didn't fly carrying that stuff did you?"

Merlin gave Doc a look of disdain.

"Yeah, right. It came by courier and was waiting for me when I got here. You know, one of the perks of office."

"By the way, what did Samuels say when you told him you were going to do this one?"

"What could he say? As of yesterday, he and I are both out."

"What are you talking about?"

"We're out. As in your dedicated services are no longer required."

"Really? Exactly what nasty business did the two of you get up to in Brazil?"

"The two of us? Samuels didn't even make the trip. It was all me. But since, technically, I reported to Samuels, he got caught up in the blowback. The bastards. I give them enough intel to keep them busy for a couple of years, and this is the thanks I get."

Merlin proceeded to divide the pile into two large lines. He reached into his pocket and removed a plastic bag containing a small glass tube. Doc watched as the white lines quickly disappeared. Merlin sealed the glass tube back in the plastic bag, sat back, sniffed and sipped his vodka.

Doc shook his head and lit a cigarette. He caught Merlin staring and pointed to the ceiling.

"Don't worry; the ventilation is great in here. You won't even catch a whiff."

Merlin watched the smoke rapidly drift upwards. Mildly satisfied, he relaxed and resumed work on his drink.

"So if you gave the Company that much stuff to work with, what's the problem?"

"Well, after I finished, I got… sidetracked."

"Uh oh. What did you do, Merlin?"

"I devalued the Brazilian currency a bit."

Doc remembered the news stories about the value of the Real inexplicably dropping forty percent over the past week.

"That was you?"

"Yeah… but it was their Finance Minister's fault. You wouldn't believe what that prick's policies are doing to the people down there. He pissed me off."

118

Merlin cut up and knocked back two more lines.

"How the hell did you manage to devalue their currency?"

Merlin shrugged.

"It's easier than you think, Doc. Money's all zeroes and ones these days. I hacked in and started moving some shit around. But I will say that there are some happy, but rather confused, charities down there at the moment."

"Jesus, Merlin. How did you get caught?"

Merlin frowned at him.

"I didn't get caught. Samuels just knew it was me, and he thought he'd kill two birds with one stone. Make himself a hero and fuck me in the process. But, like I say, he miscalculated. So he's out."

"And very pissed at you."

"Sure. But what can he do? I know more about him than he does."

"Don't fuck with Samuels, Merlin. Didn't I teach you anything?"

"Yeah, you taught me to always be prepared for any contingency. Trust me; I'm very prepared and Samuels will just have to get over it."

Merlin refreshed both their drinks.

"Okay, so what's the deal here?"

Doc recounted the events of the past week that led to his running the project. As he revealed various details, he closely watched for Merlin's reactions. When he finished, he glanced at the tape on the table but decided to wait.

"Almost two years to put in a financial package and a data warehouse? Another great testimonial for the technology consulting industry, huh?"

"Nice work if you can get it, I guess."

"How's Lawrence doing?"

"Apart from the fact he takes his women two at a time now, he's the same. He'll have to give back several million on this one, but he'll make it back by Tuesday. Just a momentary blip on the balance sheet."

"That's the only way he knows how to keep score these days. Billy Boy giving money back. That must have been fun to watch."

"No, he went quietly. I'm sure he thinks Hedaya could hurt him in the Chinese market if he got pissed enough."

"Could he?" Merlin said, momentarily pausing from his powder work.

"I'm not sure. Hedaya seems to be a genuine anticommunist but who can ever know for sure. Nationalism and commerce create some pretty strange bedfellows."

Merlin nodded.

"So why is Barrier still here? You'd think the old man would have his head on a spit."

"Until this afternoon, I wasn't sure. Now, I've got a pretty good idea."

Merlin leaned forward. "That sounds promising, but I thought you said this was a straight project."

"It is. At least as far as you're concerned. But you need to watch this."

Doc got up and put the DVD in the player. The image of Jenkins in the conference room appeared.

"That's Jenkins. He's the CIO."

Merlin nodded, and both men watched the scene play out.

"Run it again," Merlin said, dumping another small pile of powder on the table.

Doc pressed play, and they watched in silence.

"Money laundering," Merlin said.

"Yes. Very good. And here I was thinking that shit was rotting your brain."

"Not surprising given the amount of cash flowing through this place. But what about Jenkins and Barrier? How did they get involved with the Feebs?"

"From what I've heard, Jenkins has a major gambling problem. Maybe Gentry offered to help him out."

"Stupid man, our Mr. Jenkins," Merlin said.

"Yeah. And as far as Barrier goes, we both know some of the business deals he's done in the past. My guess is he crossed the line and got caught. He's probably trying to cut a deal to save his ass."

"So, they're after the old man."

"Yeah, and that's when some of the decisions they made about this project started making sense. They fucked it up on purpose to buy more time."

"Well, these projects are the perfect excuse for poking around in somebody's computer system," Merlin said. "Unfortunately, they don't look like they're very good at what they do. Two years and they still haven't found anything. Or maybe there's nothing there and they're just fishing."

"No, I'm sure there's something there, but the Caribbean reference doesn't make any sense. Hedaya is Chinese. Take a look around. Everything about this place is Asian. Except for the curling."

Merlin looked at Doc with a puzzled expression.

Doc shrugged his shoulders and said, "You'll see."

"Maybe he's just bouncing money through the Caribbean on its way somewhere else."

"I thought about that, but on the tape Gentry has that tone of authority in his voice. I think some money must have landed there and stayed. But why would Hedaya screw with the Caribbean banks? I'd worry about even setting up a Christmas Club account down there."

"You worry about everything," Merlin said, refilling his glass. "What do you know about Gentry?"

"Not much. I interviewed him last week, and something about him bothered me right from the start. I pulled his resume and called some of the companies he listed as former clients. They'd never heard of him."

"Amateur hour. Gentry should have called me. I would have set him up with a network that bounced all calls for reference checks directly back to him."

Merlin removed a handheld device from his pocket and began scrolling with his thumb. He sniffed and waited for the page to load.

"Here we go." He read from the screen. "Roger Gentry, currently attached to the Las Vegas field office, pay grade GS-11, that's around 65K a year. Seven years with the Bureau and dying to work on anti-terror initiatives, but is still assigned primarily to white collar crime. Got a Does Not Meet Expectations on his last performance review."

Merlin glanced up and smiled.

"Listen to the comment his supervisor made: It's not like Roger is a has-been, he's more of a won't-ever-be. However, Roger believes that he should go far, and in my opinion, the sooner he starts, the better off we'll all be. I recommend him for transfer to North Dakota, where his delusions of adequacy and room temperature IQ may find themselves in perfect harmony with native species such as the catfish and moose. It is my sincere hope that Roger ingratiates himself with the local residents and often accompanies them on hunting trips, preferably as prey." Merlin glanced up from the screen. "Brutal, huh?"

"Wow. That's the real comment?"

"Yeah, his supervisor refused to change it and ended up getting suspended for three days. But he said it was worth it if it ends up saving the Bureau from Roger."

Doc laughed.

"How did you get your hands on his performance review?"

Merlin gave Doc a blank stare.

"Never mind," Doc said. "I'm sorry I asked. What about his girlfriend, Grace?"

Merlin glanced down at the small screen and scrolled.

"She's FBI too. Also assigned to the Vegas office. She's one level below Gentry, and they've been living together for about a year now. She's a widow with two teenage daughters and carries the nickname of the Undercover Lady. But not for the reason you might think."

"She's… active?"

"Yeah. According to one of my sources, she's downright prolific. She got the nickname because every time she gets assigned surveillance, she often ends up-"

"Under the covers. Got it." Doc chuckled. "Who said the Bureau doesn't have a sense of humor?"

Merlin looked up with a mischievous grin.

"So, what would you have me do?"

Doc sipped his drink, deep in thought.

"Nothing with them for the moment. Let's wait until Gentry tips his hand. But keep poking around in your spare time And while you're at it, see what you can dig up on a guy named Summerman Lawless."

"Where have I heard that name?"

"He's some ex-rock star who knows Hedaya."

"And?"

"And I don't know if he's completely crazy or if he's someone we need to get to know a lot better."

Merlin knocked back another line, sniffed, and wiped his nose with a tissue.

"It's nice to be back in business with you, Doc."

"We're not back in business. Until I tell you otherwise, we're on the old man's side. Okay?"

"Sure. You know me. Anytime I get a free pass to mess with the Feebs; I'm a happy guy. So what's up with you and the old man?"

"I've gotten attached to him."

"Are you going to tell him?"

"Yeah, I think so, but I'd like to have more information first."

"Barrier won't give you anything. You know that."

"I thought I'd start with Jenkins."

Chapter 27

Doc put the menu down and looked across the table at Maya, who was still trying to decide. She casually brushed the hair away from her face and sensed the pair of eyes focused on her. She looked up from the menu and smiled at Doc.

"You're smirking."

"Was I? Sorry. You always take such a long time to make up your mind."

Maya gave him a dirty look and went back to her menu. Merlin approached the table and Maya, not looking up, slid over. He sat down next to her and Maya gently patted his hand.

"Okay," she said, putting down the menu. "I've decided."

"I know exactly what I want," Merlin said. "I've been dying for a cheeseburger."

"Jesus, Merlin, you just came from South America," Doc said. "They've got some of the best beef in the world."

Merlin shook his head in disgust.

"I don't eat meat in foreign countries. Their inspection systems are a joke."

Maya laughed and looked at Doc.

"Here we go," she said.

The waitress arrived. Maya ordered the sushi buffet and Doc a Caesar salad with chicken. The waitress nodded and looked at Merlin.

"And what would you like, sir?"

"I'd like a cheeseburger, but first, I need to know at what temperature your chef cooks the burgers," Merlin said.

"Excuse me?"

"The temperature the hamburger is cooked at. You need to make sure that the middle of the burger is cooked for at least fifteen seconds at a minimum of a hundred and sixty degrees."

"Do I now?" She forced a smile.

"Yes, you do. That's the only way to be sure that all traces of Escherichia coli are killed. It's a new bacteria strain that can be deadly."

"You're joking, right?" the waitress said, looking around the table.

Doc and Maya, well versed, sat quietly waiting out the exchange.

"My dear, just by coming to eat in your establishment, I have already increased my chances of getting food poisoning over four times what it would be by my eating at home. Trust me; I am not joking."

"Well, sir, I assure you that our grill is very hot. Would you like to come into the kitchen and test it for yourself? I'm sure the chef wouldn't mind," the waitress said, making no effort to keep the sarcasm out of her voice.

"No, that won't be necessary. Just make sure it's very well done."

"Oh, I will, sir. Anything else?"

"Perhaps a side salad."

"You can have the salad bar for an additional four dollars."

"Salad bar? Sure. And after that, I'll just stick my head in a toilet to freshen up. No, I think not. I have a policy against eating anything that's been sneezed on by a couple of hundred people. I'll have a garden salad from the kitchen, thank you."

"You got it."

The waitress took one more look around the table and walked off shaking her head.

Merlin watched her go and turned back to the table.

"Amazing. If anybody should know about restaurant germs, it would be a waitress."

Doc looked around the restaurant.

"It looks pretty clean to me."

"Yes. But it's a different world back there," Merlin said, nodding towards the kitchen.

Maya stood. "Well, I'm going to get some raw fish. How does that sit with you?"

Merlin got up to let her out of the booth.

"Stay away from salmon and Ahi. Anisakis is on the rise."

Maya paused at the edge of the table.

"Okay, I'll bite. What's Anisakis?"

"It's a disease caused by ingesting worms in raw fish. A lot of salmon and tuna are infected with a fish parasite, and if the sushi chef isn't inspecting each slice, you might end up eating worms."

"I see," Maya said. "And if I do, how will I know?"

"Oh, nothing too serious. In a couple of days, your guts will start to burn as the parasites try to bore their way out through your stomach lining."

"Thanks. And all this time I thought I missed having you around."

"Well, you asked," Merlin said, shrugging his shoulders.

Maya looked at Doc. "Next time, let's stick to cocktails, huh?" She turned and walked in the direction of the sushi.

Merlin watched her go.

"God, she's beautiful. You know, if I ever did decide to have sex, she'd be exactly the type of woman I'd want to try it with."

"Get in line," Doc said, watching her cross the room.

"Did you talk to Jenkins yet?"

"No, we're meeting after lunch," Doc said. "He doesn't look good today. I think Hedaya has been putting the wood to him. Are you happy with your technical team?"

"Yeah, they're okay. I guess," Merlin said, flicking away an unidentifiable speck from the table.

Doc smiled and knew the comment was high praise coming from Merlin. His technical assessments were always based on how others compared to his own ability.

Maya returned, and Merlin slid across the booth. He quickly rearranged the place settings. Doc looked at the pile of food on her plate and noticed Merlin warily eyeing it. Maya looked at both men, and they gestured for her to start eating. She reached down and picked up a very thin slice of fish with chopsticks. She looked at Merlin, who was staring at the piece of fish.

"What?"

"Hold it up to the light," he said.

"For what?"

"To see if it's moving."

Maya shook her head and raised the chopsticks to her mouth. She stopped and looked at Merlin, who was still fixated on the piece of fish. She pursed her lips and held the chopsticks up in the air in the general direction of an overhead light.

"Do you see anything?" Merlin said.

Maya dropped the piece of fish into her mouth and chewed slowly.

"Just a friggin moron," she said, swallowing. "Now kiss me, you fool."

She leaned over, planted a quick kiss on Merlin's cheek and licked the side of his neck. He gagged, picked up his napkin and vigorously wiped.

126

"Fuck me. What did you do that for? Raw fish and a kiss? Do you have any idea how many germs you just gave me?"

"Keep it up and next time I'll force feed it to you with my tongue."

The waitress arrived with the men's lunch. She watched in silence as Merlin cautiously inspected his food.

"Is there anything else I can get you right now?"

Doc and Maya shook their heads and looked at Merlin, who was busy eyeing the contents of his salad. He looked up and saw the three people staring at him.

"What? No, I'm fine. Thanks."

He smiled at the waitress who walked away, shaking her head.

Doc started working on his salad after declining Maya's invitation to sample the sushi. He chewed slowly and then got down to business.

"So, what do you guys think?"

Maya looked at Merlin, who was busy chewing a carrot stick. He motioned for her to go ahead.

"Well, the biggest problem is the energy level. The consultants can carry most of it, but the business decisions have to come from the staff and right now they're just worn out."

Merlin nodded in agreement.

"The week off will help, but we've got a lot to do over the next month," she continued. "That concerns me a bit, but I think we'll make it."

"She's right. But the good news is the consultants are fresh, and the technical side is a piece of cake," Merlin said, picking at his salad.

"When will you have the new instance of the database ready?" asked Maya.

"It's done," Merlin said, cutting his cheeseburger into quarters.

"With the projects module included?"

"Of course. It's all there," Merlin said, nibbling a corner off one of the quarters.

Maya looked at Doc, who shook his head. She turned back to Merlin.

"What about the data conversion?"

"What about it?" Merlin asked.

"When do you plan on running some test data?"

"Are you going to change any of the financial set-ups?"

"The chart of accounts in the general ledger won't be changing, but nothing has been decided on the projects side. We just started discussing it this morning."

127

"I know, but that's fine," Merlin said. "I've already created some dummy projects that we can use until you folks figure out how you want to set it up. Is that okay?"

"Sure. When can I see some data?" Maya said.

"I'm running it tonight," Merlin said, removing the onions from his salad and building a small pile on a nearby plate. "I hate these things."

"How about the purchasing data? When can I expect to see the first cut of that?"

"I just told you. I'm going to run it tonight. You'll have it in the morning."

"You've got all of the conversion data remapped already?"

Doc and Maya, amazed, shared a glance.

"Sure. Once I eliminated that stupid multi-vendor nonsense, it was simple."

Merlin looked up from his food and saw the looks he was receiving.

"What?"

"You've been here a day and a half, and you've got all that done already?"

"Jesus, Doc. I've got six people working on it." He shook his head in disgust. "That's the thing that drives me nuts about this industry. Anytime somebody does their job well; people get suspicious. Have our expectations gotten that low?"

"But how could you re-map everything already? We just started to review the original decisions yesterday," Maya said, grabbing another piece of fish.

"Look, folks," Merlin said, condescendingly. "It's purchasing and financial data. We've all done this stuff many, many times before. Let's not make it out to be more than it is. I had to make some assumptions about where stuff would go, but if it's not at least ninety-eight percent accurate, next time, I'll eat sushi. And if you do change anything, we'll just re-map it."

He sat back, pushing his plate away.

Doc smiled at Merlin.

"You're lucky you're as good as you are."

"Why's that?"

"Because you're such a prick, if you weren't, somebody would shoot you."

Doc and Maya laughed loudly. The waitress arrived, refilled their coffees and left with the plates. Doc looked at Merlin, who nodded.

"There's something we need to tell you," Doc said.

Maya looked at Doc and then at Merlin, who was staring off into space.

"It's about what's going on around here."

"Okay," Maya said, confused.

"I need to let you know because before the project's done, you might find yourself in some difficult spots."

"Go ahead."

Doc rubbed his forehead and looked around the room. He pulled a pack of cigarettes from his pocket and waited.

"Go ahead," Maya said.

Doc lit a cigarette.

"Thanks. It's Gentry. He's an FBI agent."

He waited for Maya's surprise to register then continued.

"He's a plant. Jenkins hired him at the start of the project, but his resume is completely fabricated. Barrier's involved as well. We think the investigation is focused on money laundering."

Doc stopped and waited.

"May I ask how you know about this?"

Doc proceeded to explain the tapes from the conference room. Maya bit her lip, deep in thought.

"That's why you interviewed me downstairs."

"Yes."

"And that explains why the project was such a mess. They purposely screwed it up so it would take longer."

"Such a smart woman," Merlin said.

"Why Barrier? How did he get involved in something like this?"

"I don't know yet."

"Yet? You're feeling some compulsion to find out why?"

"Yes," Doc said.

"Isn't this a little out of your league, Doc?"

Doc looked at Merlin, who stared back in silence. "Probably. I guess it's my inquisitive nature," he said.

"Bullshit." Maya looked back and forth at both men. "I think it's out of control testosterone."

"Look, if you don't want to be around while this plays out, I'll understand completely. No hard feelings."

"No hard feelings, huh. It's a little late for that?"

"Maybe I should leave for a few minutes," Merlin said, starting to get up.

"Sit down, Merlin," Maya said, gently.

She sat back in the booth and folded her arms. Eventually, she continued.

"What could happen to me?"

"Nothing," Doc said. "Just do your work and, if you get asked, deny you've ever heard of the FBI."

"So my boys are going to play detective," she said. "How much time will that leave for us?" she said, staring at Doc.

Doc caught off guard, stammered his answer. "As much as possible, I guess."

You never could hit a curveball.

"I've got to go. I've got a meeting." She stood and shook her head at both of them. "Just keep me out of it."

She walked out of the restaurant, and Doc watched her head towards the elevators that led to the second floor.

"Is she pissed?"

"Oh, yeah," Doc said, sinking back into the booth.

Chapter 28

"But you're not on the technical team."

Barrier, exasperated, glared at the FBI agent sitting across from him.

"Why can't you get that through your thick skull?"

"Be careful with your tone, Jimbo," Gentry said. "I don't see why I should have to change the way I've been working."

"I'm telling you. The man watches everything. Until he turns a system over to the client, he considers it his personal property. If you keep poking around in there, he's going to know about it, and it will make him suspicious."

"I think you're giving him way too much credit. He can't be that good."

"Jesus, you're a pain in the ass," Barrier said. "Look the guy has Ph.D.'s in applied technology and mathematics. Plus he picked up two or three other masters along the way. All by the time he was twenty-four. I'll say it again just so we're clear. Merlin's a goddamned genius."

"Maybe I should recruit him," Gentry said. "The Bureau is paying recruiting bonuses these days. I could use the money."

"Yeah, right. Like he would ever work for what you guys pay. We had him for two years, and he turned down a quarter million a year when he left. And that was a long time ago. He's probably making three grand a day by now."

"Five," Jenkins said.

"Five? Really?" Barrier said.

"Yeah. And he negotiated a seven-day billing week."

"Thirty-five grand a week? Damn, that's serious money."

"Then I'll use your account to log on," Gentry said.

"Yeah, that's good," Barrier said. "Then I get all the questions."

Relax. You're the technical advisor on this project. You've got every right to be in there poking around."

Barrier shook his head in disgust and looked at Jenkins, who shrugged his shoulders. All three men looked up when they heard the knock on the door.

"Come in," Jenkins said.

Doc entered and glanced around.

He turned to Jenkins.

"See no evil."

He smiled at Gentry.

"Hear no evil."

Doc turned to face Barrier.

"And, of course, evil."

Jenkins laughed loudly. It was cut short by Barrier's glare.

"Come on in, Doc. We were just finishing up," Jenkins said, trying to remove the smile from his face.

Barrier and Gentry stood up and started to leave.

"How's it going, Doc?" Gentry said.

"Good. By the way, when can I expect to see the new training plan?"

"How's two weeks from Friday?" Gentry said.

"Not as good as next Friday," Doc said.

Gentry frowned and looked at Barrier, who nodded. Doc caught the exchange and smiled at the thought of Barrier having to put in some real work.

"You got it," Gentry said.

He and Barrier walked out the door. Jenkins motioned for Doc to sit down across the desk from him.

"We were just talking about Merlin. Apparently he is quite the genius."

"Yes, he's a special case."

"It must be difficult being that intelligent," Jenkins said.

"In some ways. But I'm sure it beats the alternative," Doc said, smiling. "How are you holding up?"

Jenkins snorted and leaned back in his chair.

"I've been better. Let's just say that my relationship with Hedaya is not good at the moment."

"Well, professional relationships always ebb and flow. I think it's probably still salvageable."

"Doubtful," Jenkins said. "Are you making good progress?"

"Yeah, I'm pretty happy so far. Merlin is running a first cut of the data conversion tonight."

"So soon? That's impressive."

"Well, it's pretty straightforward, you know. You just have to follow the money."

Jenkins' face flushed

"Yes," he said, looking out the window.

"At this pace, we might even finish early," Doc said, deciding to push the man a little harder.

"I see. That would make people happy."

"Some, I suppose," Doc said, casually checking the outside view.

Jenkins stood up and walked to the window.

Keep it up and he's going to jump.

"How long have you and Merlin worked together?"

"We were at Prophecy together for about a couple years. Since then we've worked on some projects together. Having him around is like having good insurance coverage."

"Expensive insurance wouldn't you say?"

"Yes, he is. But before it's over, I think you'll agree he's worth every dollar. Besides, when it comes to work, I don't like to gamble."

Jenkins sat back down at his desk and looked at Doc.

"So you think most of the risk has been eliminated?"

"Well, let's say most of the potential problems are identified. As you know, that's the hard part. Knowing where your problems are going to come from."

"I hope you don't think any problems will come from my office."

"No, George. I imagine you'll do everything that's expected. Let's hope that's enough for Hedaya."

Jenkins frowned.

"I have another meeting with him this afternoon. Any suggestions?"

"I would try to be as straight with him as possible," Doc said, checking his watch.

"Yeah," Jenkins said. "What's the worst thing that could happen?"

You could end up buried in the desert.

Doc fought back a smile.

"Well, I'll let you get ready for your meeting." He stood up to leave.

"What's on your agenda this afternoon?"

"Oh, you know, just some more digging in the dirt," Doc said, departing with a wave.

Chapter 29

Barrier, struggling to deal with his hangover, dove deeper and felt the temperature of the water drop. He covered the width of the pool and touched the far edge. Popping to the surface, he stretched his arms out and leaned with his back against the pool, breathing heavily. The sun baked his shoulders, and he poked his chest. Satisfied that the sunscreen had done its job, he surveyed the scene surprised by the size of the crowd for a Thursday afternoon. Probably another busy weekend he noted as he gestured to the waitress who had been serving him the past few hours. She nodded and continued her journey through the maze of lounge chairs scattered around the pool.

He looked back across the pool in the direction of his lounge chair. A man dragged a vacant chair next to his. Barrier squinted against the sun and realized it was Gentry. He stuck his head under the water, resurfaced, and slicked his hair back.

Gentry disrobed down to his swim trunks and the softness invading the man's body was evident. Under the water, Barrier checked his own stomach roll and did a quick comparison, factoring in the age difference. Once again resolving to get into better shape, Barrier dropped down into the water and pushed away from the wall with both legs. He covered the width of the pool underwater and popped up on the other side a few feet away from Gentry.

"Looking for me?" Barrier said, clearing his nostrils in the water.

"Hey, Hollywood," Gentry said, coating his body with white lotion. "I want your job."

Barrier floated on his back and swam in a small circle.

"I'm just following orders, Gentry. What do you want?"

"We need to talk."

"You always need to talk. Sometimes I think that's all you know how to do."

Barrier sucked in his stomach and pulled himself out of the pool. He stretched out on the lounge chair, leaned over to finish the last of his Mai Tai and put on his sunglasses. He combed his hair back and looked at Gentry, who was still covering himself with lotion.

"I didn't think it was possible for you to get any whiter."

Barrier laughed and looked around for the waitress.

"I need to build up a base and then I'll tan. I can get pretty dark."

"Whatever you say, Gentry," Barrier said, watching two young women in small bikinis enter the pool. He stretched and smiled. "Not bad for the middle of the desert, huh?"

The waitress arrived with a fresh Mai tai. Barrier sat up, smiled at her and turned to Gentry, who was wiping the excess lotion off with a towel.

"Excuse my friend," Barrier said to the waitress. "He doesn't get out much."

"I can see that," she said, her own skin bronzed from the sun.

"What'll you have, Gentry?"

Gentry looked over at Barrier's drink.

"That looks good. I'll have one of those, please."

The waitress nodded and Barrier watched her walk away. Gentry was still preoccupied with the mess he had made with the lotion. Barrier leaned back and closed his eyes.

"The Bureau is thinking about walking away from this one."

Barrier opened his eyes but didn't move.

"Why on earth would they do that?"

"Because we haven't come up with anything. Washington is saying there's nothing here. Either that or I'm not very good at what I do."

"It took them this long to figure that out?"

"Fuck you, Barrier."

Barrier grinned and closed his eyes.

"Well, there's something here. You've got proof of that."

"All we've got is two small wire transfers from a couple of years ago."

"Four million bucks worth of wire transfers," Barrier said, sitting up. "That's got to mean something."

The waitress approached carrying Gentry's drink. Both men sat quietly while Barrier signed the check. She strolled away, and Gentry resumed the conversation as soon as she was out of earshot.

"Initially, sure it meant something. But the more I look into this guy, I realize how well connected he is politically. He's tight with a lot of politicians, especially a certain Senator from Nevada."

"Big deal. Since when does the FBI give a shit what some Senator from Nevada thinks?"

"When he's Chairman of the committee that approves the Bureau's budget, that's when."

Barrier sipped his drink and dove back into the pool. He surfaced and swam back to the edge looking up at Gentry.

"Washington feels that the longer we're here, the better the chances are that Hedaya will figure out we're up to something. Now that we're out of the loop, my bosses are getting nervous."

"Just tell them to be patient. We'll figure something out."

Gentry shook his head.

"No, I got the word today. Either we get Doc on board, or we're going to walk."

"Doc? Mr. Straight? Good luck."

Barrier ducked his head under the water. Gentry waited until he surfaced.

"You're the one who needs the luck, Jimbo," Gentry said, quietly. "That's going to be your job."

"My job? Why not you? You're the FBI agent," Barrier said.

A beach ball bounced off his head. Barrier picked up the ball and threw it back in the direction it came without looking away from Gentry. Gentry casually sipped his drink.

"Yes. And you're the guy who's facing four counts of fraud."

"Not anymore. You said that if I helped you out, the charges would disappear," Barrier said.

"Keep your voice down," Gentry said. "What have you done other than show up for work each day?"

"What have I done? Christ, I bought you guys two fucking years. It's not my fault you can't find your own ass with both hands and a flashlight. Do you have any idea how much I've screwed up my career because of this?"

"That's not my problem, Jimbo," Gentry said, diving into the pool.

Barrier stood in the water waiting for him to surface. A few seconds later, Gentry popped up directly behind him.

"What about Jenkins?" Barrier said, wheeling around.

"No, he's already on the edge. And he doesn't have the stomach for this stuff."

Gentry poked a finger into his shoulder.

"Geez, I'm burning already."

Gentry got out of the pool and sat down pulling on his tee shirt. He looked down into the water.

"You better get busy, Jimbo. You aren't the only one with career problems here. Either get Doc in…"

"Or?"

"You're a smart guy. You'll figure something out."

Gentry drained his glass, gave him a short wave and walked away. Barrier watched him go, paddled to the edge of the pool and rested his chin on the hot tiles.

Chapter 30

Doc walked Maya to her door and softly kissed her good night, capping a perfect evening. He strolled towards his suite in a great mood. The voice had been quiet all night. Stress related indeed. At the elevator, his cell phone went off. Cursing himself for bringing it, he looked at the display and saw it was Merlin.

"Are you still working?" Doc said.

"Just finished. Have you got a few minutes?"

"Sure. I'll be in my room. Come on up."

Doc disconnected and entered the elevator. By the time he arrived at his suite, Merlin was already waiting outside the door.

"That was quick," Doc said.

"I'm finally starting to get the layout of this place. It's like a maze. Easy to get into, but impossible to find your way out."

Doc opened the door and turned his phone off. Merlin headed for the refrigerator and removed a bottle of vodka. He raised the bottle toward Doc, who shook his head no. Merlin poured his drink, sat down on the couch, wiped down the tabletop and drew two small lines of coke. He quickly devoured both, sipped his drink, and leaned back.

"Feel better?" Doc said.

"Enormously. It's been a long day."

Merlin prepared two more lines but left them sitting untouched in front of him.

"And in answer to the question I know you're dying to ask, no, I never do this during the day."

Merlin sipped his drink and sniffed.

"You're a big boy, Merlin," Doc said, lighting a cigarette. "So, what's up?"

"About two years ago, Hedaya moved two separate wire transfers to a bank in the Caribbean. Two million dollars each."

"And?"

"He bounced it through Europe, then to the Caymans, and it ended up in Costa Rica."

"Is it still there?"

"It certainly is. He hasn't touched it."

"You didn't find that out just by poking around the second floor did you?"

Merlin shook his head and knocked back a line.

"Do you want to tell me how you found it?" Doc said.

Again, Merlin shook his head and inhaled the remaining line.

"Okay. How hard was it?" Doc said, too tired to play Merlin's game.

"For mere mortals, almost impossible. For me, it was hard enough, but it was still traceable. He left some footprints that I think were intentional."

"What about the money?"

Doc reconsidered the drink offer and grabbed a glass. Merlin poured.

"It looks clean. He used one of his personal accounts. Given the rate his personal accounts grow, it's hard to tell if he replaced the four million with dirty money. At least, it's hard for now. In a couple of days, I could probably figure it out."

Doc thought for a moment and shook his head.

"No, don't worry about it. I'm sure it's clean."

"Why do you say that?"

"Because Hedaya is smart. I don't think there's anything illegal with those transfers."

"So you don't think there's anything going on here?"

Doc finished his cigarette and sipped his drink.

"No, I didn't say that. I think he did those transfers for another reason."

"Enlighten me, Bodhisattva."

"I think the transfers were a test. Hedaya put them out there to see if anybody was watching."

Merlin shrugged and refilled his glass.

"Well, they were."

"Yes," Doc said, deep in thought. "A successful test wouldn't you say?"

Merlin started to reach into his pocket but decided against it. He sipped his drink instead.

"But why would anybody purposefully try to attract the attention of the FBI?"

"Oh, they were already watching. I'm sure they watch all the casinos constantly. There's so much money floating around, the temptation to cheat must be enormous. This is the sort of stuff the Bureau loves. I think

Hedaya wanted to know how closely he was being watched. The one mistake he made was ignoring the possibility of getting infiltrated."

"Who expects their own CIO to sell them out?"

"Still, he should have seen it coming."

"How's Jenkins holding up?"

"He's close to the edge. I talked to him again today and pushed a little harder. He's convinced that I know something is up. Something will pop soon."

"You don't think the Bureau would send Jenkins after you?"

"No, absolutely not. My guess is they'll send Barrier."

"Why on earth would they do that?"

"Because he's their last hope. If they had anything tangible, they would have come in as soon as Hedaya brought me on board. Now we've locked them out, and they're running out of time. Gentry's got no shot with me, and they know that. And using Barrier gives them some degree of deniability. They could sell him out tomorrow and walk away, which is something I'm sure they're considering."

"What about the political route? Hedaya's a billionaire. He must be well connected. A certain senator on a certain committee could get the Feebs to back off."

"I'm sure he's very well connected. But he doesn't want to play that card."

"Afraid of attracting even more attention?"

"You are a smart guy, aren't you?" Doc said, draining his glass. "By the way, what are you doing Sunday night?"

Merlin pointed to the cocaine and vodka.

"Probably this. Why?"

"There's somebody who's dying to meet you."

"Well, that's a first."

Chapter 31

Doc stared at his diminutive friend and looked at Maya.

"Merlin," Maya said. "You're unbelievable. Stop whining."

"All I said was that I hope he doesn't serve anything raw or any household pets for dinner."

"Merlin, Hedaya's a billionaire. I don't think you have to worry about being served dog stew," Doc said, looking around the magnificent sitting room.

"Trust me, the richer they get, the weirder their tastes. Remember that Saudi prince with the propensity for-,"

"I remember everything, Merlin," Doc snappe, giving him the 'shut your mouth' look.

"Saudi prince?" Maya said.

"He's babbling," Doc said. "When was the last time you powdered your nose?"

"Just before I came up," Merlin said.

"Don't babble, okay? I'm pretty sure Hedaya doesn't forget much either."

"For some reason," Merlin said. "I don't think he likes me."

"Now there's a shock," Maya said.

Hedaya and Rose entered, and all three stood to greet them. Hedaya, wearing his trademark silk, smiled and bowed.

"Doc. Welcome to my home, Maya."

"It's amazing," Maya said. "Thank you for inviting me."

"It was overdue," Hedaya said.

He turned and studied Merlin.

"Good evening, Merlin."

"Hedaya." Merlin bowed slightly, then wiped at his nose on the way back up.

Hedaya cocked his head.

"Are you catching a cold?"

"I think it's all the time I'm spending in the air conditioning. I don't even want to think about the collection of germs and disease those things are pumping out."

"Indeed." Hedaya's eyes narrowed as he turned to Rose. "My dear, I would like to introduce you to Merlin. He's Doc's right-hand man."

Hedaya glanced at Doc and smiled.

"The choices we make in life. Right, Doc?"

"I question mine all the time, Hedaya," Doc said, glaring at Merlin.

Rose, wearing a red silk pantsuit, took a step towards Merlin and extended her hand.

"It's nice to meet you, Merlin. I've heard a lot about you. I'm Rose."

She continued to hold his hand and smile.

"Nice to meet you, Rose."

Merlin stared at the tiny, yet beautiful, woman who was almost identical in size. Rather than lustful, it was a stare of curiosity.

Merlin sniffed and stiffened when Rose placed her other hand on their handshake and returned his stare. There was no mistaking what was behind the look. Rose's engine was about to redline.

"Come. You're sitting next to me at dinner. I'll take you to your seat."

She led him away. Merlin glanced over his shoulder and caught Hedaya's glare. The old man frowned then looked back at Doc and Maya.

"I believe dinner is served." He extended his arm. "Go ahead. I will join you in just a minute."

Hedaya pulled the buzzing phone from his pocket and took the call in a corner of the room.

"Did you see that?" Maya said as they walked towards the dining room.

"See it? I thought she was going to throw him to the ground and start riding him right there."

"But he was staring right back at her," Maya said. "I've never seen Merlin give a woman a second look. I mean, in a sexual way."

"That wasn't sexual. That's how he looks when he's curious about something. She's probably the first adult he's ever met who's shorter than he is."

"She's smitten. Wow. Talk about love at first sight."

"Unfortunately for her, it's all downhill from there."

Maya laughed.

"Maybe he'll be interested."

"Yeah, sure. Maybe when the earth stops spinning. The guy worries about putting ketchup on his cheeseburger unless it comes from a fresh bottle."

"I don't know. I recognize that look. And she's got Hedaya's determination. Maybe she'll wear him down."

142

"Never happen," Doc said. "Too bad. Their children would be short and afraid of their own shadow."

"I wonder if their kids would even be big enough to cast a shadow."

"At least Merlin's lack of interest will make Hedaya happy."

"He doesn't like Merlin. That's for sure," Maya said.

"I can't imagine why. He's such a sweetheart."

**

Doc accepted the after-dinner drink from the waiter and took a sip. He recognized the taste and sipped again. While he waited, he examined the photos adorning the walls of the old man's private office. The majority were pictures of Hedaya posing with celebrities, athletes, and well-known politicians. In each of the photos, Hedaya was beaming. Hedaya entered and sat down in the chair across from Doc. He sipped his drink and nodded.

"I love a good digestivo after dinner. Do you recognize this one, Doc?"

"Limoncello, right?"

"You are indeed a man of the world. Another wonderful contribution from the Italians."

"I used to date a French woman who loved it. She said that it should be called liquid panty remover."

Hedaya laughed.

"Another very good reason to acquire a taste for it."

"Speaking as a man of the world, yes."

Hedaya roared with laughter, then paused.

"Let's hope Rose doesn't develop a fondness for it."

"You don't have to worry about Merlin, Hedaya."

"Perhaps not. But I find the man troubling on many levels."

"We all do. Tell me," Doc said, pointing at the photos. "Were you always this happy or did it happen after you got rich?"

Hedaya chuckled as he glanced around at the photos.

"Well, money certainly improves one's mood. But since coming to this country, I've been happy most of the time."

Doc looked at his watch and saw that it was almost midnight. Despite the late hour, he was wide awake.

"Thanks for agreeing to stay behind after dinner," Hedaya said.

"No problem," Doc said. "What's on your mind?"

"Can I trust you, Doc?"

Doc sat back in his chair and looked at the old man who sipped his drink without taking his eyes off him. Doc lit a cigarette and watched the smoke disappear into the ceiling.

"Yes, Hedaya. You can trust me."

"That makes me happy," he said, setting his drink down on the coffee table. "Since I can trust you, I believe that you have some things to tell me."

Doc noticed the hard expression on the old man's face.

"Have I done something to offend you, Hedaya?"

"That very much depends on what you decide to tell me." Hedaya's face softened. "I received a phone call today from a friend of mine in Costa Rica."

Doc felt his face flush.

Easy. Relax, but stay sharp.

"And?"

"It was almost identical to the phone call I received from him two years ago."

"I see," Doc said, extinguishing his cigarette.

"A most disturbing phone call."

Hedaya reached under the coffee table. Doc watched as Hedaya's hand disappeared under the table and felt the panic surge through him.

Son of a bitch. Get ready.

Doc leaned forward in his chair not taking his eyes off Hedaya's movements. Hedaya's hand reappeared holding a small metal can.

"Cashew?" he said, offering the can of nuts to Doc.

Doc resumed breathing and took a small handful.

Sorry about that.

"The call was most disturbing," Hedaya said, resuming his stare. "So?"

"Your friend in Costa Rica must be a banker."

"Yes."

"And he called you to let you know that someone had been poking around his computer system."

"Very good. But unlike the first time, when I was able to trace the intruder back to my casino, this attack was untraceable."

Despite the direction the conversation was headed, Doc was pleased to hear that Merlin's skills were as sharp as ever.

"This one came from here, too," Doc said.

"As I imagined," Hedaya said. "Please continue."

He picked up his drink, then sat back and waited.

"Two years ago you bounced two different wire transfers totaling four million dollars across Europe and into this bank where it has been collecting dust ever since. I suppose you'd like to know how I how that."

"Yes. I would very much like to know how you know that."

"I started to get suspicious right after I got here. The project was such a mess, and I knew that Barrier, despite his other shortcomings, was very good at what he did. I figured somebody was purposely stalling to buy time."

"Do you mind if I have one of your cigarettes?" Hedaya said, reaching for the pack. He lit one, took a long drag, and leaned back in his chair. "Don't tell Rose."

Doc smiled at the thought of Hedaya being afraid of his niece.

"Anyway, I got lucky when I reviewed my interview tapes. Apparently you weren't the only one who didn't know there was a camera in the conference room."

"I see. And what did you find on the tape?"

"It was Jenkins, Barrier, and Gentry discussing the FBI and money going to the Caribbean."

"Gentry. Of course." He shook his head. "I should have figured that out."

"Yeah, you probably should have. He's the agent who's been planted. Jenkins and Barrier have been sucked in for the ride. Jenkins must be in trouble from his gambling, and my guess is that Barrier got caught with his hand in the cookie jar on some other business deal. He's probably helping the Feds out so he can stay out of jail."

"He's facing multiple counts of fraud involving some kickbacks."

"Can you tell me how you know that?"

"No, I can't," Hedaya said.

Hedaya smiled and got up to refill the drinks. Doc lit another cigarette and waited until Hedaya had refilled the glasses. Hedaya sat back down and nodded for Doc to continue.

"So, two years go by, and they can't find anything other than those two original transfers. Soon you're down about thirty million on a computer system that doesn't work, and I show up. You decide to use me to push their buttons. Once you learned about my relationship with Barrier you knew I'd do everything possible to make his life miserable. You played it perfectly, Hedaya."

Hedaya smiled, but let the compliment pass. He leaned forward in his chair.

"Do you work for the FBI, Doc?"

Despite the serious tone of the question, Doc laughed.

"Absolutely not, Hedaya. You're wondering if my showing up here was some big set up?"

"The thought did cross my mind."

"No, my being here was the luck of the draw. Believe me; I am no fan of the FBI. They have never bothered me, although I suppose they're about to start. But they have gone out of their way to screw with many of my colleagues."

Hedaya relaxed and lit another cigarette.

"So what mischief do you think I'm up to, Doc?"

"I don't know, Hedaya and, in all honesty, I don't care. I do think you've been watching this project a lot closer than anybody realizes."

"Yes."

"The wire transfers were a test weren't they?"

Hedaya's eyebrows went up momentarily.

"Why do you say that?"

"Because you wanted, perhaps needed, to know how closely you were being watched. You haven't done any transfers since then, so my guess is they were a trial balloon. You got your answer but forgot about the possibility of infiltration. That was a mistake."

"Yes," Hedaya said. "Mistakes happen."

"Yes, they do. And I also need to mention another mistake you made. It's about Grace."

"Grace from Guest Relations?"

"Yes."

"What about her?"

"She's FBI too."

"Really?"

"And she's Gentry's girlfriend. They live together."

"The lucky bastard," Hedaya said. "You'd think he'd be in a better mood given that he sleeps next to her."

146

Hedaya shook his head.

"I must be slipping. Two agents working on my staff."

"As you say, mistakes happen."

Hedaya nodded and stared off into the distance.

"After you figured out something was going on with the project, rather than kill it, you decided to let it play out," Doc said. "That's why you kept Barrier around and didn't fire Jenkins."

Doc stood and stretched, feeling the fatigue set in.

"I won't keep you much longer," Hedaya said, stifling a yawn. "Tell me about your friend Merlin."

"What about him?"

"Does he have any particular allegiances here?"

"Only to me. He did what I asked him to do."

"And why did you ask him to… poke around?"

"Because I don't want to get caught in the crosshairs. You've had the Bureau hanging around your life long enough to understand it's something I want to avoid at all costs." Doc looked directly at Hedaya. "Plus, I needed to know if you were setting me up."

Hedaya, surprised by the comment, stared at Doc.

"You worry about being a fall guy? That's funny, Doc. You don't seem like the paranoid type."

"Appearances can be deceiving, Hedaya. I'm just a guy looking for a quiet life, and this has the potential to get ugly."

"Usually, people searching for solitude are trying to put something behind them. Or perhaps they want to hide. Have you done bad things in the past, Doc?"

"Haven't we all?"

Hedaya laughed and stood up. "Of course." He turned serious. "So, where do we go from here?"

"I'm expecting a visit from the Bureau soon."

"Yes," Hedaya said, nodding in agreement. "And?"

"I would think whatever allegiances I have should be clear to you by now, Hedaya."

"That pleases me, Doc. It truly does."

Hedaya smiled and extended his hand.

"Yes, well, from this point forward, just assume somebody is always watching," Doc said, shaking the old man's hand. "Good night, Hedaya."

"Good night, Doc."

Doc walked alone down the hallway and exited through the elevator. He arrived in his room around three and napped on and off for the next two hours.

Chapter 32

Doc flipped through the large document, pleased at what he was seeing. Maya, sitting on the couch a few feet away, was focused on the same report. Merlin knocked back two large lines from the glass top. Doc and Maya looked up at the noise and shook their heads at Merlin's silent invitation to join him.

"That shit is going to kill you," Maya said, going back to her reading.

"She's right," Doc said, lighting a cigarette.

"You're one to talk," Maya said, waving the smell of smoke away. "What total are you showing for purchase orders the last three years?"

Doc flipped through the document and gave her three numbers. She reviewed her figures and looked up.

"They tie out to the penny. Good work, Merlin."

Merlin shrugged and sipped his drink.

"All projects should be this easy."

"Well," Doc said. "We're not home free, but I'm feeling good. Data conversion wrapped up in less than a month. I'll take that any day."

Doc picked up a bottle of wine and refilled Maya's glass.

"Trying to get me drunk?" she said, not looking up.

"Of course."

"I think it's working," she said, taking a sip. "Well, now I know how much it costs to rent a cruise ship for three weeks. He invites over a thousand people a year on a cruise?"

"Yeah. He calls it his high roller cruise. I'm guessing he ends up making enough on the gambling to pay for the ship."

"This guy is worth some serious money."

She leaned back into the couch and rubbed her eyes.

"He's perfect for you, Maya," Merlin said, preparing two more lines. "Rich and old."

"Funny. I thought you were the one working his way into the family tree."

She looked at Doc, and both smiled as they watched Merlin's face turn bright red.

"Yes," Doc said. "Do tell. Have you been deflowered yet?"

"Not in this lifetime," Merlin said. "Although lately she's becoming pretty insistent. The other night she forced my hand up her skirt. You

149

wouldn't believe what it… well, you two would. She says it would be the best I've ever had."

"Given your situation, she'd be right," Doc said.

"Says it would be beyond comparison."

"Compared to what?" Maya said. "Your right hand?"

Doc and Maya laughed. Merlin turned indignant.

"Maya, you can be a real bitch." He turned to Doc. "How do you put up with her?"

"She has her moments."

Merlin finished two more lines and leaned back in his chair.

"Nothing yet from our Mr. Barrier, huh?"

"No. He's been way too quiet," Doc said.

"We should have gone to watch his hockey game. Seeing his head bounce off the ice would have brought so much joy," Merlin said. "But I have enjoyed watching the amnesia scam he's been trying to pull off."

Merlin chuckled.

"I'm sorry. Have we met before?" he said, mimicking a dazed and confused Barrier.

Doc and Maya roared at Merlin's impression.

"How about when he walked up to Maya and said, 'Mommy?' The look on your face was priceless."

"It was just an excuse to nuzzle my breasts," Maya said. "It's sad. I almost feel sorry for the guy."

"Fuck him," Merlin said, getting to his feet. "I'm going to leave you two alone. I have a date this evening."

"Going clubbing again?" Doc said.

"No, I'm going upstairs for dinner with her and the old man."

"Oh, tell Hedaya the entire project team has confirmed for the party."

"Will do. See you guys tomorrow."

Merlin departed, and Doc looked at Maya, who had stretched out on the couch. Doc slid down and soon her head was resting on his lap. He pushed her hair back and softly stroked the side of her face.

"Feel like going out?"

"No, not really."

Maya closed her eyes.

"Good," he said, quietly continuing the gentle strokes.

"Have you decided what you want for your birthday?"

"I've given it a lot of thought."

"And?"

She opened her eyes and looked up at him.

"I want to be inside you at the stroke of midnight and stay there for the next twenty-four hours."

Maya smiled and closed her eyes.

"I don't know," she said, sleepily. "I was thinking more along the lines of a sweater."

She drifted off to sleep. Doc sat still, softly stroking her hair, trying to remember the last time he had been this content.

Chapter 33

Barrier waved a finger, and the dealer flipped another card in front of him. He stared at the five cards lying face up and frowned.

"That's thirteen showing, sir," the dealer said, resting his hand on the card shoe.

"I can count, thank you,"

Barrier checked his down card for the fourth time. It was still a three. Barrier waved his finger at the dealer who proceeded to flip a six next to the other cards.

"Twenty-two. Sorry, sir."

"Damn," Barrier said, sitting back.

The dealer removed the cards and Barrier's money.

"That's too bad, sir," the dealer said, unable to hide his small smile.

"Yeah, I can tell it breaks your heart," Barrier said, fidgeting with his remaining chips.

"How's it going?"

Barrier turned to the voice.

"What do you want?"

"We need to talk."

Jenkins shifted back and forth on his feet as he ran a hand through his hair.

"Jesus Christ, Jenkins. I'm trying to win some money here."

"We need to talk."

"Jesus Christ. All right. Just let me finish this hand."

Barrier looked at his cards and slid them under his chips.

"Good play," Jenkins said, peering over Barrier's shoulder.

"It's fucking nineteen. What did you expect me to do?"

"Jesus, you're in a good mood. How much are you down?"

"Eight hundred."

"That's all? Shit, I'm down three grand today."

"Is that supposed to make me feel better?"

Barrier watched the dealer reveal twenty. He shook his head and grabbed his remaining chips.

"I need a drink."

They walked into a nearby lounge and sat across from each other. The waitress arrived, took their orders and headed off toward the bar. Barrier looked around the empty lounge and focused on Jenkins.

"Okay, what's up?"

"I'm thinking about going to Hedaya."

"To do what? Beg for forgiveness?" Barrier said, shaking his head.

"Basically, yes."

"Excuse me, Hedaya I need to let you know you I'm responsible for planting an FBI agent in your casino in the hope of bringing down your empire. Are you fucking nuts?"

"It's our only hope."

"What are you talking about?" Barrier noticed the wild look in Jenkins' eyes. "What on earth is the matter with you?"

"Gentry's planning on taking us out."

"What?"

"I heard him on the phone today. I was outside his office, and I heard him say, 'Don't worry, I'm planning on taking them out later.' He's going to kill both of us."

"You're crazy," Barrier said, waving a hand at Jenkins.

"And then he said, 'It's time to teach them a lesson. I'm through cleaning up their messes.'"

Jenkins sat back quietly as the waitress returned with their drinks.

"That'll be nine fifty," she said.

Barrier tossed a ten dollar chip on the waitress's tray.

"Keep the change."

The waitress stared at the chip.

"Gee, thanks," she said, walking away.

Barrier rubbed his head.

"Why would he do that? It doesn't make any sense."

"Yes, it does. If they take us out, they can walk away from the whole thing, and nobody is the wiser," Jenkins said. "We're the only two who know what's been going on. It makes perfect sense."

"That sonofabitch," Barrier said. "What else did he say?"

"Nothing. But you should have heard the tone of his voice. It scared the shit out of me."

"What a surprise," Barrier said, taking a long swig from his beer.

"What do we do?"

Barrier's attention was drawn to Jenkins' feet.

"Are those new?"

"Yeah," said Jenkins, proudly holding one of the cowboy boots up for Barrier's approval. "They're a size too big, but I couldn't resist."

Barrier rubbed the outside of the boot.

"Nice. What is it? Snake?"

"No, lizard. Cool, huh?"

"Yeah, not bad. How much?"

"Got them on sale for nine hundred. I haven't done anything for myself in a while so I figured what the hell."

"Well, if you have to go, it might as well be in style. So let's hope you die with your boots on."

Chapter 34

"I beg your pardon?" Merlin said, choking on his wine.

Hedaya leaned across the table and repeated his question.

"I said I would very much like to know what your intentions are with respect to my niece."

"Isn't that a little personal, Hedaya?"

"Yes, it is," Hedaya said, smiling with narrowed eyes.

"Don't you have more important things to worry about?"

Merlin immediately regretted the comment as well as the last two lines of coke he'd done just before arriving for dinner.

Hedaya, his mood now dark, sat back in his chair. Rose returned to the table and surveyed the two men sitting in silence.

"Bofu, what have you done to upset Merlin?"

"No," Merlin said. "It's my fault. Please accept my deepest apologies, Hedaya. There is nothing worth worrying about more than Rose's happiness and well-being."

Rose beamed and kissed Merlin on the cheek.

"That is so sweet."

"No, I was… never mind."

"You're such a sweetheart."

She sat down and placed her hand on Merlin's forearm. He stared at the hand but said nothing.

Hedaya got up from his chair and tossed his napkin on the plate in front of him.

"If you'll excuse me, I have a few things I need to take care of."

He kissed Rose on the cheek, glared at Merlin, and left the room.

Rose watched him leave and turned to Merlin.

"I don't know what you said, but he's very angry."

"I'm sorry. I was flippant with him. Does he stay angry long?"

"Usually not. Unless it concerns business or me."

Merlin frowned and picked at his food.

"Then I think I'm in the doghouse."

Gentry knelt and gagged from the smell. He gently pushed the two puppies away and covered the four brown piles with paper towels.

"Okay, guys. Just wait a minute. Yes, Daddy is happy to see you too."

He tossed a tennis ball across the room and they dashed away in hot pursuit. He picked up the piles, dropped them into a plastic bag and began scrubbing the carpet.

"It's about time you got home," Grace said.

Gentry sighed and continued to scrub the carpet.

"Hello, dear. It's nice to see you too. How was your day?"

"Apart from that?" she said. "It was just fine, thank you. Make sure you get all of it."

"I told you on the phone this afternoon I would clean up their mess as soon as I got home. And that's what I'm doing."

"You had to go and get *two* dogs, didn't you?"

Gentry scrubbed the carpet harder.

"I thought I'd like to experience unconditional love," he said, under his breath.

"What?"

"Nothing, dear."

"When you finally do get them housebroken, I expect new carpeting. And they need their walk so don't forget to take them out."

Grace wheeled and headed for the kitchen. From upstairs came the pounding of bass and drums, courtesy of Grace's teenage daughters. As much as he hated their constant practicing, he had to admit that they were getting good.

Now if he could just figure out a way to put a smile back on Grace's face, maybe she would finally cave and agree to marry him.

Gentry remained deep in thought until he heard both puppies race across the carpet, trailing footprints that contained the contents of the now overturned plastic bag. He shook his head at the brown paw prints and waited. Grace returned from the kitchen, saw the new mess, and shrieked.

Gentry sighed and began the second round of cleaning.

"And as soon as you're done," she said, "I want you to-,"

"Jesus Christ, Grace. I told you I was going to take them out. And I will." Gentry said, too loud for any hope of a quick resolution to the argument.

Grace pointed at him and flashed an evil grin.
"You have puppy shit on your face."

Chapter 35

"I thought you said there was an ice rink down here," Maya said, looking around the room.

"There is," Doc said. "It's under the floor."

He saw Merlin and Rose wave to them. They were sitting alone at one of the many large tables that filled the back half of the room now set up for a large party.

"There they are," he said, lightly touching Maya's arm.

They wove their way through the multitude and sat across from the couple. Rose's hand rested on Merlin's thigh.

"Hi guys," Rose said, beaming. "Maya, I love your dress."

"Thanks," Maya said. "You look great. Silk, right?" Maya reached across the table and felt the material.

"It's a present from you know who," she said, patting Merlin's hand.

Merlin's eyes were scanning the room.

"He's over at the bar," Doc said.

Merlin looked over and picked Hedaya out of the crowd.

"If he comes this way, let me know," Merlin said. "He's still pretty frosty."

Doc smiled, remembering his recent conversations with Hedaya about his concerns about Merlin. He knew his friend would eventually climb out of the hole he'd dug, but the process would be long and painful.

Doc lit a cigarette and looked around the room. A large stage dominated one end. In front of the stage was a dance floor big enough for several hundred people. The tables were elegantly set for dinner and candlelight filled the room. He watched dozens of servers effortlessly handle all the requests.

Doc stood and leaned over the table to be heard above the noise.

"I'm going to say hello to Hedaya."

"Want me to order a drink for you?" Maya said, pausing from her conversation. She reached out and gently touched his hand.

"Sure. Cabernet, please. I'll be back in a few minutes."

Doc carefully worked his way through the crowd stopping at the table filled with his project team.

"Hi, folks. Quite a party, huh?"

"Doc." Jerome, the Casino's purchasing manager, waved to him. "Sit down and have a drink. I've got a bone to pick with you."

"Not tonight, Jerome," Doc said. "I'm off the clock."

"Firrrsth thing Monday then," he said. "S-s-some people have next week off. Unfortunately, I am not one of them."

"That was your choice, Jerome. Personally, I'd love to see you take the week off."

"Huh? Oh, I get it. Good one, Doc."

Jerome finished his drink and immediately began scanning the room for signs of his waiter. Doc waved goodbye to the group and continued in Hedaya's direction. He approached the bar and found Hedaya chatting quietly with a young Asian man.

"Doc," Hedaya said. "I've been looking everywhere for you. I'd like you to meet a friend of mine, Mr. Roger Matasha. Roger, this is Doc White."

Doc recognized the face immediately.

"It's nice to meet you, Roger," he said, shaking the man's hand.

Jesus Christ. What is he doing here?

The man, not sharing Doc's recognition, returned the handshake.

"It's nice to meet you, Doc. I understand you're quite the computer consultant."

"Unfortunately, most of my clients don't."

Both men laughed.

"He's too modest," Hedaya said. "What do you think?"

"I think you have way too much money," Doc said.

"Yes. I'm sure I do," Hedaya said, scanning the room. "Senator. It's so nice to see you."

Hedaya turned back to Doc and Matasha.

"Please excuse me, gentlemen. There's someone I need to say hello to. I'll stop by your table later, Doc."

Hedaya wandered off.

Doc looked at Matasha, who was scanning the room with a big smile on his face.

"What do you do for a living, Roger?"

"Import-export," he said. "I'm afraid I'm partly responsible for the trade imbalance we've been reading about lately."

"Do you do business in China?"

"Yes. All of Asia actually," Matasha said, smiling past Doc in the direction of the main entrance. "Would you excuse me, please? I think I see Jackie Chan. I'm a big fan."

He waved goodbye and started to wind his way through the crowd. Doc watched him for several moments before working his way back to his table.

"Did Hedaya say anything?" Merlin said.

"He said he would see us later."

Doc leaned across the table and started to whisper to Merlin. "You'll never guess who's-"

"Doc," Rose said. "I'd like you to meet some of my friends."

Doc sat down and smiled at Rose. He looked at Maya, who was sitting quietly with a small smile etched on her face that refused to go away. He looked at Rose and then around the now full table.

"Starting from your left is Jasmine, then Rosalie, Marjorie, Nashville, Gladys, Audrey, Phyllis, and next to Maya is Petunia."

Doc followed Rose's introductions around the table. All the women were in their twenties and extremely attractive.

Stripper alert.

He leaned forward in front of Maya to put a face next to the last name. Startled, he almost recoiled, but was stopped by Maya's nails digging into his leg.

Whoa! Check, please.

Doc looked around the table and recovered his smile.

"It's nice to meet you, ladies."

"You were right, Rose," Jasmine said, giggling. "He is cute."

Doc felt his face redden, and he looked at Maya, her bottom lip turning white. Petunia stuck a meaty paw in his direction. Doc returned the handshake and grimaced from the pressure.

"It's nice to meet you, Doc," Petunia said.

How nice. She's a baritone.

"You too... Petunia," Doc said.

Maya's nails went deeper into his thigh, and Doc took a deep breath.

"This is Petunia's first time out," Rose said. "Doesn't she look gorgeous tonight?"

Maybe for a linebacker.

The other ladies at the table gave Petunia a golf clap and Doc nodded at Rose and Petunia.

"Thanks. I finally let the girls - they're all dancers at my club on the North side - talk me into a public event," Petunia said, blushing. "I was afraid I would look slutty."

"Not at all," Doc said. "Nice dress."

Petunia smiled and picked up her drink. The glass disappeared inside the hand.

"To good friends."

They completed the toast just as a drunken Barrier staggered up to the table.

"Well, well, well," he said, glancing at Maya, Doc, and Merlin. "If it isn't the Princess, the Pawn, and the Phobic."

Barrier looked around the table and caught the eye of Nashville, a petite blonde sitting next to Rose.

"My, my, my. Aren't you a cutie? What do you say you and I go off and get better acquainted?"

Petunia slowly stood up, towering above the table.

"Is there a problem?"

A confused Barrier looked at the hairy figure in the cocktail dress standing a few feet away.

"No," he whispered. "No problem at all. I was just asking if she would care to join me for a drink."

"She's with me." Petunia's baritone reverberated around the table.

"Okay then," Barrier said, trying for composure. "Then I guess I'll be going."

Barrier took one more look around the table and staggered off.

"What a disgusting man," Rose said.

"Amen, sweetie."

Petunia sat down and smiled across the table at Nashville. The woman beamed back at her date.

Maya leaned over and whispered to Doc. "At least the weird part of the evening is over."

Before he could respond the lights went down and a voice came over the public address system.

"Ladies and gentlemen, direct from Hong Kong, please put your hands together for the King."

A loud round of applause went up as an Asian Elvis impersonator hit the stage and launched into a raucous version of Viva Las Vegas.

Maya looked at Doc and shrugged her shoulders.

"Well, maybe it's not."

They sat back and enjoyed the next hour along with the rest of the audience.

**

"Two glasses of Cabernet, please," Doc said to the bartender.

He let go of Maya's hand and reached his arm around her waist and drew her close for a soft kiss. The bartender poured their wine while they watched the dance floor gyrate to the band.

"Pretty good band to have for a party, huh?"

"Pretty good party, period."

Doc looked around and saw the solitary figure sitting quietly at the end of the bar. He nudged Maya gently, and she followed as Doc approached the King. He was still dressed in his sequined blue velvet jumpsuit, sipping a martini.

"Great show," Doc said.

"Thank ya very much."

The King slurped his martini.

"He's hammered," Maya whispered.

Doc nodded.

"Is this your full-time gig?"

"Yeah, everybody loves the King."

"What's it like to go through life impersonating somebody else?" Doc said.

Looking for some pointers?

"It's a beautiful thing," the King said. "If you're gonna spend your life being somebody else, you couldn't make a better choice than Elvis. Know what I mean, Babe?"

"I sure do, King," Doc said. "I sure do."

"Is this your lady?" the King said, looking at Maya.

Doc looked at Maya, unsure how to answer. Maya shook the King's hand.

"Yes. I'm Maya. It's nice to meet you."

"She's a beautiful lady," he said, looking at Doc.

"Yes, she is. Say, can I order you another martini?"

"You can do anything you want," the King sang, staring at his empty glass. "But stay offa my blue suede shoes."

162

Rose and Merlin approached. Rose was flushed with excitement. The King slowly turned in his seat.

"Ah, the beautiful Miss Rose. The wonder of wonders."

"Hi, King. Great show."

"Thank ya very much," he said, cautiously picking up his fresh martini with both hands.

Rose shook her head sadly and looked at Doc and Maya.

"It's tragic," she whispered. "What'll you have, Merlin?"

"Another champagne, please. Excuse me for a moment, folks. I need to go visit the powder room."

Rose watched him leave and shook her head. She looked at Doc.

"I hate that he does that shit. Isn't there something you could do make him stop?"

"Me? Gee, Rose, I didn't know it was my week to watch him."

"Yeah, I know. He's an adult. I'm sorry, but I just don't like it."

"Well, he's been doing it ever since I've known him. So far he seems to have it under control. What can I tell you? He's one of those people who loves cocaine."

Rose frowned. Then she brightened and beamed at them.

"After the show, we're all heading upstairs. You must join us."

"Doc says he will only go if Petunia is going to be there," Maya said.

"You are so bad." She leaned closer and whispered. "Pretty frightful, huh? Next week I'm putting Gerald, that's his real name, in touch with the person who does my electrolysis."

"Better bring a lawnmower," Doc said, shaking his head.

"Stop it," Rose said, laughing. "He just loves wearing women's clothes. Which seems odd since he spends all day watching naked women."

She paused and considered the idea.

"Or maybe it does make sense. Either way, it took a lot of balls to come dressed that way tonight."

"Yes, unfortunately, I couldn't help but notice," Doc said.

163

Chapter 36

The elevator opened, and Hedaya stood waiting to greet them.

"Hello, my dear." Hedaya hugged Rose then turned to Maya.

"Maya, you look magnificent. Doc is a very lucky man."

His smile turned into a cold stare.

"Hello, Merlin."

"It's good to see you, Hedaya," Merlin said, bowing. "I must thank you and compliment you on the party. It's a wonderful evening."

Hedaya accepted the compliment with a curt nod and turned back to Rose.

"Your friends are already here, my dear. I must ask you, who on earth is the tall one in the floral dress?"

"That would be Petunia, Bofu."

"Petunia? How unfortunate. It's such a beautiful flower. She, he... pardon my ignorance, my dear. Which one do I use?"

"Tonight you would use she, Bofu."

"Yes, I was afraid of that," Hedaya said, glancing at Doc. "Given how hard life is as either a man or a woman, I can't imagine why anyone would want to do both."

He turned back to Rose.

"She is, of course, most welcome, but please do your best to keep her away from me. She makes me nervous."

"Yes, Bofu."

Rose led them into the massive living room. Doc guessed around a hundred people had been invited upstairs. Maya handed him a glass of champagne; they gently touched glasses, and Doc watched her expression as she looked around the room.

"This is incredible," she said, staring up at the ceiling. "My whole Brownstone in New York could fit in here." Maya noticed his reaction. "Sorry. I mean my old Brownstone."

"I would have thought you'd be used to this kind of luxury."

"Doc," she whispered. "It's been a perfect night. Let's not ruin it."

"All I was saying-"

"I know what you were saying. Leave it alone, okay?"

"Okay," Doc said. "What would you like to do? I see some blackjack tables in the corner. Feel like gambling for a while?"

"No, I'd like a tour of the place if Hedaya wouldn't mind. And then I want to meet Bugsy."

They approached Hedaya, who was still greeting people coming out of the elevator. They waited quietly until he finished.

"Excuse us, Hedaya," Doc said. "Would it be all right if I take Maya on a tour?"

"Of course, enjoy yourselves. But you might want to avoid the area where the Irish pub used to be. There's some construction going on back there, and it's quite a mess."

"Construction? The place was immaculate the last time I was there."

"Yes, but my Irish friends had a particularly unsuccessful visit a few weeks ago, and they've decided to change casinos in the hope of improving their luck," Hedaya said. "Such is the life of a casino owner."

"What are you building there?" Doc said.

"A ski lodge."

Doc and Maya glanced at each other then back at the old man.

Hedaya laughed at their blank stare.

"I recently acquired a new customer who loves to ski as much as she loves to gamble. I stole her away from a competitor by promising to fly her to and from Vail every day and build her a ski lodge where she could gamble at night."

Hedaya flashed a mischievous grin.

"As I'm sure you've noticed we don't get much snow here in Vegas. And she doesn't like the Indian casinos in Colorado. It's just part of the cost of doing business, Doc."

He turned to face the man stepping out of the elevator.

"Good evening, Mr. Gentry. How nice to see you."

Chapter 37

"I'm saying we need a plan," Jenkins said. He tossed a large shot of tequila down the back of his throat. "Bartender. One more time."

A frenzied man in a black tux grabbed a bottle of Patron and placed it on the bar in front of Jenkins. "Help yourself." The bartender departed shaking his head.

"Thank ya very much," the King said, talking directly into the mahogany covered bar.

"Shit, he's alive," Barrier said, attempting to get up off his stool. "Hey, King. How about an encore?"

"Maybe later, Babe." The King rested the side of his face in a small puddle of tequila.

"Lightweight," Barrier said. "You can't quit already. You're the King."

"The King's on break."

Barrier laughed and slapped the King on the back. He poured another shot of tequila and tossed it back. "Ah. Good one." He looked at Jenkins, who was about to force down another of his own. "What were you saying?"

"Was I talking?" Jenkins said, confused. "Sorry."

"No, you moron. Something about a plan?"

"Oh, yeah. We need one." Jenkins tossed down the tequila that immediately threatened to return. He placed one hand on the bar and waited. He belched and turned to Barrier.

"So what are we gonna do?"

Barrier pondered the question as he looked around the increasingly blurry room. He squinted into the distance and frowned.

"Shit. He's here."

"Who's here?" Jenkins said.

"Gentry," Barrier whispered.

"Who?" Jenkins said, leaning closer.

"Gentry."

"That prick. What about him?"

"He's here."

"He is? Damn. What do we do now?"

Barrier tossed back another shot.

166

"We either run or hide."

Jenkins burped again.

"I don't feel much like running right now."

"Me neither. Do you know your way around this place?"

"Nope. Never been up here before. I've worked for that ingrate for six years, and he's never once even invited me up for a drink. Can you believe it?"

"Not now. We can hear about your career problems later," Barrier said. "We've got to get out of here. Let's try that door over there."

Barrier shoved Jenkins toward a far corner of the room. Tequila bottle in hand, Barrier staggered the short distance and led Jenkins through the door.

**

"I think he's cute," Maya said, looking down over the six-foot wall separating them from the lizard that lived below. Bugsy sat staring up at them.

"I think he's wagging his tail."

"He's probably hungry. We should go get him something," she said.

"How many thousand canapés do you think it would it take to fill him up?"

"He's adorable. Hi, Bugsy. Who's the good boy, huh?"

"Shall we continue?" Doc said, glancing around the indoor rainforest.

"Sure," Maya said, pointing into the distance. "What's over there?"

"I don't know. I haven't been over there. Let's check it out."

Doc, carrying a champagne bottle, led her across the bridge to the other side.

"This is amazing." She took in her surroundings and pointed up. "Look."

Doc followed her line of sight and saw a large red and blue parrot sitting on a tree branch a few feet above them. The bird, appearing groggy, fluffed his feathers and looked down at them.

"I think we woke him up," Doc said.

"Hello."

"Hello," squawked the parrot. "You dirty rat."

Maya laughed. "I think he's talking to you."

"That's the worst Cagney I've ever heard," Doc said, staring up at the parrot. "Who's the pretty bird? What a pretty bird."

"Thank ya very much," squawked the parrot, shifting its weight from one foot to the other. "Thank ya very much. You dirty rat." The parrot bounced up and down on the branch now very much awake.

Another parrot used its beak and feet to work its way down the tree. The yellow and blue parrot stared at them and flapped its wings.

"Kiss your ass goodbye, sucker." The parrot bounced around the branch trying to look tough.

"Got a smoke?" said the first parrot.

"Don't tell Rose. Don't tell Rose," squawked the second.

They were still laughing when they reached a set of automatic glass doors. The doors silently slid open, and they walked through the opening and found themselves facing another set of identical doors. The second set opened, and they stepped outside, realizing they were standing on one end of the rooftop garden. They stood silently taking in the view of the city displayed in front of them.

They both noticed the pool intertwined with a series of elaborate waterfalls at the same time.

"Feel like a swim?" Doc said.

"You read my mind," Maya said, quickly disrobing.

**

Jenkins took a swig of tequila, shook his head to clear the cobwebs, but remained bewildered by his surroundings.

"Jiiiim?"

"What?" Barrier said, stumbling over a rock.

"How did we end up in the jungle?"

"Beats me," Barrier said, staring off into the distance. "I was following you."

"I think we're lost."

They approached the platform and sat down. Barrier took a swig of tequila and offered the bottle to Jenkins. He waved it away.

"What the hell is this place?" Barrier said.

"I don't know," Jenkins said, wiping sweat from his face. "But it sure is hot in here."

"We're in the jungle. What'd you expect?"

168

"What was that?" Jenkins whispered.

"I didn't hear anything."

"Shhh. Listen. Hear that?"

Barrier tilted his head and listened carefully. "Yeah," he whispered. "I hear a voice. But I can't make it out."

Jenkins leaned forward in silence. "You dirty rat. Kiss your ass goodbye, sucker." He stared at Barrier. "Shit, we're fucked, Jim."

"I don't believe it," Barrier whispered. "That bastard Gentry went and hired thugs to do his dirty work. The friggin guy is too lazy to do his own hits."

"The FBI is contracting out basic services? What is the world coming too?"

Barrier stood up and looked around.

"I don't have a clue," he whispered. "But I'm not sticking around to find out. C'mon."

Barrier pointed to the wall behind them, and Jenkins staggered to his feet. They peered down into the foliage.

"Gee, I don't know, Jim."

"Don't be a baby. It's only about six feet."

Both men climbed from the platform onto the granite wall and dropped softly to the ground below.

**

Doc opened his eyes and looked at the waterfall cascading a few feet away. Submerged to their shoulders, Maya was straddling him and kissing his neck. She noticed him watching the waterfall, got him refocused with a passionate kiss, and whispered, "I want to do this all night."

Doc broke the kiss and cocked his head.

"What?" she said.

"We've got company," he said, peering around the edge of the waterfall.

She turned her head and looked out toward the edge of the pool. "Think they can see us?"

"I doubt it," Doc said, looking out at Rose and Merlin arguing.

"Good." Maya repositioned herself for a better look. "She sounds pissed. What's she doing?"

"Well, right now she's getting undressed," Doc said.

Maya extracted herself from Doc and looked out at the pool. "Jesus. She's amazing. She's like a miniature version of some Greek goddess."

"Except for her being Asian."

"Well, sure. That goes without saying." Maya laughed. "How does she manage to walk upright?"

"I think her ass provides counterbalance."

"Oh, so you've noticed her ass, have you?"

"I'm paid to pay close attention to detail."

"You think those things are real?"

"I'm not sure. You want me to go check?"

"Why don't you start by checking mine first?"

Maya watched Rose angrily shake her head, dive into the pool and swim towards the far end until she was out of sight.

"What do you think they're fighting about?" Maya said, returning Doc's nuzzle.

"Who cares?"

**

Jenkins stared straight ahead in the darkness and whispered.

"Jiiiim?"

"What?"

"Could you move your hand? Your nails are digging into my leg."

"My hands aren't anywhere near you. And besides you moron, I'm sitting over here, ten feet to your right."

"Oh," Jenkins said, glancing over. "Yeah, I see you."

He slowly turned his head left, his eyes eventually focusing on the face of the giant lizard staring at him. He saw the huge paw resting on his left leg. The lizard flicked a gigantic tongue against the tip of Jenkins' nose.

"Jiiiim?"

"Now what?" Barrier snapped.

"We've got a problem."

"No shit, Sherlock. I'm working on it. Now be quiet and let me think."

"I'm not talking about that problem. There's a giant lizard sitting next to me."

"A lizard? It won't hurt you. Just brush him away."

170

"I don't think I can do that, Jim," Jenkins said, looking back at the lizard.

"Why not?"

"Well, for one thing, he's at least ten feet long."

"Ten feet?" Barrier whistled softly. "Shit, that's a big lizard."

"Yes, it is, Jim. What should I do?"

"Don't make any sudden movements."

"That won't be a problem, Jim."

"What he's doing?"

"He's staring at me."

"Does he look like a friendly lizard?"

"I guess he seems pleasant enough," Jenkins said, forcing a smile in Bugsy's direction. "What should I do?"

"Maybe we can distract him."

"That would be good, Jim."

Barrier thought for a moment.

"Okay, here's what we'll do. I'll throw the tequila bottle over to the other side. Maybe he'll go over to check out the noise. As soon as he moves, we head for the wall."

"Please hurry."

Barrier drained the tequila and hurled the bottle. It crashed into a collection of ferns. Bugsy turned his head in the direction of the noise and slowly lumbered away. As the lizard turned, it flipped its tail striking Jenkins sharply on the side of his face.

"Ow," Jenkins said, scrambling to his feet.

Both men staggered across the short distance, struggled over the wall and collapsed face down on the platform. Jenkins, breathing heavily, sat up and patted his pockets as he scanned his immediate surroundings.

"Shit," he said, peering down over the wall.

"Now what?"

"I dropped my Blackberry."

"So what? Just get another one."

"My whole life is in that thing," Jenkins said.

"Don't you have it backed up on your computer?"

"I've been meaning to do that." Jenkins staggered to his feet and looked down at the device lying next at the base of the wall. "I've got to get it back. If you hold my feet, I think I can reach it."

"Are you out of your fucking mind?"

"I've got notes in there from all of our meetings with Gentry."

Barrier nodded and stood. "Okay, let's do it."

Jenkins leaned over the wall as Barrier clutched his legs. Slowly, he lowered Jenkins down.

"Have you got it?" Barrier said, struggling with the man's weight.

"Almost," Jenkins said, frantically stretching his arm out. "Just a little further."

"Stop wiggling," Barrier said, repositioning his hands on the man's legs. As his hands slid towards Jenkins' feet, Barrier felt the man's weight slip away.

"Ow," Jenkins said, landing hard on the far side of the wall.

"Oops," Barrier said, looking at the cowboy boots he was holding. "These are nice boots."

"Jiiiim?"

Barrier leaned over the wall and looked down. The lizard lumbered toward the latest noise.

"Hang on; I'll distract him again."

He stepped off the platform, pulled a rock from the ground cover and climbed back onto the platform. He peered over the wall and saw the lizard staring at the frozen Jenkins. The lizard had returned its paw to Jenkins' leg and was flicking its tongue.

"You know, I think he likes you, Jenkins." Barrier laughed and tossed the rock over the wall into the undergrowth.

The lizard turned its head and again wandered off towards the noise. Barrier grabbed Jenkins' arms and pulled him up onto the platform. Jenkins pulled on his boots, brushed the hair away from his face, and sat staring off into space.

**

In the surveillance room, Joe and Sam listened to the howls that refused to subside. Several people were huddled in front of the monitor. A few others were rolling on the floor doubled up with laughter.

"Okay, guys," Joe said, regaining his composure. "Show's over. Time to get back to work."

Hedaya, amazed by what he'd just witnessed, shook his head and waved goodbye to the surveillance staff as he headed back upstairs for what was left of the party.

Chapter 38

Doc sank deeper into the thick leather chair, leaned back and rested his feet on top of his desk. He glanced at Jerome, the purchasing manager, who had his head down and was rapidly reciting numbers from a thick document. Doc turned his head away and closed his eyes.

He smiled at the memories from the party. It hadn't ended until early Sunday afternoon, capped off with a brunch Hedaya had served poolside on the rooftop garden. Doc and Maya hadn't had to travel far to get to their table. Around four in the morning, they'd discovered an air mattress and drifted aimlessly across the pool in a deep sleep until the smell of French toast woke them.

Doc turned towards Jerome, who continued to rattle off numbers. He closed his eyes and wondered how the events of a single day could so easily be permanently etched into memory. And why it was so hard to sustain those events past a single day? Doc pushed the question away and turned his attention to Jerome, who was finishing his recitation.

"So what do you think?" Jerome said, taking off his glasses.

"About what?" Doc said, taking his legs off the desk. He rolled forward and sat with his arms folded on the desk

"About these numbers. Certainly they show justification for a minimum of three new staff once the system goes live."

"Jerome, you're going to need fewer people once we go live. But taking people out is not part of my job here. So keep what you've got and be happy."

"You just being difficult, Doc."

"I told you I was a pain in the ass."

"Well, at least you're honest."

Doc took a long swig of water and rubbed his forehead.

"Are you okay?"

"Yeah, I'm fine. Still fighting a bit of a hangover."

"It was a great party," Jerome said, reshuffling his papers for another volley. Before he could get started, they heard a knock on the door.

"Come in," Doc said.

Merlin stuck his head halfway through the door.

"Excuse me for interrupting, but we have a complex technical issue I need to discuss with you at your earliest convenience."

Doc, immediately grasped the true meaning of Merlin's comment and felt a rush of adrenaline surge through his body. Merlin, obviously concerned, stared and waited. Doc nodded and looked at Jerome. "We're done, right?"

"For now," he said. "But this isn't over. I'll be back."

"And I'll be waiting for you."

Doc motioned Merlin into the office. Merlin shook his head. Doc followed him out into the hallway.

"What's up?"

"Not here. Outside."

Merlin walked down the hall towards the elevators. Doc trailed behind, his good mood shattered.

They rode down in silence surrounded by the buzz of the casino. Merlin nodded in the direction of the front doors. Doc reluctantly followed him outside into the summer blast furnace. They walked down the long driveway and sat down on an empty bench at a bus stop. Doc lit a cigarette. Merlin looked at him bewildered.

"Jesus, Merlin. You're scaring me."

"This is bad, Doc. This is very bad."

Doc took a deep breath and tried to prepare himself.

Here we go again, huh?

"I spent last night looking around after the party and about three o'clock I found it."

"Found what?"

"You're not going to believe it. I still don't believe it."

"For chrissakes, Merlin. What the hell are you talking about?"

"Hedaya has a copy of Run Rabbit Run."

Doc sat stunned. "Say that again."

"You heard me. He's got the whole thing. Except for the second layer of firewall."

"How the hell did he get his hands on it?"

"Don't look at me," Merlin said. "I didn't give it to him."

"Until we know otherwise, I'm going to assume Roger Matasha gave it to him. I knew there had to be some reason why he was at one of Hedaya's parties."

"How would he get his hands on a master copy? Shit, I built the thing, and even I couldn't get it."

"I have no idea, Merlin," Doc said, his mind racing across several fronts. "Maybe Matasha got compromised. Maybe the Company has something going with Hedaya nobody knows about. Or maybe Matasha has flipped and is working both sides."

One thing at a time, Doc. One thing at a time.

"Hey," Merlin said, attempting to lighten the moment. "Do you remember the time we tracked down Matasha? We were sitting in a van across from his house getting the satellite feed that showed him barbecuing steaks on his back patio."

"Yeah."

Doc tossed his cigarette into the street and immediately lit another. He remembered the complex technical challenges inherent in building the new system that had been needed because a proliferation of highly-skilled hackers had regularly compromised their existing computer systems. Run Rabbit Run's primary objective was to prevent any unauthorized user from getting into the Company's computer systems ever again. Merlin had overcome that challenge without breaking a sweat.

It had been Doc's idea to create the second firewall as a decoy, allowing hackers to believe they had successfully invaded the computer system. But it was Merlin's technical brilliance that enabled the second firewall to be built. While the hackers poked around the system looking at believable, yet bogus, data, the Run Rabbit Run program captured the invading computer's address and transmitted it to a satellite equipped with global positioning software. In seconds, the intruder's location was pinpointed to within a few feet.

On that particular day, Matasha, the man Doc recognized at the party, had been only a few miles from Langley headquarters. They, along with several agents, had driven to his home and parked across the street.

"That was a fun day," Merlin said.

"Yeah. I remember calling him on the phone and telling him his steaks were burning. I'll never forget the sound of his voice."

"Another hacker successfully brought into the fold," Merlin said.

"Well, it was either work for the Company or go to Federal prison for fifteen years. It's not a hard decision. And it was the same one you had to make, right?"

"Yeah. Who knew some stupid fraternity prank would end up with me working for the CIA?"

"That's what you get for joining a fraternity at fourteen."

175

"What else was I going to do? You try being a teenage freak on a college campus. And I do still hold the record for the fastest infiltration ever."

Merlin stared off into the distance.

Doc looked at his friend, knowing how devastating it was for him to have the crown jewel of his technical career compromised.

"It's not your fault, Merlin."

"It doesn't matter. The fucking thing is compromised. You know what that means."

"Yeah," Doc said. He looked up at the sun that was nearing its apex. He closed his eyes and leaned back against the bench, bone weary.

"We have to call Langley. You know that," Merlin said. "The Company's data is secure, but there's no way they're going to allow a copy of that software to float around."

"Yeah, I know. We'll call them, but not right away."

"Doc," Merlin said. "We can't screw around with this one. Especially since we don't even work for them anymore. People get killed over shit like this."

"I thought you said you had so much stuff tucked away; you weren't worried about them coming after you."

"I wasn't talking about me."

Doc tossed his cigarette into the street. A city bus approached, slowed and then continued on its way. He ran a hand through his hair and wiped the sweat collecting on his forehead. He shook his head and looked at Merlin.

"We don't say anything for now. We need to get a better handle on this before we do anything. And that includes calling Langley. If this is sanctioned and Matasha is running the show, we don't want to blow his cover. On the other hand, if he has gone renegade we need to go slow and play it carefully, or he and Hedaya will run and hide."

"I don't like your plan, Doc."

"I don't either. I'm supposed to be retired."

"Yeah, sorry about that. Let's hope you get to live long enough to enjoy it."

"You're a big help." Doc took a deep breath. "Okay, first things first. Once you discovered the software, did you try to get in?"

Merlin frowned, and his eyes narrowed. "Please. Do I look like an amateur? Of course not."

"So our first problem will be getting in to find out what the hell Hedaya is using it for."

"That won't be a problem," Merlin said, grinning. "When I built it, I left a back door open."

Doc nodded, his longtime suspicion confirmed. Developers often added back door access to their software that could remain undetected forever.

"Good. What sort of footprints could you leave?"

"Well, Run Rabbit Run always grabs the ID used to access the software, but that won't be a problem as long as I use the back door and don't change any data. When do you want to go in?"

"Tonight."

"I'll need a few things to cover our tracks just in case anybody is watching. I'll head over to Radio Shack. They should have everything I need. It'll take me a couple of hours to get ready."

"A couple of hours? Is that all?"

"Sure. It's a piece of cake. You should have seen what I pulled off in Rio."

"I'm having dinner with Maya, so we'll get started around nine. We'll do it from my suite."

"Shit," Merlin said. "I forgot about her. How do we handle that?"

"The usual. Absolute and total silence."

"I'm sorry, Doc."

"Yeah, me too."

"So I guess we're officially back in, huh?"

Doc crumpled the empty packet of cigarettes and tossed it into a nearby trash container.

"Let's hope not."

Doc stood and waited for Merlin. They slowly walked back towards the Casino through the unrelenting heat.

"This might end up being the shortest retirement in CIA history." Merlin picked at his sweat soaked shirt. "I hate this place. I need a long shower." Merlin paused to wipe his sunglasses dry. "What do we do about Matasha?"

"Nothing for now. Let me see if I can get Hedaya to tip his hand. But Matasha is very lucky he's never actually met us. That would not be good for him."

"It would certainly complicate things."

177

"Samuels would want to put a bullet in his head."
Merlin nodded as they strolled up the long driveway.
"Is it just my imagination, or is it getting even hotter?"

Chapter 39

Doc stood behind the chair, unwilling to sit down.

"What are you worried about?" Merlin said. "You haven't been away long enough to get rusty."

"That's not it," Doc said, gripping the back of the chair with both hands. "In a few seconds, I'll officially be back in, and I'm not happy about it."

"Yeah, I know," Merlin said, staring at the laptop in front of him. "But admit it. Your juices are flowing aren't they?"

"Yeah," Doc said. "I am curious to know what he's up to."

"Me too. Ready?"

Doc sat down next to Merlin and lit a cigarette, making sure the smoke was drifting away from his friend.

"Let's go," he said.

Merlin thought for a moment and recited the number from memory. He kept repeating it as he entered the number and soon the casino's computer system's welcome page appeared on the monitor.

"I've bounced this number back and forth across several time zones to confuse anybody who might be being paying attention downstairs."

"What are the odds of that?"

"Very low. I gave project assignments to the night staff that will keep them busy for about three days."

Doc, confused, looked at Merlin.

"I said it will take them three days." Merlin chuckled. "I told them I needed it by tomorrow morning. Trust me; they're a little preoccupied right now. Okay, here's where they've hidden Run Rabbit Run."

Merlin guided Doc through an elaborate set of file directories with strange numbering schemes.

"I've been all over this system, and I've never noticed those before," Doc said.

"You need senior system administrator access to get at these," Merlin said.

"How many people have it?"

"Five," Merlin said, not looking up from the screen. "Me, the casino's three database administrators and one unidentified user ID."

"It can't be Hedaya."

"Doubtful. He's no techie. Whoever that ID belongs to is the one using Run Rabbit Run."

"Can you get at the passwords?"

Doc couldn't miss the look of disdain Merlin gave him.

"Sorry. Dumb question. How about we just use that person's ID and password to get in?"

"No, it's safer to backdoor it. Every time you log on, the date and time of your last session appear in the log in window. That way you can tell if someone has accessed the system using your ID."

Doc nodded.

"That's right. I remember the fights over that when we were defining the system requirements."

"In the time it took you guys to decide what you wanted the system to do, I could've built three of these things."

Doc focused on the file directories displayed on the screen.

"All the files have zeroes in the file size column."

"Yeah," Merlin said. "That's an override. To create a file for one of those directories you have to use the mandatory numbering scheme. Every time a file gets created or modified, the size indicator defaults to zero. Nice touch, huh?"

"Don't you worry about somebody seeing a bunch of apparently empty directories and deleting them?"

"Doc, were you asleep during all those design sessions?"

Doc thought for a moment and remembered the motto they created about halfway through the development of the software.

"Be careful what you create."

"Right. Archive, always. Never delete. It's virtually impossible to get rid of something once it's in there. Especially the master directories."

"All right. Take us in," Doc said, extinguishing his cigarette. "What, no coke tonight?"

"Maybe later," Merlin said, bringing up an image very familiar to Doc. It was a picture of a brick wall which appeared to be a simple screen saver.

"Why are you screwing with that? I thought you were going to use your back door."

"I am. But I want to check something first."

Merlin sat back in his chair deep in thought.

"Damn, I can never remember this. I shouldn't have made it so hard."

"The date and year the Agency was created and today's date and time. Add all the digits together and multiply it by itself twice," Doc said, reciting from memory.

Merlin nodded and typed a seven-digit number into individual bricks on the bottom row of the wall on the screen. The screen remained unchanged.

"How the mighty have fallen." Doc laughed. "That's what you get for trying to do it in your head."

Merlin sat quietly, deep in thought.

"Shit, this thing's on Greenwich Time, and it's already tomorrow over there."

He recalculated the number in his head and typed the new number. The brick wall disappeared. Merlin glanced at Doc with a 'take-that' expression.

They looked at the login window on the screen. Merlin typed the word magician and hit the enter key. A small pop-up window appeared. Merlin studied the information and leaned back in his chair.

"It's version three point two," he said. "An upgrade I did about two years ago. Worst case is they've been using it since then."

"How many little features did you put in just for you?" Doc said, nodding at the screen.

"Enough," Merlin said. "The good news is if they were trying to hack into Langley, people carrying big guns would have descended on this place by now."

Merlin exited the program and the cursor sat blinking.

"Sorry, Doc. But would you mind giving me a few seconds?"

Doc, surprised, stared at his friend.

"It's nothing personal. But nobody gets to see this."

Doc crossed the room and stared out the window. When the typing stopped, he looked at Merlin, who nodded for him to return. Doc sat down and saw a familiar screen in front of him. The neat, crisp design, one of Merlin's trademarks, was identical to the one he had seen virtually every day for several years.

"Whatever you do," Merlin said. "Don't try to access the e-mail system. Any attempt is immediately logged. I'll use another technique to get in there later."

"Will we be able to read any of the e-mails?"

181

"Well, since I don't have access to the keys they're using here, I'll have to hack it."

"How long will that take?"

"It could take some time. I wrote the algorithm, and I've built additional software that uses a powerful random number generator. Even with that, I'm not sure how long it will take."

"How much computer processing will you need to run the random number generator?"

"A lot more than is available here," Merlin said.

Doc caught the Langley reference immediately.

"No," Doc said. "There must be another way to get around the e-mail system."

"I could go into the system and get at the master file where the keys are stored, but you might as well put a flashing neon sign up announcing my presence."

"Then we'll wait on the e-mail. Hey, if they would know you were poking around looking for the access keys, why wouldn't they know you were hitting the system with the random number generator?"

"They would unless I made a copy of the data first."

"Made a copy?"

"Sure. That's not a problem," Merlin said.

"C'mon, Merlin. You've just spent the last several minutes telling me everything that system knows about itself. Are you now telling me you could make a copy of all the data in this system, and it wouldn't be tracked anywhere?"

"Yes, Doc," Merlin said, nodding his head. "That's what I'm telling you."

"How on earth is that possible?"

"I never told it to do it."

Doc scratched his head with a confused look on his face.

"Do you mean in all the time we sat around the table defining this system, we forgot that."

"Either you forgot, or you guys assumed it would automatically be there," Merlin said.

"Why didn't you say something?"

"Let's say I thought it would be a nice feature."

"For who?"

"For me," Merlin said, staring at Doc.

Doc's eyes widened.

"Don't tell me."

"Yeah," Merlin said, shrugging his shoulders.

"You don't?"

"Oh, I do. At least once a week."

"You copy everything out of the Company's system?"

"Well, not all of it. But enough."

"Why on earth would you do that?"

"I call it my life assurance policy. Don't look so surprised, Doc. We both know a lot more about what goes on around the world than either of us ever wanted to. And we've both seen how careers with the Company can go south in a hurry. Out here in the real world I might be a technical genius, but inside those walls, I'm considered a phobic geek who does a shitload of coke and knows an awful lot about a lot of people."

"Jesus, Merlin, you built this thing by yourself, and you're still the first one they call whenever something needs to be done to it."

"Yeah, maybe. But if the Company ever does decide to try and put me out to pasture, I'll need every tidbit I can get my hands on to save my ass. So each week I save off a copy and do a little light reading in my spare time."

"You already have access to the system. Why bother?"

"Because I don't like them knowing what I do or when I'm doing it."

Doc laughed.

"It sounds like you've got a bit of a death wish."

"Actually, it's an anti-death wish."

Merlin leaned forward in his chair.

"Let's get back to work. You want to start with the financials?"

"Yeah."

"Fire away."

Doc entered Run Rabbit Run's financial application, and the screen was filled with a list of available files. Doc stood up and began pacing the room. Merlin started to ask a question, but Doc stopped him with a wave of his hand. He continued to walk back and forth deep in thought.

One at a time.

"Well, maybe just a little one," Merlin said.

Doc heard the familiar tapping sound of razor blade on glass. He sat down and looked at Merlin, who was wiping one nostril with the soft side of his thumb.

"You sure you don't want some?"

Doc laughed softly and shook his head.

"If this gets any worse, I may."

He looked back at the screen and opened a file called Demomaster. An enormous financial spreadsheet filled the screen. The font was small and dozens of tiny columns spread horizontally across the screen.

"Jesus," Doc said, staring at the numbers. "Whoever is using this has better eyes than I do."

He moved the cursor to the top of one of the columns and clicked on it. The column expanded, and the number 3 that previously filled the available space in the top cell was now followed by six zeroes. Doc expanded the other columns and found the same result.

Merlin peered over Doc's shoulder.

"Go down to the bottom. I want to see the total."

Doc scrolled down the spreadsheet until he located the designated cell. He expanded it, and the number twenty-seven was joined by nine zeroes.

"That is twenty-seven billion I'm looking at, right?" Merlin said, blinking.

"It certainly is."

"Makes the four million he bounced to the Caribbean a rounding error."

Doc jumped back to the page that listed the files. He reviewed the naming conventions. Each of the file names began with Demo, followed by a two-digit alpha and an eight-digit numeric.

"It was nice of them to make it easy to follow along," Merlin said. "The numeric sequence is a date field. Those files are weekly summaries."

"Yeah. I think you're right."

"But what does the two digit alpha signify?"

"They're cities," Doc said, not looking up. "See," he said, pointing to one of the files. "LV. That must be Vegas. Want to see what Hedaya has been throwing in the kitty?"

Not waiting for a response, Doc opened the file. He scrolled to the bottom and revealed the total.

"He's been busy the past couple of years," Doc said, whistling softly at the number.

"A couple of million here, a couple there and pretty soon you're talking about real money, huh?"

Doc laughed and tried to do the math in his head. Merlin watched him for a moment and then interjected.

"If he's been doing this for a couple of years, it's a couple million a day."

"Thanks. Two million a day. You could hide that fairly easily if the denominations were big enough," Doc said.

"Denomination? You think this is a cash operation?"

"Absolutely. Remember the Caribbean test?"

"Yeah."

"He's said to me several times he doesn't trust technology. Calls it a necessary evil. This is a low-tech operation. I'd bet anything on it."

"How do you move that much cash around without being noticed?"

"I have no idea," Doc said, getting up from his chair.

"What about the file name? Demo." Merlin said, drawing another small line on the glass. "Demonstration? Maybe this is another test he's doing."

"No, this is the real deal. Besides, Demo doesn't stand for demonstration," Doc said, remembering what he thought at the time was a casual conversation. "It stands for democracy."

"And all this time here I was thinking we already had one."

Merlin laughed and knocked back the line.

"What do we do now?"

Doc walked to the refrigerator and poured two vodkas. He handed one to Merlin and stretched out on the couch, resting the glass on his chest.

"Well, you need to make a copy of those files, and I need to get started figuring out what's going on."

"It doesn't make any sense," Merlin said. "You'd need a lot more money than that to fund the type of operation he's thinking about."

"Yeah, but remember who we're dealing with. The Chinese take a much longer view than we do. We bumble along quarter to quarter, but they think in decades."

"I guess you're right, but what makes Hedaya believe he could pull something like this off?"

"Because he's Hedaya."

Chapter 40

Barrier and Jenkins sat huddled next to each other in a booth near the back of a dimly lit bar. Jenkins, not taking his eyes off the door, absent-mindedly played with a pile of quarters on the table.

"Stop it." Barrier, annoyed, placed his hand over the pile of quarters.

"Are you boys having a good time way back here?"

The waitress grinned at the two men who appeared to be holding hands.

"What?" Jenkins said, glancing back and forth between the waitress and the front door.

Barrier quickly removed his hand.

"If you don't mind, we're a little busy at the moment."

"Yes, I can see that." The waitress laughed and wandered off.

"Move the fuck over," Barrier said.

Jenkins slid across the booth.

"He's late."

"Good. Maybe he won't show," Barrier said.

"You don't think he'd try anything here do you?"

"No. But it's a short drive to the desert," Barrier said. "There he is."

Gentry entered the bar and spotted them. He walked over and sat down across from them.

"Good evening, gentlemen. How nice of you to show up. I've been getting the impression you've been avoiding me."

"I've been busy," Barrier said.

"Yeah, me too," Jenkins said

"I'm afraid I have some bad news for both of you," Gentry said, motioning to the waitress. "The Bureau has decided to pull the plug on you."

The waitress wandered over, and Gentry ordered a beer. As soon as she was out of earshot, Gentry continued.

"I went out on a limb for both of you. I gave you plenty of time to handle our boy Doc, and I got nothing. Fucking amateurs."

"Well, excuse me, Bureau boy, but I don't do this stuff for a living," Barrier said.

"What exactly do you do, Jimbo?" Gentry said. "That's still a mystery to me. Maybe I should join the private sector. Using you as the example, it seems like an easy way to make a lot of money."

"Wouldn't work for you, Gentry. You'd need to have a tangible skill set," Barrier said.

"Easy guys," Jenkins said, starting to stack the pile of quarters. "We're all on the same side here."

"We were," Gentry said, not taking his eyes off Barrier. "At the rate the project is moving now, it's going to be done before we know it. Then I'm looking at a transfer to North Dakota. And my girlfriend isn't very happy about it."

"I hear North Dakota is a real hotbed of crime." Barrier grinned. "Say, Gentry, what's the difference between Moosehead in Canada and Moosehead in North Dakota?"

"I wouldn't have a clue."

"In Canada, Moosehead is a beer, but in North Dakota, it's a misdemeanor."

Barrier roared at his joke and slapped the table. Gentry glared at him. The waitress arrived, and Gentry took a long swig from his beer.

"As of this afternoon, Jimbo, your problem is officially back in play. And you, George, are on your own. The money tap has been turned off."

"What?" Jenkins said. "I'm into those no-necks for two hundred grand. If I stop making my weekly payment, I'm screwed. You guys have to give me some more time."

"Too late," Gentry said, draining his beer. He waved to the waitress for another. "By the way, I didn't see you at the party."

Jenkins looked at Barrier, then back at Gentry.

"I guess we missed you. We were there."

"Yeah," Gentry said, smiling. "So I hear."

Chapter 41

Doc sunk back into the couch, uncrossed his ankles, and shifted his weight wondering how he could feel so completely at peace in such an uncomfortable position. He sipped his wine and dimmed the light on the table. Hooking one foot back over the other, he gently resumed stroking her face.

"You okay?" Maya said. "You seem fidgety tonight."

"A little I guess, but I'm fine." He brushed the hair away from the side of her face and looked down at her. A powerful wave of emotion surged through him.

Tell her.

Doc shook his head as he continued exploring her face. His eyes worked their way down to the top of her bare shoulder peeking out from the blanket that hid the rest of her. He closed his eyes and remembered the fresh-faced young woman he'd met so long ago. He opened his eyes and returned to her face, wondering which of the small lines had been caused by his own inadequacies.

Tell her.

She opened her eyes and caught his stare.

"What?" she said, smiling.

"I love you."

That's not what I meant, but it'll do.

Maya snuggled deeper into him and closed her eyes. "I know you do," she said. "What time do we fly out tomorrow?"

Doc leaned his head back and spoke to the ceiling. "I can't go."

She sat up and brushed the hair away from her face.

"What? Why not?"

"Something's come up. I need to spend the weekend working through it with Merlin."

"What are you talking about? Everything's fine."

"I'm not sure yet," Doc said. "Something about the database backup and recovery plan." His eyes darted down, then away.

You're going to have to come up with something better than that.

"Backup and recovery? Jesus, Doc. Merlin can do that in his sleep."

She slid down the couch. She crossed her legs and stared at him.

"I'm sorry."

"Here we go again," she said, shaking her head.

"What do you mean?"

"You. I'm talking about you," she said. "Every time we get to a certain point, you do this. And you wonder why I'm always holding back."

Unable to run, he tried to prepare himself for what was coming. "What do I do, Maya?"

"Shut down. Run away. Hide. Call it whatever you want, Doc."

"That's not it, Maya."

"Then what is it, Doc? I'm out on a limb here and I could use some help."

'Tell her.

"I don't know. But that's not it." Doc fell silent and took a deep breath.

Goddamn it, Doc.

She shook her head sadly and continued to stare in the hope of locking eyes, but he seemed resolved to look everywhere except at her.

"Maybe I should go by myself. Perhaps I'll find out what you find so appealing about going solo. Do you really enjoy going through life alone?"

You get used to it.

"No, I don't." A flash of anger, borne of frustration, surged through him and faded away. "I'm sorry."

He tried to fight the feeling that, once again, she was inexorably slipping away.

Chapter 42

"Hello, Hedaya," Doc said, looking up from the daily racing form.

"Good afternoon, Doc," Hedaya said, smiling as he looked around the room filled with a disparate collection of hopefuls. "You seem out of sorts today."

"You can tell that from hello?" Doc said, cocking his head at the old man.

Hedaya laughed softly.

"No. I was up on the second floor, and the cameras picked you up, so I followed you for a while. You bet every game on the board, and now you're betting the horses. Feeling a little restless?"

"My life on parade, huh?"

"What did you tell me not long ago? Always assume someone's watching."

"Yes. That's a safe bet these days, Hedaya."

Hedaya squinted and then the smile returned.

"Yes, I'm sure it is. Speaking of safe bets, you might want to try Hedaya's Dream in the fifth at Santa Anita."

Doc scanned the racing form and found the horse in question.

"Hedaya's Dream? Your horse?"

"No, a namesake. One of my friends paid me the honor of naming it after me."

"Fifteen to one? I don't know. The odds are pretty long."

"I'm a big believer in long shots. Besides, life is so boring if you only bet the favorite."

"Well, maybe I'll try it for a hundred."

"I really shouldn't say this since you'll be taking money out of my pocket, but if I were you, I'd go at least a thousand."

"A sure thing, huh?"

"Doc, I'm surprised. By now you should know they don't exist."

"I'm wondering how far your influence stretches, Hedaya. That's all I'm saying."

"Yes. Well, it looks like everything is under control in here. I need to take care of a few loose ends."

Hedaya smiled and continued to stare at Doc.

"Hedaya's Dream, huh?" Doc said.

"Yes, Hedaya's Dream."

He waved and walked out of the sports book into the main casino.

Doc turned his attention back to the betting window. He watched the bettors come and go. An elderly woman wearing a large hat adorned with flowers approached the window. Doc got up and walked to the betting window next to her.

Noticing him, she looked over.

"Having any luck?"

"I'm hoping it changes soon."

Doc laughed and pulled out his wallet and approached the attendant working the window.

"Three thousand on Hedaya's Dream in the fifth at Santa Anita."

Doc quickly counted out the cash and set his wallet on the counter as he waited for the man to process the bet. He looked up at the small round glass globe directly above the betting window and smiled for the camera. The attendant printed the betting slip and handed it to him. Doc walked away from the window and left the sports book.

Two hours later, after a solitary lunch and two beers, Doc took the elevator to the second floor and knocked on the surveillance room door. Sam's head appeared from behind the partially opened door.

"Hey, Sam. How are you doing?"

"Nice to see you, Doc," Sam said, peering out. "What's up?"

"I need a small favor. I lost my wallet somewhere downstairs. I think I left it on the counter when I was betting a horse. Would you mind checking the tape for me?"

Sam considered the request, then pulled the door open.

"Sure. C'mon in."

Doc followed him to the bank of video monitors.

"Do you remember which window it was?"

"It was somewhere near the middle of the room," Doc said.

Sam gave a woman sitting at the console the instruction, and she quickly rewound the tape. Doc saw himself at the window speaking to someone on his right. The camera tracked in as the attendant counted Doc's money and pulled back to reveal Doc standing next to a man in shorts and a tee shirt. Doc saw his wallet sitting on the counter, but his attention was drawn to the image of the man standing next to him.

"There it is," Sam said. "You should be more careful, Doc. When you get back down to the casino, check with the front desk. We always run the name against the computer first to see if it's a guest. I'm sure it's there. If not, let me know."

"Thanks, Sam. I appreciate it."

**

"I don't know, Doc," Merlin said. "Why would Hedaya bother with that? And in plain view. I don't know. It sounds goofy."

"I know. But there's a sense of style to it. That's the way he does everything. If something's not elegant, it doesn't hold his interest. It's classic Hedaya. The thing that makes the most sense is that it's done on his turf on his terms. He's such a control freak and this way he can keep a very close eye on what's going on."

"But he knows the FBI is all over the place. And he's got the Gaming Control Board to deal with. They count every nickel to make sure they get their nine percent or whatever it is these days."

"Nobody ever sees that money," Doc said, holding up a bottle of vodka. "I'm out of Grey Goose. Ketel One okay?"

"I'll suffer through it," Merlin said, holding out his glass.

"I'd be surprised if it ever found its way into a bank," Doc said, pouring the drinks. "At least in this country. If you get a chance, tomorrow take a look at the design of the betting counters."

"Yeah. I'll add it to my list." Merlin yawned and looked up at the ceiling. "Review the backup and recovery plan, refresh the database, create the production environment, eat lunch, save the world. I'm beginning to understand how you burned out on this double-life stuff. Jesus, I'm fried."

"You're not allowed to get tired yet. We've got a ways to go yet."

"I know," Merlin said, sipping his vodka. "And that's all before we deal with the Langley problem."

Doc frowned and finished his drink, grimacing from a headache that refused to go away despite two small handfuls of Advil.

"We'll get to that when we need to. Okay. What have you got?"

Merlin leaned over the top of the table, inhaled two large lines and fired back a large shot of vodka. He shook his head, sniffed loudly and rubbed his eyes.

"It's massive. And the places the money comes from seem pretty random."

"There's nothing random about any of this."

Doc pointed at a folder on the table.

"Is that the list?"

"Yeah," Merlin said, sliding it across the table.

Doc opened the folder and scanned the list of cities. He sat back, sipped his drink and closed his eyes.

"There must be some logical connection between them," Merlin said.

Doc looked back at the list that included cities from a variety of countries including Canada, the Philippines, Australia, Sri Lanka, the Dominican Republic, Vietnam and South Korea.

"Of course. How could I be so stupid?" he said, shaking his head. "You know what these places all have in common?"

Merlin picked up the list and looked at again.

"Other than the fact that I've been coked to the gills in all of them, I wouldn't have a clue."

"Casinos."

"Hedaya's put together a network of casinos to fund this thing?"

"Yes. And that's not all. I'll need you to check it out, but I'm sure we're going to find that those casinos are owned by a certain type of individual."

"Overseas Chinese," Merlin said.

"How you can do so much of that shit and still stay sharp amazes me," Doc said, getting up to grab a new bottle of vodka.

"You figured it out. How hard can it be?" Merlin said.

Merlin offered his empty glass to Doc. Doc refilled both glasses and stretched out on the couch.

"Say, how are you and Rose doing?"

"She's pretty steamed. She doesn't understand how someone can go through life not wanting to have sex."

"She's not the only one."

"Yeah," Merlin said. "But I've got enough germs. Sex is Germ-World on steroids."

Doc shook his head.

"I've seen you turn down some pretty amazing women over the years, so I know it's not Rose."

"Try to convince her of that. She puts up a good front, but she's pretty fragile."

"It's too bad. I like her."

193

"I do too. But she'll get over it. You know, sometimes I think that whatever amount of sexuality humans are usually born with went to my brain instead."

They sat in silence, listening to the music playing in the background. Suddenly, Doc sat upright.

"Where's that purchasing data conversion report?"

Merlin looked through the stack of papers on the table and located the document. He handed it to Doc, who quickly found the page he was looking for.

"This guy sure pays a lot of money for vegetables."

Merlin looked at Doc with a puzzled expression and watched him repeatedly run his fingers through his hair.

"You have plans tonight?" Doc said, finally looking up.

"Not really. Rose is going out with her friends. I thought I'd stay in my room, get whacked, and watch a movie."

"Feel like dinner?"

"After four lines of coke? That's not gonna happen. What? No, Maya tonight?"

"No, she went to Colorado with Sally from her team."

"That's right. You guys were supposed to go away this weekend. How'd she take the news?"

"Not well."

"Are you tempted to tell her about your previous sordid life as a spy?"

"Constantly."

"It's risky, but she could probably handle it."

"I can't do it. I couldn't put her in that kind of jeopardy."

"Man, you guys can't catch a break can you?"

Doc shook his head and stood up.

"I think I'll hit the tables. I had a bit of a windfall this afternoon."

Chapter 43

Doc wiggled his finger in the direction of the dealer who flipped a six in front of him. He waved away another card, leaned back and lit a cigarette. The dealer flipped her hold card over revealing nineteen. Doc took a slow drag and watched the dealer count out a large stack of purple chips.

"You're on fire," said the man sitting next to him, looking admiringly at the stack of chips in front of Doc.

The adrenaline continued to surge. Doc took a deep breath and tried to remain calm. He looked down at his chips and smiled. He'd taken the forty-five thousand he'd won on Hedaya's horse and added another ninety thousand to it over the past hour. Doc glanced up at the dealer as he riffled his stack of chips. He stared down at the two yellow chips. Stacking one on top of the other, he slid them forward.

Haven't you learned anything?

Doc shook his head at the voice and lit a cigarette.

"You're gonna bet twenty thousand on one hand? Shit, I get sweaty palms playing twenty bucks."

The man who made the comment reached behind him and tugged the shirt of one of his friends. Soon, a small crowd was standing behind Doc.

"You feel like playing along on this one?"

"Sure," the dealer said, knowing that if Doc won the hand, she would add the total of whatever side bet Doc made on her behalf to that evening's tips. Doc looked down at his stack and tossed a thousand-dollar chip out in front of him.

"You sure?" the dealer said, raising an eyebrow.

"Thanks to you, I'm up ninety grand in an hour. I think it's the least I can do."

The dealer smiled and began dealing. She dropped a six in front of Doc.

"Damn," he whispered.

The dealer dealt herself a five and pointed to the person at the end of the table.

Okay, a five. We're still in this.

The dealer flipped another six in front of Doc. She stood back and waited.

No guts, no glory.

"I'll split those," he said, counting out another twenty thousand in chips plus an additional thousand to match the dealer's side bet.

The dealer separated the pair of sixes and rearranged the chips to indicate he was playing two separate hands.

"Man, you've got balls," said the man sitting next to him, standing on a twelve of his own.

Doc ignored the comment and focused on the next card. He knew he was going against the odds with the dealer showing a five, but he hated standing on twelve. He watched the dealer flip the next card in front of him.

It must be the work of the devil, laddie.

Doc stared at the three sixes displayed in front of him and looked around the table. All eyes were riveted on his next move.

"Split it," he said, reaching for more chips.

"Sixty thousand. Jesus Christ, I don't believe it." The man sitting next to him glanced excitedly around the table. He tugged at Doc's sleeve. "Don't panic. Just stay cool, man. You gotta focus."

Hey, Gomer do you mind? The man is trying to play cards here.

Doc shook his head and tried to regain his focus. He looked at the table and waited. The dealer flipped the next card, and a gasp went up around the table at the fourth six. Doc shook his head in amazement.

"Well, there's something you don't see every day," he said, looking up at the dealer. "How many times can I split?"

"Up to four," the dealer said. "That's your last one."

"What the hell." He reached down and counted the chips remaining in front of him. He looked up at the dealer. "I'm getting a little short here. I'll need a marker."

The dealer turned away from the table and called to the man standing behind her.

"Request for a marker here, Stan."

The pit boss strolled over to the table, reviewed the situation and smiled at Doc.

"What sort of mess have you gotten yourself into, Doc?"

"We'll see, Stan. I need some cash to play this hand."

The pit boss filled out a form and gave it to the dealer.

"Give him what he needs."

He moved behind the dealer and watched as she counted out fifty thousand dollars in yellow chips. The dealer reached for the next card and flipped a five next to the first six.

"Showing eleven," the dealer said, raising an eyebrow.

Do it.

"I'll double that," Doc said, sliding another twenty thousand in chips forward.

"That's a hundred thousand," said the breathless man sitting next to Doc.

"Thanks for reminding me," Doc said.

The dealer smiled and said, "One card. Here we go." She flipped a ten down in front of him.

Doc looked at the twenty-one and felt the rush of adrenaline. He shifted his attention to the second hand. The dealer turned another five.

"Eleven," the dealer said.

Doc shook his head and pushed another twenty thousand toward the dealer.

"Double it."

Doc was oblivious to the stares he was receiving around the table. The dealer flipped a queen next to the eleven.

"Unbelievable," said the man looking back at his friends.

The dealer reached into the shoe and flipped a four next to the third six. Doc looked up at Stan, who was intently watching the proceedings.

"Showing ten."

"Double it," he said, looking up at Stan.

Stan smiled and made a notation on the marker sheet. The dealer counted out another fifty thousand, placed twenty next to the third hand, and slid the other thirty toward Doc. Doc tossed another thousand dollar chip toward the dealer. She placed it next to the bet on her side of the cards.

"I think there's an ace there," Doc said.

The dealer chewed her bottom lip and reached for the shoe. She flipped the ace down next to the six and four.

"Sonofabitch," the man said. "That's three twenty-ones."

"One more to go," Doc said, looking into the dealer's eyes.

She pursed her lips and glanced over her shoulder at Stan, who nodded for her to proceed. She flipped another four next to the remaining six. She waited while Doc pushed another twenty thousand next to the cards. He flipped a thousand dollar chip towards the dealer's side bet.

"Think there's another one there?" the dealer said.

"There's only one way to find out."

The dealer flipped the ace over. A loud shout went up around the table. Doc leaned back in his chair and looked at the four hands of twenty-one displayed in front of him. He fought back a massive rush of adrenaline surging through his veins.

"A hundred and sixty thousand, right?" Doc said.

"Yup," the dealer said. "Plus the eight you put out for me."

"How quickly one's life can change, huh?"

Doc took a long drag on his cigarette and exhaled towards the ceiling. He closed his eyes and heard the voice behind him.

"Hey, Doc. Sorry to bother you."

"Hi, George. Haven't seen you around for a couple of days," Doc said, not turning around.

"I need to talk to you."

"I'm a little busy right now, George."

Doc felt the tap on his shoulder. He turned around and saw Jenkins' heavily bandaged face. The bandages surrounded his wild eyes and completely covered his nose except for two small holes left for breathing.

"Jesus Christ, George," Doc said. "What the hell happened?"

"A small incident of my own doing I'm afraid," Jenkins said, scanning the table. "Holy shit. That's the hand of a lifetime. That's what you've got there."

Jenkins looked around the table and nodded knowingly, feeling very much the expert. Other people standing near George took a step back or shuffled away.

The dealer looked at Doc with a smile frozen on her face.

"I think it's your turn now," Doc said.

"Nervous?"

"Absolutely. How about you?"

"What do you think? I've got eight grand riding on this."

She looked at the five in front of her and flipped her second card over. The table groaned at the six.

Doc shook his head at the eleven. The dealer looked at Doc again.

"Any ten and we push. That would be a lot of work for a tie, huh?"

"That's not going to happen," Doc said. "This one's mine."

The dealer slowly reached into the shoe and flipped a nine down next to the eleven. A long slow breath escaped Doc amid the loud shouts around the table.

"In the blink of an eye," Jenkins said.

The dealer removed the wagers from the other players and counted out the hundred and sixty-eight thousand. She dropped eight thousand into the box that held the dealers' tips and pushed the balance to Doc.

"Thank you," she said, beaming.

"No, thank you."

"Nice play, Doc," Stan, the pit boss, said. "See how fast your life can change around here? You're lucky Hedaya's so fond of you," he said, tearing up Doc's marker. He looked at the dealer who was trying to maintain her composure in the midst of her own excitement.

"I think it's time for your break," Stan said to the dealer.

"I'm done," Doc said, getting up from the table.

He tossed another thousand-dollar chip to the dealer and waited while she put his winnings in a tray. He picked it up, said goodbye to the table and walked to the cashier with Jenkins trailing close behind.

**

"Did somebody do that to you?" Doc said.

"Yeah, but I asked for it."

"Is there anything I can do?"

"No, eventually it'll heal. So what are you gonna do with the money?"

"I don't know."

Doc realized he had not only fully recovered from Sylvia's withdrawal and his initial losses at blackjack, but was now up about a hundred grand. He looked at the frazzled Jenkins and around the crowded lounge. The noise began to hurt his ears.

His thoughts traveled to an intimate stretch of sand in Belize. His mind wound its way to the mountains of Colorado, and he was forced to wonder about what she was doing and, more importantly, what she was thinking. He desperately missed her and fought the urge to jump on a plane, find her, and vanish from the world's eyes and ears.

How hard could it be?

"Too hard," Doc said, deep in thought.

"What?" Jenkins said, confused by the outburst.

Doc castigated himself and focused on Jenkins.

"The money," he said, smiling. "It's too hard a decision to figure out what to do with it right now."

"A quarter million is a lot of money."

"Yeah, but it's still only money, George."

Doc drifted away and saw blonde hair resting on his suntanned shoulder.

"That's easy for you to say."

Doc looked across the table and lit a cigarette.

"What was it you wanted to talk about, George?"

Jenkins shifted in his chair.

"I'm in real trouble, Doc."

Doc nodded and waited for him to continue.

"I have this thing with gambling. Lately... I've hit a bad patch. I'm sure it's going to turn around soon, but I'm running out of time."

Jenkins looked around the room.

"Are you asking me for a loan, George?" Doc said.

"No, of course not. I couldn't do that," Jenkins said. He paused and raised an eyebrow in Doc's direction. "Could I?"

Doc smiled.

"No."

"Yeah, I figured that," Jenkins said, the brief flicker of hope vanishing. "Actually, I was looking for some advice."

"I've got tons of that, George," Doc said, laughing. "I don't know what it's worth, but I have a lot of it."

Jenkins tried a smile, but it didn't take.

"Ever find yourself in a place you desperately want out of, but each alternative seems worse than where you are?"

Constantly, George.

"Yes I do, George. All the time."

"I find that hard to believe. You seem somehow blessed by life."

Doc leaned forward and crushed his cigarette out.

"I used to believe that."

"And now?"

"Now? Now I'm happy to break even."

"Can I trust you, Doc?"

Jenkins gave him a hard stare. Doc considered the question.

"Do you want my honest answer?"

Jenkins frowned, surprised by the question.

"Yes."

"It depends, George."

"I see," Jenkins said, sipping his beer. "On what?"

"On a lot of things," Doc said, forcing the man to go first.

"There are external forces at work here."

"External forces? Have you been reading a lot of science fiction lately, George?"

"Very serious external forces," Jenkins said.

"What kind of external forces?"

Jenkins paused. "I don't know if I can tell you."

"Well, then it's going to be hard for me to give you any useful advice."

Doc lit another cigarette and watched the bandaged man continue to scan the room.

I've seen glaciers move faster than this guy.

"I'm involved in something I can't handle."

"Okay," Doc said. "That's a start. And?"

"And I have very few alternatives."

"Stay and keep doing what you're doing. Stay and try something different. Or leave."

Jenkins bolted upright in his chair.

"Yes. How did you know that?"

"When you boil it all down, George, those are the only choices we ever have."

"Interesting."

"What's the worst thing that could happen, George?"

"I could die," Jenkins said, fighting back tears.

"I see." Doc realized that he felt genuine sympathy for the man across the table.

"If I ran, do you think they would ever find me?"

"I guess that depends, George."

"On what?"

"On who's looking for you."

"Yes," Jenkins said. "I could go somewhere. Get a new identity. Just start over."

"It's been done before," Doc said, trying to calculate the number of people he knew who had chosen that route. "If you decide to do that, remember one thing."

"What's that?"

"You'll still have to live with yourself."

"Yes, I need to fix some things."

"Do you have a family, George?"

Doc was surprised to realize how little he knew about the man's personal life.

"No. Forty-nine and single. First, it was my career and then I just got too self-absorbed. As time went by I kept ignoring the little voice inside my head telling me to settle down. Know what I mean?"

Doc sat silently in his chair.

We're waiting.

"Sure. I ignore mine all the time. Besides, who's to say the voice has a clue what it's talking about?"

Very funny.

Doc felt relieved to hear that George's problem, despite its severity, could be dealt with solo.

"I imagine being on your own might make your decision easier."

"Yes," Jenkins whispered. "Maybe it's time I found a special woman and an isolated stretch of sand."

"That sounds nice, George."

"Lately, I've been thinking that I might like to be a bartender."

Doc smiled and considered the idea.

"Spend the rest of your life in a tropical paradise making umbrella drinks for happy vacationers? That doesn't sound bad, George."

"It's a noble profession," George said. "So you think I should run?"

"I'm not saying that. You need to make whatever decision will keep you on the planet for the longest time possible. Your life might suck at the moment, George, but it still beats the alternative."

Amen, brother.

"I'm sorry," he whispered.

"For what?" Jenkins said, confused.

Doc realized he had been speaking to a far corner of the room. He looked across the table. "For you." Doc felt his own reality rapidly slipping away. "I'm sorry you find yourself in such a bad spot." Doc picked up his glass and noticed his hand shaking.

Jenkins sat back in his chair. "I should get going. Thanks, Doc."

"No problem, George."

"If I don't see you again, you take care."

Jenkins started to walk away but stopped.

"Doc, you might find it hard to believe, but I'm very good at what I do."

"I believe you." Doc studied the bandages that dominated the man's face. "Circumstances sometimes get the better of us."

"Yeah," Jenkins said, discreetly wiping the corner of his eye. "Thanks again, Doc. It's been a pleasure getting to know you."

"Me too, George. And remember, life doesn't give you any do-overs, but there's always second chances. Give yourself permission to move forward from here."

Jenkins nodded, got his smile working and slowly walked away.

Good advice. Maybe you should take it.

Chapter 44

"It sounds beautiful."

"It was."

"I wish I could have gone with you and not come back."

"Really? Let me get this straight. You desperately wanted to go with me, but couldn't find the time. And despite your busy work schedule, you somehow managed to squeeze in a night of gambling?"

Doc had been waiting for the question. In the midst of her hard, unblinking stares, he had looked for the best possible time to bring it up. Some way to soften the blow, some way to make it possible for them to survive the conversation intact. He needed to know they could move forward, that he could somehow repair whatever damage she would soon be reporting.

Unable to step into the void of silence that followed her clipped responses, he waited. But he'd waited too long. Now the question delivered quietly from behind the wine glass hovered over him.

He remembered a similar conversation five years ago. The details were different, the circumstances almost identical. Contrary to the serendipity that landed him in Vegas, that project had been carefully orchestrated from the beginning. He, along with Merlin and two other agents, had infiltrated a South American terrorist group using a variety of financial institutions as their base.

The consulting company he concocted to win the project was a total fabrication. By the time the team had been assembled and references created for bogus prior projects, the competition had fallen away. Doc remembered filling out the balance of the project team with consultants oblivious to the primary objective. He had been searching for a lead person who could both handle an enormous workload and effectively relate to anyone regardless of title or personality. He processed the requirement through the massive database the Company had of innocent bystanders who worked in the industry, and her name appeared at the top of the list. Out of the blue, he called and asked her if she wanted to go to Brazil for six months.

They started working together. During long days of intense focus followed by warm nights they fell in love. They stayed that way until the project turned dangerous. Then, like now, his behavior, driven by a dark secret, had turned her away.

He returned her stare across the table. The word of his run of luck spread quickly. Who had told her didn't matter. The real issue was someone had gotten to her first. Before he had the chance to couch it in his own terms. Before the whole thing completely unraveled.

"What is it, Doc? Another woman?"

Doc stared back at her bewildered.

"How could you even say that?"

"Think about it," she said.

Doc closed his eyes, desperate for the waterfall. The memory wouldn't take hold.

"I had too much work to do, Maya. I played for about an hour. That's all."

"Yes. That's all."

Her tone of finality engulfed him.

Tell her.

"I'm thinking about getting out of here early, Doc," she said.

"I see."

"Do you?"

Doc looked across the table at the woman, now a million miles away.

"Yes, I do."

"How's the view?"

"It's cloudy."

**

Hedaya focused on the ice in front of him and rubbed the bottom of the polished granite rock. When he noticed Doc standing at the other end of the rink, he waved and pointed toward the couch.

Doc sat down and looked around the massive room. He smiled as his eyes drifted past the King's bar stool and his thoughts returned to chatty parrots and a flesh-colored waterfall.

It's amazing what a good memory will do for your mood.

"Yeah."

"Good morning, Doc."

Startled, Doc looked around and saw Rose standing behind him wearing ice skates and a skintight black leotard. Her hair was tied in a single strand that trailed the length of her back.

The eighth wonder of the world.

Doc nodded and stood up. He gave her a warm hug.

"Hi, Rose. I haven't seen you in a while. You look great."

"Thanks," she said, holding the hug. "I was on vacation."

"Oh, yeah? Where did you go?"

"Sri Lanka, of all places." She laughed. "It's a long trip, but productive."

Doc felt the adrenaline surge.

This woman is full of surprises.

"Sri Lanka? That's an interesting choice."

Doc made a mental note to tell Merlin another piece of the puzzle had fallen into place.

"I have a few friends working over there. It was my turn to visit them," she said. "It was fun. How about some coffee?"

"Sure. That sounds great."

Rose held up two fingers to the man behind the bar. She stretched her back and sat down. Doc slid back into the couch and sat watching her in a new light.

"What?" Rose said, smiling at him.

"I was sitting here thinking about how much you remind me of your uncle. I never really noticed the resemblance before."

Rose glanced over to the curling rink and watched Hedaya as he slid down the ice, one foot in front of the other, barking commands to the sweepers.

"Thank you," she said, glancing back at Doc. "I consider that high praise."

Doc nodded, watching the ice in front of him. The server arrived with the coffee, placed the tray in front of them and departed. Rose picked up a small container.

"How's Maya?" she said.

"She's pretty pissed at me right now."

"Really? Have you been a bad boy?"

"It's a long story, Rose. Let's say that I was playing blackjack when I should have been in Colorado."

"Yes, I heard you had a quite a run the other day. Congratulations."
Rose stood up holding her coffee. "I have to practice. It was nice seeing
you, Doc." Rose winked at him and sauntered away.

Doc watched her walk toward her patch of ice and shook his head in
amazement at the delicate flower that was Rose.

I've seen bowling balls that weren't that round.

"Or as hard," Doc said.

He lit a cigarette and sipped his coffee.

"Having impure thoughts, Doc?"

He looked up at Hedaya, who had appeared next to him.

"Morning, Hedaya. Yes, you caught me. I was admiring the scenery."

Hedaya smiled and motioned to the man behind the bar. He sat down
and stretched his legs in front of him.

"Damn, I hate getting old."

"That'll never happen, Hedaya. You've got decades left."

Hedaya looked at Doc with a touch of sadness in his eyes.

"Doubtful. How many eighty-five-year-olds could believe that?"

Doc cocked his head in surprise.

"You? Eighty-five? No way."

"Yes. Sad, but true."

Hedaya nodded to the waiter who arrived with a strange looking
concoction in a large glass, then departed. Hedaya sipped the drink and
grimaced. "Too much ginseng." He frowned and motioned to the man who
quickly returned.

"Yes, Hedaya?" the man said, bowing slightly.

"Let's try this again, Will. The recipe is somewhere behind the bar."

Hedaya handed him the glass.

"My deepest apologies, Hedaya."

Dejected, the man walked off carrying the glass.

Hedaya looked at Doc. "He's new. Thanks for stopping by."

"It's not a problem. I'm clear until ten."

"I've meant to tell you. I've been very impressed with your work. The
project has moved forward just as you said it would and while everyone is
busy, it's no longer frantic. I like that."

"Thank you," Doc said. "I have a good team. They're doing most of
the work."

"Yes, but you have provided the essential leadership." Hedaya winked
at him. "You are a man of many talents."

Hedaya accepted a fresh glass from the bartender who stood waiting while Hedaya sipped the drink. "Perfect," Hedaya said. The man bowed slightly and left.

"Any word from George?"

"No," Hedaya said, setting the glass down. "I'm afraid George is gone, and he won't be back."

"Do you think something bad happened to him?"

"I imagine you have a better idea of what happened to George than I do, Doc." Hedaya gave him another knowing smile.

Doc remembered the conversation he had had with George in the lounge.

Cameras.

"Do you watch everything I do, Hedaya?"

Hedaya smiled.

"Only what you let me see, Doc."

"Well, we've already had the trust conversation."

"Yes, we have, haven't me?"

"Jenkins ran. He believed he was out of options," Doc said.

"I know. He's fortunate the loan sharks he's involved with are local. If he used another group that had, how shall I say it, more of a global reach, he would be in serious trouble."

"They won't go after him?"

"For two hundred thousand? Doubtful. They could easily spend more than that trying to find him. But I'm sure we'll never see George in Vegas again."

"What about the FBI?"

"Ah, yes, the Bureau." Hedaya sighed. "We'll have to see what happens with that, won't we?"

Hedaya cocked his head and stared at Doc.

Doc stared back.

"You would have made a great cop, Hedaya."

Hedaya laughed loudly, and it echoed through the room.

"A cop? After everything I've done for you, and still you hold me in such low regard?"

Doc chuckled as he extinguished his cigarette. "By the way, I'm meeting with the Bureau this evening." Doc paused to let the comment sink in.

"Fascinating," Hedaya said, leaning forward. "How did they approach you?"

"I kept expecting Barrier to be the one to broach the subject, but it came from Gentry. He said he needed to speak with me privately."

"Did he mention the FBI?"

"No, that'll come tonight."

"What will it be? A threat to your livelihood or an appeal to your patriotism?"

"Oh, I'm sure they'll start out nice, but that will change in a hurry. They'll try to be subtle about potential IRS problems or mention they have a knack for being a nuisance. When that doesn't work, they'll drop a tidbit about something from my past."

"Do you have a checkered past, Doc?" Hedaya said, smiling.

"Don't we all?" Doc lit another cigarette. "But even if I didn't, they'd just make something up."

"Do they worry you?"

"I'll survive."

Doc looked around the room. It began to spin slowly.

"How are you going to handle them tonight?"

"If it's okay with you, I thought I might agree to play along for a while."

"Ah, misdirection," Hedaya said. "Interesting. That might be fun to watch."

"You need to get out more, Hedaya."

Chapter 45

Gentry passed the time by wondering what was taking so long for his beer. The man across the table incessantly rattled off a list of Gentry's deficiencies that required attention. He looked around the darkened bar and shook his head in disgust.

The waitress arrived with his beer and the man's Diet Coke. He stopped reading, smiled at the waitress and waited for her to leave.

"Get another ready for me," Gentry said, as the waitress emptied the ashtray. She nodded and strolled away.

"And another thing," the man continued. "I don't like it when my agents drink on duty."

Gentry looked at the man over the top of his beer as he took a long pull, then belched and set the bottle down. He continued to hold it with both hands.

"Yeah, I should be more like you. Come to a dive like this and order a goddamn Diet Coke. Aren't you the one always talking about how agents shouldn't make themselves conspicuous?"

The man pursed his lips tightly and decided to let the comment pass. He looked back at the document and resumed reading.

"Next, your paperwork is very shoddy at times. You can do much better. Also-"

"Isn't this a strange time and place for my annual performance review?" Gentry said.

"You think so?" the man said, genuinely surprised. "I thought since we were meeting we'd just take care of it. Besides, Washington wants them all done by Friday."

Gentry shook his head at the man he was forced to call his boss. He wondered, once again, how the Bureau could consistently promote people whose sole skill was their ability to push paper through the bureaucracy.

"Cut to the chase, Freddie," Gentry said, checking his watch.

"Okay." The man folded his hands on the table. "I'm giving you an overall rating of Does Not Meet Expectations."

"Again? Fuck me. That's two years in a row you've done this. So I'm not eligible for a bonus again this year?"

Gentry drained his beer.

"Cocksucker," he whispered.

"What did you call me?"

"Cock-suck-er," Gentry said, carefully enunciating the word.

"I could add that to your file if you like."

"Is there a form for that? Cocksucker form, seven-dash-A?"

"I could recommend a suspension followed by probation if you prefer."

"No, that's okay. Since I'm already failing to meet your expectations, I'd hate to make more work for you," Gentry said, grabbing the beer off the waitress's tray.

"Is that our boy?" the man said, looking towards the entrance.

Gentry squinted and recognized Doc. He waved and settled back into the booth. Doc approached and nodded at Gentry, waiting for an introduction to the other man.

"Doc White. This is Fred Williams,"

Williams stood and shook Doc's hand.

"Nice to meet you, Doc. My friends call me Shorty."

"That's good to know, Fred," Doc said, sitting next to Gentry. "Okay, I'm here, and it's late. What can I do for you?"

Williams looked at Gentry, who shook his head, indicating it wasn't his meeting. Williams pursed his lips and smiled at Doc.

"I thought we should meet."

"Are you in the technology business, Fred?" Doc said, attempting to catch the waitress's eye.

"Actually, no," Williams said, the smile pasted his face.

"I didn't think so. Nobody who works in this industry smiles that much. What do you want?"

The smile disappeared, and Williams looked across the table at Gentry. Gentry nodded and looked at Doc.

"We need some help, Doc."

"Help? You need a fucking miracle, Gentry."

Doc held up Gentry's beer to the waitress.

"You guys want to tell me why the Bureau is suddenly so interested in me? What's the matter? Finally get tired of waiting for Barrier to deliver?"

Doc sat back in the booth and watched the reaction of both men.

Williams looked down and played with the document in front of him. Gentry ran a hand through his hair.

"I'm surprised," Williams said. "I wasn't aware our cover had been blown."

"Cover?" Doc laughed loudly at the two men. "Gentry couldn't cover himself with a blanket."

"Careful, Doc," Gentry said. "I'm already in a bad mood."

"Do you mind telling me how you found out about us?" Williams carefully placed the straw to his lips and sipped his Diet Coke.

"Let's just say he forgot he was being watched."

"Cameras?" Williams said, leaning forward.

"Now what do you think, Sherlock?" Doc said.

"Where?" Gentry said, staring down at the table.

"The small conference room."

"Shit," Gentry said.

"Yes. And quite deep," Doc said.

"Who else knows about this?" Williams said.

"Nobody."

"You're sure about that?" Williams said, glancing at Gentry.

"Yeah. I just happened to get the tapes so I could review the interviews I did when I first got here. Hedaya and his hatchet men had completely forgotten there was even a camera in there. I'm the only one who knows you guys are sniffing around."

"Why haven't you gone to Hedaya?" Gentry said, recovering. "You two seem pretty close."

"Jesus Christ, Gentry. Haven't you figured out anything about this business yet? The guy writes me a big fat check every week. You think I enjoy pushing forty pound rocks down a piece of ice?"

Doc sat back, paused for effect, then pressed forward.

"Besides, whatever is going on is between you and Hedaya. It has nothing to do with me."

"So you're just a disinterested bystander. Is that what you're telling us?" Williams said.

The waitress returned with Doc's beer. He took a long sip and looked at the man across the table.

"That's what I'm telling you, Freddie."

"So then you might be willing to help us out if you considered the cause to be just?" Williams said.

Doc laughed.

"A real just cause, or are you screwing with Hedaya just 'cause you feel like it?"

"At the moment, all I can say is there are national interests at stake. As a good American I'm sure you understand why we need to rally together in times like these," Williams said.

"Yeah, you look like a real fucking patriot, Freddie. The only thing missing is your flag pocket protector."

"I told you he was a cocky son of a bitch," Gentry said.

Williams shook his head at Gentry and sat back into the booth with his arms folded. He looked at Doc.

"How's the project going?"

"How's the project going?" Doc said. "You've probably been talking about this meeting for weeks now, and that's the best you two could come up with? How's the project going? What's next? Are we gonna talk about the weather? Where I come from, people usually prepare for meetings."

"I'd like to kick your ass," Gentry said.

"Get in line."

Doc looked back at Williams.

"The project is going just fine. In fact, in a couple of weeks, it'll be done. At which point you guys are going to have to find another excuse to hang around."

"What do you know about money going to the Caribbean?"

"Well, I usually budget about ten grand for a week," Doc said. "But you guys look like buffet and happy hour types, so I'm sure you could do it for less."

Williams leaned forward and continued with a series of rapid-fire questions.

"What do you know about wire transfers?"

"Nothing."

"Nothing about money illegally moving out of the country?"

"Nope."

"How about a third world slush fund?"

"Nothing."

"The casino cooking its books?"

"You're talking to the wrong guy."

"What do you know?" Williams sat back, disgusted.

"For one thing, I know you guys are costing me money every second I sit here."

Williams paused and studied Doc carefully. Doc lit a cigarette and was pleased to see the smoke drift across the table. Williams waved it away and shifted in his seat.

"Okay," Williams said. "Let's talk about the niece. What do you know about her?"

"Well, I know she looks a lot better in a dress than J. Edgar."

"That is a vicious, totally unfounded rumor," Gentry said. "Hoover was a great man." He looked across the table. "Fred, why don't you let me take him outside where I'll proceed to kick the shit out of him?"

Doc smiled at Gentry and looked back at Williams.

"Tell me, Freddie. Do they come like that, or do you have to train them?"

"Be careful, smart ass. I might just let him do it." Williams sucked on his straw. "You do know that Hedaya is up to no good, don't you, Doc?"

"No, actually I don't know that at all. All I see is an old man who runs a very successful business and does it in a way that makes the people working for him feel good about themselves. That's pretty rare these days. By the way, Gentry how do you feel about your job?"

"Apart from the scum I have to deal with, it's fine."

Doc looked across the table at Williams.

"Is he referring to you or me, Freddie?"

"I don't think you should underestimate us, Doc. There are a few things in your past that appear somewhat unresolved," Williams said.

"Yeah. Well, getting closure can be tough sometimes."

"A little case of wiretapping up in San Francisco, for example," Williams said, smirking.

Doc let the comment sit. He knew what Williams was referring to. To infiltrate and gain the trust of a network of Chinese companies in San Francisco moving large amounts of money and weapons to a variety of Asian countries, Doc had created a story about his arrest on wiretapping charges. The ruse had worked perfectly and at the end of the mission, the charges were erased. He had to give the Bureau some credit for finding it.

"That was a long time ago."

Doc faked a cough and nervous laugh. He glanced at both men and went silent.

"Didn't the charges disappear in a hurry? You must have had a good lawyer," Williams said. "We've done a little checking and believe that it might be possible get the case reopened. Trust me, Doc. You don't want that to happen."

Doc lit another cigarette with a trembling hand.

"Okay, what do you guys want me to do?"

"We need more evidence of the wire transfers. Hedaya has been hiding his tracks pretty well," Williams said, glaring at Gentry. "But I know it's still going on. I can feel it."

Doc took a drag on his cigarette waving the smoke away from the table.

"And if I do help you guys out?"

"You go back to whatever it is you do. We're not after you, Doc. I mean, look at you. You're just another computer geek. What could we possibly want with you?"

Williams and Gentry laughed at Doc's expense. He sat quietly and let them have their moment.

"Okay," Doc said. "I'll look, but I don't know if anything is there."

"It's the thought that counts, Doc. Okay," he said, standing up. "I think we're done here."

Gentry chugged his beer, and Doc stood to let him out of the booth. He sat back down and looked up at the two men who now towered over him.

"Nice meeting you, Doc," Williams said. "Stay in touch."

"Yeah."

The two men started to walk off when Doc called after them. They slowly walked back to the table. Doc looked up at them with a frown on his face.

"I do have one question. If Hedaya is involved in illegal international stuff, why are you guys here? I thought that was the CIA's job."

"Fuck the CIA."

Doc smiled at Gentry.

"Did you catch that, Gentry? Freddie said a bad word. It must be the Diet Coke talking."

Williams and Gentry looked at each other, then left the bar. Doc lit a cigarette and ordered another beer. He sunk into the booth, closed his eyes and forced himself to relax.

That was fun.

"I guess this job does have its moments."

Chapter 46

The issue was decided, but some people couldn't let it go. Advocates continued to grind their points even as the dissenting arguments faded. Maya sat back and listened to the back and forth. She closed the folder in front of her and looked at her watch. The final two combatants who'd fallen in and out of lust during the project, but were now sworn enemies, were stuck in an endless loop of will-too, will-not.

"Okay," Maya said. "Let's move on."

"Oh, I've moved on. You can be sure about that."

The woman folded her arms and glared at the ex-love-of-her-life.

Maya looked around the table at the faces she had come to know over the past several weeks and wondered how many of them she would ever see again. She reopened the folder in front of her and scanned the list of agenda items, but found nothing. Every issue came back completed. Despite her best effort to find a reason to stay, the evidence was overwhelming.

She was done.

"That's it," she said, forcing a small smile. "Good work. I'm going to miss you guys."

"I can't believe you're leaving us," Sally said. "We've still got almost two weeks to go."

Maya smiled at the woman and gently patted her forearm.

"There won't be any problems. Other than watch, there's nothing left for me to do here."

"But you'll miss the party," Sally said.

Maya smiled, remembering the waterfall.

"Goodbye parties are overrated."

The participants started to leave and, one by one, Maya accepted their goodbye hugs and promises to stay in touch. Soon, only Sally remained.

"Have you decided where you're going?"

Maya sat in her chair, tossing items into her bag. "I have to go back to New York for a few days to meet with my lawyer. Then I think I'll take a vacation."

"A nice beach in the tropics?"

"No. That's not going to happen."

Maya picked up her bag and slung it over her shoulder.

"I can't believe I thought that son of a bitch was a good guy."

Maya let the comment pass and hugged her friend.

"Just remember to do everything in sequence, one step at a time. You won't have any problems. But if you do get stuck give me a call, and I'll walk you through it." Maya smiled at her friend. "Thanks for everything, Sal."

"Call me."

"I will. Bye."

Maya walked down the hallway towards the elevators. She stopped in front of Hedaya's office and poked her head inside.

"Hi. Is he in?" she said.

"Hi, Maya. Yes, he is." She paused from her work. "Oh, that's right. You're leaving today."

"Yes, I'm out of here. I just stopped in to say goodbye."

"Let me check." She picked up the phone, spoke briefly and hung up. "Go right in. You take care of yourself."

"Thanks, I'll try."

Maya walked down the hall to Hedaya's office. She knocked on the open door, and Hedaya looked up from behind his desk. He stood and beamed at her.

"Come in, Maya. Can I get you something?" Hedaya said. "A glass of wine perhaps?"

"You know me too well, Hedaya. I will if you join me."

"Of course."

Hedaya motioned for her to sit and stepped behind the bar. He poured two glasses and sat down across from her. He raised his glass.

"What shall we drink to?"

"How about to the project?" Maya said, raising her glass.

Hedaya frowned.

"You can do better than that, Maya. Nothing that mundane. How about to better days?"

Maya smiled and touched his glass.

"To better days."

She sipped her wine and set the glass down.

"So. How are you, my dear?"

"I've been better."

Maya studied the framed photos adorning the walls.

"You certainly know a lot of famous people, Hedaya."

Hedaya glanced at the photos.

"Yes," he said. "I guess that comes from being in my line of work. Still, they are just people. About the only difference is that they are the type of people other people want to have their picture taken with."

Hedaya smiled and winked at her.

"I've noticed a lot of people wanting you in their photos."

Hedaya laughed.

"No, fame is something I do not seek."

"I think it found you anyway," Maya said, sipping her wine.

"Perhaps, but fame is overrated. One's legacy is much more important."

"Legacy?" Maya shook her head. "Lately, I've been struggling to make it through the day, let alone worry about a legacy."

"You'll know what yours is to be when you see it. Someday it will find you."

Maya returned the old man's smile.

"What's your secret, Hedaya? How do you do it?"

"Do what, my dear?"

"All of it. I see people all the time who have shut down. Some of them very young. Even my parents have stopped… well, stopped *living*."

"That's tragic. I see it all the time in the faces of many people who come here. They think a sudden run of luck is all they need. I'm afraid many have forgotten why they're put here in the first place."

"Which is?"

"To leave a legacy of course," Hedaya said.

"So what's your legacy, Hedaya?"

"As of yet, it is undetermined." Hedaya picked up the wine bottle and topped off both glasses. "If I may ask, how are you and Doc?"

"I'm afraid we're done," Maya said.

"I'm very sorry to hear that. You seem to fit so well together. Like a…"

"Jigsaw puzzle?"

Hedaya laughed.

"No. But if that's your preference, we'll go with that."

"We have this space we can't seem to fill."

"I thought you young people wanted others to give you space. Rose uses that phrase all the time."

"That's it. But it doesn't apply to this particular piece of space."

Maya felt a tear roll down her cheek. Hedaya handed her a box of tissues.

"Thanks." Maya dabbed at her eyes. "I'm sorry."

"No apology required. He's a very troubled man, Maya."

"I know."

"Talented, yet troubled. I will miss him."

"Me too." Maya checked the time then stood. "I'm sorry, Hedaya, but I need to go."

Hedaya stood and hugged her warmly. He handed her another tissue and stood quietly while she composed herself.

"Thank you, Hedaya. Thanks for everything. It's been an honor working for you."

"You take care of yourself and don't worry. It will find you."

She was grateful for the empty elevator. Back in her room, she started packing. A half-hour later she was sitting on the couch surrounded by her luggage. She got up to close the blinds, checked her watch and sat back down.

He was late.

**

The knock was soft. She crossed to the door, pulled it open and nodded. She silently returned to her position on the couch. Doc watched her walk away and stepped inside. He silently closed the door. He sat down across from her.

"All set?"

"Yeah."

"Here we are again."

"Yeah."

Doc took a deep breath.

"I thought it might be easier this time."

"Don't worry, Doc. You won't have to go through this again. This is our last goodbye."

Tell her.

"Yeah. I know," Doc said. "A glass of wine?"

"No."

Doc flashed back to how angry she'd been when she returned from Colorado and learned that, instead of exploring the mountains with her,

219

he'd been gambling. Eventually, the anger disappeared, only to be replaced by impenetrable silence.

"Do you remember what you told me in Belize that night?"

Doc raised his head and looked at her.

"I told you a lot of things."

"There aren't any do-overs, but there are always second chances."

"Yeah," Doc said, running a hand through his hair. "I tend to overuse that line."

He tried a weak smile. Nothing.

"Well, Doc this was your second chance. And you failed miserably."

Tell her.

"We had it. It slipped away."

"Same old Doc," she said, shaking her head. "As soon as I give myself to you, you decide you're no longer interested. What is it? Conquest? The thrill of the hunt? Is that it?"

"No," Doc whispered.

"Then what the hell is it, Doc? I've spent too much time trying to figure it out on my own. You need to help me out. You owe me that much."

Doc looked back at the stare that was refusing to succumb to tears.

"You're asking me to go somewhere I can't."

"I see," she said. "Is it that hard?"

"It's impossible."

Doc looked down at the carpet.

Maya nodded and waited. "How bad is the voice these days?"

Doc looked up at her. "It's bad."

Maya shook her head. "I'm sorry, Doc. The next time you talk to him, tell him I said he gives shitty advice."

Great. Now it's my fault.

"Will do."

Maya looked at her watch.

"I need to get to the airport."

"Can I take you?"

"No."

"Okay. Can I call you sometime?"

"No. I'll call you."

Promise?"

"Yes. But don't wait up."

She stood and went to the phone. She dialed the concierge and waited.

"Yes, I need some help with my baggage."

She put down the phone and walked over to Doc. She reached out and gently touched his face.

"And you, sir, definitely need some help with yours."

Doc hugged her and refused to let go. Eventually, she gently pushed his shoulders away. She kissed him softly on the cheek and touched his face one final time.

"Be good to yourself, Doc. You're all you've got."

"I love you."

"I love you, too."

Doc took one last look and walked slowly toward the door. He stopped and turned back.

"I almost forgot to tell you what a great job you did on the project."

"It was just what you said it would be."

"What's that?"

"A piece of cake."

Doc nodded and turned toward the door. He pulled it open, stepped through and closed it silently behind him. Maya watched him go.

Leaning against the closed door, she finally gave her tears permission to begin flowing.

Chapter 47

"Oh, here's a good one," Merlin said, laughing. "Did you know last year there were over 150,000 attempts of hackers trying to break into the Pentagon's computer systems?"

Doc was stretched out on the couch working his way through a water glass of vodka.

"150,000?"

Doc closed his eyes and tried to find some meaning in the number.

"Does it say how many got in?"

"You don't want to know."

Merlin looked away from the screen and raised an eyebrow in Doc's direction.

"And you wonder why I'm so nervous about hanging around the Internet," Merlin said.

"I thought you were just afraid of catching something."

"You're funny for a burned out spy."

"It doesn't matter-"

"My life's already on parade. All I need is somebody stealing my identity." Merlin thought for a minute. "Boy, wouldn't they get a surprise?"

He laughed. Doc took a sip of vodka and closed his eyes.

"Yes, Merlin, you convinced me. Big Brother is watching."

"Watching? Shit, he's moved in," Merlin said.

Doc laughed and sipped again. The Advil was slowly taking effect. He knew what his friend was trying to do, and he was grateful. Merlin roared with laughter, and Doc lifted his head from the couch.

"What's so funny?"

"Listen to this. Recent studies have shown that homely criminals get prison sentences fifty percent longer than good-looking ones. Unbelievable."

"I don't know what's stranger. The fact that's it probably true, or that somebody took the time to study it."

"Please, Judge," Merlin said. "Don't hate me because I'm beautiful."

Doc laughed hard from the couch. It felt good.

"This country should carry a Surgeon General's warning."

Merlin continued reading from the screen.

"Recently, while vacationing in the mountains of Utah, Margaret Titwilly, from Omaha answered an incoming call on her cellular phone when the electromagnetic interference activated her power wheelchair sending her over a cliff."

"Jesus," Doc said. "Talk about bad luck."

"I really can't talk right now, Suzie. I'm in the middle of plunging to my death. Leave a message," Merlin said.

"What the hell are you reading anyway?"

"Just some lighthearted facts and figures the Company has started compiling."

"Merlin, if a bunch of guys knock on my door carrying guns, I'm gonna get pissed. If anybody finds out you've hacked your way into Run Rabbit Run…"

Doc trailed off, too tired to argue.

"They won't find out. And I didn't hack it. I simply went in through an unlocked back door."

"Whatever." Doc got up to refresh their drinks. "Since when does the Company have a lighthearted side?"

"Probably since you and I left. Shit. This is scary. Organized paramilitary groups now have branches in 29 states. Recently, a man in Wyoming was arrested for buying frozen bubonic plague bacteria over the Internet. When questioned, the man replied he was only following orders from God who had spoken to him through a waitress at Denny's."

Merlin stopped reading and dumped a pile of coke onto a small mirror on the desk.

"There are some scary motherfuckers out there."

"They're everywhere. Haven't you heard?"

Merlin sniffed back a long line and leaned back in his chair.

"Do you remember the time we were talking about six months before 9/11?"

"Yeah. We were in Turkey doing that hit."

"You were doing the hit," Merlin said. "I was screwing around with his computer system."

"An insignificant distinction."

"No, major distinction. I don't kill people. That's your job."

"It used to be my job."

"Now that is an insignificant distinction."

Merlin laughed, then turned serious.

"Do you remember what you said when I asked you about how people would handle it when this country finally realized how vulnerable it was?"

"I think I said; not well."

Merlin finished the second line and sat down in the chair across from Doc.

"At the time, I thought you were just being flip. It turns out, you were most prophetic."

"When they get scared, people tend to forget about things like privacy and civil liberties. They spend their time worrying about their kid's safety or getting blown up on an airplane."

"As they should."

"Yeah. You can't blame them. The politicians blather on about protecting and preserving personal freedom, but people like us in the underbelly of the beast pretty much have carte blanche. Even if people had an inkling of some of the shit we do, it's way too late to stop us."

Merlin sipped his drink and drummed his fingers on the arm of his chair.

"What's the matter, Merlin? Having a crisis of confidence?"

"Nah. I'm just wondering about what I'm going to do now that I'm out."

"I've been asking myself the same question. I certainly don't want to do these projects anymore."

"No. Me neither. It's time to make some real money."

"More money? Jesus, Merlin, how much do you need?"

"For what I want to do, a lot."

He sniffed and sipped his drink. Doc turned his head and saw the frown on his friend's face.

"What?" Doc said.

"You think Hedaya's right?"

"What? His theory about the decline of civilizations?"

"Yeah."

"Sure. To believe any different is wishful thinking."

Doc took a long swallow of vodka.

"Why don't I get you a bucket?" Merlin said, nodding at the size of Doc's glass.

"I'm trying to cut down to one drink a day."

Merlin laughed and sniffed loudly. He put his feet on the table and leaned back in his chair.

"So, how are you doing?"

Doc closed his eyes.

"I'm a mess."

"You should have told her."

Amen to that.

"I thought you were going to give me a break tonight," Doc said.

"What?" Merlin said, confused.

"Huh? Oh, sorry. I was just thinking out loud," Doc said.

Merlin stared at his friend.

"Whatever you say. Say, why don't we take the night off? Go downstairs and hit the tables."

"No," Doc said, getting up off the couch. "We've got work to do." Doc arched his back, hoping to find some energy. "Did you finish generating the sports book yet?"

"Yeah. Want to check it out?"

Doc nodded, grabbed a chair and carried it to the desk. He sat down and waited. Merlin began working the keyboard. A photo image of the sports book appeared on the screen.

"Okay," Merlin said. "Here's the photo I started with."

"Did you take it from dead center of the room?"

Doc caught the frown.

"Sorry. I was just asking."

"Then I took the digital and mapped it to this."

Merlin tapped the keyboard, and the photo was replaced by a blueprint representation of the sports book.

"Jesus," Doc said. "What a cool piece of software."

"Thanks. It's my latest creation. Pretty slick, huh?"

"You're unbelievable," Doc said, admiring the blueprint.

"Yeah, I know."

Merlin drew another line and snorted. He sniffed and wiped his nose, took a sip of vodka, then continued.

"See how the betting counter is V-shaped?"

"Yeah," Doc said, nodding his head.

"Take a look at this."

Merlin called up the next image.

"Sonofabitch," Doc whispered. "Where did it go?"

"I gotta give Hedaya credit. This was a nice touch. This image is what the cameras down there see. See the two red dots at the top of the image?"

225

"Yeah."

"Those are the camera positions from the betting windows on either side of the center one. Watch this."

Merlin superimposed the two images and sat back in his chair.

"He's eliminated the center window."

"Yeah, the camera angles blend perfectly with the architecture of the room. It's seamless and virtually impossible to detect with the naked eye."

"Unless you get lucky," Doc said, remembering the woman in the floral hat.

"Only the well prepared get lucky, Doc. Or don't you remember teaching me that?"

"I remember," Doc said, still staring at the screen. "This software is amazing."

He leaned over and began working with the images. He zoomed in, then out. He clicked a function key that changed the image to an overhead shot. Another click produced a detailed map of coordinates with distances clearly marked in feet and inches.

"It also does metric," Merlin said, smiling.

"So this is why you kept telling me to be patient about the sports book?"

"Yeah, the program the Company uses for this sort of stuff sucks. I finally got tired of it and built this. It's just a geometry problem surrounded by several thousand lines of computer code."

"Are you gonna share this?"

"I haven't decided yet."

"They would love to get their hands on this," Doc said.

"Now there's a surprise," Merlin said, chuckling. "So Hedaya has people walk up and slide envelopes of cash to whoever is working that window?"

"It certainly appears so. One of the same four people is always assigned to that window."

"Yeah, I noticed. During a day, it wouldn't take that many envelopes to come up with a couple of million."

"No, it wouldn't. And with the amount of daily traffic going in and out of there, who's going to notice?"

Doc sat back in his chair.

"Well done. Well done, indeed." He looked at his friend in admiration. "How long did it take you to build this?"

"Ah, only a couple of weeks. I had a bunch of code lying around that I knitted together. It's still in Beta, so it's a little buggy."

"How much sleep have you gotten the past month?"

"Who's got time to sleep?" Merlin said, chopping a small pile of coke on the mirror. "What I can't figure out is what he does with the money. I've run traces on every financial institution from here to Beijing, and there's nothing. I don't get it."

"Me either. But we will. Keep thinking low-tech."

"I can't even find any evidence of money exchanges. What the hell is he doing with it?"

"You won't find any. He's not spending it. He's still building the account."

"Until when?"

"Until he has a competitive advantage."

"The last time I looked China was sitting on about 300 billion of hard currency."

"Yeah, I know," Doc said. "But Hedaya's betting that the Chinese economy will cool off. And at the pace he's setting, Hedaya thinks he can catch up."

"Well, it would go a lot faster if he invested some of it."

"Too much potential for visibility. Hedaya is way below the radar on this one, and he plans on staying there," Doc said, lighting a cigarette. "He's either a genius or completely out of his mind."

Doc moved back to the couch and stretched out.

"I don't know if you want to hear this now, but I've got a few things to discuss the project."

Doc sighed but nodded.

"Go ahead."

"I've got the final transition plan done for when we go live. I need confirmation of the date and time Hedaya wants to start cutover."

"I'll ask him tomorrow morning when we meet," Doc said, rubbing his eyes.

"Since Jenkins took off it's impossible to get a friggin decision out of these people. By the way, who is the CIO around here at the moment?"

"Probably you."

"I wouldn't be a CIO for all the tea in…." Merlin trailed off at the irony. "It's an awful job."

"You still going to LA tomorrow?"

"Yeah, but I should be able to get back by three or four in the morning," Doc said.

"Just in time to get up."

"Yeah."

Doc drifted off into sleep. Merlin looked at his friend, draped a blanket over him and quietly packed up and left.

Chapter 48

Doc trudged through the main floor of the casino oblivious to the early afternoon action. The headache had merely rested while he slept and then joined him in the shower. He headed towards the casino's main kitchen and pushed through one of the swinging doors into a collection of people scurrying back and forth.

"Move it or lose it, sugar," barked a waitress carrying a large tray.

"Sorry," Doc said.

But she'd already departed and was immediately replaced by another.

"I'd get behind the line if I were you," the second waitress said.

Doc stared at her, confused by the comment.

"Hey," said the man standing in front of several broilers. "Who are you and what are you doing in my kitchen?"

Doc turned to face the man screaming at him. He stared around the kitchen dazed.

"I asked you a question," the man said, pointing a large pair of tongs at him.

Pick it up. You're too sluggish.

"I'm looking for Hedaya. I was told he might be back here."

"Not even Hedaya is allowed to cross that line so move your ass."

The chef turned to flip a steak.

Doc looked down at the piece of red tape on the cement floor. He took two steps back and looked at the chef wondering how anyone wearing such a silly hat could be that menacing.

"He's not in here. Try out back."

He nodded towards the back door and scanned the room, wild-eyed.

"I'm waiting for a baked potato for this New York. C'mon people." His face turned bright red. "Lift your fucking games."

He banged the tongs on a stainless steel counter and, unbelievably, the pace quickened.

Doc headed toward a back door that opened onto a loading dock. The temperature outside was almost identical to the kitchen. He saw Joe and Sam standing near a large refrigerated truck. They were, as always, engaged in heavy debate.

"Hey, Doc," Sam said. "Slumming it today?"

Doc tried to focus on anything other than the pounding in his head. "Is he always like that?" he said, nodding his head toward the kitchen.

"Who? Chef?" Sam laughed. "Shit, he's in a great mood today. You should see him when he's losing."

"I'm looking for Hedaya," Doc said. "I was told he might be out here."

"No," Joe said. "I saw him in the count rooms, but that was a while ago."

"Well," Doc said, glancing at the truck. "I'll try his office again."

"Say, Doc," Sam said. "We need you to settle something."

"Don't you guys ever quit?"

Doc shrugged his shoulders, put his hands in pockets and waited.

"You seem to have a pretty good take on things," Joe said. "So, we've been debating aliens. Numb nuts over there is convinced they exist, but I think he's out of his mind. If aliens do exist and can visit Earth, they must be a lot more advanced than us with respect to technology, right?"

"Probably," Doc said, exhausted.

"Then why wouldn't they take over?" Joe said.

"Maybe they're being neighborly. Or maybe it's the lack of challenge. How would I know? Why don't you call the NSA? I'm sure they'd be happy to talk with both of you."

"NSA?" Joe said.

"National Security Agency," Doc said. "The most secretive government agency on the planet."

"Never heard of it."

"And that's just the way they like it." Doc took a quick look at the truck, waved goodbye, and headed back into the kitchen. Chef's screaming stopped him in his tracks. He walked around the back of the casino until he found another entrance.

**

"Are you okay, Doc?"

He's talking to you.

"What's that, Hedaya?"

"I asked if you were okay."

Doc looked around the office at the photos covering the walls and squinted as he tried to put names to familiar faces. He looked at the

230

cigarette that had burned and extinguished itself. He dropped the butt into an ashtray and sat forward on the couch rubbing a hand through his hair.

Behind his desk, Hedaya sat quietly, a look of concern etched into his face. He walked across the room and sat in a chair across from Doc.

"Talk to me, Doc."

Doc looked up initially surprised by the old man's proximity. He stared into the intense, yet soft, eyes fixed on him.

"Sure, Hedaya. What would you like to know?"

Doc eyes drifted away and returned to the photos.

Hedaya leaned back in his chair and studied his friend.

"I'd like to know what I can do."

Doc looked at Hedaya. "Right now, there's nothing you can do, Hedaya."

Doc took a deep breath and wondered if this would be their last conversation as friends.

"Is it Maya?"

"She's the primary symptom."

"Symptom? I see. Would you like to discuss the cause?"

"More than anything, Hedaya."

Hedaya waited for him to continue. Doc shook his head slowly.

"Okay," Hedaya said. "I'd like to help, Doc."

"You've already done enough, Hedaya."

Doc stood, deep in thought. "I know there was something else."

Transition and LA.

"Right. Thanks," Doc said, oblivious to the stare he was receiving. "We need to pick the time for the final transition and cutover schedule."

"Okay," Hedaya said, continuing to study Doc's face. "What do you suggest?"

"Start Friday evening around six. It'll be ready to go first thing Monday morning," Doc said, reciting from memory.

"I'll make sure everyone is aware. Why don't you get some rest? Go lie out by the pool. Use the one on the rooftop garden."

"The waterfall?" Doc whispered. He shook his head and looked at Hedaya. "Sounds nice, but I have to go to Los Angeles this afternoon. But I'll be back in time for work tomorrow."

"L.A.? Is anything wrong down there?"

"Sure. Lots of things. It's a big city."

"Are you driving?"

"Yeah."

"I don't know if that is such a good idea, Doc."

"Me neither, Hedaya. But it has to be done."

"Why don't you let me put you in one of the stretches and get you a driver?"

Doc slowly shook his head. "No, but thanks, Hedaya. I'll be fine."

"Okay, Doc," Hedaya said. "But be careful. I'll check in with you tomorrow morning."

"Sure." Doc walked to the door. "You know, one of these days you and I need to sit down and have a long talk."

"I'd like that, Doc."

Don't bet on it.

Chapter 49

Joe stood chatting with Sam near the back of the truck when they heard a loud noise. Instinctively, both men reached inside their jackets but stopped when they looked inside the truck and saw the forklift on its side. The driver stared at the overturned machine, confused. Joe shook his head and looked at Sam who shrugged his shoulders.

"Nice. Would you mind telling me how the fuck you managed to do that?" Joe said, glaring at the driver.

"I think I tried to take too many boxes at one time," said the chagrined driver.

Sam peered inside the truck to make sure none of the boxes had popped open.

"Take your time and try not to kill yourself. Or me."

He called two other men over to help the driver turn the forklift right side up.

"Fucking moron," Joe said. "Who's he related to again?"

"He's the son of one of Hedaya's buddies. He's okay. Just a little too eager to please."

Joe turned around at the noise behind him on the loading dock. Again, he reached inside his jacket. The homeless man staggered toward him.

"Every time I'm in L.A. I have to deal with these people," Joe said.

The man lurched forward and stopped a few feet away.

"Got a dollar?"

"Go away," Joe said, turning his back on the man.

"Easy, Joe," Sam said, reaching into his pocket. "Give him a dollar. Christ almighty, don't be such a prick."

Sam handed the ratty man a dollar who glanced at it then back at Joe.

"Here," Joe said, handing over a dollar. "Now go away."

"God bless you," said the man, peering into the back of the truck. "Got any food in there?"

"See what I mean? You give these scumbags an inch, and suddenly you're their best friend."

He turned and grabbed the man by the shoulder. He jerked him away from the truck.

"No, there's no food in there. Now beat it. Go buy your bottle."

233

The homeless looked from one man to the other, pulled his ragged coat around himself tightly, and trudged away clutching the two-dollar bills.

Joe watched him go and looked at the hand he used to grab the man.

"Ahhh," he said. "Where has this guy been? I'll be right back. I have to go wash my hands."

Joe continued muttering as he walked into the back of the darkened store.

**

The homeless man trudged slowly down the sidewalk and smiled wondering what he could get for two dollars. He crossed in the middle of the street and headed in the direction of a nearby parking lot. The few people he encountered cut a wide path as he passed. He walked into the unattended lot and stopped suddenly when he heard the voice.

"Hey, old man. What's up?"

"Would you look at what we have here," said a second youth.

The man stood watching two skinheads standing a few feet away on either side. He looked down at the boots they were wearing and recognized the steel toes, perfect for dismantling faces and snapping ribs. Not moving his eyes, he took a step back.

"Easy there, big fella," said the first youth, smiling through several tattoos on his face. "This won't hurt for long."

The second youth laughed and pulled a knife from his pocket, flipping the blade open. The man saw it glint briefly against the dim light. The second youth slowly started moving towards him, gently waving the knife back and forth.

The man focused on the knife and shifted his feet to maintain his position in the slow moving circle. The knife flicked at his face, and he jerked his head back as he grabbed the young man's wrist. The knife clattered to the ground. With his other hand, he grabbed the young man by the shoulder. Simultaneously raising his knee and pulling down viciously with both hands, he snapped the man's arm backward against the elbow joint. The arm cracked like kindling, and the young man fell to the ground in agony staring in wonder at the bottom half of his arm gently swinging in the air.

234

The homeless man quickly picked up the knife and saw the boot heading for his groin out of the corner of his eye. He slid away and felt the boot graze the outside of his leg. Seconds later, the second boot came rushing toward his face, and the man caught it with one hand and used the other to drive the knife deeply into the back of the young man's thigh. The youth fell onto the pavement, and the man watched blood spurt from the wound. He dropped onto the young man with full force and drove the knife into the same spot on the other leg.

"You fucking animals," he whispered into the young man's ear. The young man trembled as he continued to bleed. The homeless man turned his attention back to the youth with the ruined arm.

Doc. Let it go.

Doc breathed heavily as he stared down at the two young men. He wiped the knife down and put it in a pocket of the torn, urine stained overcoat he was wearing. He tossed the coat into a nearby dumpster.

Doc angrily pulled the keys out of his pant's pocket and unlocked the door of his rental car. He got in, his hands trembling as he started the car, and squealed out of the parking lot.

Are you going to call an ambulance?

"Fuck em," he said, staring into the rear view mirror.

A very different reflection stared back.

Chapter 50

Sleep deprived, but freshly showered, Doc walked into the conference room and noticed everyone was already there. He dropped his bag on the table, took out several copies of a document, and passed them around.

"I'm sorry I'm late. I had a couple of problems I had to deal with," Doc said, glancing at Merlin.

Doc tapped the top of his watch, their shared signal that they needed to talk immediately after the meeting. Doc looked down at the document in front of him.

"Okay, let's talk transition."

The room settled, and everyone sat quietly waiting for him to begin. He looked around at the faces and took it as a good sign he could still put a name next to each face.

"First of all, I need to thank Jim Barrier for helping out with the transition plan. We had a couple of last minute issues with the technology, and you got us out of a jam. Thanks, Jim. Nice piece of work."

A surprised Barrier stared at Doc, but smiled and acknowledged the light round of applause he received from the group.

"Next," Doc said. "We need to thank Sally. You stepped up after Maya left and your stuff is in great shape."

Another burst of applause broke out, and Sally beamed.

"Actually, all of you have done a great job. This thing has gone as smoothly as possible, and unless we completely shoot ourselves in the foot over the weekend, it's going to be a-"

"Piece of cake?" Sally said.

Doc looked at the woman who had turned cold toward him and tried a smile.

"Yeah. A piece of cake."

She glared at him. Doc nodded and refocused on the group.

"Okay. Starting Friday morning, we move to rotating twelve-hour shifts through Monday night. Merlin and his team will start the final data conversion at midnight Friday, and unless somebody forgets to feed the squirrels, it should finish early Saturday morning. Merlin's cutover schedule for the technical team is on page ten. You guys are on a roll so keep doing what you've been doing. Monday morning those folks assigned to hold the hands of the users should get here early. Be nice, be patient, and expect them to hate it. That's the way it goes. Everybody loves change, except when it impacts them."

Doc stopped and reviewed his notes, waiting for a kick of adrenaline. Nothing came back.

"The last thing I should mention is that we'll be meeting every four hours over the weekend starting at eight o'clock Saturday morning. No agenda. Just be prepared to let us know how things are going. Any questions?"

Doc waited.

"All right. Thanks again, folks. Good stuff all around. Don't forget about the wrap-up party Hedaya is throwing for you Tuesday night."

"Do you think it will be as good as the last party?"

Doc choked back the emotions.

"I doubt it."

Merlin stood by his chair until the room emptied, then approached Doc.

"Nice job," he said. "Where did that come from?"

"Where did what come from?"

"Lucidity."

Doc laughed and shook his head. He slung his bag over his shoulder.

"I have no idea."

"So, you gonna make it?"

"I've only got a few days to go. I can do that standing on my head."

"Let's hope you won't have to."

Doc smiled at his friend.

"C'mon. I'll buy you breakfast."

**

"This must be my lucky day," said the waitress as she approached the table. "What are you worried about today, Sweetie? Whether I'm wearing clean underwear?"

Merlin rolled his eyes in the general direction of the waitress.

"Actually, you can keep that particular piece of information to yourself."

Merlin looked at Doc and winked.

"But you should be aware that it's been scientifically proven that underwear only stays clean for about a minute and a half."

237

"Honey, you need to get yourself a girlfriend."

She turned to Doc while pouring two coffees.

"Morning, Doc. What'll you have?"

"Hi, Suzie. The usual."

"You got it," she said, then turned back to Merlin. "How about you, Princess?"

"Corned beef hash. Sourdough toast. Side of homefries."

Merlin grabbed his napkin and used it to hand the menu back to the waitress.

"The eggs on the hash come over easy."

"Not on my plate they don't," Merlin said, frowning. "Make sure they're cooked."

The waitress shook her head, smiled at Doc and walked away. Merlin looked across the table.

"Raw eggs. That's all I need, Salmonella poisoning."

"I thought that was chicken," Doc said.

"Where do you think eggs come from?"

Too tired to debate or even listen to the current topic, Doc turned serious.

"It's the trucks. They come in after hours, unload the cash, and reload with the Chinese vegetables Hedaya's always raving about."

"Did you get a look inside the truck?"

"Just a quick one. But it's what I thought. A false floor. It looked about a foot deep, and I saw a bunch of long flat boxes that would fit."

"Interesting," Merlin said, sipping his coffee. "So it went off without a hitch?"

"Apart from my brief encounter with a couple of Hitler youth."

Doc proceeded to tell Merlin about the previous evening. Merlin sat listening intently.

"Did you hurt them?"

"Yeah," Doc whispered. "I broke one of the kid's arms."

"The one where you snap it backward at the elbow?"

"Yeah."

"I hate that one. The bottom half of the arm just flops around."

"It certainly does. Then I sliced the other kid's hamstrings."

"With what?"

"With the knife he was using to take my face off."

"Serves him right."

238

"Hate groups preying on homeless people. What the hell is going on?"

Merlin sat quietly for a moment.

"Well, they should probably consider themselves lucky. I've watched you do a lot worse."

"Yeah."

"Remember the time you… sorry." He brightened. "Hey, you'll never guess what I got today. An invitation for Hedaya's cruise. I thought he was still pissed at me."

Doc stared off into the distance deep in thought. "Sonofabitch."

"What?"

"He sure has some set of balls."

"What the hell are you talking about?"

"I think it's time I had my little chat with Hedaya."

Doc smiled.

"And then Langley, right? We have to bring them in, Doc." Merlin paused and then continued. "I'm feeling a little exposed, what with your current bout of…"

"Insanity?" Doc said, raising an eyebrow.

Merlin looked directly at Doc and shrugged his shoulders.

"What the hell, we're both adults. I was going to say instability, but your word will do. Are you going nuts on me, Doc?"

Doc watched his cigarette smoke drift toward the ceiling.

"What do you think?"

Merlin leaned back into the booth.

"I think you came back too soon. I mean, after your last bout."

"Yeah, probably," Doc said.

His smile disappeared.

"Who can blame you?" Merlin said, shaking his head. "Having to take that kid out like that. Sometimes it's just part of the job, Doc."

Merlin saw the tears beginning to well in Doc's eyes.

"Hey," he said. "It was either you or him."

"He was nine."

"And firing a machine gun at you."

"Whatever happened to Little League?"

"They grow up pretty fast these days."

"But into what?"

Doc slumped further into the back of the booth and saw the waitress approach. He moved his coffee cup to make room for the food. She put the plates down and watched briefly as Merlin began carefully wiping his fork with a napkin.

"I've got some Formula 409 in the kitchen," the waitress said.

Merlin glanced up and dismissed her with a curt smile. Doc missed the exchange as he sat staring at his pancakes. He picked up his fork and had another thought.

"I'll need you to keep a close eye on Rose tonight while I'm talking to Hedaya."

"Jesus, Doc," Merlin said, picking at his eggs. "Why?"

"Because, if all hell breaks loose, we don't know what she might do. Maybe they've got a system worked out. Maybe the security staff is in on it. Who knows? Just keep her occupied for a couple of hours."

"Why don't we call Langley in now? Get some backup. Know what I mean?"

"No," Doc said, shaking his head. "I owe Hedaya that much."

Merlin set his fork down on the edge of his plate.

"You're a very strange man, Doc White."

Merlin nibbled a piece of toast.

"How do you suggest I get Rose to agree to see me? She's barely speaking to me."

"Offer to sleep with her," Doc said, through a mouthful of pancakes.

Merlin laughed, then turned quiet when he realized Doc wasn't joking.

"No way."

Doc looked up from his plate.

"Merlin, I'm afraid it's time for you to take one for the team."

"No way," Merlin said, shaking his head vigorously.

Doc slowly chewed another mouthful of pancakes.

"No fucking way, Doc."

Doc poured more syrup on the dwindling stack and resumed eating in silence. A smile remained frozen in place.

"No… fucking… way."

Doc sipped his coffee.

"Are you just gonna sit there and stuff your face or are you going to say something?"

240

"Have a nice time," Doc said. "And be sure to take your time warming up. The first one usually doesn't last long."

"You can be a real prick, Doc."

Merlin pushed his plate away. He sat back in the booth and folded his arms.

"The things I do for this country."

Chapter 51

Doc sat on the couch, lit a cigarette and watched the old man gently glide the rock down the ice and begin barking commands to the sweepers.

Now that's the definition of focus.

Doc nodded and watched as the rock slowed and stopped. Doc admired the precision of Hedaya's movements and took a sip of beer.

Stay sharp.

"Well, it's a little hard with you buzzing at me constantly. Why don't you take a break?"

Well, excuse me.

Doc smiled at the voice's indignation and gazed at the empty ice rink on the other side of the room. Doc watched Hedaya wave goodbye to his team members and casually stroll in his direction. Doc watched him approach, knowing the upcoming conversation would irrevocably change their relationship. From his previous experience with similar discussions, he knew the odds weren't good that it would change for the better. Hedaya stepped into the lounge area, removed his shoes and put on the familiar slippers.

"Nih hao a, Doc."

"I'm fine, Hedaya," Doc said. "Thanks for agreeing to meet on such short notice."

"Not at all. I always have time for you, Doc. I see you already have a beverage." Hedaya started off in the direction of the bar. "The staff has the night off so I will be right back."

Doc lit a cigarette and smoked in silence until Hedaya returned with his beer.

"You seem better today, Doc. I was worried about you yesterday. How was your trip to Los Angeles?"

Hedaya put his feet up on the table and stretched out.

"It had its moments."

"Are you okay?"

"I'm a little crisp around the edges I guess."

"But no doubt still tender in the middle," Hedaya said, winking.

Like a pancake.

"Yeah, just like a pancake," Doc said.

242

"Yes, I see." He looked at the expression on Doc's face and turned serious. "What did you need to see me about?"

Trying to forget the fact that he was about to reveal himself to a friend, Doc took a deep breath a final drag off his cigarette. He leaned forward in his chair.

"We have a problem, Hedaya."

Hedaya smiled and shook his head.

"I knew this project was going too smoothly. What is it?"

"It's not the project, Hedaya. I wish it were. I hope you believe that."

The smile disappeared from the old man's face.

"I believe you, Doc. Please continue."

"I would very much like for you to tell me how you came into possession of Run Rabbit Run," Doc said.

And in that briefest of moments, the two men's shared reality shattered. Doc watched the color in the old man's face fade into a pale white. Hedaya's eyes widened and then narrowed dangerously.

**

Rose pulled the top sheet back and gently patted the mattress. Merlin sat in a chair in a far corner of the room with his arms folded. He then leaned forward to devour his fourth line of the evening.

Rose, wearing a black thong over matching garter belt and stockings, walked over to the chair and sat on the arm twiddling Merlin's hair. He wiggled against her touch, but couldn't escape. The erect nipple of her left breast, only inches away, beckoned.

"I have to give you credit, Merlin," she said. "You get an A for calling me tonight."

Merlin sat rigid, staring straight ahead.

"What grade do I get for just sitting here and talking?"

Rose leaned in and softly flicked her tongue inside his ear, her nipple pressing into his shoulder.

"An incomplete," she whispered.

**

"You're a man of many surprises, Doc."

"I think we share that trait, Hedaya."

"Yes. Apparently we do. It will be interesting to see how many more surprises tonight holds for us."

"I don't imagine either one of us will ever forget this conversation if that's what you mean."

Hedaya looked at Doc's cigarettes. Doc tossed the pack to him.

"Tell me, Doc. Are you with the NSA or the CIA?"

"Neither," Doc said. "But I used to be CIA. When I got here, I was officially out, but your activities put a crimp in my retirement plans."

"By all means, please accept my sincerest apologies."

Hedaya smiled.

Despite the gravity of the situation, Doc laughed.

"Jesus Christ, Hedaya. Most guys your age, if they're lucky, play golf, and eat dinner at two in the afternoon. Why are you doing this?"

"Because I can." Hedaya sat back and blew smoke up at the ceiling. "What do you know?"

"Enough. Pretty much everything about how you get the money in and out. Thanks to the stuff on your copy of Run Rabbit Run, we've got a lot on your network of casinos and the amount of cash you've been generating."

"We?" Hedaya said.

Doc thought for a moment, then decided Hedaya would find out about Merlin soon enough.

"Merlin and I."

"Merlin? Very interesting. Isn't he a little too smart to be working for the CIA?"

"Thanks a lot, Hedaya."

"Oh, my. I'm sorry, Doc. What I meant was it that he's so brilliant, one would expect to find him in a university or perhaps a research setting."

"No. The perks aren't good enough. He's one of us. Was one of us... one of them. Shit. I'm babbling. Merlin is now officially out of the Company as well."

"Isn't he a bit young for retirement?"

"He recently left under different circumstances."

"I see. Did he get into some trouble? I must say that prospect doesn't surprise me."

Hedaya laughed.

244

"Well, sort of. He's always been a contract employee, or at least that's what they called him. Since I recruited him, he's been pretty much able to pretty much define his own terms."

"He's that good?"

"Yeah. He's the best I've ever seen. He's a rock star."

"Right down to the cocaine," Hedaya said, frowning. "So was this a setup from the start? Please don't tell me you've been lying to me all this time, Doc."

"Absolutely not," Doc said, shaking his head. "It was bad luck for you that I happened to end up here and brought Merlin in to work the project."

Hedaya stared hard at Doc then decided to believe him.

"So you just happened to stumble across the software program?"

"Yes. But I didn't ask Merlin to start digging around until I saw Roger Matasha at your party."

"I guess that makes sense. But Roger has never mentioned either one of you."

"He doesn't know us. But we're the ones who caught him trying to hack into our system."

"That was you?" Hedaya said, genuinely surprised. "What a small world. I still can't believe how well that worked."

Doc cocked his head.

"Are you telling me you planned that? For Matasha to try and break in and then be recruited?"

"Of course," Hedaya said.

"How long have you been planning this?"

"Oh, a long time, Doc. A very long time. So you and Merlin are a team?"

"Pretty much. At least we were. Nobody ever liked working with us. I have this… affliction that makes people nervous. And Merlin, well, I'm sure you can understand why people don't like working with him."

"I certainly can." Hedaya said. "So seeing Matasha that night at the party made you suspicious?"

"Yeah, I'm afraid it comes with the job. Up until that point, the only thing I knew was that the FBI was screwing with you. Then I saw him talking with you and I knew something was going on."

"And now you're back in?"

"No. That won't be happening. But I will need to call someone as soon as you and I finish here."

"So, as of this moment, the only two people who know about this are you and Merlin?"

Whoops.

Doc slowly sat upright in his seat. Hedaya noticed and laughed.

"Relax, Doc. I'm no thug," Hedaya said. "But this does complicate my life."

"I'm sure it does, Hedaya. Why don't we sit here and see what we can come up with." Doc relaxed into the couch. "I have to tell you; I'm impressed. Almost thirty billion in three years."

"It's a start. But we have a long way to go. How do you think I get the money in and out of the casino?"

"You're using the horse racing area in the sports book."

"How on earth did you figure that out?"

"Initially, I just got lucky. Remember the tip you gave me on Hedaya's Dream?"

"Yes, I've meant to speak to you about that. Give you an inch and you'll turn it into a quarter million. That was a nice run you had there."

"Yeah. Anyway, I lost my wallet, so I went up to the second floor to see if I left it at the betting window and something I saw on the video didn't make any sense."

Hedaya frowned.

"Don't worry, Hedaya. I'm no stool pigeon."

**

"Get on the bed, Merlin. It's a little hard to do this all by myself."

"It appears to be working okay for you so far."

"Merlin," Rose said. "Get over here. Jesus Christ, it's like you've never done this before."

"Actually, I haven't," Merlin whispered.

"Really? How wonderful." She softened her tone. "That's okay, sweetie. Everyone's nervous the first time." Rose stretched out languidly on the bed. "You're really a virgin?"

"Yeah."

"Well then," she said, holding her arms out. "Come to Momma."

"That one was pretty obvious, Hedaya," Doc said, sipping his third beer. "I don't care how good they are; nobody pays that much money for vegetables. It was a nice touch to figure out a way to make whatever you're paying the in L.A. to hold your money tax deductible."

Hedaya's smile was almost childlike.

"The cost of doing business, right?"

"Yeah. I like that one. A nice touch, Hedaya. In fact, I like all of it. Particularly the low-tech nature. The entire world is falling over each other for technology, and you've got people carrying envelopes of cash and refrigerated trucks rumbling down the highway."

"How am I getting the money out of Los Angeles?"

"That took me a long time to figure out. Probably longer than it should have." Doc said. "Merlin and I tried every possible scenario we've ever seen. And we've seen a lot. This morning at breakfast it hit me. Your annual cruise."

Hedaya leaned back in his chair and shook his head.

"Unbelievable."

"You know, if I hadn't been able to cross reference the casinos listed in Run Rabbit Run with the cruise ship itinerary, I would have never put it together. As soon as it finally clicked it made perfect sense. Every year you take that ship and a bunch of your best customers around the world. They you pick up money at each port and sail into Hong Kong like you're Marco Polo. You've got a real sense of style, Hedaya. I like that."

Doc reached for his beer and took a long swallow.

"Where the money goes from there or what sort of operation you're building on the ground over there, I don't know."

"I'm impressed. It appears I underestimated your organization's capabilities," Hedaya said.

"This wasn't anyone except Merlin and me. But they'll be involved very soon." Doc turned serious. "And never forget one thing, Hedaya. They take world domination very seriously."

"You can't be serious. You want me to do what?"

"Look," Rose said, stretching out on the bed. "It's very simple. Hold your fingers like this and then just…"

Rose closed her eyes and moaned as she continued her lesson. Merlin stared down in disbelief. She opened her eyes and held out her hands.

"Okay, now you try it."

Merlin cocked his head.

"Try what?"

"Touching it."

Merlin's hand shook as it slowly made its way towards Rose's upper thighs.

"How's that?"

"I've had eye blinks that lasted longer."

Rose grabbed Merlin's hand and placed it where she wanted it.

"Try leaving it there, okay?"

"If you say so."

"I say so." Rose repositioned herself under his hand. "There. Now how hard is that?"

"Is that a trick question?"

Rose giggled.

"Okay, let's move to round two."

"Round two? You mean there's more?"

"Yes, there's a lot more."

"How many rounds are we going?"

"What?"

"Rounds. You know, like a boxing match."

"Merlin, we're not boxing here. Certainly not the first time anyway."

Merlin's eyes widened as he stared down at her.

"What?"

"I'm joking," Rose said. "No boxing, but a little wrestling certainly isn't out of the question."

"You promised you'd be gentle, Rose."

"I'm just having some fun with you. Gee, Merlin. You sure know how to treat a lady."

"I'm not so sure this qualifies as a treat. For either one of us."

"That's because we haven't gotten to round two yet."

"I didn't hear the bell."

"What?"

"Never mind."

Merlin moved his hand away, thought about brushing his hair back with it, then glanced at his hand and wiped it on the sheet. He exhaled loudly.

"Okay, Rose. What's round two?"

"Lean down and give it a little kiss."

"Are you out of your fucking mind?"

"Merlin."

Merlin stared down at Rose and shook his head.

"You do know you're dealing with somebody who changes his toothbrush every day, don't you?"

**

"Tell me, Doc," Hedaya said, returning from the bar with two fresh beers. "Is your specialty Asia?"

"I pretty much worked everywhere, but I've done a lot over there."

"And you always used a technology project as your cover?"

"The first several years I did. But I've added some other covers over the years."

"Fascinating," Hedaya said, reaching for another cigarette. "How do you handle the double life aspect?"

"Usually not well."

"Yes, I understand. I find it quite difficult at times myself. Trying to keep it straight in my mind about who knows what and what I can say at what time. It's not a lifestyle I would recommend. How did you get started?"

"I raised my hand."

"I see. Do you consider yourself a patriot, Doc?"

"Well, I did at one time." Doc thought for a moment. "Yeah, I guess I still do. Somebody has to win and from what I've seen this place still holds the most hope for the planet. But in many ways, it's fading fast."

"Midnight in America?"

"Well, it's certainly way past happy hour."

Hedaya laughed and lit another of Doc's cigarettes.

"I don't know Hedaya. You're the guy with the long view. You tell me."

"There's a lot of life left in the old girl, but I worry about having so few people carrying the load. The priorities of many people seem strange to me."

"What's the phrase you use? I should have remembered that one. It struck a chord."

"Personality over performance. Fashion over form."

"That's it," Doc said, committing it to memory.

**

"Merlin, get your ass back on this bed."

Rose glared at the closed bathroom door.

"I'll be right out."

Rose shook her head as she removed the single band that held her hair back. She leaned back gently arranging the hair over and around her breasts. The bathroom door slowly opened, and Merlin peered out.

"C'mon, Merlin," she said. "You're making me work way too hard here."

"That's strange," Merlin said, slowly walking back to the bed. "I was just thinking the same thing."

Rose stretched her arms over her head and arched her back.

"You call this work? I want your job."

**

"I think I'm getting a little buzzed, Hedaya."

Hedaya burped and stared down at the table.

"Do you have anything scheduled for the morning?"

"No," Doc said, finishing his sixth, or seventh, beer.

"Then let us enjoy ourselves tonight."

Hedaya staggered in the general direction of the bar. "Who knows what tomorrow will bring?"

"Tomorrow's going to suck, Hedaya."

Doc repositioned himself on the couch.

"That much I do know."

**

"Shhh," Rose said. "Listen. Our hearts are beating in rhythm."

Merlin, paralyzed with fear from the neck down, opened one eye.

"Then yours must be beating really fucking fast."

"Yes," Rose whispered. "And it's magic."

"You like magic?"

"Not really."

"Wanna see a card trick?"

"No."

She licked the inside of his ear.

"Ahhhh," Merlin said, cringing as he felt her saliva run down the side of his neck.

"Good, isn't it?"

"Oh, it's delightful."

**

"So who's going to win, Doc?"

Hedaya was stretched out on the couch, staring up at the ceiling.

"Win what?"

"The battle for world domination."

"Probably nobody. I've been telling them that for years. Just call it a tie and be done with it. But they won't buy it."

"That's easy for us Americans to say."

"Why do you say that?"

"It's always easy to be magnanimous when you're winning."

"Yeah, I guess you're right."

Doc removed the last cigarette from his pack.

"Oh, before I forget. You need to start sending a bunch of money to the Caribbean."

"Why on earth would I do that?" Hedaya said, barely able to lift his head off the couch.

"Because we need to give the FBI something to do."

"Okay." Hedaya belched loudly. "How much?"

"A lot. Just make sure it's after-tax dollars."

"Okay. What time should I expect a visit tomorrow?"

"Don't worry. I'll make it as late as possible."

251

"That was incredible," Rose whispered.

Merlin pulled the sheet up under his chin and stared at the ceiling. He turned his head and looked at the pair of deep green eyes staring back.

"What are we supposed to do now?"

"We cuddle and then go to sleep, you silly," Rose said, snuggling close.

"Okay. I think I can handle that," Merlin said, fully prepared for a sleepless night.

"Are you sure it was special?" she said, nuzzling his neck. "The first time should be memorable."

"Oh, I'm pretty sure I'll never forget it."

**

Doc picked up the receiver finally sure he would be able to hear over the noise of the casino. The crowd was dwindling, and he was the sole user of the long row of telephones that stretched along the outside wall near the elevators. He put the receiver back in its cradle and removed a bottle of Advil from his coat pocket. He swallowed a small handful, washing them down with a mouthful of club soda and lime. He opened a fresh pack of cigarettes, lit one, and leaned against the wall surveying the scene.

He checked his watch and realized it was four in the morning in Washington. He and Hedaya had spent over six hours talking.

And drinking.

Doc smiled at the memory of the old man, the architect of the grand plan and purveyor of democracy in the distant land he used to call home, hammered and snoring loudly from the couch. Doc hadn't even bothered trying to wake him. At a minimum, he owed Hedaya the pleasure of a good night's sleep.

Doc removed the receiver and punched in the number. It rang several times and eventually a sleepy voice answered.

"Hello."

"Could I please speak with George Tirebiter?"

The pause was long enough for Doc to know the name had registered.

"I'm sorry, but there's no one here by that name."

"Gee, that's odd," Doc said. "This is the number he gave me. I'm supposed to meet him this afternoon at three in the lobby of the Bellagio, but I haven't heard from him."

"Bellagio? What city are you calling?"

"Vegas, of course."

"That's the problem. This is Washington. The area code here is 202. I believe the area code for Las Vegas is 702."

"I'm sorry. I must have dialed the wrong area code. Sorry to get you out of bed."

"No problem. It happens all the time."

Doc heard the click, hung up the phone and went to bed.

Chapter 52

Doc saw the man wearing plaid shorts and a Hawaiian shirt casually stroll through the front doors of the Bellagio. A floppy sun hat and sunglasses completed the outfit. Doc couldn't suppress his short burst of laughter. He nodded at Samuels then headed towards a long row of slot machines. Doc watched him walk to a cashier cage and exchange some bills for several rolls of quarters.

The man strolled to a quiet area along one side of the casino, sat down at a slot machine, and began feeding it. Doc followed his lead and sat down next to him. Doc slid a twenty into the adjacent machine.

"These things do accept bills you know," Doc said, staring straight ahead.

"Not on my budget they don't," Samuels said, dropping another quarter into the machine. "Judging by the look of you, if that's what retirement has in store, I'll keep working."

"We need to talk."

"That's why I'm here," Samuels said, watching the clanging machine spit coins. "Must be my lucky day."

"I doubt it," Doc said, offering the man a folded twenty. "Here. I think I owe you this."

The man took the money and noticed the small slip of paper tucked inside.

"What time?" he said, looking back at his machine.

"Give me an hour."

Doc stood up and cashed out the machine. The coins noisily collected in a tray underneath.

"Feel free to play these."

Doc strolled away. He walked outside feeling the intense afternoon heat and stood quietly under the soft, cool mist drifting down from above.

**

Doc opened the door and smiled. Samuels looked down the hallway in both directions, stepped inside and gave him Doc a quick hug.

"Nice outfit," Doc said, leading him into the living room.

"When in Rome, huh? Don't worry, I've got a change of clothes," he said, taking in the plush surroundings. "Nice place." He settled into the couch. "Are you sure it's safe to talk here?"

"Yeah, it's fine," Doc said. "Can I get you something to drink?"

"Maybe later."

Samuels watched Doc fix a drink and light a cigarette.

"I was more than a little surprised to hear from you this morning, Doc."

"I imagine you were. I hated having to call you at home, but I don't have any of the normal channels available anymore."

"No problem. Why am I here, Doc?"

"Well, Samuels, you are here because of a little Chinese man named Hedaya."

"Hedaya? That rings a bell. Casino owner. Is this one his?"

"Yeah."

"What's he done? Screw some bus tour out of their hard earned nickels?" Samuels said.

"He's got a bootleg copy of Run Rabbit Run." Doc sat back and waited.

Samuels' eyes widened.

"What? All of it?"

"Everything except the box and shrink wrap it came in."

"Okay," he said. "Now I know why I'm here. I hope you don't mind telling me what he's using it for."

He took a cigarette from the pack on the table and lit it.

"Hedaya's using the software to coordinate a global network that, at some distant point in the future, will try to orchestrate a democratic revolution in China," Doc said.

Samuels sighed.

"Oh, is that all. I was worried he wanted the software because he like the way it handles email."

He sat back and smoked in silence. He rubbed his forehead deep in thought.

"Shit."

"Yeah," Doc said.

"How did he get his hands on it?"

"Matasha gave it to him."

"Roger Matasha? My Roger Matasha?"

"Yeah."

"Goddamn it. What is it with these cowboys? Do they think we're playing a video game? Okay, Doc. Start talking."

**

Hedaya dialed the phone and waited. Rose sat on the other side of the desk absent-mindedly flipping a quarter from one finger to another using only one hand. Hedaya hung up and looked at her.

"He's not answering," Hedaya said.

"Do you know where he's supposed to be?" Rose said, focusing as she trapped the quarter with her thumb and rolled it into her other hand.

"I think he said Los Angeles," Hedaya said. "But I'm not sure."

"How much danger could he be in?"

"I don't think anything would happen to him immediately. But I'm sure there are people very interested in talking with Roger. It would be nice to warn him."

"How much danger are we in, Bofu?"

Hedaya saw the fear in her eyes. He reached across the desk and gently patted her hand.

"We are very safe. Don't worry."

"Was Doc angry with you?"

"Remarkably, no."

"What did you talk about then?"

"We discussed many things, my dear."

"I can't believe they're CIA," Rose said, the quarter resuming its slow roll across her fingers.

"They were CIA."

"Regardless, I hope they don't ruin everything. So you and Doc just talked all night."

"Well, we also drank. I'm afraid that's the reason for my low energy today."

"You know I don't like it when you drink. You always smoke cigarettes."

"You worry about me too much, my dear."

Hedaya laughed.

"Besides, can't an old man have a little fun now and then?"

"Fun, yes," Rose said, refocused on the quarter. "Cigarettes, no."

256

Chapter 53

Doc finished telling Samuels the story, sat back in his chair, and waited for the question he knew was coming.

"And you're just now getting around to telling me this?" Samuels said.

"Yeah. I wasn't sure if Matasha was sanctioned. If he was, I didn't want to blow his cover."

"Sure, Doc. Like I'm just going to hand over a copy of our computer system for some casino owner to play with."

Samuels crossed to the wet bar and fixed himself a drink.

"Stranger things have happened," Doc said.

"I should have said yes to my mother when she asked if was planning on spending the rest of my life just taking up space."

Samuels took a long sip of bourbon.

"So what are we supposed to do about this?"

"We deal with it," Doc said.

"How? Neither one of us works for the Company anymore."

"Yeah, I heard about your situation."

"From who?"

"Merlin."

"Merlin?" Samuels said, rubbing his forehead. "Please don't tell me Cokehead is involved in this."

"Okay, I won't tell you."

"Goddamn it. I should have shot him when I had the chance."

"He's the one who found out Hedaya had a copy of the software."

"Of course, he did. You can't keep anything secret from the little prick. That's why he's completely…"

Samuels pursed his lips, then took another long sip of bourbon.

"That's why he's completely what? Completely safe? That's it, right?"

"Yeah. He's got stuff on everybody. And I mean everybody. And I'm sure he's got copies of what he knows stashed all over the place. How he got it, I have no idea."

Doc smiled at the thought of Merlin having back door entry into the Company's computer systems, but said nothing.

"Do you have any idea how big a shit storm will hit if this leaks? I may be out, but Roger is one of mine. This would be my second major problem in six months. Unlike Merlin, I don't have enough information to save my fat white ass."

Samuels took another sip of bourbon.

"Please tell me you've got some ideas," Samuels said.

"Yeah, we got some ideas. Merlin's not very happy with one in particular, but he'll play. And it probably won't get you back in, but it should take some of the heat off."

"Shit, I don't want back in," Samuels said. "The place sucks."

"What are you going to do?"

"Good question. Right now, I'm raking leaves and playing with the dogs. I suppose I'll do some consulting at some point. Isn't that what everybody else does? You and Merlin put this together all by yourselves?"

"Yeah."

"Nice piece of work, Doc."

He drained the rest of his bourbon, added fresh ice and poured.

"How is our little coke monkey anyway?"

"He's a little dazed today, but brilliant as ever. And still a total pain in the ass."

"The bastard drives me nuts. But you should have seen what he pulled off in Brazil. It was frightening to witness the damage he can do when he's motivated. Their currency went south like that."

Samuels snapped his fingers to accentuate the point.

"Did you know that he can do the Sunday New York Times crossword puzzle in his head?"

"Yeah. Last week, I watched him take five grand off a guy who bet Merlin couldn't calculate square roots in his head," Doc said.

"I wonder how smart he'd be if he quit doing so much blow."

"Shit, I hope he doesn't do that," Doc said, chuckling. "I have enough trouble keeping up with him as it is."

"Well, get him up here. We've got work to do."

Doc dialed Merlin's suite. He spoke quietly into the phone, hung up and sat back down in the chair.

"So, how are you, Doc?"

"Well, it's been pretty bad lately. But the past few days I'm feeling a bit better. I'm not sure, but I think it had something to do with an encounter I had in L.A."

"What about the voice?"

"Comes and goes. Lately, it does pretty much whatever it wants."

Samuels stood and stretched, trying to shake the fatigue of the long flight. He walked to the refrigerator and poked around until he found a candy bar. He sat back down and chewed slowly.

"You mentioned the FBI was sniffing around up here. Who's working it?"

"They've got a guy named Gentry on the ground. He's way out of his league, but don't try telling him that. Here in Vegas, he reports to a guy named Williams."

Samuels cocked his head. "Short little guy, officious, ugly little pushed in face? His nickname is Shorty."

"Yeah, that's him. Do you know him?"

"I met him a couple of times. What a little prick. He used to be based in DC, but he took a field assignment when he heard it would accelerate his career advancement."

Doc was surprised by the comment, knowing a key component of upward mobility at the Bureau was the ability to stay close to influential people working out of Headquarters.

"Who on earth told him that?"

"The people he worked for in DC." Samuels laughed. "How are you handling them?"

"Don't worry, I've got it teed up. They're getting desperate."

"Did they piss you off?"

"Oh, yeah. Do you want to hear about it?"

"No, surprise me," said William, smiling. "Is it good?"

"It's beautiful," Doc said, nodding his head. "I'm leading them right where they're dying to go."

Samuels stretched out on the couch and yawned.

"I guess this means you want back in."

"I don't think so," Doc said, lighting a cigarette. "It's changed too much. I miss the work, but hate the bureaucracy."

"Amen to that."

Samuels checked his watch.

"I wonder what's keeping Cokehead?"

Chapter 54

Doc looked around the table already knowing the outcome of the upcoming discussion. He'd played the scene out so many times in his head, he felt he'd already lived it.

Rose fidgeted in her seat, and Doc felt sympathy for her. Her reaction was predictable. Everyone was nervous the first time they were invited to a meeting with government officials who had something on their mind. Merlin walked in and sat in the chair next to Doc.

"No sign of Matasha?" Merlin whispered.

"Samuels said they picked him up a couple of hours ago. He's on his way."

Merlin nodded and settled into the chair. He glanced across the table at Rose, who managed a small smile. The conference room door opened, and Hedaya walked in. All four got up from their chairs and waited. He nodded once and gestured for them to sit back down. Hedaya sat at the end of the table closest to Samuels, his arms folded, elbows resting on the table.

"Hedaya looks almost Presidential today," Merlin whispered.

"That's because he's got a hangover that could kill a horse."

"I'm assuming you're Mr. Samuels," Hedaya said.

Samuels, dressed in a dark suit, stood and bowed.

"Please, just call me Samuels. It is a pleasure to meet you, Hedaya. Although, I would have preferred different circumstances."

Hedaya rose slowly from his chair, bowed slightly and shook the man's hand.

"The pleasure is all mine," he said, settling back into his chair. "I'm assuming that it's not customary to exchange business cards during meetings of this nature."

Samuels smiled, shaking his head.

"No, it's not. Before we go any further, I need to ask you if this room is equipped with any recording devices."

"No," Hedaya said. "This is my personal conference room."

"I see," Samuels said. "I can take you at your word on that?"

Hedaya blanched at the question. His eyes narrowed.

"Yes, you can," Doc said.

"May I ask what your position is with the CIA, Samuels?" Hedaya said, mildly annoyed.

" I'm no longer with the CIA, but if I were, would it make any difference?"

Hedaya thought for a moment and smiled.

"No, I imagine it wouldn't. Would it be safe for me to assume these two gentlemen used to work for you?"

Samuels looked down the table at Merlin and Doc.

"They did. Although on more than occasion, it was hard to tell that one of them did."

He glared at Merlin. Hedaya caught the exchange and laughed.

"Let it go, Samuels," Merlin said. "For chrissakes. You're such a baby."

Hedaya watched the brief stare down between Merlin and Samuels and then continued.

"Would it also be safe to assume you are, were part of the covert operations group?"

"I see Mr. Matasha hasn't been shy about providing you with background information. By the way, Hedaya. Mr. Matasha will be joining the meeting soon."

"So Roger is safe?"

"For now, yes," Samuels said, staring at the old man.

"Tell me, Samuels," Hedaya said. "Do you specialize in handling sensitive issues with respect to China?"

"I specialize in many things, Hedaya," Samuels said. "All of them sensitive."

"I see. And how many people are aware of the specific details of your activities?"

"How many people are aware of yours, Hedaya?" Samuels said through a small smile.

"Yes," Hedaya said, returning the smile. "Your point is well taken."

The Dance of the Scorpions.

Both men fell silent and leaned back in their chairs staring at each other. A long silence filled the room. Eventually, Samuels leaned forward on his elbows.

"I'm sure you're aware you've put all of us in a difficult position, Hedaya."

"Yes," Hedaya said. "Just as your people have done to me."

261

"The difference is they were doing what they've been trained to do. It's their job."

"Yes, I can see why you might feel that way, Samuels. But I am merely doing mine."

"I applaud your efforts on this operation, Hedaya but, with respect, I think they are somewhat misguided."

"Do you?"

"Yes, I do. I can understand, given the situation in China and your heritage, why someone like yourself might attempt such an effort, but there are people much better equipped to handle it. I think this one should be left to the professionals."

Hedaya blanched, and Doc recognized the anger.

"I see," Hedaya said. "So tell me, Samuels, what are these *professionals* doing on China?"

"They undertake assignments that support and advance our country's policy."

"Policy?" Hedaya flashed his smile. "Yes, that has always fascinated me. Over the years, I've closely followed the dual and rather fluid policy on China. I believe the terms used are containment and engagement. Tell me, Samuels, which one is it this week?"

Doc looked down, unable to suppress a smile. He shot a quick glance at Merlin, who was also smiling and watching Samuels. Samuels leaned back in his chair and rocked gently.

"Well, Hedaya," Samuels said. "Perhaps there have been inconsistencies in that regard. I'm sure you would agree it's a very difficult situation."

"Yes I would," Hedaya said. "I would also think you'd welcome all the help you could get."

Hedaya continued to stare across the table. Samuels rocked in silence for several moments.

The sharp knock on the door caught everyone by surprise. A sheepish Roger Matasha entered the room, walked silently to a chair directly across from Samuels and sat down. He looked around the room, nodding to the others.

"Hello, Roger," Samuels said. "It's been too long. What have you been up to?"

"Hello, Samuels," Matasha said.

He glanced around the room and nodded at Hedaya and Rose. He gave Doc and Merlin blank stares. He turned back to Samuels.

"Look, I can explain."

"Let's hope so," Samuels said. He turned his attention back to Hedaya. "With respect, Hedaya, many people might assume you've simply lost your mind. I hope you don't mind me being blunt."

"No, I don't mind. Over the years, I've learned to appreciate a certain degree of bluntness. As far as people believing I'm insane, that is something I can't control. So I don't worry about it. Besides, a long time ago in this country, many felt the same about another group. I believe it was called the American Revolution. I must ask you. Which comes first? The insanity, or the patriot?"

Samuels nodded, then softened.

"What's your timeframe, Hedaya?"

"As long as it takes. We're not going anywhere, and we've got nothing better to do."

"You know I could shut this whole operation down, don't you?"

"I know you could try," Hedaya said. "Why on earth would you want to do that? It's the best chance you've got to avoid the inevitable."

"And what would that be, Hedaya?"

"War with China, of course."

"I think you're underestimating some of our abilities, Hedaya."

Hedaya chuckled softly.

"Mr. Samuels, do you really believe that a group of ex U.S. officials flying in and out of Beijing to chat and collect fat consulting checks in any way influences how Chinese officials think or behave?"

"No, I don't," Samuels said. "But there are many possible alternatives."

"I'm sure you believe that. But if it appears to the Chinese people the U.S. is actively promoting real democratic change in China, it will only harden their position. Given China's current growth and development, it won't be long before the people are ready for something truly different. For now, all we can do is keep working and wait."

"Wait for what, Hedaya?"

"An opportunity."

"I see," Samuels said, rubbing his forehead. "I don't know if I can let you do that, Hedaya."

"Samuels, you're asking me to abandon something many people have invested a great deal in. To you, this operation, as you call it, is just another in a long line your organization uses to manipulate and control the world agenda. If things don't go well, you go back to the people controlling you and say things like if we'd only had more time, or people, or money. Spin it, regroup, and move on to the next. For us, it is different. This is our dream. It is our legacy, not yours. However, misguided you believe it to be, it must be allowed to run its course."

"And what makes you think I would be willing to let that happen?"

Samuels leaned back and rocked slowly in his chair.

"Because it's time, Samuels."

"For what?"

"For organizations like yours to put up or shut up. All I hear coming out of Washington are patriotic promises about making the world safer for democracy. Well, Samuels, with all due respect, patriots come in all shapes and sizes. And just so we're clear on this point, they don't all live in Washington, and they most certainly are not all white males."

Doc felt the air leave the room and looked at the two men at the other end of the table staring intently at each other. He glanced at Merlin, who was watching closely.

"What bothers you the most, Samuels?" Hedaya said. "The potential embarrassment this could cause, or that you didn't think of it first?"

Once again, a deep silence fell over the room and lingered. Eventually, Hedaya broke his stare and leaned back. Samuels dropped his stare and glanced at Doc.

"I'm sorry, Hedaya," Samuels said. "You're asking too much. I can't turn a blind eye to this. At the bare minimum, we need to be able to watch it closely."

"I see." Hedaya exhaled and sighed. He looked back at Samuels. "You're suggesting I allow someone from your organization inside."

"You already have someone from my organization inside," Samuels said, giving Matasha a dark look.

"But the circumstances have changed considerably."

"Yes, they most certainly have," Samuels said.

"That's asking a lot," Hedaya said, shaking his head. "Who on earth could I possibly trust to handle this?"

"Me."

The entire room fell silent again. Doc stared down at his hands folded on top of the conference room table.

"You?" Hedaya said. "Doc, I appreciate the offer, but I know how badly you want out. Why on earth would you make such an offer?"

"It's what I do," Doc said.

Hedaya sat back in his chair, glanced around the room, then back at Doc. He folded his hands under his chin deep in thought. Turning his attention back to Samuels he said, "Please explain how you see it working."

"Doc is your primary point of contact. You keep him informed. It will be his responsibility to do the same for me. Believe me, Hedaya," Samuels said, glancing at Merlin and Doc. "You won't be the only one making a leap of faith on the question of trust."

"What will you do with the information?" Hedaya said.

"I will be telling three people," Samuels said.

"Can I ask who they are?"

"No, you may not. But, don't worry. You'll be meeting one of them very soon."

"Obviously, senior people."

"Very."

"So this will be an officially sanctioned operation within the CIA?"

"Probably not," Doc said. "None of us work there anymore."

"Now I'm confused," Hedaya said.

No more than the rest of us.

"I'll explain it to you as soon as I get it all clarified," Doc said.

"And what happens to Roger?" Hedaya said.

"Roger will be coming with me to Washington for some very serious converstions. After that, if he doesn't end up in federal prison, he'll be chained to his desk for a very long time," Samuels said.

"I see," Hedaya said. "Is that everything?

"Almost," Samuels said. "We still have the problem with Run Rabbit Run. I can't have a copy of our software floating around. It puts too many people in jeopardy."

"Would you like me to give it back?"

"No, you can keep it. It's compromised so I'm afraid we need a new system."

"I see," Hedaya said. "I'm assuming you don't just buy something like that from a catalog."

"No, unfortunately, we'll have to start from scratch."

"How long will that take?"

Samuels looked over at Merlin, who took his cue.

"About a year," Merlin said.

"So it's safe to assume that you'll be paying very close attention to what we do with the existing program," Hedaya said.

"Oh, we'll be doing more than that, Hedaya," Samuels said, a smile on his face.

He gestured in Merlin's direction.

"I'd like you to meet your new Chief Information Officer."

"Merlin?"

Hedaya shook his head.

"You're not alone, Hedaya," Merlin said. "I'm not very happy about it either."

Rose beamed.

"Effective immediately, Merlin is assigned here until the new system is implemented. He will take direction directly from you on all matters related to casino operations. He will be coordinating the development of our new system from here and will be working closely with the development team at Langley until it is done. I strongly urge you and everyone else within a twelve and a half thousand-mile radius of this place to completely, constantly, and vigilantly ignore each and every one of his activities in that area. I trust I have made myself very clear on that point."

Hedaya smiled and looked around the table.

"Yes, I think we all got that one."

Samuels stood up and extended his hand. Hedaya grasped it, closing the deal.

"Hedaya, it's been a pleasure. Try not to forget you have a new business partner," Samuels said.

Samuels looked at Doc and Merlin.

"I'll see you two upstairs later. I need to have a little chat with Roger first."

He nodded at Matasha, who got up, walked to the door and waited. Samuels turned to Rose.

"It was a pleasure meeting you, Rose. Hopefully, the next time will be under more pleasant circumstances."

"It was nice to meet you too," Rose said, glowing from the news about Merlin.

266

Samuels headed toward the door, stopped and turned to Hedaya. "Good luck at the Olympic trials. I hope you bring back the gold."

Chapter 55

The midday sun was brutal but from the comfort of his lounge chair, Doc was a man at peace. He sipped cold, crisp Chardonnay and gazed around the rooftop haven. He watched Hedaya barbecue chicken in the shade; the old man shrouded by the cool mist floating through the breeze. Tongs in hand, Hedaya swayed to the jazz piano playing in the background. He flipped a piece of chicken, caught Doc's eye, and bowed in his direction. Doc waved and studied the old man's movements, wondering where the pleasure he took in everything he did came from.

"What do you think?"

Doc looked at Merlin, who was sitting next to him covered in suntan lotion. Doc laughed, unable to decide whether Merlin's skin or the lotion was whiter.

"I think you need to get out more, Merlin," Doc said.

He settled into the lounge chair and closed his eyes.

Looking for a place to put the excess lotion, Merlin wiped his hands between his toes.

"You want some of this?"

"No, I'm fine."

"A year," Merlin said. "As fucking CIO." He stretched out and pulled his hat down until it touched the top of his sunglasses. "I should have kept my mouth shut."

"Quit bitching," Doc said. "I don't know about you, but I could certainly get used to this."

"Well, we're both going to get a chance to find out."

"Yes, we certainly are," Doc said, smiling. He opened his eyes and sat up in the lounge chair. "Hey, I forgot to ask you. How was your date the other night?"

"It had its moments," Merlin said.

"What? No details? I go to all that trouble to fix you up, and this is the thanks I get?"

"I don't kiss and tell," Merlin said, shifting in his chair.

"C'mon, Merlin. I'd tell you."

"No, you wouldn't. But frankly, I don't see what all the excitement's about. If I had wanted to gyrate like that, I would have taken up gymnastics."

Doc laughed and reached for his wineglass. He lit a cigarette and stared out at the pool watching Rose effortlessly swim laps.

"I must say. This is a first," Doc said.

"What's that?"

"Well, here we are getting ready to go live with a new system tomorrow, and all we have to do is wait. In the past, we were always up to our eyeballs scrambling to get ready."

"Yeah," Merlin said. "We did good."

"I like the way it turned out."

"Piece of cake, Doc. A piece of cake."

"Yeah," Doc said.

"That's not the only first, Doc," Merlin said, removing a small vial from inside his shirt pocket. He glanced over at Hedaya, still preoccupied with the chicken, and sniffed back a small spoonful.

"What's that?"

Merlin dropped the vial back inside his shirt pocket.

"All the time we've been up here, there hasn't been one car chase, no shots fired, and nobody died."

"You're right," Doc said. "Nice work if you can get it, huh?"

Rose pulled herself out of the pool, removed the elastic band holding her hair, and let it cascade down her back. Doc nudged Merlin and they watched the topless wonder, without a trace of self-consciousness, stroll towards them. She was wearing a tiny black thong accented with a simple gold chain that hung from her hips.

"She fills that outfit out nicely, wouldn't you say, Merlin?"

"Fuck you."

Rose approached, bent forward and kissed Merlin on the cheek.

"What are you boys up to?" she said, wringing the water out of her hair with a towel.

"I'm just enjoying the view." Doc smiled up at her. "Doesn't she look amazing, Merlin?"

"Yeah," Merlin said. "She's something else."

He gave both of them a weak smile.

Rose winked at Doc and stretched out face down on a lounge chair. Doc's eyes slowly worked down the muscles in her back to the taut curves that threatened to rip apart the tiny strand of fabric surrounding them. Doc looked at Merlin, who was squinting up at the sky. He gently nudged him.

"Now what?" Merlin said.

"That," Doc whispered, nodding his head in the direction of Rose's firm, round bottom.

Merlin looked over.

"What's the big deal? Everybody's got one."

Doc shook his head at his friend.

"Not like that they don't."

Hedaya called them to lunch, and all three collected their belongings.

"Great," Rose said, pulling on a large shirt and buttoning it halfway. "I'm starved."

They joined Hedaya at a table sitting under a large awning and watched as two waiters filled the table with a variety of salads. Hedaya pulled a large bottle of champagne out of an ice bucket and poured four glasses.

"Ooooh, champagne," Rose said. "Yummy."

Hedaya handed them their glasses and looked around the table.

"What should we toast to?"

"How about world domination?" Merlin said.

Hedaya frowned.

"Too harsh."

Hedaya looked at Doc and waited.

"To good friends?"

Hedaya shook his head.

"Really, Doc. I'd expect something better from you."

Hedaya smiled and winked at him. He turned to Rose.

"How about you, my dear?"

Rose thought for a moment and squeezed the top of Merlin's thigh under the table.

"To days and nights ahead."

"Perfect," Hedaya said, raising his glass.

Chapter 56

Merlin stared wide-eyed and pulled his legs up onto his lounge chair. He nudged Doc, who was dozing in the lounge chair next to him.

"What?" Doc said, grumpy about being woken.

"Does Hedaya have a personal zoo around here?"

"What are you talking about?"

"Unless I'm hallucinating from the coke, I think I see a tiger. And he's heading straight for us."

Doc opened his eyes, saw the bounding dog, and waved at Summerman.

"That's not a tiger. It's Murray."

"Oh, that makes me feel so much better."

The massive dog nudged Doc's arm and waited for a head scratch. He then focused on Merlin and draped both front paws over his shoulders. Merlin tentatively reached out to pet the dog who returned the gesture with several licks to the face. Merlin, trapped beneath two-hundred pounds of dog, wiped his face but managed a laugh.

"C'mon, Murray. It's too hot for him to wear you like a coat. Why don't you go for a swim?"

Summerman, hands on hips, waited patiently. The dog cocked his head at the word swim, gave Merlin one final lick, and dove into the pool. He surfaced, woofed loudly, and spied two young women splashing nearby. Soon he was enjoying their company in the shallow end.

"He's got the magic touch with women," Doc said. "You back for another round of consultation, Summerman?"

"Actually, I've been waiting for a chance to speak with both of you." Summerman turned to Merlin and extended his hand.

"I'm Summerman. It's nice to meet you, Merlin."

Merlin, confused, returned the handshake.

"My pleasure." The name registered. "Summerman Lawless."

"Yes. And you're the famous Merlin."

"Fame's a relative term."

"Yes. Especially where I come from."

Summerman smiled and waved to a waitress holding up two fingers. He dragged a chair between the two lounges and sat down facing them.

Merlin glanced at Doc, who shrugged and wiped sweat from his brow with a towel.

"I thought it was time for the second part of our conversation," Summerman said.

"I'm still trying to recover from our first," Doc said.

Merlin started to get up.

"I'll get out of here so you two can talk."

"No, Merlin," Summerman said. "This very much concerns you. In fact, you're quite central to what I'm about to propose."

Doc snorted.

"Look, Summerman, I appreciate what I think you're trying to do here but, if you don't mind, we're a little busy at the moment."

"Yes, achieving Hedaya's goal of a democratic China must be a full-time job."

Summerman smiled and glanced at the pool. His voice turned sharp.

"Murray, stop pulling that."

Summerman waved to the laughing woman who was trying to retie her bikini top and fend off the energetic dog at the same time.

"I'm sorry. But he's very good with knots."

The woman smiled and waved back then vigorously rubbed the dog's head. Summerman turned back to both men.

"What was I saying?"

Doc removed his sunglasses.

"How do you know about Hedaya's plans?"

"Where do you think he gets his advance intelligence? You guys in the CIA?"

"We're ex-CIA," Doc said, glancing at Merlin.

"Of course," Summerman said. "My mistake."

"Who is this guy?" Merlin said, watching Summerman but talking to Doc.

"Merlin," Doc said. "Summerman claims to be what he calls, a part-timer. Part-time human, the rest of the time he's a...what, ghost?"

"I prefer the term spirit," Summerman said. "But that's close enough."

Merlin laughed and took a long swallow of vodka.

"I guess crazy comes in all shapes and sizes. But the dog is a nice touch."

"By the way, Merlin, your mother says hello and asked me to tell you to go easy on the coke. She says it will rot your brain."

"My mother has been dead for-"

"Eleven years. Yes, I know. But she sends her best. The rest of your family as well."

"Doc," Merlin said. "Make him go away."

"But you haven't heard my proposal."

Summerman glanced up at the approaching waitress carrying two Guinness, one in a glass, the other in a metal bowl. Summerman whistled, and Murray climbed out of the pool and shook. He trotted over and began lapping at his bowl. Summerman stroked his wet coat and took a sip of his drink. He set it down on the table and leaned forward.

"Gentlemen, both of you have spent the majority of your lives working behind the scenes trying to root out evil in the world."

"Doc?" Merlin said.

"It's okay, Merlin."

Doc nodded at Summerman. "Continue."

"Finally, a receptive ear." Summerman exhaled. "I was beginning to wonder if I'd chosen the wrong people."

"Chosen?" Merlin said. "For what?"

"For the opportunity of a lifetime, Merlin."

Summerman took another long sip of Guinness then poured the remainder into Murray's bowl.

"That's all for now. When you finish, why don't you go lay down in the shade?"

Murray cocked his head and appeared to nod. Doc and Merlin stared at the dog dumbfounded.

"He's such a great dog. I don't know what I'd do without him."

"Is he...?" Merlin said.

"A part-timer? Yes." Summerman smiled and nodded at Merlin. "Don't worry, Merlin. Sometime soon I will tell you the whole story."

"This is nuts," Merlin said. "Doc?"

"I know, Merlin. I had the same reaction when he first approached me."

"Why didn't you say something?"

"You're already worried I've completely lost my mind hearing voices. I was supposed to tell you I got a visit from the ghost of Christmas past?"

"Ghost of Christmas past," Summerman said, laughing. "Good one, Doc. Never heard that one before."

"So, what's this plan?"

"A small organized group of like-minded individuals, let's call it a posse, intent on identifying and hunting down bad people."

"Oh, is that all?" Doc laughed and looked at Merlin, who joined in. "I think that's what we already do, Summerman."

"Yes," Summerman said. "But you don't make millions of dollars in the process?"

"How do you propose making money hunting down these bad people?

"Rewards and bounties for terrorists and people on the most wanted lists. Inside information on whatever company we decide to target. And from the truly evil making fortunes doing incredibly bad things around the planet, we just steal it."

Summerman waved to the waitress and made the gesture for another round of drinks.

"Hedaya has perfected customer service. His staff is amazing."

Doc stared at Summerman, then glanced at Merlin who was deep in thought.

"I know you're still not convinced, Merlin," Summerman said.

"No, I'm not. But I have to say I am intrigued."

"Think about it, gentlemen. With my ability to hover in on the real world nine months out of the year and then return with a wealth of information and insight into what's going on, combined with your skill set, we'd be unstoppable."

"I'm going to need some proof," Merlin said. "This could be one of Samuels' setups just to pay me back for the shit I've put him through."

"Samuels," Summerman said. "Yes, I see a role for him as well."

"Do you now?" Doc said.

"Yes, I'm not sure he would be of much use working on projects, but it certainly wouldn't hurt to have some cover and protection at the most senior levels of government."

"Samuels is out," Merlin said. "We're all out."

"I know," Summerman said. "And what could be better than that? We form an independent group that is completely unknown except to a handful of people. And as long as we produce results, no one is going to come looking for who we are and what we do."

Summerman wiped his forehead.

274

"Damn, it's hot out here. And if someone did get a bit overzealous in their attempts to root us out, I have a variety of ways to deal with that the nine months of the year when I'm on the other side."

Merlin laughed.

"What do you do, haunt their houses?"

"My friends from the other side terrorize them."

Merlin caught Summerman's cold stare and held it as long as he could. Eventually, he returned to the safety of his vodka tonic. Summerman handed Merlin a piece of paper.

"What's this?" Merlin said, examining the note.

"That's the key code you've spent the last year looking for."

Merlin glanced up at Summerman.

"Where did you get this?"

"It came to me in a dream," Summerman said, sipping his fresh Guinness. "Where the hell do you think I got it, Merlin? I hovered into his office three months ago and watched him type it into his computer."

"Sonofabitch," Merlin said, sliding the note into his pocket.

"You're welcome." Summerman said, shaking his head at Merlin. "Well, Doc, what do you think?"

"How many people know about your situation?"

"Six. Two members of my family, Hedaya, the two of you. And Captain Wilbur. For obvious reasons, I'd like to keep it at that number. And I must know that you'll be sworn to secrecy."

"Captain Wilbur?" Merlin said.

"He's my pilot."

"Your pilot?"

"Yes, I have a Gulfstream. And while I'm on the other side, you'd be free to use it for your work. And play."

Summerman smiled at both men and winked.

"Assuming you ever learn how to play, Merlin."

"Hey, watch it, Ghost Boy."

Doc waved at Merlin to be quiet.

"And if we were to bring Samuels into it?"

"No, for now, Samuels cannot know about my situation. He's too close to the upper echelons of power. I have no desire to become a lab rat in some government research facility. If Samuels ends up providing cover for our operations, you will be the front person as far as he is concerned."

"How would it work?"

"You'd spend a great deal of your time working on things I've uncovered the previous year. During the summer when I'm back on this side, we get together for some work, but, hopefully, we also have time for some fun. We split everything three ways, minus expenses plus whatever cut Samuels decides he wants for his effort."

Summerman handed Doc a large sealed envelope.

"In there you will find three initial prospects I believe are worthy of our efforts. If we're successful, I'm anticipating a return of around seventy million dollars. Maybe more. And that's just the first year."

"Seventy million?" Merlin said. "Finally, you're speaking a language I understand. What do you think, Doc?"

"Why are you doing this?"

"I'm going to need some clarification here, Doc."

"If your situation works the way you say it does, why go to all this trouble? You could easily steal all the money you'd ever need and spend your time on this side playing your piano and chasing women."

"I already have all the money I'll ever need. And don't worry about me. I still make time for the piano and women. Just try to think of it as my way of giving back," Summerman said. "Besides, I get bored if I'm not doing something useful."

Doc continued to review the contents of the envelope. He flipped through the pages and rubbed his forehead.

"I would love to get my hands on these guys."

"Yes," Summerman said. "I know you would."

"Is there anything you don't know?" Doc said.

"There is one thing I've been struggling to understand." Summerman glanced at Merlin. "I was wondering why Rose has fallen head over heels for you. I've been trying to get her horizontal for three years without any success."

"Maybe she just likes my brain," Merlin said.

"Perhaps," Summerman said. "I thought she just decided to pick on somebody her own size."

He flashed a huge grin at Doc, who burst out laughing.

"You're pretty funny for a dead guy," Merlin said.

Summerman stood and whistled. Murray, sleeping under a massive palm, stretched and trotted over. Summerman patted his head.

"You ready to head to Chicago, Murray?"

He looked back at Doc and Merlin.

"Think about it, gentlemen. I need your help. And we can make a ton of money and have a hell of a good time, doing good."

He and the dog started to walk away, but Summerman stopped.

"Oh, Merlin."

"Yeah?"

"He always takes lunch at 11:30. You missed today's window, so you might want to wait until tomorrow. Remember, 11:30 sharp."

Merlin nodded silently and managed a weak goodbye wave.

"I'll be in touch, Doc. And feel free to use Hedaya as a reference. I'm sure he'll vouch for me."

Doc and Merlin watched him and the dog stroll towards the far end of the rooftop. They heard the noise before they saw it. A large helicopter approached and slowly landed on the roof. Summerman watched Murray hop in and then he turned and spread his arms wide and smiled at them. He shouted, and Doc smiled and waved him away.

"What did he say?" Merlin said.

"He said welcome to my world."

"He's got style," Merlin said. "I have to give him that."

"Yeah," Doc said, nodding his head. "Rich and blessed with eternal life. Nice work if you can get it."

"Yeah," Merlin said. "The dog's cool too."

Chapter 57

Doc strolled out of his office, nodding and chatting briefly with several people. He knocked on the open door and waited in the doorway.

"Hey, Doc."

Barrier, haggard, sat behind a small desk surrounded by large metal cabinets filled with office supplies.

"Come on in."

Doc sat at a small table and looked around the office. Barrier scrunched himself into a chair at the table.

"Jesus," Doc said. "This is where they put you?"

"I thought it was your idea," Barrier said.

"No, it wasn't me." Doc said. "How the mighty have fallen. Why didn't you say something?"

"Would it have made a difference?"

"Probably not," Doc said. "When are you getting out of here?"

"I've got meetings with my lawyers next week, so I'll be here for a few more days. Don't worry. I won't be at the farewell party."

"How's that thing going for you?"

"You mean the Bureau thing?" Barrier said, making no attempt to hide his contempt.

"Yeah."

"It's going to get ugly. They've got a real mean streak," Barrier said.

"Maybe this will help," Doc said, sliding a large manila envelope across the table.

"What's that?"

"It's a gift."

Barrier unwound the string holding the envelope closed and removed a single piece of paper. He began reading, his eyes growing wider by the second.

"Jesus Christ," he whispered. "Why are you doing this?"

"Like I said, it's a gift."

"But why?"

"Let's say I got sick and tired of all the crap going on around here and leave it at that. Whatever Hedaya is up to is of no interest to me, and I certainly don't want the FBI in my life," Doc said.

"But why are you giving it to me? Why not give it to them yourself?"

"I don't want anything to do with those people."

"You know what this is going to do for me don't you?"

"Yes, I do," Doc said. "And I suggest you turn it over, get them off your back, and go back to chasing skirt and whatever else you're good at these days."

Doc stood up and extended his hand. Barrier returned the handshake.

"But why would you do this for me, Doc?"

"To tell you the truth, I'm not sure. Maybe I'm just tired of people bringing out the worst in me."

Barrier smiled.

"Yeah," he said. "Friends?"

Doc smiled back and shook his head.

"Never."

"Yeah," Barrier said. "Too much history."

"And all of it bad."

Doc took a final look around the cramped office.

"Start taking better care of yourself."

"You too," Barrier said. "Thanks, Doc."

"Don't mention it. To anybody."

**

Barrier sat on the edge of his chair listening carefully to the voice coming through the speakerphone. Gentry, a huge smile planted on his face, glanced back and forth from the phone to Williams, who was excitedly pacing the room.

"Nah, that won't be a problem," Williams said, coming to a stop. "We've got enough."

"I don't know, Fred," said the voice on the other end. "It seems a little sudden for him to start moving that much money around. Gentry, what's your take on that one?"

Gentry cleared his throat and looked at Williams, who nodded for him to speak.

"Well, sir, I have to agree with Fred. We're convinced that it's got something to do with the new system, and the recent payments were some test to make sure it's working. Don't forget about the rest of the document that outlines a dozen more scheduled for the next two weeks. This is it. I can feel it."

Gentry sat back in his chair and looked at Williams, who was smiling and nodding. He pumped a fist triumphantly in Gentry's direction.

"What about this guy running the project? What did you say his name was? Doc White?"

"Yes, sir," Williams said. "Nothing to worry about on that side. He's oblivious. This information came directly from Jim Barrier."

"Well, I guess we're good to go. Nice work, guys. Okay, go get him."

"Yes," Gentry said, clenching his fist tightly.

"Is that all you need from me?" the voice said, already bored.

Barrier cleared his throat and looked at Williams.

"Oh, yeah," Williams said, looking at Barrier. "One more thing, Chief. I'm assuming the Bureau is too busy dealing with other matters to bother with Jim's situation."

He looked at Barrier and winked conspiratorially.

"Yeah, I'll take care of that on my end. He's free to go. Mr. Barrier, are you still there?"

"Yes, sir," Barrier said, sitting up.

"It's been a pleasure doing business with you," said the voice. "Let's make it the last time, shall we?"

"Yes, sir. Thank you, sir," Barrier said, smiling broadly.

The voice clicked off, and Gentry and Williams whooped loudly.

"I'm going to be back in Washington before you know it," Williams said, squeezing both hands tightly into fists.

"Congratulations, Chief," Gentry said.

"And you can forget about North Dakota. You're coming with me, Gentry. We're going right to the top."

He looked at Barrier.

"Thanks, Jim," he said, extending his hand. "I appreciate all your help. Now if you'll excuse us, we've got some work to do."

280

Chapter 58

"What's that?" Doc said, holding the cell phone close to his ear. "Yeah, it is a great party. What? Yeah, I'll see you when you get up here."

Doc turned off the phone and tossed it into his bag.

"Who was that?" Merlin said.

"That was Jerry. His replacement is ten minutes late, and he wants to get up here."

Merlin looked around the room. He spotted the man in question, chatting up a pretty blonde.

"There he is," Merlin said. "I better get him down there. God, I hate being responsible for other people's behavior."

"You'll get used to it," Doc said.

"If he thinks I'm going to babysit him, he's in for a surprise."

Merlin headed off to track down his tardy staff member. Doc walked over to the bar and ordered a glass of wine.

"Gentry," Doc said, recognizing the man's back. "Who let you in?"

"Doc. How nice to see you," Gentry said, already slightly toasted. "I'd like you to meet my fiancé."

The woman turned, saw Doc, and choked on a mouthful of wine. She began a coughing fit that lasted long enough for her initial shock and embarrassment to pass. Doc smiled and waited. She wiped her mouth with a napkin and extended her hand.

"It's nice to meet you. I'm Grace."

"Hi, Grace. I'm Doc."

Doc smiled as he glanced back and forth between the couple.

"Actually, I'm Roger's girlfriend." She turned to Gentry and spoke through clenched teeth. "I asked you not to do that."

"Sorry, dear. I can't help myself."

"Maybe it just seems like you're already married," Doc said.

"Funny guy," Gentry said. "He's the pain in the ass I've been telling you about."

"I'm sure that's a harsh assessment, Roger." Grace said, fully recovered.

"I have my moments," Doc said. "Roger tells me you work in Guest Relations."

"Yes."

"Do you enjoy your work?"

Doc continued to smile and glance back and forth between them.

"It has its ups and downs."

"And its ins and outs as well, I assume."

"Absolutely. Sometimes simultaneously."

She sipped her wine and glanced at Doc over the top of the glass.

"Up, down, in, out," Doc said. "Sounds like the job puts you in some challenging positions."

"Yes, several of them take some getting used to, but I enjoy it."

"Yeah," Gentry said, forcing his way into the conversation. "Those pesky guests can be pretty demanding."

Grace smiled at Doc.

"Yes, they certainly can."

She finished her wine.

"I'm going to get another of these and chat with Hedaya. He said he had something he wanted to talk about. Nice meeting you, Doc. Maybe I'll see you around later."

"That would be nice."

She waved and strolled away. Both men watched her disappear into the crowd.

"I love that view," Gentry said.

"What? Watching her walk away from you?"

"No, smart guy. Not walking away from me. Just watching her from the back."

"It is quite impressive," Doc said.

"You got no idea."

I wouldn't be too sure about that, Goober.

Gentry turned back to Doc and sipped his beer.

"So when are you leaving?"

"First thing tomorrow morning."

"Too bad."

He drained his glass and snapped his fingers at the bartender for another.

"You're gonna miss the fireworks. Where you headed next?"

"That's none of your business, Gentry."

"Yeah, I guess you're right," he said, leaning back against the bar. "Well, I hope you realize you proved to be absolutely no help."

"Sorry to disappoint you." Doc accepted his wine from the bartender and started to walk away. "Oh, be sure and give my best to Grace."

"Will do."

"You're a lucky man, Gentry."

"Luck is for suckers. Finding a woman like Grace requires skill."

"Or incredible timing."

"What?"

"Nothing. See you around, Gentry."

Doc walked off, grinning ear to ear.

That wasn't very nice.

"No, it wasn't. But I don't like him."

He worked his way through the room pausing several times to say goodbye to various people. He picked Sally out of a small group, shared a nod, and watched as she turned her back to him. He made a beeline for an empty chair in a corner of the room. He sat down, lit a cigarette, and watched the revelry from behind his glass of wine.

"There you are. I've been looking everywhere for you."

Rose stood directly in front of him wearing a silk blouse and a very short skirt. She sat down on the arm of the chair and rested her hand on his thigh.

"Great party," she said, glancing around. "Are you enjoying yourself?"

"Yes, it's nice. I'm just quiet tonight. I always feel the same at the end of a project. They seem like they'll never end, and then suddenly it's over. Nothing left to do except say goodbye."

Rose brushed the hair away from her face.

"I think you know we are far from done here, Doc. We have much work left to do."

"Yes, I know."

Rose watched Hedaya, chatting up a storm and entertaining a large circle of people.

"Do you think he's crazy, Doc

"No. He's just a guy with big dreams."

"I don't know what I would do if anything ever happened to him."

Rose sighed as tears filled her eyes.

"He's my life," she whispered.

"He's not going anywhere, Rose. He won't go until he's good and ready."

He handed her the napkin wrapped around the bottom of his wineglass.

Rose turned her head and wiped her eyes.

"Look at me sobbing like this," she said. "I must look a mess."

"You look beautiful."

Doc gently stroked her back. They sat silent for several moments until Doc spoke.

"Do you believe in what he's trying to do, Rose?"

"If it keeps him alive and well, I'll believe anything."

"Well, you're helping him out. And that takes courage on your part."

She laughed loudly.

"Courage? Me? Oh, Doc. You're priceless."

Her laughter subsided, and she took a sip of wine from his glass.

"I lead a life of total privilege because he rescued me from what would have been either enslavement or an early death. Maybe both. The least I can do is support his dreams. That's not courage, Doc. That's love and loyalty."

She took another sip of his wine.

"Doc, do I have to remind you to never underestimate the persuasive skills of a beautiful woman?"

Doc and Rose looked up at Hedaya, who seemed to have appeared out of nowhere.

"Oh, Bofu," Rose said, blushing. "Doc and I are merely good friends. Besides, you know my heart belongs to another."

"Yes," Hedaya said, frowning. "Thanks for reminding me."

"Oh, stop it. Merlin's wonderful. He's just momentarily confused," Rose said.

"Yes, my dear. And speaking of confused, your friend Petunia just arrived."

Hedaya grimaced at Doc.

"Really? How does she look tonight?"

"Well, whenever I see her, my goals seem more attainable.

Doc started to laugh but stopped when he saw the look he was getting from Rose. Hedaya stood silent, quietly amused.

"You two are mean," Rose said, departing in a huff.

Hedaya sat down. He made sure Rose was out of sight, then nodded. Doc got the message. He lit two cigarettes and gave one to Hedaya, who leaned back blowing smoke up at the ceiling.

"How are you, my friend?"

"I'm good, Hedaya," Doc said. "But still working on getting better."

"I'm glad to hear that," he said, looking at the cigarette wedged softly between his fingers. "Are you ready for your trip?"

"Yes, but don't worry. I'll be back in a week or two."

"Take your time," Hedaya said, waving Doc off with the hand holding the cigarette. "This is a marathon, Doc. It's essential you learn to pace yourself."

"It's a massive effort, Hedaya."

"No, I'm not talking about that. I'm talking about life."

Hedaya blew a perfect smoke ring.

"In the end, it's merely a collection of small moments. If you rush past them and don't take the time to enjoy and learn from them, what will you have when the clock strikes twelve?"

Doc choked back a flood of emotions. Hedaya watched in silence. He waited until Doc reached for his wine before continuing.

"Sometimes when I see what goes on in the world, I wonder why I bother. Why do we do the things we do, Doc?"

Doc sat quietly, then shrugged his shoulders.

"Because we can, Hedaya. Just because we can."

Hedaya smiled, finished his cigarette, then stood.

"Come. I have two seats saved in the front row."

"I didn't know we were having entertainment. That's great. Who's playing?"

"Why the King, of course."

Hedaya led him across the room.

"For some reason, I thought he was the perfect choice."

Chapter 59

Doc worked his way through the crowd doing his best not to trample his fellow passengers. He entered the gate area and walked to the large electronic board that listed departures and saw he had an hour before his flight to Belize City. He searched for several minutes, eventually locating what appeared to be the last airport bar in Dallas that allowed smoking. Dropping his garment bag on a chair, he ordered a beer and stretched his neck. His flight from Vegas had been on time and uneventful, thereby achieving Doc's definition of the perfect flight.

He lit a cigarette and looked around the crowded room understanding why non-smokers hated being around lit cigarettes. Whatever amount of smoke the remainder of the airport was being spared, this small bar was making up for.

The waitress arrived with his beer.

"That'll be seven dollars."

Doc looked at the small glass and raised an eyebrow.

"What can I tell you? It's a captive audience," the waitress said, tapping her foot.

Doc smiled and waved her away with a ten. A buzz went through the room, and he looked around trying to identify the cause. A television hung high on the wall seemed to be the center of attention. He looked up at the screen and saw a female news anchor sitting behind a desk.

"Oh, good they're running it again," said the woman at the next table.

Doc turned toward the woman.

"Have you seen this yet? They've been running it all afternoon," she said, laughing.

The news anchor began talking, and Doc strained to hear the audio. The bartender pointed the remote at the screen, and the volume went up.

Today, a bizarre set of events in Las Vegas sent shockwaves through the corridors of power in Washington when an elderly man was victimized by an overzealous, and apparently out of control, Federal Bureau of Investigation. This morning at a press conference, representatives of the FBI announced a major investigation into alleged Caribbean money laundering operations being controlled by casino owner, Bernard Hedaya. Hedaya, an eighty-four-year-old Chinese immigrant, who arrived penniless on these shores as a small boy, is one of the most respected businessmen in Las Vegas and seemed visibly shaken when the announcement was first made. Reportedly in failing health, Hedaya's personal physician responded angrily and openly questioned the FBI's moral character.

Only two hours later in a remarkable turn of events, Hedaya, represented by famed attorney, William R. Gold, responded to the charges at his own press conference. Announcing that, while indeed, Mr. Hedaya had been sending money to various bank accounts in the Caribbean, the funds were being used for the creation of the Rose Foundation, whose mission is to foster education and economic development throughout impoverished parts of the region. Adamantly and aggressively challenging the FBI to get their facts straight, Mr. Gold insisted that Mr. Hedaya's contributions to his Foundation came solely from his personal fortune. When asked about the secretive nature of the Foundation, Mr. Hedaya cited his desire for anonymity.

Reaction from elected officials throughout Nevada and many other parts of the country was swift and marked by anger as the FBI was strongly chastised for their actions. One Senator, requesting anonymity, said he was surprised the FBI had nothing better to do than smear the reputation of a valuable and admired immigrant industrialist. In a statement just released by the White House, officials have announced that the President will be flying to Las Vegas in the near future to deliver a personal apology to Mr. Hedaya. As of yet, the FBI has been unavailable for comment.

Doc sat back and sipped his beer. He smiled at the image of a forlorn Hedaya hobbling to the bank of microphones and cupping his ear with his hand to better hear the questions being fired at him.

"Those bastards," said the woman at the next table. "How much do you think he'll get out of them for that?"

"He won't sue," Doc said, shaking his head.

"Well, I sure would. I bet the FBI will be keeping their distance from him for a while."

"One would hope," Doc said.

He finished the last of his beer and collected his bags. He left the bar and casually strolled through the throng of travelers. His plane was loading and he was soon standing next to his seat in first class.

"Excuse me."

Doc nodded to the businessman in the other seat and tossed his garment bag into the overhead bin. He sat down, ordered a beer from the attendant, and looked out the window at the tarmac below.

"You going to Belize for business or pleasure?"

"Purely pleasure," Doc said, smiling at the man.

"Good for you. I, however, will be working the whole time."

"That's too bad."

Doc settled into the comfortable seat and sighed.

"So," said the businessman. "What do you do?"

Doc thought for a moment.

"Everything that's expected I guess."

The man laughed.

"I hear you there. I mean what industry?"

Doc thought about the question. Technology was the safe answer, but might lead to a lengthy discussion he preferred to avoid. Part of him wanted to say spy just to see the man's reaction. He glanced at the man, then looked out the window at the runway.

"Human behavior," Doc said.

"Oh, you're one of those," the man said, nodding. "You got a specialty?"

"I'm going to need a little clarification here."

The man frowned but continued.

"Is there any particular type of people you deal with?"

"Yeah."

Doc leaned his head back and closed his eyes.

"Damaged ones."

Chapter 60

Ending the one-hour journey from Belize City, the water taxi cruised into Ambergris Caye, idled alongside the long dock, and came to a stop. A young man tied the boat and Doc, along with a few other weary travelers, climbed out and walked the short distance to the main entrance of the resort.

Doc stood outside the main door and looked around at the familiar scene, finding it hard to believe another year was over. He watched his bags get loaded onto a hand trolley and followed them into the registration area. He smiled when he saw the man standing behind the desk.

"Hey, Doc. Welcome back."

Doc warmly shook the young man's outstretched hand.

"Nice to be back, Miguel. You have no idea how good it is to be back."

"You missed the excitement."

Doc looked around the quiet elegance of the resort that, in total, comprised forty-two private villas. The lobby was virtually empty. "Yeah, I guess I did."

"No. I'm talking about the television show," Miguel said.

Doc's senses sharpened as he prepared himself for bad news.

"I'm sorry. I don't know what you're talking about."

"Temptation Island," Miguel said.

Doc remembered hearing about a show that put couples in a tropical setting. The objective was to see how their relationships would withstand the pressure of attractive people whose sole mission was to create infidelity. Doc had seen enough of it in real life to know the last thing he wanted to do was watch it on television.

"Please don't tell me they shot it here, Miguel," Doc said.

"Yes, it was incredible. It should put us on the map."

"Damn. One more hidden treasure made bare."

"What's that, Doc?"

"Nothing. I'm just babbling."

"Your villa is all set, and you're bags are on their way. I'm sure you remember the way. And may I say, well done."

Miguel winked at him. Doc, confused, waved and walked toward the bar. A solitary customer sat chatting with the bartender at one end. Doc walked to the other end and sat down. The bartender strolled over and greeted him with a smile, then frowned. Seconds later, the smile reappeared.

"What can I get you?"

"Anything with rum and an umbrella, thanks," Doc said, lighting a cigarette.

The bartender smiled and began mixing the drink. Doc frowned as he tried to recall the memory. He looked at the bartender who was busy preparing the drink, but kept glancing back in Doc's direction.

"How long you here for?" the bartender said above the noise of the blender.

"A week. Maybe two."

Doc's frown deepened.

The bartender placed the drink in front of him and stood waiting as Doc took a sip.

"Wow," Doc said. "Unbelievable. What is this?"

"It's my creation."

"It's great. What do you call it?"

"My Little Secret."

The memory of a bandaged man flashed through his mind, and he smiled. He looked at the man's eyes, their youthful tautness natural to the untrained eye. The nose was smaller, the lips fuller. His hair was longer and now blonde from dye or daily sun. The neatly trimmed beard and glasses sat comfortably on his face. The loss of at least fifty pounds completed the transformation. He gently chewed his bottom lip as he watched Doc sip his drink.

"I'm Doc," he said, extending his hand. "What should I call you?"

"Willie," said the bartender. "Call me Willie. Nice to meet you, Doc. Where are you coming in from?"

"Las Vegas."

"Vegas. I wonder if it's still hot up there," Willie said, raising an eyebrow.

"Lately it's cooled off quite a bit."

"Glad to hear that. The heat can be brutal. What's been keeping you in Vegas?"

"Working on a project," Doc said, rapidly working his way through his drink.

"Yeah? I hope everything turned out okay."

"Everything is just fine, Willie," Doc said, nodding. "So, how did you end up down here?"

"Oh, I heard a friend talking about this place and thought I would check it out. They needed a bartender, so here I am."

"I'm glad to see you took your friend's advice. It's a place you could stay for a very long time and never be bothered."

"You think so?"

"I'm sure of it, Willie."

Doc finished his drink in silence. He waved off the offer for another and shook the bartender's hand.

"I'm going to walk the beach and go to bed. Let's see if we can get to know each other a little better while I'm here."

"I'd like that, Doc."

Doc casually strolled out of the bar as Willie began restocking the coolers.

Chapter 61

Doc stood silently at water's edge, felt the water lick his feet, then disappear. He looked out at the sailboats and yachts moored safely offshore and watched their lights, one by one, disappear into the night sky. He wondered what those on board were thinking and feeling inside their private cocoons and what had brought them to this particular place at this specific point in time. His phone rang, and he checked the number.

Merlin.

"What's up?"

"Hey, Doc. You won't believe what I just watched."

"Okay. I'm game."

Doc lit a cigarette and waited.

"I just watched Summerman and Murray cross over to the other side. Well, I didn't see them… but I saw… shit. Doc, I gotta tell you. I don't know what I just saw. But I'm convinced this guy is for real."

"You actually saw it?"

"One minute he and Murray are swimming in the middle of the St. Lawrence River and then they both submerge and don't come up."

"Merlin, I hate to tell you, but that doesn't sound like crossing over. That sounds like drowning."

"I know. It's strange. And spooky too. But you're going to love the plane."

Doc laughed.

"Oh, I am, huh?"

"Yes. We have to do this, Doc."

"It is tempting."

"And I talked to Samuels. He's in."

"You didn't tell him about Summerman did you?"

"Do I look stupid? I told him you and I and a few others were going into business for ourselves and that we needed someone to provide some cover in high places."

"And?"

"And Samuels said he'd do it. We'll need to complete the new project in Vegas. But after that, we're good. Samuels wants ten percent. I was going to hold out for five, but figured what the hell? Why piss him off before we even get started?"

"It never stopped you before," Doc said, laughing.

"Yeah, that's true. Hey, I gotta run. I need to get back to Vegas. We'll talk more about this when you get back. Enjoy your week of solitude."

"Thanks. See you soon."

He slid the phone back in his pocket and, after a quick glance in both directions, decided to stroll away from the hotel. It felt strange to be at such peace. Only a few days ago, he'd been on the edge, unable to move forward, too terrified to step back.

I knew you'd make it.

"Well," Doc said. "Where have you been?"

We both needed a break.

I see. And now you're back?"

No. It looks like you've got things pretty well under control.

"We'll see," Doc said, looking up at the dark sky.

I guess I should be going. Take good care of yourself.

"You too."

And listen to Summerman. He knows what he's doing.

Doc remembered a hot day and a bloody street. And the face, his face, staring up at him, through him, into space. He stopped walking and waited as the emotion surged and passed. He stood listening. Waiting for the voice to return. The only sound he heard was the soothing calm of late night tropical.

"Stay in touch."

He started walking again and noticed a solitary figure strolling in his direction. Her walk was unmistakable. She came closer and smiled. In her eyes, he saw sadness, yet contentment. Frustration, yet hope. He reached out and gently brushed the side of her face, staring at the incredible gift, this vision appearing out of nowhere.

"What are you doing here?"

"To give you your birthday present."

She softly kissed his cheek.

"But why?"

"I got a note in the mail."

Doc felt a surge of panic.

"From who?"

"I have no idea. It had a Vegas postmark."

Instinctively, Doc knew it had been Hedaya.

"What did it say?"

"Enough to get me down here," she said. "I still have many questions."

"Whoever did it shouldn't have," Doc said. "It could put you in danger."

"No, it should have come from you, Doc," Maya said. "I think I get it, but I have so many questions."

"I'm sure you do."

"Will you answer them?"

"Every one I can," Doc said.

"Then let's start," she said. "Those few weeks in Vegas, when we were really good together. That was during the time you were out?"

"Yes," Doc said. "Is that it?"

"No, but that was the big one," she said, hooking his arm with hers. "I have others, but I guess they can wait."

She looked around taking in the surroundings.

"It's so beautiful here."

"Yes."

"Let's enjoy the hell out this place, okay?"

"Absolutely," Doc said. "When did you get in?"

"This afternoon. I sat in the sun and took a nap. After dinner I stopped by the bar. Wait until you try this drink called My Little Secret."

"I'm way ahead of you."

Maya laughed.

"It's great, isn't it? And that bartender is a hoot."

"Yeah, he is," he said, deciding this was one secret she would forgive him for keeping to himself.

"So what's going on with you and your husband?"

"Oh, that. He's begging me to come back."

"And?"

"I'm... undecided."

She stared out at the moonlit ocean.

"And you thought coming here would help you decide?"

"That's exactly why I'm here. How this goes will force me to choose."

"Nothing like putting a little pressure on a vacation."

"From what I understand, you're used to working under pressure."

She smiled and squeezed his hand.

"So, how did things up in Vegas?"

"All things considered, not bad I guess."

Doc smiled at the memories of Barrier and George. One barely escaping prison, the other now serving cocktails a few hundred feet away.

Damaged people.

And so many in one place.

Again, his mind wandered.

To the memory of overzealous Federal agents.

To soft kisses amid a moonlit waterfall.

And the voice.

Thanks for remembering.

And the piano playing part-timer and his dog.

And Merlin and Rose.

And Hedaya.

Especially Hedaya.

The little old man with dreams of freeing souls and winning gold, living in a giant castle safe from the outside world while still trying to make the world a better place for everybody.

"So, Doc," Maya said, stroking the side of his face. "What is this for us? The beginning of the end, or the end of the beginning?"

"I have no idea," Doc said, shaking his head. "But I'm looking forward to finding out."

"Me too."

"C'mon. It's time to go."

He took her hand and gently led her back towards the resort.

"It's almost midnight."

Be sure to follow the adventures of the Damaged Po$$e in the next installment:

Larrikin Gene

Gene has a bit of a problem. Several actually. He's wrapping up a year-long, high-end matchmaking scam that has proven to be most profitable but, in the process, he's lost the love of his life to a billionaire. Now to help mend his broken heart, he's back in Las Vegas finishing up another lucrative scam. But the FBI is on his trail and Gene discovers that the agent in charge is none other than the hapless Roger Gentry, a high school acquaintance with whom he shares a tenuous past. To make matters worse, Gene is soon sleeping with the other agent on the case who turns out to be Gentry's fiancé.

To cool things off, Gene decides it's time for a well deserved vacation Down Under. He brings his father along, an ex-convict whose biggest wish in life is to work one scam with his son before he dies. And before Gene can even get a chance to catch his breath and enjoy his time off, he finds himself running the ultimate con; one that threatens to irrevocably change his life. Fortunately for Gene, the Po$$e needs his help and Doc, Summerman and Merlin follow him to Australia to do a little recruiting and provide Gene with a possible way out of his current predicament.

"Cold beer, beachfront property, elaborate double crosses and exploding pigs. What more could you want? Larrikin Gene delivers a touching but hysterical take on the question of nature versus nurture. This second installment in the Damaged Po$$e series provides additional testimony to what was said about the series' first book, American Midnight; this is a series to watch out for."

Amazon link to Larrikin Gene

http://amzn.to/10tqmMa

Chapter One

I stared into the mirror at the man in the dark blue suit. It could have been any man, any suit. Unfortunately, for him, it just happened to be this man, that suit. And after three and a half martinis, the man's mood matched the suit's color. I studied him as he stood, removed and folded his jacket, and draped it over an empty barstool. He checked his hair in the mirror, brushed some stray hairs back in place, and sucked in his stomach. He cast a slow furtive look around the bar then sat back down.

I almost felt sorry for the man in the blue suit. I often manage to find some degree of sympathy for men like him. At first glance, that might appear to be one of my better traits. Actually, it's just me looking for my good side.

Soon the man in the blue suit would firmly believe fate had brought me to this bar, at this time. In fact, not only would he believe it, he would tell me so. Somewhere into his next martini, he would turn his head toward me, touch my arm, and speak in hushed tones in an attempt to display confidentiality and a sense of intimacy. But I would know that the softness of his voice was designed to conceal weakness. And fear.

He would profess genuine gratitude and pronounce eternal friendship in the manner that only sad drunks have truly mastered. He would be verbose, then morose. Charming, then sullen. One minute, a playful young boy. And then he'd dissolve into a world-weary old man. And at the exact moment when he truly believed I was the best friend a man like him could have, I would order another round and make my move.

For I was far from becoming this man's best friend. The savior role he had in mind for me, even at this early point in our friendship, was misplaced. But misguided men, driven by ego and a misplaced sense of their destiny, make bad decisions all the time.

Perhaps when surrounded by bank statements or the comforts of their chosen profession, they feel less vulnerable.

Perhaps when surrounded by others of their ilk, they feel more protected.

Perhaps others surrounding them simply don't notice. Mirror images offer true reflection only to those searching for it.

Perhaps.

I finished the last of my martini, sucked the pimento from the olive, and ordered two more with a casual wave. The man in the blue suit slumped forward and ran a hand through his dwindling hair. The creative comb over on display earlier had disappeared and two large bald spots threatening a merger shined under a bank of overhead lights. He wiped his hands with a napkin and sipped from his fresh martini before it even had time to get comfortable on the bar.

I lifted mine by the stem and savored the frigid stream that trickled down my throat. The first taste of frostbitten Grey Goose, like one's initial encounter with any fresh object of desire, was always the most satisfying. No matter how much pleasure one took from the overall experience, after the initial sensory overload, everything was pretty much downhill from that point forward. I carefully returned my glass to its place of honor on the bar and swiveled ninety degrees.

**

"I know, John." I nodded in sad agreement. "I know exactly what you're talking about."

John forced a smile and refocused on his drink.

"Most people would spend all night debating that."

He glanced over at me. "Debating what?"

I nodded at his drink. "Whether your glass is half full or half empty."

"I always thought that it was a good question. Which is it for you?"

I smiled as he bit the hook. I decided to let him run and tire himself out before reeling him in.

"For me, John, that question has always been irrelevant. The real issue is about control. Most people go through life debating half-empty, half-full with pop culture concepts they've picked up from self-help books. And if you get advice from a book someone else has written, that's not self-help, that's help."

"That's good."

"I was quoting George Carlin."

"I love Carlin. I saw him at the MGM in Vegas one time, and he did this bit about-"

"Yes, I know, John." I placed a hand on his forearm. "But I want you to stay with me. Okay?"

"I'm with you, buddy. I'm with you."

4

"Good. As I was saying, most people don't get what I'm about to tell you. Whatever amount is in the glass is completely under your control. Too much in the glass? Pound that baby back. Drain it dry. Not enough in it? Order a fresh one."

"Just like that?"

"Just like that."

"Are you telling me it's my round?"

"No, John." I laughed and squeezed his forearm. "What I'm telling you is that you control everything. You have the power to control how much is in your glass. Except, of course, with one very big exception."

He looked up at the ceiling then glanced back at me and held my stare. "Love?"

"Precisely. Love. In the end, it's the only thing that really matters to people of substance. Sweet, but evasive. Tender, but heartbreaking. The eternal quest beaten back by the demands of daily life."

"Amen."

"Yes. Amen, my brother. But even prayer has failed you on your quest for love. Hasn't it, John?"

"Yes," he whispered. He drained his glass and waved a finger in the direction of the bartender.

I looked away as he dabbed a napkin at the corner of one eye. This close to closing the deal, I didn't want him embarrassed. I needed him strong and decisive. Let him feel weak and powerless on his own dime.

I waited until the fresh martinis arrived then recaptured his stare in the mirror. "And when everything including prayer fails, you're forced under cover of darkness to confront the question all of us face at one time or another."

He turned his head towards me and waited.

I took a slow sip of frostbite.

"What's the question?"

"Is this all there is?"

"Yes." He nodded and exhaled. "Yes, that is the question isn't it?"

"And it's at that precise moment, in that perfect moment of clarity, when the question of whether the glass is half-full or half-empty becomes meaningless. If you've got the wrong glass, John, why would you care how much is in it?"

"That's so true."

"I know you, John. I meet men like you all the time. It's my business to meet men like you. And when I meet them, do you know what I do?"

"No," he said, raising an eyebrow.

"I help them, John. I help them."

"That's very nice of you."

"Well, thank you, John. That's nice of you to say. Would you mind if I told you a little bit about yourself."

"I wish somebody would."

I slowly began to reel him in. I tested the hook. Secure. He wasn't going anywhere.

"Right now, you're at a point in your life where you should be jumping out of bed at the crack of dawn every day."

"But I do," he said. "Well, actually I don't jump. Lately, it's been more of a crawl."

"That's precisely my point, John. You should be on top of the world, but you feel like life has nothing to offer. Despite your success, you feel like you're wasting away. You're getting up at five because you feel you have to, not because you can't wait to see what the day will bring."

"How do you know that?"

"Like I said, John. It's my business to know. You're in your thirties. You've killed yourself getting to this point. And now the people in your firm believe that even if you don't walk on water, you at least know where all the rocks are. You've got a nice place on the Westside worth in the neighborhood of three million. You've got the Jag or the 740 for work, and the SUV for the weekend, just to show everyone you're still a regular guy. You go to Vegas and stay at the Bellagio because they make you feel like a high roller. You usually take along some fresh wannabe starlet with juices sweet enough to put in your coffee. But in the back of your mind, you know she's only there because it's a free weekend and maybe, just maybe, you'll spring for a new boob job. And after giving her a couple grand to gamble, then dinner and a show, she fulfills the unspoken demands from her side of the deal."

"And cocktails."

"What?"

"Don't forget all the cocktails."

"Well, sure. That goes without saying. Try to stay with me here, John."

"I'm with you. I'm with you."

6

"Finally, you're there. And it's fresh and new. But mid-stroke, you're either trying to convince yourself she's worth the effort, or you're fantasizing about Peggy Sue from high school who took your cherry in the backseat of your father's Ford."

"Chevy."

"What?"

"It was a Chevy. Dad worked for GM."

"Chevy. Got it. Stay with me here, John. So while you're sipping your nightcap in solitary because she just had to have a shower, you smile to yourself and say *at least she's not a hooker*. Because you've convinced yourself that you've never paid for it before in your life. Haven't you, John?"

"Yes," he said, nodding. "I've never paid for it."

I smiled and sipped my drink. It was deteriorating rapidly. I motioned to the bartender.

"Can you please shake what's left with fresh ice?"

The bartender nodded and left with my glass. Moments later he returned with a fresh glass of frostbite. I took a sip, found it lacking and turned back to my new friend. He, too, was in desperate need of fresh ice.

"Every one of those weekends, unless you get lucky at the tables, costs you around ten large. Maybe more depending on how much shopping you let her do. In a year, those weekends, plus the other trips to Europe and Hawaii, end up costing you, what, maybe a hundred grand? I hate to say this, John. But you've been paying for it for a long time. "

I fell silent and went back to my drink. Through the mirror, I watched him chew on his lower lip.

"But what you crave is one woman," I whispered. "One woman you could be sure loved you. Someone you'd be happy to spend all your money on and spoil rotten."

"Yes. I do."

"I do."

I smiled.

"Your deepest desire is to be able to repeat that phrase in the most traditional of settings. To find a woman who's beautiful and smart. A woman you can have an intelligent conversation with. A woman successful in her own right. Not a wannabe, but an already is. Someone mature. Someone who can captivate a room full of heavyweights over dinner, then takes you home and fucks you like a whore. Someone who wants you inside her, not out of obligation, but just because she loves it. Needs it. That's what you crave, John. That's what you need. That's what all of us need, John. And all you have to do is have the courage to change the glass."

"Change the glass," he whispered.

"I have that glass, John."

He suddenly turned all business and swirled his glass in front of him. I waited patiently. I was about to pull him into the boat and didn't want any extreme movements that might snap the line or let him wriggle away. I sipped my drink and waited out the silence.

"I don't know," he said. "Twenty-five thousand is a lot of money."

"Yes, it is." I placed a hand on his shoulder. "But tell me, John. How much money have you spent the past five years looking for the right woman?"

"Probably half a million," he whispered. "Maybe more."

I whistled softly. The bartender glanced up from his magazine and caught my eye. I shook my head, and he disappeared back into the World's 50 Most Beautiful People.

"Half a million? Jesus Christ, John. If you're looking for a way to blow your money on cheap thrills, cocaine's cheaper."

"So, if I sign up what guarantee do I get?"

"You get a guarantee that I will personally identify three extraordinarily successful and beautiful women who fit your personality and lifestyle perfectly. You will mutually decide what type of first date the two of you would prefer and, once I am satisfied that the logistics are finalized to both parties satisfaction, you're on your own."

"That's it?"

"That's it? Let me ask you, John. How many women like the type I just described have you met, let alone gone out with the past year?"

"I meet successful and beautiful women all the time."

"Let me rephrase it. How many have you met that are not only available but are looking for exactly the same thing you are at this precise moment in time?"

"None."

"None."

I drained my martini.

"Change the glass, John. It's time to change the glass."